THE ISLAND *of* LAST THINGS

THE ISLAND *of* LAST THINGS

Emma Sloley

FLATIRON BOOKS
NEW YORK

This is a work of fiction. All of the characters, organizations, and events portrayed in this novel are either products of the author's imagination or used fictitiously.

THE ISLAND OF LAST THINGS. Copyright © 2025 by Emma Sloley. All rights reserved. Printed in the United States of America. For information, address Flatiron Books, 120 Broadway, New York, NY 10271.

www.flatironbooks.com

Alcatraz illustration © Zirochka/Shutterstock

All emojis designed by OpenMoji—the open-source emoji and icon project. License: CC BY-SA 4.0

Designed by Jen Edwards

Library of Congress Cataloging-in-Publication Data

Names: Sloley, Emma, author.
Title: The island of last things / Emma Sloley.
Description: First edition. | New York: Flatiron Books, 2025.
Identifiers: LCCN 2024025650 | ISBN 9781250329240 (hardcover) | ISBN 9781250329257 (ebook)
Subjects: LCGFT: Novels.
Classification: LCC PR9619.4.S58 I85 2025 | DDC 823/.92—dc23/eng/20240701
LC record available at https://lccn.loc.gov/2024025650

Our books may be purchased in bulk for promotional, educational, or business use. Please contact your local bookseller or the Macmillan Corporate and Premium Sales Department at 1-800-221-7945, extension 5442, or by email at MacmillanSpecialMarkets@macmillan.com.

First Edition: 2025

10 9 8 7 6 5 4 3 2 1

For Adam

THE ISLAND *of* LAST THINGS

Alcatraz

That day all we could think about was the elephant. Everyone had been counting down the months, then the weeks, then the days, until only a few scant hours stood between us and the arrival of the *Elephas maximus indicus* on which we had pinned all our hopes. We didn't know anything about Sailor then, didn't even know she existed, so no one was anticipating her arrival. But there she was anyway, a new keeper at the breakfast table. Defiant in her aloneness. Hyperalert to her surroundings, like a deer hearing the undergrowth crackle. She was tall, and I guessed a lot older than me—maybe forty—and wore a strange little smile, like she had been proven right about something and was pleased about it. But not in an arrogant way. More like the quiet pleasure that comes from feeling the sun on your head after a day spent toiling in the darkness of the cells.

On a normal day, we would all have been abuzz at the arrival of a new keeper. The whole intricate social puzzle would need to be taken apart and reassembled to fit this new piece, this potential ally or rival, and while some keepers hated these disruptions to the status quo, I lived for them. Every new person was a small blast of helium into my balloon of hope. I'm not sure exactly what I was expecting or whose attention I aimed to catch with this balloon. A savior of some kind, I think, although I never expressed that to anyone else. In the three years I'd been working at the zoo I hadn't met a person whose company I preferred to the animals, but that didn't stop me from dreaming. Of someone who might make the empty hours between shifts bearable. Of someone who might feel the way I did.

But this wasn't a normal day, so I didn't spend long examining the new keeper. I was too preoccupied with imagining what the elephant would be like. He was called Titan, which we all thought an unimaginative name, considering he was likely the last Asian elephant left on Earth. His previous handlers at Singapore Zoo had named him, though, and that had been the most respected of the five zoos before it closed, so the administrators said the name had to stay.

After breakfast, we left the mess hall to receive our assignments. There's a big screen near the entrance to the rec room where we check our names and the sections we've been allocated to work. This system has the potential to yield the occasional ripple of excitement; for instance, if you're a keeper who lives for the Great Apes, your heart might lift to see you'd been assigned the enclosure containing Stella, Bruno, Alicia, and Bones, our chimpanzee troop. If you're feeling lazy, you might be relieved to find yourself paired up with the golden frogs, who are clean and low-maintenance and tend to just quietly sit there, only perking up when we bring them their breakfast of fruit flies and dead crickets dusted with reptile vitamins. Or if you fancy yourself an ailurophile, that is, someone who digs big cats, you might experience a small frisson to see your name alongside that of Beyoncé the Bengal tiger, or the serval cat. But even the ailurophiles blanch at being assigned to Feliz.

Feliz is our lone jaguar. The last jaguar we had before him died of despair. That wasn't the official cause of death, of course not, but we all knew it. The rumor goes that the zoo's owners, the Pinkton family, paid an obscene amount to acquire another jaguar, probably the only one on Earth, given the state of the countries in which the creature's natural habitat once existed. Feliz was plucked out of the last few acres of the Amazon as the bulldozers waited, like customers impatiently hovering while a buffet is prepared. So Feliz is kind of a big deal. He doesn't appear cognizant of this fact, however. If anything, he looks to be on a mission to wear away the floor of his enclosure until he drops right through the earth and out of this life. He paces without cease. His nails are worn to stubs and his mouth hangs open in a perpetual rictus that wrecks your heart. He longs to forget all this, and to be forgotten.

The day Titan was due to arrive, I lingered at the tail end of the crowd as it surged to the assignment screen—it makes my eyes twitch to be crammed elbow to elbow with other people. By the time I arrived to check my assignment, there were only a few other stragglers left. One of them was the new keeper. Hands planted on her hips, she swayed her head a little as she peered at the screen, like she was memorizing all the names and data. She was wearing a regular civilian getup of white T-shirt and denim shorts, with sturdy work boots going ragged at the top. Soon she'd be relegated to the zoo uniform: a long-sleeved thermo-regulated top that protected from the sun while wicking away perspiration, a floppy hat for outside work, and a pair of black overalls. Black because it was better at hiding the various stains. She'd be allowed to keep the boots. They would already have been disinfected at the dock when she arrived. We all had to wear those; you could get fired for being seen in open-toed shoes. Deportation, we called it, because Alcatraz was our own little country.

I stood a respectful distance away and scanned down to my own name. At any given time there are around two hundred keepers living on the island, taking care of our 2,318 precious residents. (The screen doesn't even list the dozens of guards, vets, tech workers, and admins who share this rock with us—they sort themselves out.) At first I was confused because the lists are alphabetical, and my name wasn't in the usual place. Then I saw it out of the corner of my eye, in an unfamiliar spot, under a heading called SPECIAL ASSIGNMENTS. CAMILLE PARKER, followed by the words TOUR GUIDE ASSISTANT / ORIENTATION OF NEW KEEPER, SAILOR ANDERSON.

I was momentarily elated—I hardly ever got to go on the tours, which were considered a high-status posting and tended to be filled by the same elite employees every week—but the feeling was chased by irritation. Showing a new person the ropes meant I couldn't get on with my duties, and fulfilling those duties was my entire purpose. I shiver now to think about it, how easily it could have been someone else randomly assigned to accompany her that day.

I turned to Sailor. "Looks like I'm showing you around."

It's possible I didn't use the most welcoming of tones. But instead of answering my coldness with a chill of her own, she looked so pleased I immediately regretted being unfriendly.

"Ah, so *you're* Camille. You don't look like a Camille."

"Wait, what do Camilles normally look like?"

"Well, the ones I've known were all tough, chain-smoking French broads, so consider yourself a breath of fresh air! I'm Sailor. Have you met any sailors before? Wait, scrap that, it sounds creepy."

She laughed—a short, startling sound like a corvid's greeting—and extended her hand. I was struck by how soft her skin was and pulled my own hand back quickly, a little embarrassed at how dry, cracked, nicked, and generally beaten-up it was. I had wrenched a splinter out of my palm a few days before and still bore a stigmata-like mark. I shoved my hands in my pockets and we walked outside together. I kept my respirator slung around my neck. It was a rare low-pollution morning and there were patches of blue sky and plump cumulus clouds and a breeze that played with the hems of our clothes. Waves gnawed at the cliffs below us. The perma-fires in the Marin hills were less intense than usual—the only evidence a smudgy orange haze on the horizon. Funny how the mind has a way of freezing a significant day in place, its discrete details trapped forever under glass, like those insect displays people used to hang on their walls.

"So, when I was on the ferry coming here," Sailor said as we walked to the admin center, "some guy called Coates told me my first assignment would probably be the jaguar, because that's what the new keepers always get. Is that true?"

As I was contemplating how to answer, an ungodly stench wafted up to greet us. Worried this would be her first impression, I began to stutter out an explanation. "So when we've had a few warm days in a stretch, the jellyfish in the bay get cooked in the warmer waters and . . ." But Sailor was already nodding.

"Yeah, I got acquainted with that lovely phenomenon when I was in the city. I've never seen so many jellyfish. Are you from around here?"

"I grew up over there"—I gestured toward the mainland, shimmering across the water like a bad dream—"and it started happening a few years ago. I'm used to it now." Sailor shielded her eyes with her hand to look out at the water. For some reason I was in a garrulous mood. "When the water got too warm and everything else died, they flourished. We actually call it

Jellyfish Bay now. They're the reason we don't go in the water. They can give a nasty sting. Not fatal or anything, but still." I assured her the cleaners would be around soon to spray the island with the scents they use to mask the stench on bad days.

"So, tell me more about this jaguar," she said. "Never dreamed of getting one of the big cats so early on."

"Well . . ." This was my chance to warn her about the jaguar, but I was wary as a waterbuck about saying the wrong thing. "His name is Feliz. But you won't likely be looking after him for long."

"Can't have keepers bonding with the prisoners . . . I mean, the animals, am I right?"

She flashed me a big smile like we were already in league.

"To be honest," I said, "because you're new you'll probably end up with the reptiles or the frogs." Her expression didn't give away what she thought about that. "You'll get upgraded to the more charismatic animals later on," I added encouragingly, not wanting her to feel despondent.

She tilted her head and gave me a quizzical look. "Ah. What makes an animal charismatic?"

"Oh." I was flustered, not having ever had to define it before, we all just agreed on which creatures qualified. "I don't know. Size, mostly. Rarity. Level of beauty." I was thinking of the ocelot, with its exquisite pelt and limpid black eyes, beautiful as a movie star. "Any of the big cats. The bear. The elephant, of course. Elephants, after today." Saying those words sent a little thrill over my scalp.

"Isn't Feliz a big cat? He sounds charismatic to me."

"Well, yeah. But you'll see."

She nodded along politely, as if she were taking notes in her head. It was obvious she already knew all this—every keeper knew what "charismatic" meant in the zoological sense—but for some reason she was interested in hearing my version of it, and I was happy to pretend I was educating her. I could tell her amused smile wasn't designed to alienate, but to draw me in, and I felt something like gratitude pass through me.

We approached the entrance of the admin center, a forbidding yellow building that originally contained the guardhouse, chapel, and repair shop for the prison, back in the era when the island was a repository for men society considered worthless. It functions today as headquarters for the administrators, who carry out the will of the Pinktons, like priests are supposed to be vessels through which God can pass. The admins dictate the rules and the guards enforce them. Civilized authority backed up with the threat of violence: one of the oldest arrangements. There were also rumors about a dungeon cell used for holding unruly employees in solitary confinement. Keepers joked about it sometimes, but the idea made me uneasy, and I didn't share it.

We presented ourselves at the employee office—I averted my eyes, as always, from the rifle slits in the thick brick walls—to get Sailor's paperwork sorted out and to pick up her uniform. She signed for it, and the clothes and equipment were slid in a neat pile through a gap in the glass screen.

"Just like being in prison," she said, flashing me a wink. I waited outside the barracks while she got changed, and when she emerged, twirling to show off her new gear, I smiled and said, "One of us now."

As we approached the dock, the protestors came into view. There were a lot of them that day, thanks to the agreeable weather and calm water. I explained to Sailor that the protestors were here because they object to the expense and labor that goes into keeping the animals alive when so many humans are suffering. Guards in black Kevlar are posted at intervals all around the shore, so the protestors can't actually get onto the island, even if they were somehow able to slip through the cordoned-off free-speech zone that extends about twenty feet into the bay. Instead they sit or stand, wobbling, in small boats, holding up signs and chanting. They travel out here every morning from the mainland and then back again at night, spewing diesel fumes into the already choked air. As with many things that start off being irritating, they soon melded into the fabric of my days and ceased to even register, so it was almost startling to see the scene through a newcomer's eyes.

"Did you have them too?" I asked her. "At your last zoo?"

"Not so much. It reminds me of the crazies who used to wave their placards around outside abortion clinics." Then she gave me a quick glance, as if she realized she shouldn't speak of such things in front of me.

"I have a theory," I said.

"Well, spill it. I love a good theory."

"The real reason a lot of them come out here is that when the wind blows a certain way, they can smell the flowers and plants in the Arboretum."

"No kidding?" She dropped her shoulders, closed her eyes, and inhaled deeply. Curious to test out my own theory, I mimicked her, clenching my eyes shut and breathing in through my nose. And for a second I could detect it, the subtle scent of some flowering plant—jasmine, maybe?—threaded beneath the omnipresent smell of burning garbage drifting across the bay. I opened my eyes and met her gaze, triumphant.

"Night lilies," Sailor said decisively. "Haven't smelled one of those in years." She wagged her finger at the protestors. "You wily little fuckers, sneaking in here to get a free whiff of our flowers."

I spotted the glossy black guest boat in the distance, zipping its way toward the island and carrying a cargo of well-heeled visitors. Some days you couldn't sight the boat at all through the haze, only hear the eerie slapping of hull-on-wave as it approached.

"They're coming," I said, reflexively standing up straighter. Even the days without tours were bent toward the big occasion—prepping the enclosures, polishing the zoo to a shine, practicing our welcoming faces.

"Why only once a week?" asked Sailor, gazing out at the water. "I mean, don't get me wrong, I'm not complaining about seeing visitors so infrequently, ha, but still."

"Because the tours are so expensive, I suppose," I said. "Kind of makes the experience more exclusive."

"Why Tuesdays?"

"Mrs. Pinkton says Tuesday is the most auspicious day."

Sailor looked puzzled, and I realized it had never occurred to me to question this. "Is that why they're flying the elephant in today as well?"

"Must be," I said faintly. It was overwhelming to have so many things happening at once, and I wasn't sure how many more questions I could handle.

Maybe sensing this, Sailor ceased her questioning and offered a few biographical details. She was from Florida originally and used to live with her family on the edge of the Everglades. I nodded, but I honestly hadn't been sure that was a real place. It sounded impossible, a vast wetland teeming with animals and fish and insects. I couldn't believe I was with someone who had been alive to see that. She had worked for ten years in a senior role at the Paris Zoo, the last zoo in Europe, which is why she'd been qualified for the transfer. I didn't ask her why she'd wanted to leave Paris. You didn't ask questions like that, or at least I didn't. People had their reasons and often those reasons were private, or painful.

"Why do they call it a 'funicular'?" Sailor seemed tickled at the sign near the loading station, with its curly gold letters on black. She traced her fingers along its raised contours.

"I'm honestly not sure. I think it just sounds fancier?"

"Yeah, that follows. This whole enterprise has a real Gilded Age vibe going on. What's it like living here, anyway?"

"Weeellll." I wasn't sure what kind of answer she was looking for, but the truth is I had turned this question over many times in my mind, and it felt like I had just been waiting for someone to ask me. "It's somehow both lonely and unbearably crowded?"

She nodded, and I could tell the answer satisfied her, as if that's how she already felt about it too.

An employee approached with two steel boxes for us to take up the hill. I signed for them and placed the boxes carefully on the ground, then Sailor and I stood on the staff side of the track, waiting for the visitors to off-load. After they had been searched, presented their vaccination papers, had their phones collected for safekeeping (only old-fashioned cameras allowed, with an agreement to never share images publicly per our NDA), and exchanged their mainland shoes for special one-use footwear, they headed toward the funicular. They were a boisterous bunch that day, enlivened perhaps by the rare good weather. The tours were small by design, twenty guests maximum, but those entry fees funded the whole enterprise, as Sailor called it.

Sailor and I waited for them all to be seated before we boarded the funicular. It was more like a small train, enclosed by a clear domed roof and with big windows so the guests could see the bay growing smaller and more dollhouse-like as we glided up the hill. It was all unnecessary theater, I suppose, because it would have taken the same amount of time, maybe even less if you count all the palaver of boarding, to simply walk up the hill to the zoo. But this was one of the highlights of the tour for a lot of guests: it made them feel special, to be whisked to the top of the rock like superstars. We stood at the back, legs apart to brace against the movement. I had given Sailor one of the steel boxes, and I held the other. Before boarding, I'd told her we would open them on the count of three and explained how the mechanism would work, and she looked both reverent and apprehensive as to what was inside. It felt good to keep it secret, like a little treat to make her first day memorable.

As soon as the funicular started moving, the MC, a guy called Kyle, stood up to start his welcome spiel. Kyle was from Kentucky, but during the tours he spoke in a languid, properly enunciated English accent inspired by David Attenborough. The guests lapped it up. I nudged Sailor and held up my fist to count to three. As Kyle finished saying the words "Ladies and gentlemen, I would like to proffer a warm welcome to the most wonderful place on Earth . . . Alcatraz Zoo," I mouthed "three," uncurled my last finger, and Sailor and I opened the boxes.

Hundreds of painted ladies spilled out and filled the air. A collective gasp, then murmurs and exclamations of surprise and delight as the butterflies fluttered around or landed on exposed flesh—heads and hands and faces and calves—bestowing soft butterfly kisses. (They're just attracted to the sweet saltiness of perspiration, but the guests don't need to know that.) All the faces almost cracked from smiling so wide. I knew it was cheesy, I knew it was just for show and wasn't what butterflies should naturally be doing, but I couldn't help it: I loved the butterfly release then, and I love it still. Even if it falls to me to sweep up the little papery corpses at the end of the shift.

Let me have this one thing.

The funicular pulled to a stop on the parade grounds at the southern tip of the island, with panoramic views of the city and the two bridges majestically straddling the bay. The octagonal concrete lighthouse looms over the scene, lonely in its perpetual, sleepless vigil. I've heard one of the most torturous things for the prisoners was to be so close to San Francisco, a mere mile and a half away, to be able to see it and hear it and smell it—fireworks flushing the city with light on New Year's Eve; fumes from cars driven by people who took their freedom of movement for granted; even the sound of voices occasionally wafting across the waves—while knowing they could never go back.

Sailor and I brought up the rear as the guests piled out of the train and into the arrivals hall, a small, modern building containing change rooms and an elevator that descended into the bowels of the zoo.

"What happens now?"

"Decontamination showers," I said. "Unfortunately, we have to take them too, since we've been in contact with people from the mainland. We stay outside until the guests have gone down, then we follow. Wait!"

This last word was yelped at Sailor's departing back. She had sprung up the stairs and was standing at the guest entrance to the zoo, just beyond the lighthouse, squinting up at the imposing white building. When the Pinkton family first purchased Alcatraz Island, they decided to update the exterior of the cellhouse, which had historically always been painted yellow, to this brilliant white. It was intended to convey cleanliness and modernity, to assure guests that whatever happened within these walls was as far from the island's most famous traditions as it was possible to get. The problem being that the rock is perpetually pummeled by salt and wind and storms, and it only takes a few months for the jaunty white to start flaying off in patches. A team of painters has to be brought over from the mainland every few months to do touch-ups.

Torn between my duty to supervise Sailor and reluctance to leave my post, I joined her, hoping Kyle wouldn't notice our absence. The arched entrance was designed, like so much of the island, to strike awe. There were two massive black iron gates sporting an ornate peacock design, and the words ALCATRAZ ZOO were emblazoned above in the same gilded script as the funicular. Impassive armed guards stood at either side. Only their eyes moved as we approached.

After a while Sailor spoke. "So this is it, then, huh? The end of the road." I gave a nervous nod, given she was technically correct. In the literal sense we had reached the end of the path and there was nowhere left to go but inside or back down the hill. "The animal kingdom's last stand."

"I don't think of it like that," I responded stiffly. Her characterization stung my pride, somehow. "We're giving the animals a future."

To a stranger, the words must have sounded like propaganda, the parroting of lines we'd been trained to say. That wasn't far off the mark. We all knew the correct way to talk about captivity if it came up. The idea was to be armed with a ready line for any guests who might feel uneasy about the whole animals-in-cages thing. We rarely encountered unbelievers among the guests, though: the tours were so wildly expensive and conferred such status that they tended to attract a self-selecting group of people easily convinced of the virtues of conservation.

I too was a believer. The choice, however regrettable, was binary: the remaining animals out in the once-wild could either fend for themselves in a world that no longer offered them safety, or they could be cared for in a place like this, where all their material needs were met and there was at least a small hope of securing the survival of their kind. Better to lead a confined life than no life at all, that was the line we all swallowed and regurgitated like parent birds.

"A future," echoed Sailor, as if she was trying to figure out what that word meant.

"We should go," I said, tugging gently at her sleeve. We headed back to the arrivals hall, and as we reached the lighthouse Sailor turned around and made finger guns at the guards.

"Are you trying to give me a heart attack?" I said, hustling her inside the building and into the elevator, but her bold grin was infectious, and I couldn't stay mad.

Downstairs, we arrived just in time to see the guests emerge from changing booths wrapped in towels and robes. The showers still emitted the haunting utilitarianism of a prison, and I'm convinced the Pinktons intended it this way. Obviously, they could have afforded to retrofit the area into a gleaming, palatial spa if they had wanted to. Retaining the creepy features of the original space—the vertical rows of showerheads bolted to the roof and streaked with rust; the institutional green tiled floors; the sickly overhead lights—reinforced the idea that the guests were required to undergo a kind of ritualistic cleansing before entering the sacred space of the zoo. There was something primal about it. All the perfumes and cosmetics and cloaking smells stripped away, all the clothes and external status symbols shed like snakeskin. Reduced down to their human animal.

As the decontaminations began, Sailor stared wide-eyed at it all: attendants ushering men and women into separate areas, sluicing them down with bars of black soap and huge evil-looking scrubbing brushes, then leading them to the shower jets, after which they shuffled to a series of booths where they were given protective visors and sprayed by robot arms with a powerful disinfectant. Finally, the guests emerged, born-agains with damp hair and shy smiles, to be returned upstairs.

"Well, this is . . . debasing," said Sailor. She seemed amused rather than horrified as some people are when they witness it for the first time. "Can't help but think most of them are kind of into it, though. Like, it makes the experience more authentic or something." I was impressed that she had struck on it exactly.

After all the guests had gone back upstairs, we workers got misted in the decontamination tank as well, fully clothed—no showers for us, which only confirmed my suspicions that most of what happened here was a show for the benefit of guests. By the time we returned to the arrivals hall, most of the guests were ready for their big adventure.

"What the fuckety-fuck," said Sailor softly as the first of them emerged from the changing rooms in the safari gear the zoo provided for their use, spinning around to show one another and posing for souvenir photos. "Have to admit, 'cosplaying colonial explorers' is a twist I definitely wasn't expecting."

I stifled my laugh. They did look ridiculous, doughy businessmen in pith helmets with multipocketed khaki vests straining across their bellies, their wives in headscarves and leopard-print trousers with binoculars around their necks. When everyone was ready, we led the guests to the entrance. The iron gates swung open silently. No one spoke as we passed through that grand portal. Even the wind died down. Inside, we ushered the guests up a narrow, steep staircase and into a small waiting room with black walls and black tentlike fabric draped from the ceiling. There were low murmurs of excitement.

Kyle opened the door with a showman's flourish and stepped out onto a steel catwalk, beckoning the guests to follow him. One by one we passed through the door and into the main zoo, which had been dramatically darkened. Flickers of light played around the dark walls, and the catwalk itself was illuminated so people could see where they were stepping, but otherwise the thrilling, slightly dizzy feeling of sensory deprivation continued for a few more moments as we all huddled close together at the beginning of the walkway, shoulders touching, breaths mingling. Suspended in space and time. Sailor nudged me, and I nudged her back.

Kyle turned to face the group. He raised his eyebrows and performed a brief, secretive smile. "Is everybody *ready*?"

Couples reached out to clutch one another's hands. Kyle made a theatrical unfolding gesture in front of his face and the entire space grew a shade lighter, like when you stay up all night and watch dawn bleed over the horizon. Then, out of nowhere, a large herd of pure-white antelope materialized around us and galloped down the catwalk, tails twitching and slender bodies leaping, hooves clattering on the metal until they faded away into darkness at the other end. Guests gasped, hands to chests.

After the antelope disappeared and their hoofbeats faded, the light kept gradually getting brighter until the entire zoo was illuminated. Everything had changed. We were no longer standing on the steel catwalk of a former prison but had been transported into a lush jungle-scape twitching with sound and life. The formerly empty corridors and blank walls were now festooned with trees and ferns and flowers and waterfalls, all of it so lifelike you felt you could reach out and pluck a trembling blossom. The air reverberated with the sounds of rustling leaves, of creatures calling to one another. Kyle let the guests soak it all in for a minute, then cleared his throat. He spun to face the uppermost row of cells, spreading his arms wide.

"Behold, the canopy! This, ladies and gentlemen, is where the exotic birds of Alcatraz make their home."

The cells had been obscured in shadow, but at his words they too began to brighten, and a new vision appeared. The birds flocking and squawking and roosting and twittering and preening in front of us weren't projections this time, but real flesh and blood and feather. Most were brilliantly colored (plumage and ability to get along with other birds were the main criteria for their placement here), and each sang a different tune. Some had voices like bells, some like squeaking doors, some like catcallers whistling at women on the street. The enclosures contained real plants and trees too—I knew because I often helped Gill, the head arborist, with greens dressing, moving the plants around or replacing them, which had to be done often because they didn't get enough light. But they were also overlaid with masses of magical projected foliage that made it appear the birds were deep beneath the canopy of some ancient rainforest. Dappled sunlight filtered through trees. Droplets of water sparkled like diamonds on leaves. The forest gave the impression of stretching for miles, to a distant horizon where a range of snowcapped mountains jutted into clouds.

Kyle led the spellbound group slowly along the path, pointing out birds of interest, sometimes hitching up his khakis and squatting on his haunches to show guests some shy creature on the forest floor, answering enquiries with a sonorous, "That is a *very* interesting question, thank you."

Amid the clamor, I heard Sailor's voice close to my ear. "How do they do that, with the cages?"

"A trick. I'll tell you later." She looked disappointed but I could somehow tell it wasn't with me. With herself, maybe. The trick was that during the tours, the cages look as though they've magically vanished. The bars and the wire are more visible when the 3D simulator is off, but even then, they're pale and shimmery, some kind of polymer that seems to disappear at certain angles. They designed it that way so that even if the simulator isn't working or the power goes out, there's still a blurring effect. With the simulator on, the bars and the walls melt completely away.

There was debate in the early days of keeping the guests in some kind of enclosed vehicle, but it was decided they wouldn't have liked that distance from the rare creatures they had come to gawk at. They wanted to not only see them but also smell them, hear them, maybe even feel their hot breath as they went by.

When the guests had finished blissing out on the birds, we moved to the staircase to descend to the next level. There was a glass elevator too, but no one that day needed it. As we brought up the rear of the pack, I nudged Sailor to turn around. We both watched as the rainforest disappeared and the canopy went dark, blinking off cell by cell. The guests were focused on a new set of wonders ahead, the birds already forgotten. Now all they cared about was visiting with the lions, cheetah, giraffe, and gazelles on the African savannah, a relatively large habitat spread across the cavernous former kitchens and mess hall of the prison. Or swinging with monkeys through the jungles of Southeast Asia. Or watching the solitary old grizzly bear fishing for salmon in the whitewater rivers of Canada as a soft rain from the sprinklers above misted us with a spray that might have been blown right off the river.

It was our job as guides to wind our way unobtrusively through the scene, checking on guests, answering questions, making sure everything was shipshape. Sailor stuck close to me, and at every new section she would whisper wry commentary in my ear.

"Check it out, here come the Small Dick Guys," she said when we reached the big cat section and several older men brandishing long telephoto lenses jostled their fellow gawkers out of the way to get their shots.

Kyle stood with his back pressed against the fenced section of the catwalk so as not to obscure anyone's view. "Witness the magnificent lioness grooming her pack mate, no doubt hoping for a return favor at some later time, perhaps an extra scrap of meat during a kill."

"How many Bengal tigers are left?" someone shouted to him when we were in the vicinity of our glorious tiger, Beyoncé.

"This is the *very* last one," answered Kyle without missing a beat. There was a reverent gasp. I was probably the only one who clocked Kyle's discomfort. He went ever so slightly red where his ropy neck muscles met the collar of his polo shirt. I knew he used to answer this question honestly, if vaguely, based on scientific estimates as they evolved out in the world. "Maybe a hundred?" He used to say. Or: "We actually think fewer than a dozen now. Eight or so." Until one day he got called into the admin office and after that he only ever answered in this way. "This is the *very* last one."

Sailor mouthed at me: "Is that true?"

I gave a tiny shrug and under my breath said, "We don't know for sure. Maybe."

"Sounds better this way, though, huh? Gets them all wet."

I had to look away so I didn't laugh. Guests didn't like it when we laughed. She was right, though. There was something distasteful about how much the guests perked up when you told them an animal was the last of its kind. Like it conferred a special status on them to be so close to an extinction.

The only ones who aren't fooled by all the pageantry are the animals, because the technological marvels swirling around mean nothing to them. As far as they're concerned, they're still sitting or lying or pacing or flapping in the same environment they've always been in. That's why the ownership decided to use a few low-tech tricks with the animals too, like installing treadmills as the entire floor for the big cats to give the impression they're striding along the plains or stalking in the jungle. Behind the scenes, there are keepers switching on the treadmills as the tour approaches.

When we arrived at the elephant enclosure I involuntarily moved toward the bars, although we were supposed to let guests go first. Kira was a sweet-natured twelve-year-old cow, and she had been inconsolable in the four years since her longtime companion, another African elephant called Shambala, had died. It tore at my heart to see her standing stock-still day after day. During the tours the enclosure leaped into vivid and animated movement around her, a pretend herd magicked up to keep her company on the pretend savannah, so the guests didn't tend to notice her sadness. But I did. It was exhilarating knowing today was the last day she'd be alone.

"Elephants are your favorite, aren't they?" Sailor was scrutinizing me rather than Kira, as if in that moment I was the more interesting animal.

"Oh, I don't know," I said. I'd trained myself to pretend I didn't have favorites. But my training crumbled because I blurted out, "My dream is to get to touch one someday."

"You've never touched her?"

"'Course not," I said, shocked she didn't know this. "Only her dedicated keepers are allowed to interact with her. Same with Achilles the crocodile."

"So those keepers don't swap around like the rest of us?"

"No. They have those assignments for life."

"Who decides which keepers get assigned those positions?"

"The ownership. The admins." I was surprised she didn't know all this stuff. Maybe it had been different in Paris.

"So that's just the way it is, huh?"

I nodded. I couldn't tell what she thought of this. Maybe it struck her as unfair. I suppose it was, in a way, but we were all used to things being unfair, so no one ever fought against it. That didn't mean you couldn't nurse secret hopes, though, in the privacy of your own head.

Finally, we ushered the guests into a large space on the ground floor. It was set-dressed as an old-style lounge, with sofas, ottomans, velvet curtains, and framed oil paintings. Sailor raised her eyebrows, but I just gave her a Mona Lisa smile. Beyond the velvet-draped wall at the back was the multi-room gift shop—where guests could stock up on big-ticket souvenirs like fake swordfish bills, real bird feathers, and bags of manure from the exotic animals, a perennial bestseller—and beyond that the Arboretum. But instead of passing through, all the guests remained chattering happily and making themselves comfortable. Sailor and I stood against the wall near the entrance. "Just watch," I whispered to her.

Kyle moved toward the front of the room. He rubbed his hands together, grinning mysteriously. "And now, ladies and gentlemen," he said in his plummiest voice, "for the final surprise, each and every one of you"—he slowed his enunciation down even further—"*each and every one of you . . . is going to get the chance to hold an animal who is the very last of its kind.*"

A murmur of anticipation rippled around the room. After a few suspenseful minutes, a keeper entered holding something, and the room began to buzz. I couldn't even tell which keeper it was because they were wearing a full hazmat suit.

"This is Precious," Kyle explained to the group, sweeping his palm through the air in the direction of the large gray, exceedingly fluffy domestic cat cradled in the keeper's arms. "She is the only remaining member of the once-robust prison cat colony that thrived on the island of Alcatraz in days past. As the keen-eyed of you might notice, she has six toes on each paw, making her what is known as 'polydactyl.'"

The keeper carried Precious to a sofa in the center of the room where an elderly man was waiting, knees together, lips pressed against an emotion you could see bubbling up in him. The keeper set Precious down on the guest's lap. The cat settled in, gently kneading the man's thighs and purring loudly. (A mic attached to her collar filled the room with a hypnotic hum.) The man lifted his hand tentatively, as if not daring to hope it was real, then lowered it into the cat's fur. Tears began leaking down his face. Around the room, people sniffled and wiped their eyes, leaning their heads on one another's shoulders.

It never fails. I mean, it's a poignant moment, even when you know, as we all do, that Precious isn't the last one at all, but part of a thriving colony. We breed them in a warehouse at the northwestern end of the island. The cats are pliant, friendly, and extra-resilient for some reason, immune to the usual diseases, and every batch of kittens is near-identical, so it's easy to swap out a new Precious when the current performer gets too old or dies. Do the guests really think we'd let outsiders handle her if she were truly the last? Well, never mind. In my experience, people just see what they want to see.

We trailed the guests to the gift shop entrance, and then that part of our day was over. The only things left to show Sailor were the boring parts of the island where we keepers lived out our lives—the laundry room and other parts of the barracks she might not have encountered. The long, low-slung hospital building on the untouristed side of the island, which even has a tiny human wing in case one of us gets injured or sick. Although if there's even a hint of illness, especially something contagious, something that could jump species, you're out of here so fast your head would spin. Dumped on the mainland. Someone else's problem.

"So, what did you think?" I asked her as I wrapped up the orientation.

"Of the tour, I mean?" For some reason I was anxious to be told she'd had a good time, as if I were a hostess waiting to hear how a dinner party was received. She let her breath out through puckered lips, as if weighing up how much was safe to say.

"I think . . . it's like the Ringling Circus on acid."

"Shhh," I said, half amused, half scandalized. "No one says the C word around here."

"Circus, circus, circus," Sailor whispered, her lips so close to the side of my head the words reverberated in my eardrum, and I tried not to laugh.

At 4:00 p.m. we all gathered at the parade ground to wait for Titan. Everyone but essential personnel had been granted time off to witness this historic moment. We stood in a loose bunch, faces raised to the sky, although Titan and his crew weren't due until five. We didn't talk much. Usually an occasion like this would have been a chance to gossip and talk nonsense, to complain about our days or tell a funny anecdote about one of the animals. But we all understood the gravity of this particular arrival, representing as it did the last, unlikely hope for averting the extinction of one of the most incredible creatures to ever roam this earth.

When a lone bull had been found in a tiny corner of jungle in the Golden Triangle a while back—disoriented and defeated-looking, walking in circles—he had been whisked to the Singapore Zoo and displayed as their star attraction. After rumors surfaced that the zoo was close to shutting down, the Pinktons made their move. The deal to bring Titan to Alcatraz to attempt a mating with Kira had been struck on, the papers signed, the vast sums of money transferred into some Swiss bank account, and after a series of excruciating delays, finally Titan was on his way to us.

In the barracks after-hours we all agreed that a baby elephant was never going to come out of the arrangement, mainly because the elephants are different species, from different continents, and the chance of them producing offspring was vanishingly small, even if the optimists did try to bring up other dubious hybrid success stories from history, like Pizzlies and Ligers. We'd all been burned before, hoping for the survival of some exquisite creature only to watch the last one or two members of the species grow apathetic, fade away, and disappear forever.

Still, it was hard not to get swept up in it anyway. The original plan had been to bring Titan over from the Embarcadero on some kind of custom-built barge, accompanied by a celebratory flotilla, crowds cheering him on from the shore, a whole big spectacle, but the scheme was scrapped. No one knew for sure if elephants got seasick, but the consensus was it wouldn't have been a good look to have the zoo's prize elephant barfing on the first day of his new life, or worse, have him freak out and capsize the barge. The ownership procured a military helicopter instead, one of those huge, open-sided ones in whose belly Titan would travel. Frankly, that didn't strike me as any more dignified or less terrifying than the barge, but no one consulted me.

The helicopter had just come into sight above the bridge and a rousing cheer had risen from the assembled crowd when Joseph elbowed his way to my side, reaching down and pinching my butt.

"Hey."

"Ow," I said, rubbing the spot. "Hey."

Joseph was one of the other keepers, and we had sex sometimes—that's why he considered himself to have butt-pinching privileges. My mind had been blown when Joseph started paying attention to me, because he could have had anyone. He was one of the keepers who looked after Achilles the crocodile, and I couldn't imagine anything more appealing than that. His artfully scruffy good looks and general swagger—the other qualities that made him a big hit around Alcatraz—weren't as important to me, but I doubt any of the other keepers believed that. Joseph was related to the Pinktons, so he was basically untouchable as far as getting fired or even reprimanded went. I think everyone thought I was a social climber. As if there was anywhere to climb to apart from the top of this rock, windblown and hemmed in by a stinging sea.

"Big day, huh?" Joseph put his arm around me. "Titanic, one might say."

"I can't believe it's here." I squeezed his arm, and he instinctively flexed his bicep. "I just can't believe it. Can you believe it?"

He normally got annoyed when I prattled, but he just smiled, like it was endearing this time. "Yes, babe, it's a very big deal."

It felt good seeing him misty-eyed and sincere, like when we first got together and would talk for hours about the animals and what we loved most about working with them. I didn't notice Sailor had arrived on the other side of me until she bumped me with her hip.

"Oh, hi," I said, glad she'd sought me out. "Joseph, say hi to Sailor. She just arrived."

"Hey," he said, turning his brazen gaze her way. Sizing her up. Sailor was at his eye level, though, which seemed to put Joseph at a disadvantage. He radiated curiosity and wariness, like a wolf inspecting an intruder, whereas Sailor appeared perfectly comfortable, even bored.

"Joseph works with Achilles, the crocodile," I announced into the slightly tense silence.

That got her attention. "No shit? Must be nice."

"It ain't too bad." He flashed a grin.

The chopper slowed as it approached the island, its massive blades a blur of movement, its steely gray body hanging like a malignant wasp. A collective sound went up when the helicopter opened, something between a gasp and an exhalation. Slowly, while the chopper hovered over the rec yard, the elephant was lowered out of the hatch, his enormous belly girdled by a thick rubbery harness, his wrinkly tree-trunk legs dangling out the bottom. The sight was somehow both awe-inspiring and comic. With painstaking care, the personnel in the helicopter lowered the elephant until he was only a few feet off the ground. Kira was inside the elephant house (the two elephants would be introduced and acclimatized to each other over many days), so she was spared the sight of her potential paramour's undignified arrival.

My eyes filled as Titan made landfall. It was like watching man set foot on the moon for the first time. Something you knew you could tell your grandchildren about, if you were ever to have any. I startled a little when I felt a touch on my left hand. There was a fair bit of movement and jostling in the crowd as everyone watched the descent, so I thought it was an accident at first, and I politely shifted my hand closer to my body. But Sailor's hand was back again a few seconds later, searching for my own, and when she found it she held on tightly, her fingers warm. That was the last time her hands would ever be that soft again: soon they would be as calloused and nicked as my own.

We never looked at each other. As soon as the elephant was fully standing on the ground, a group of keepers ran to unchain him from the harness, and the crowd erupted in a giant storm of cheering and clapping. Sailor casually dropped my hand and joined in. They dispersed us quickly after that, the guards hustling everyone back to the barracks so the stewards and vets could maneuver Titan up the rec yard ramp and into his enclosure.

The feelings of the group were mixed. I heard some keepers breathlessly recapping the event, already shaping it into a treasured tale, while others complained it was anticlimactic. Impossible to tell what the elephant thought of it all. No one ever asked him.

If you were given the chance to do it again, knowing how it all ends, would you take it? What if it promised to let the tiniest sliver of joy into your otherwise dreary life? What then?

The questions stew in my mind, whoever I am demanding answers from never responding. But in the end, I realize I'm only asking myself, and I already know the answer. I have always known it.

Paris

Eight Years Earlier

Florida was two years behind her now. There was plenty to love about this new place but she could never quite forgive it for not being home. She didn't feel French and she didn't feel American anymore either, rather something in between, a wanderer across oceans and landscapes of opportunity. She was thirty-five years old. Her body and mind were good and strong, she had landed her dream job, and on the nights she couldn't sleep it struck her as sharply unfair that the world appeared to be more or less ending just as she was coming into her full powers.

The blights had started by then, striking simultaneously at points around the world: Southeast Asia, Eastern Europe, Australia, along the border of Canada and the United States, the UAE, South America. A virulent strain of mold that attacked tree roots, thinning out forests and jungles. Then a fungus that morphed from a mostly harmless strain of candida into a deadly and fast-acting disease against which thousands of animals and birds were defenseless. For many species already teetering on the edge, it was the last push they needed to tumble into the extinction abyss. The disease didn't appear to be zoonotic, a silver lining everyone was too freaked out to fully appreciate. Maybe the fungi just hadn't found a way in to the human body yet.

It was Anouk, her closest friend at the zoo, who delivered the news. She darted over to Sailor, who was bent over the washing station, sluicing her arms under the jet.

"Sailor, did you hear?" Anouk's curls bounced and her dark eyes were wide and bright as a squirrel's, solemn with the weight of secret knowledge.

"No, what?"

"They blew up the San Francisco Zoo."

"What? Who did?"

"*Je ne sais pas.* Some lunatics. Can you believe?"

It turned out a group calling themselves "humanism defenders" had left homemade bombs in six trash cans around the zoo. Only two had detonated, just before the zoo opened, which was considered a mercy, as there were no human fatalities, just one injured security guard, a Central American anteater called a tamandua who was rushed to the hospital to have pieces of shrapnel removed from its forelegs, and three crowned pigeons who flew panicked and disoriented into a glass curtain when one of the devices exploded near their enclosure. The bombing was new but the amorphous rage that sought a target was not. Sailor could feel it constantly vibrating beneath everything, like an approaching train that sets the rails humming. Soon it would come for them too.

After the bombing, she and Anouk and six other keepers formed a group that met for apéros every week at a divey bar in the 14th, near Montparnasse Cemetery. Loud, discordant bands played in front of a heavy red curtain every night. There was no need for secrecy, not at the beginning anyway, but when they met they instinctively chose an isolated corner table to huddle around.

The first time they just shout-talked over the music about everyday stuff—gossip and politics, mostly. A few drinks in, things got maudlin and they went around the table reciting various things they already missed: fresh peaches, the way the Jardins Luxembourg used to look in spring, skiing, the alien beauty of the Everglades. So many things they'd once taken for granted were either in peril or already memories. Oceans busy rising and forests busy shrinking, the old order of the world turning inside out.

She'd never thought of herself as sentimental, but the past began hijacking her at odd moments. One day in the sea lion enclosure, passing her hand over the velvet-slick coat of a bull hassling her for fish, she found herself ambushed by a memory and had to sit down abruptly on the cold concrete.

She was eight or nine years old and tilted over the side of a boat with the ribbons from her pigtails trailing in the water. Her father at the bow, shouting that he'd just seen the shadow of a manatee. He was always swearing he'd just seen a manatee, claiming Sailor must have been dozing to have missed it, and only years later did she realize he'd just been pretending so he could hear her joyous shrieks ring through the mangroves. Because even back then their numbers had been collapsing and sightings were becoming rarer and rarer, until the blights finished them off for good.

Scratch another entry into the book of loss. And how many more pages would be filled before all this was done?

Alcatraz

The day after Titan arrived, I shuffled out of my room to shower, testing my mood to see whether the excitement of the previous day had caused an uptick in my serotonin levels. The good feeling, I noted with pleasant surprise, hadn't yet dissipated. I knew it was still dark outside, we always got up before dawn, but the lighting inside the barracks was designed to artificially stimulate our circadian rhythms—a gradual dimming as it got closer to bedtime, a gradual lightening as our workday approached. Between dawn and dusk the lighting was set to pitilessly bright, probably to discourage furtive naps. The windows facing out to the dock were kept covered. It was like being in a casino, a place outside of time. Like the exterior of the zoo, the barracks are whitewashed every few months in an effort to combat the rising damp, but it creeps back from the ground up, staining the wall in splotches until it's time to paint it again. Just one of the many Sisyphean tasks around here.

In the mess hall, I saw Sailor eating breakfast by herself. She looked up at my approach, her face blank for a moment then softening into recognition. I didn't sit down because I've always felt like I needed an invitation to join someone, so instead I pressed my pubic bone awkwardly against the edge of the table and dangled my respirator off my fingertips.

"I just wanted to make sure you had one of these," I said. "It's going to be pretty bad out there today. There should be one in your locker. If you don't wear it you end up coughing for weeks."

Sailor's eyes went squinty, and her half-open mouth, still chewing on breakfast mush, tilted at the sides into the beginning of a smile.

"This isn't my first rodeo, kid. But thanks." There was no venom in her words, so I didn't take offense. "Appreciate you looking out for me." She continued chewing slowly and studying my face as if it fascinated her. "Feel free to join me," she said at last, tapping her spoon on the table next to her. "It's not like anyone else wants to."

I gladly accepted her offer, dropped my mask on the seat beside her to save my spot and took my place in the cafeteria line. I'm always famished when I wake up, looking forward to breakfast the way a feedlot cow might once have anticipated the first daily delivery of rancid grain from the chute. I don't blame the cooks, they do their best with what they've been given. It can't be easy to cobble together nourishing and appealing meals out of lab meat, surplus Minnesota soy protein and corn, and on the rare occasion, tiny, bony fish. The nice cooks do little things to cheer us up, like garnishing the plate with a sprinkling of sudsy-tasting herbs they grow under hydroponic lamps near the dishwashing station. I've always tried to practice gratitude. Mediocre food is better than starving, and on Alcatraz we eat better than most people on the mainland. (And the animals eat better than all of us.)

On this morning my heart lifted a little because one of the warming trays contained actual bread. Unleavened, of course, because yeast is so hard to come by, but it was still a treat. Hunter, one of the cooks, nudged an extra piece onto my plate, beneath the soy patty, and I gave him a grateful smile. I took one of the mandatory smoothies, as they call them, a nauseating slurry of a fruity vitamin/mineral cocktail we receive each day to make sure we stay healthy enough to keep doing our jobs.

"Morning, Camille." I turned to see Gill, one of my favorite people on the island. "Happy Arbor Day."

"Oh, I didn't know! Happy Arbor Day to you. How are you celebrating?"

Gill lifted a smoothie and put it on his tray, his mouth puckered with distaste. "Beloved, every day is Arbor Day for me. But yes, it's technically observed on the last Friday of April. Planting season, in our hemisphere. Spring, if you still believe in such things. You know what the riches are doing today?"

"I do not."

"They're buying tree indulgences. It's true. I read a thing."

"Do I want to know what 'tree indulgences' are?"

"Oh, boy. Well, you know how Catholics in the Middle Ages were into indulgences? Paying the church off to release them from sin and all that? Now it's the elites buying trees to offset their carbon footprint. Look"—he thrust his phone toward me—"here's a beautifully styled photo of some billionaire philistines planting a tree on their estate." I looked dutifully, shaking my head. "It's not even native! Flown in at staggering expense from Laos. It's going to be dead in two weeks!" He sighed.

I patted him on the hand in sympathetic acknowledgment of it all, then left him to his glum perusal of the chafing dishes.

I sat down next to Sailor, making sure to keep a respectable distance between my elbow and hers. I didn't want her to think I intended to take advantage of the brief moment of intimacy we'd shared while watching Titan drop in. I steeled myself, took hold of the smoothie, and drank it down in one breathless gulp. I could feel Sailor looking at the side of my face, horrified no doubt at my table manners. But she laughed and there was admiration in her voice when she said, "Yeah, that's the way to do it." I tried to smile but it came out a wince instead. Sailor speared a piece of crispy Facon on her fork, chewed it with a contemplative air. "So, what are you in for, anyway?"

"Huh?"

"I mean, how did you end up at Alcatraz? I don't think you mentioned, yesterday."

"Oh." I wanted to kick myself for being such a dull wombat. "Well, I got sentenced to ten-to-life because my parents knew the boss."

Sailor's eyes lit up with curiosity. "Really, the Pinktons? How did your folks know them?"

I hesitated. My palms itched like I'd touched something poisonous. "My dad was Mr. Pinkton's chauffeur for a while." That wasn't the whole story but I didn't want to be a downer. Not that she wouldn't have had similar stories herself: everyone did.

"And that was enough to get you the job?"

"Dad could be pretty persuasive. Spun some story to Mr. Pinkton about his daughter having a 'rare rapport' with animals."

I found being pinned under Sailor's bright, curious gaze both flattering and excruciating. Her frank interest was very disarming after living among my peers, the Great Unimpressed.

"Guess he was right, wasn't he?"

"Ah, I don't think so! No more than anyone else." Sailor frowned and stirred her bowl of mush. I made a mental note that self-deprecation wouldn't fly with her. Keen to correct my error, I said, "When I was a kid, I definitely dreamed about being a zookeeper, before I even knew what that was. My parents took me to the San Francisco Zoo once when I was maybe twelve, and I had a meltdown when they tried to drag me away. I couldn't think of any job better than working with animals. Still can't, actually."

"Couldn't agree more. Although I wonder how many other people in here feel that way? Seems like zookeeping is only sought-after because it offers a better life than anything else going. Fuck it, may as well live and die surrounded by animals than in a sweatshop or war zone, right? All I know is I had to jump through crazy hoops to get this far."

"Really? You're so qualified."

"Alas, we can't all be nepo hires like your boy Joseph." She grinned to indicate she was just kidding. I stifled a laugh but I also wondered how she knew about Joseph's background already. "People would kill for that kind of job security."

"I don't think anyone minds," I said loyally. "He's very popular."

"Yeah, I noticed. I prefer stiller waters, myself."

I didn't grasp exactly what she meant, but there was a flattering intimacy to her banter that made me feel like I was on a date. Not that I'd ever been on a date—what Joseph and I had didn't really rise to the level of dating—but I'd heard about them and seen them in movies.

Keen to prove myself worthy company, I said, "Oh, by the way, we call the vets the Squeaky Shoes. On account of—"

"Their squeaky shoes?"

I already didn't mind her teasing tone. It was different from when other people did it.

"Yes, exactly. So what was it like, working at the Paris Zoo?"

I must have sounded overeager, but I didn't care. I'd always been fascinated by the other zoos and would rush to interrogate new keepers who'd worked at one of the others. I was sad I'd never get to see them.

"It was a prison too," she said, "but at least it was in Paris." She laughed after saying it, so I couldn't tell if she was serious or not. "It's different from here. The visitors can just wander around and look at the exhibits on their own, but after a few security breaches they put all the animals behind glass, and the tourists didn't like that. They feel cut off from the whole 'nature' experience. It's been losing tons of money for years. There's just a skeleton staff there now. I was, um, transferred back to the States during the last round of staff cuts. Needed a job and pulled some strings."

"Were you sad to leave the zoo?"

"I was sad it existed, if that's what you mean."

I didn't mean that at all, and I think she knew it. I wasn't completely naive, I knew what people said about places like this. That they were cruel, inhumane; evil, even. That the zoo was a carceral state and should be abolished. There were plenty of people who celebrated every time a zoo closed down, because it was considered a victory for the rights of the animals to live free lives.

"But what about the fact the animals are doomed out there, thanks to us?" I blurted this out without caring how defensive I sounded. "The once-wild is no place for animals anymore."

"I guess you're beginning to see why no one wants to sit with me," said Sailor.

"It's not that," I said, flustered. "I just don't see what the alternative is, you know?"

Sailor pushed her food to the side, dropped the spoon into the bowl, then leaned back with a defeated sigh. "I hear you, sister, this is as good as it gets. For now."

"So . . . what's it like out there?" I asked, wanting to change the subject. It was considered gauche to ask that of new people, but I was one of the keepers who never left the island and was starved for news. There were scheduled trips to the mainland for people who needed to see family or whatever, but I never did that. There was no one there for me now. Still, that didn't stop me craving even the barest snippets of information, little details of the world beyond this island.

"Out there? It's the same. People are mean and hungry, mostly. Always fighting over something. They're worse than hyenas. Actually, hyenas are really cooperative, so that analogy doesn't work, does it?"

I didn't know whether the question was rhetorical, so I didn't answer. Alcatraz had a hyena once. Their jaws are so strong they can crush bones at a force of 1,100 pounds per square inch. Even that talent wasn't enough to keep ours alive, though. They're communal creatures, hyenas, and ours had no community left.

Sailor and I left the mess hall together to get our assignments. But even before we got to the screen, we knew something was up—the electricity generated when a group of people are presented with a new and potentially day-altering piece of information. We jostled to the front and saw the screen was empty of the usual names and assignments. Instead, there blared one simple message: ALL STAFF REPORT TO THE PARADE GROUNDS AT 0700 FOR A MESSAGE FROM A VIP GUEST.

"Will the wonders never cease?" said Sailor.

I twirled the end of my ponytail around my finger. Much like the animals, I mistrusted changes in my daily routine. The elephant had been a welcome once-in-a-lifetime disruption, but I wasn't ready for another one so soon.

"Who do you think it is?" I wasn't really expecting her to answer, not being familiar with our local VIPs.

"Well, judging by the vulgar jade-green yacht I saw anchored on the other side of the island this morning, I'd say we're being graced by a member of the Pinkton family."

I gaped at her. I wasn't sure which impressed me most, the fact that she knew what the Pinktons' yacht looked like, or the knowledge that she'd been up and roaming the island before I'd even opened my eyes.

We trooped obediently to the parade grounds. I could tell some workers were irritated at this upheaval to their day and were itching for the ceremony to be over quickly so they could get on with their tasks. Others were giddy as truants. I belonged firmly in the first camp, and I trudged alongside Sailor, shivering as a gust of wind raked the hill.

I could see Joseph's tousled hair ahead. I would usually have hurried to catch up, but there was already a small scrum of people around him and I held back. Joseph's best friend and occasional rival, Brandon, was there, as was an acerbic keeper called Louise, who'd started at Alcatraz around the same time as me but had far more social clout, and Ali, who worked with the elephants and was therefore almost a demigod. There was Carter Coates, who worked the boat, and a few others. From the moment you stepped off that ferry and touched Alcatraz soil for the first time, it was obvious who the anointed power brokers were among the keepers. If you were smart, you worked your way into their graces or at least kept a respectful distance, like I did. Yet I hadn't seen Sailor acknowledge any of them, not even with a glance.

At the top of the hill, four huge men in black sport coats and sunglasses shoved their way through the crowd. They were so immense, presenting such a solid block of humanity, it took me a moment to understand they were shielding another, smaller human who walked between them. A hush descended, and the hordes parted. At the front of the parade ground, the phalanx of large men spread out to reveal the human they had been charged with protecting: Mr. Pinkton.

The entire Pinkton family officially owns the zoo, but James Pinkton Sr. is the patriarch around which the whole concern revolves. Visits from him are rare and usually announced long in advance. Mr. Pinkton smiled and raised his hand in greeting. I noticed for the first time a hastily erected wooden platform near the lighthouse, so at least a few people had known about his visit. For someone so ancient, he took the stairs to the podium with surprising gusto, waving like a politician on the first leg of a campaign.

The day was truly rancid. Even with a respirator on, taking a breath was like drawing glass into your lungs. Workers were pulling their EZ-Breathe inhalers out of overall pockets left, right, and center, drawing that mixture of albuterol and a patented Pinkton secret chemical into their grateful bronchial tubes. It suddenly made sense why this little demonstration was being held outdoors—hard to forget in that moment how much we relied upon the inhalers on which Mr. Pinkton had built his formidable fortune. He probably loved that. Even the air quality index was on his side. Whether he was determined to project toughness or was somehow immune to the dire conditions, his own face was uncovered. Maybe elites like him had found some way to outwit the atmosphere itself.

"Workers of Alcatraz!" Mr. Pinkton's voice, no doubt booming and authoritative in the boardroom, was whipped away by the wind as soon as it left his mouth. I was close to the front and I could barely hear him. "This is a historic time for the Pinkton family, and for the human race. A magnificent and rare specimen has arrived at our zoo!" He was practically shouting by this point, his cheeks mottled. People shuffled and there was sporadic coughing. You could tell he was irritated at the widening gulf between how he'd imagined this moment and how it was going. "You were all blessed to witness the extraordinary debut of our Titan yesterday. A great and joyous moment. But yesterday, we didn't know just how significant his arrival would be. I have some other, very sobering, news to share." He paused here for effect, savoring his little moment of dramatic irony. A current of genuine curiosity rippled through the crowd. Mr. Pinkton leaned so close into the mic he was almost kissing it. "We have been informed that the Paris Zoo has officially shut down. I think you all know what that means." The ripple grew into a shock wave. "Let us share a moment of silence."

Silence? How could we be silent? A moment ago we were cold and disgruntled employees enduring a pep talk before the start of our ordinary workday, and now we were finding out we were the world's last zookeepers. While Mr. Pinkton and the admins bent their heads, the rest of us conferred urgently under our breath and clung together. Some people were crying. Sailor and I had become separated in the crowd, and I swiveled my head, looking for her, wondering how she'd react to this news. I spotted her finally, a few rows back. Her face was stony. I wasn't surprised: I could already tell she was someone who knew how to keep potentially dangerous emotions concealed.

When Mr. Pinkton deemed enough respect had been paid to the fallen Paris Zoo, he raised his head and addressed us again.

"This is a day to be somber, yes, my friends, but not to despair. Thanks to our acquisition of Titan, the magnificent elephant species has a chance at creating a new generation. New life, new hope. This place"—he paused to gesture beyond us to the zoo, his pale blue eyes watery with feeling—"is beyond doubt my greatest legacy. Long after everyone standing here today is dead, the significance of what has been built here will live on."

I noted some offended expressions on the faces around me. As if we didn't already feel insignificant enough. But he was the boss, and we all clapped politely after his speech was done, then formed a line to shake his hand. Mr. Pinkton owned all of this—the animals, the keepers, the island, even a certain amount of San Francisco Bay, technically—and without him we'd all be out on the streets, or in the case of the animals, I suppose go extinct, so there was a certain reverence we always performed in his presence. The animals were only here because of him, and we were only here because of the animals, and I think most of us were aware of that symbiotic relationship to some degree and knew we owed him our livelihoods.

As I waited in line, someone a few feet ahead started breathing in that heightened, choking way we'd all come to dread. Mr. Pinkton raised his head and blinked a few times. He gestured impatiently to one of his bodyguards, then pulled an EZ-Breathe out of his inside pocket and handed it to him with a muttered instruction. The inhaler looked pathetically flimsy in the bodyguard's meaty palm. The man approached the victim—now doubled over and wheezing, supported on both sides by concerned fellow keepers—and extended the inhaler.

"It's a new prototype," called out Mr. Pinkton. "Forty percent more effective! That's yours to keep. Feel better." He smiled benevolently. We watched as the distressed keeper was hustled off.

After, we were all ordered back to work. In the barracks, the screen now displayed our assignments, and there was a newfound gravity to the keepers, a new steeliness of purpose as they matched names with enclosures and set off to work. With the Paris Zoo gone, no one could deny the importance of what we were doing here. Like the animals, we were now the last of our kind.

As preordained, Sailor was on Feliz duty. I had been assigned to the farm, which was what it sounds like, a re-creation of a twentieth-century farmyard. I'd be looking after a cow, three sheep, four goats, an alpaca, and a clutch of hens. There was also a hedgehog, a rabbit, an injured raven whose left wing didn't work, some sparrows, and a grumpy box turtle who hated the other turtles and couldn't be kept in the same enclosure as them. Basically, the farm was the destination for any random animals and birds that turned up—often hoofstock rescues and injured wildlife close to death that weren't exotic enough to make the main enclosures. That makes it sound like a dreary assignment, but I loved working the farm. The sheep recognize and greet me whenever I enter their enclosure. Not many people realize this, but sheep have incredible facial recognition. They might all look the same to us, but it's been proven that sheep can tell the difference between up to twenty-five pairs of their own species' faces. In a study, they bleated in recognition when they saw familiar pals shown to them on a screen.

A surprising number of guests have fond feelings for this section as well, especially the older people. There's something so warm and fecund and homey about an enclosure that smells of hay and milk and chicken poop, filled with bleating and scratching and the chewing of cud. I can understand how if you'd once upon a time seen sheep and cows standing in an actual field, in the actual world, the farmyard experience could be incredibly moving. More moving than encountering even a lion in the flesh. After all, most people alive have never seen a lion. It's like a made-up creature from a fairy tale.

Sailor and I walked up the hill together as though this had always been our routine.

"Do you have your ID?" I asked between anxious breaths as I tried to keep pace. Her long legs devoured the distance like it was nothing. "You need to have your ID on you at all times."

She glanced back at me, holding up her forefinger, as if testing the direction of the wind. "You mean this? Yep, carry it with me."

"Ha, right, I mean the other one. To tell the difference between workers and guests. We've had guests try to stay behind on the island before."

"Stowaways? Interesting. Thanks for reminding me." She pulled a lanyard from her back pocket and slung it around her neck. The ID chip at the center glinted in the weak sunlight. "Poor tree." She stopped to inspect the skeletal eucalyptus tree just off the path, its long-dead arms stretched out toward the ocean like a sea captain's wife awaiting the return of her husband. The wind had torn pale strips off its trunk. I think she was really just stopping to let me catch up.

"I'm so sorry about Paris," I said.

"Thanks. Weird how something can be inevitable and still get you here." She pressed a palm to her heart, then shook her head in annoyance, as if expelling something. "It's just the animals, you know."

"Where do you think they'll end up?"

"Somewhere better than this, I hope." She glanced at me. "Sorry." I could tell she wanted to change the subject. "So I guess that Coates guy was right about me being assigned to Feliz, huh?" Her face brightened saying his name. "How does the system work, anyway? Aren't the assignments random?"

"Mostly," I said. "But the admins tweak the system sometimes. With new employees, especially."

"What's the theory behind it?"

I hesitated, unsure how to explain it. Sometimes it felt like everything I knew about Alcatraz I knew by osmosis. "Well, at the beginning, before I got here, all the keepers used to have enclosures they worked permanently. But then the tours became a big hit, and some guy—a corporate guru Mr. Pinkton had seen speak somewhere?—convinced him that letting the keepers get too close to the animals was a bad idea."

"Why?"

"Apparently it's to do with attachment theory. Like, if an animal needs attention while a tour's in progress, it's important that any one of us—whoever's closest and available, basically—can quickly handle the situation instead of having to wait for the bonded keeper to arrive. That's how we ended up where we are now."

"Perpetually adrift?" She smiled sweetly.

"Huh, I guess so." I liked how she looked at me as though I had interesting things to say, a situation I'd rarely found myself in before, and it inspired me to dig up more fun facts for her. "There's also an advisory board that's very into"—I made air quotes—"'optimal productivity.' Some theory about how productivity increases when workers don't know what their work is going to be each day. Switching from one task to another helps employees adapt and become more nimble? Something like that."

"Well that's completely psychotic," Sailor said, but in an unsurprised way. "Wonder how many members of this illustrious advisory board own sweatshop empires, am I right?"

Reluctant to agree with something that sounded so heretical, I shifted her attention to a small white building behind the zoo. "That used to be the military morgue."

"Ooh, dead soldiers, let's go see."

When we reached it, Sailor pulled her respirator down and bent to peer in the window, cupping her hands to shade her eyes.

"They use it to hatch the butterflies now," I said. Inside, rows and rows of caterpillar crates stretched to the shadowy back wall. The keepers hadn't arrived yet and the building was as quiet and still as, well, a morgue, the dim overhead lights buzzing softly. Sailor straightened up.

"And what's that building down there?" She pointed in the direction of the water tower, still scrawled with the words:

> PEACE AND FREEDOM
>
> WELCOME
>
> HOME OF THE FREE INDIAN LAND

It had been painted there back in the 1960s, when a group of Native American activists reclaimed the island. The paint dripped in places, like blood. The ownership decided to leave the message there because it added to the historic atmosphere. But I could tell Sailor wasn't talking about the tower itself but the building beyond it, on the north shore, smokestack jutting above an industrial facade.

"Oh, that's the desalination plant." She nodded but didn't look particularly fascinated, and, in the way of a comedian who feels he's losing his audience, I tried to think of something, anything, to revive her interest. "It provides all the water for the island. There are pipes that bring the water from the bay into the plant, and then pipes that run into the various buildings. There's even one that feeds the pool for the crocodile and the otters."

Her eyes lit up above her mask. "Interesting. Love all the behind-the-scenes details of zoo life. Tell me more about how Alcatraz works." I was only too happy to prattle on until we got to the employee entrance to the zoo. It didn't occur to me to wonder why she was so interested in the island's infrastructure. I was just happy to have her company.

Once we entered the security area, I pressed my forefinger on the sensor pad and my pixelated face showed up briefly on the screen, like a ghost. When I removed my finger the screen blurred as the automatic sanitizer cleaned the pad, then Sailor stepped up and presented her own finger. There were armed guards stationed everywhere around the island, but they never took much notice of us keepers, unless it was to engage the women in half-hearted sexual harassment. The two that morning gave me a cursory glance and lingered on Sailor. She didn't drop her eyes like I frequently did but stared right back at them, and they both quickly looked off.

Sailor barely waited until we were out of earshot to say, "They really love playing big tough soldiers here, huh?"

"Yeah," I said, apologetically. It was the aspect of Alcatraz I liked the least. "You get used to it after a while."

"So those guns are for the animals, right, if they get out of line?"

"No." I could tell she was teasing me, but I didn't know how to respond with anything but earnestness. "They're for the people."

She raised her eyebrows. "People like us?"

"Not really, more like thieves. People trying to steal or hurt the animals."

"Ah."

As soon as we passed through the entrance, the usual transformation took place. One moment I was an unmoored, nervous creature flailing out of my element; the next I had arrived at the only place in this world where I belonged. The air vibrated with chuffing and screeching, squawks and rustlings, the low hum of human voices beneath growls and bellowing, and my nostrils tingled with the deeply reassuring funk of the nonhuman. The zoo felt so different when the tours weren't on, it may as well have been a different planet. I worried Sailor might be disappointed, but she came to an abrupt stop beside me, took a deep breath, and exhaled with an expression of pure happiness, and I knew it was just the same for her.

Feliz's enclosure is close to the employee entrance, in A Block, on Michigan Avenue—all the corridors were named for famous streets, a hangover from the prison days—so we didn't have to go far. He lives on the ground floor of three tiers of vertical cells. The top row is so high you can barely see it from the ground. The keepers and other workers use the steel catwalks that run the lengths of the enclosures to move around and access the animals and birds on the higher levels. There were plenty of people around already that morning, gliding along the catwalks like highwire acts in a circus. We'd all become adept at speeding while hauling gear, nimbly darting out of the way when there's someone coming in the other direction, and zipping up and down the staircases at either end.

The jaguar's cage had been retrofitted by knocking out the walls between several five-feet-by-nine-feet prison cells to make one bigger enclosure. The owners liked to boast about these "spacious" enclosures. If you knew how much territory a single jaguar traverses in the wild, you'd know what a joke that was. Still, it wasn't the dimensions of his enclosure that was most disturbing. It was the fact he was there at all. No other resident of the zoo felt so starkly, egregiously out of place.

I gestured toward the enclosure. "So, this is Feliz."

Whoever named Feliz had a very bad sense of humor. Or a keen sense of irony. I averted my eyes from his pacing, but Sailor didn't balk. She kneeled on the ground in front of the enclosure, just sort of melting down to earth, legs tucked beneath her like the cage was an altar and she was preparing to pray. She stared through the glimmering bars. Feliz is a melanistic jaguar, glossy and black, and seeing his rippling pelt up close can be a transporting experience if you've never seen a specimen like him in real life before. He ignored Sailor as he ignored everything else. The world didn't exist for him outside of his own relentless locomotion.

"So sad," Sailor said softly. "Haven't seen zoochosis this bad in a long time."

"I know," I said, tapping my foot anxiously and looking around to make sure Sailor hadn't drawn too much attention. "It's weird too, the more solitary animals usually fare the best, because they've always been fated to be alone."

I realized how dramatic this sounded and felt a hot pulse of shame. I didn't normally express these thoughts in front of the other keepers. If you happened to have developed fanciful, emotive theories and philosophies on animals or zookeeping, you weren't supposed to share them. The protocol was to share factual, scientific observations or nothing at all. Sailor turned her neck to look at me.

"Yes," she said with that smile again, "I've noticed that too. The born loners and the pack animals are the only ones whose souls don't get smothered."

It was such a relief to be understood, I felt emboldened to go further. "Can I make a confession?"

Sailor's face lit up with curiosity. "Why yes, my child."

I leaned down so only she could hear, cupped a hand around my mouth. "It's kind of sacrilege, but I actually prefer Feliz to the lions."

She laughed. "Well of course you do! The lions are lazy and boring. They're like beautiful dilettantes, lying around all day waiting to be adored."

I felt so exhilarated I could hardly breathe. I wanted more than anything to stay there and work out what other things we had in common, but I had my own duties to attend to.

I've often wanted to apologize to the farm animals for being so distracted that day. I didn't neglect them, exactly, but my attention was elsewhere: How could it have been otherwise? Titan may not have appeared in public that day, but his presence was felt in every breath we all took. Every now and then his muffled bellows would echo along the avenues, a new and singular voice speaking a language we didn't yet understand. I had my own theories, though. He was trying to tell us that things were going to be changing around here.

Paris

Five Years Earlier

One of the keepers, Daniel, proposed calling their little group of concerned zoo workers the Maquis, after the rural French Resistance guerilla fighters during World War II. They adopted the name semijokingly, even though Daniel was dead serious. It made Sailor uneasy. Not just the name but also what it implied about their plans.

They continued meeting every week to discuss worrying developments at the zoo and in the wider world. The San Francisco Zoo had abruptly closed. A Bulgarian keeper called Timotei read out snatches of the story from his phone. The owners were denying the bombing had been a factor, claiming they didn't acknowledge, let alone give in to, the cowardly tactics of terrorists. Instead they cited rising costs, impossible insurance premiums, increased biosecurity hazards, public safety. The welfare of the animals was paramount, the statement declared, and as such, the remaining residents of the zoo had been sold to an unnamed but highly regarded benefactor and conservationist who would be making an announcement soon about their new home.

By that point, so many zoos had closed it didn't really make a big news splash in the wider community. But at the Paris Zoo, in the spotlight now as one of the last remaining public zoos on Earth, the news was the kind of chill wind November used to bring. No one had the time or inclination to visit a zoo with chaos raging. Animals came to be seen as harbingers of the same doom coming for humanity—not exactly the kind of cheerful family outing a zoo used to represent. Thick glass was installed to seal in the previously open-air enclosures, and decontaminations became a daily necessity. The animals were physically safe, but they withered behind their glassed-in prisons. It was like someone had installed an invisible doomsday clock above the real Art Nouveau clock at the zoo entrance.

When news arrived that the island of Alcatraz was being retrofitted as a high-security animal conservation project by some pharma-industry billionaires, Sailor and the other members of the Maquis gathered to talk it over. Most of them were skeptical, scathing even. What kind of billionaire ever did anything for the public good?

"At least we know the San Francisco Zoo residents will be safe there," said Sailor. "Safer." She wasn't sure why she was defending this place she had never seen.

"She is an *idéaliste*," said Anouk, patting Sailor's knee affectionately.

The owners in Paris tried a variety of desperate tactics to revive visitor numbers. They paid celebrities millions of euros to film endorsements for the zoo. They began accepting corporate sponsorships from pesticide companies, fossil-fuel corps, the entities whose products and activities had helped create the ideal conditions for the unfolding catastrophes. Secretly—although not so secretly that it escaped the attention of the Maquis—the owners began selling some of the most precious zoo specimens on the black market.

Even Sailor knew then that there could be no peace. She'd always stayed silent when the talk around the table would become too incendiary. She hadn't been born, as some of her compatriots had been, with the Gallic zeal for burning down the institutions of oppression. But it was becoming too stark to ignore. There was no better world just waiting for them: they were going to have to go out and make it for themselves.

Alcatraz

From the start, Sailor wanted to change things. If that seems like unremarkable behavior, well maybe I should clarify that wasn't how things worked at Alcatraz. The laws of the zoo—both spoken and unspoken—were immutable. We didn't try to change things because we knew there was no point. As someone who only ever wanted to fly under the radar, this had always suited me well enough. For my entire first year on the island, I had lived in terror of being exposed as a fraud. I faked knowing what I was doing until the day I realized I wasn't faking anymore and the work had become second nature.

Sailor didn't make it two weeks before she caused her first stir. It was a Monday, I remember, and she was working in the raptor section with our golden eagle, Maggie. Because the weekly tour was looming, the entire zoo population was on war footing. There were the usual mountains of daily animal-care tasks to be completed—cleaning, feeding, grooming, enrichment, nail trimming, medicating, more cleaning, testing for fungal infections, making sure there were no other health issues the vets need to check out—along with endless tech checks, security drills, and general beautification of the public areas. The animals tend to get more agitated as the hour grows closer. The zoo may look spectacular when the tours are in full swing, but not everyone appreciates it. The stagecraft does a seamless job of concealing this from the guests, but the animals are at their worst when the tours are in motion. Strangers make them anxious and fractious.

On this particular afternoon, I was working in the ring-tailed lemur section, which was located close to the raptors. I was happy like I always was when existence was reduced to completing a single task or series of tasks. When I ceased to be a mind in charge of a body and became just the body itself. I lived by simple mantras: Head down, do the work, be there for the animals in the moment. Share in whatever small moments of delight might be available.

I hummed as I worked, moving lightly across the soft, rubbery flooring designed to reduce injuries. Clutching raisins in my fist, I invited the lemurs one at a time onto the scale to be weighed. Their collective gaze bounced between my hand and my face as they chattered excitedly in line. They loved raisins more than life itself and happily participated in their own health care.

"Good boy, Smooth Tony," I said as the last of my masked bandits hopped off the scale clutching his prize. I booped him gently on the nose. The lemurs all smelled faintly of crayon and squeaked like chew toys. It made the enclosure feel comforting, like a toddler's playroom.

As the troop scampered and allogroomed and quarreled on the branches above, I found myself wishing I could visit Sailor. We'd sat together at breakfast, as had become our habit, but I already felt brimful of things I wanted to talk to her about. It wasn't as if visiting adjoining enclosures was forbidden exactly—keepers did it all the time, and provided you didn't visit your friend for too long or neglect your duties, the guards tended to look the other way. But I'd always avoided it. There had never been anyone whose company seemed worth the risk.

As I was emptying the ravaged food box, Sailor's voice rang out. "Hey Camille, you there?"

"Yes," I called out into the void, struck as ever by the carceral weirdness of communicating by voice between cells.

"Do you have a spare screwdriver? I can't seem to find mine, and I need to make a repair."

"Sure," I called back, scrambling in my toolbox. "Be right there. Don't do anything naughty."

"What?"

"Sorry, I was talking to the lemurs."

Her disembodied laugh was like a shot of caffeine. I practically ran between the enclosures, clutching the screwdriver as if it were a baton and I were the last runner in the relay. Sailor grinned at the sight of me, quick-breathing and alert at her door. With Maggie's talons curled around her hand, she strode through the first security door, then buzzed me in through the second external door. "You're a lifesaver." She made no move to take the tool from me but ushered me inside.

"Holy shit," I said, staring at the bird perched on her hand. "She really likes you."

Sailor blew a piece of hair off her forehead, lowered the leather glove, and stroked Maggie gently. The bird's body was larger than my head; her wingspan, had she chosen to stretch her wings, as long as a full-grown man. She closed her eyes to slits, a gesture we call Love Blinks, which often indicates an animal or bird feels at ease with you. "Yeah, we're great friends. Aren't we, *ma chérie*?"

"I've never seen discrimination like this with a new person," I said in wonder. "Well, never this quickly and never with the raptors." Discrimination is when an animal treats one person differently from others. It can also refer to an animal's ability to discriminate between two things, a game at which birds are supertalented, especially when it comes to colorful or shiny objects they might covet. Sailor was clearly the shiny thing Maggie coveted that day. Don't get me wrong, lots of animals and birds have favorites among the keepers, even though we're swapped around all the time. But it normally happens over months, even years, not in days.

I reached out and stroked Maggie's head in turn. You could feel the shape of the skull just beneath the flesh and the feathers, strong and fragile at the same time.

"She likes you too," said Sailor admiringly. "I saw her quite literally fly off the handle at another keeper."

"Thanks." I brimmed with pleasure at the compliment—there's nothing better, if you're an animal person, than being told an animal likes you—but it also made me self-conscious.

"I've worked it out," she continued. "Why the animals get calm around you. You hum at a frequency that puts them at ease." Sailor reached into a bucket and fed Maggie a piece of meat. We called it Fake Steak, a catch-all name for the fleshy substitutes that featured on the menus of both animals and humans in this place. "It's also your scent, though."

Sailor wiped the fake blood off on her overalls and picked up my left hand. She smelled the skin like she was inhaling a snifter of fine whiskey. I burst out laughing and Maggie let out a high whistle of indignation.

"Sorry, Maggie," I said. Then to Sailor: "What are you doing?"

"It's hard to describe, but you smell different from the others. Like, have you ever smelled a stone you've pulled from the riverbed as it's drying in the sun?"

"Um, no."

"Well, something like that. Clean water. Earth. Moss. Those are the scents that put animals at ease."

"So you're calling me mossy?"

"Girl, mossy is the highest compliment I can think of." She smiled and dropped my hand. "In Paris I'd sometimes get asked by visitors how they could ingratiate themselves with certain animals. People always want the animals to love them, you know?"

"Ha, I know," I said, as if I hadn't just been silently congratulating myself on my own lovability.

"So I'd tell them, next time, come dressed like we are. Our uniform was gray jackets and khaki pants. That way the animals might think you're a keeper and be nice to you in case you have food."

"I bet that only worked with the antisocial ones."

"Oh, yeah. You couldn't fool the parrots or the lions or the chimps. They either like you or they don't, it doesn't matter what you wear." Sailor carefully placed Maggie back on her perch and began scattering fresh straw from a bucket onto the enclosure floor. I helped her. After a while, Sailor straightened up and faced me. Close up, I noticed a constellation of pale freckles scattered across her nose and cheekbones.

"Do you have bad guys here?"

"You mean, like, villains? Well, some of the guards are kind of"—I cupped my hand around my mouth—"jerks."

She laughed. "No, I mean, like, in Paris if one of us had established a hard-won bond with a specific resident, we'd nominate another keeper as the 'bad guy' when it was time to catch them for a wellness check or give them a shot or anything unpleasant, really. So the animal would keep perceiving you as the person who always does positive things."

"That makes so much sense."

"Yeah, we called it the trust bank. The idea was you made 'deposits' by doing things to earn the animal's trust, like providing them with food or treats, and moving in a predictable way around them, exuding an aura of calm and safety, all that stuff. And withdrawals were anything that eroded that trust, like having to catch them for a procedure."

"So you'd act as bad guys for each other?"

"Yep. Although we preferred bribing the vets to do it."

"Good idea, I need to try that."

"Way ahead of you, sister," she said with a wink.

I couldn't decide whether to be shocked or envious that she was so new and had already worked out so many tricks.

"The thing is," I said, troubled by a newly recognized pattern, "I think maybe *I'm* the bad guy."

She laughed. "What?"

"Well, most of the time people call me when they need to calm one of the animals down. I've just never really thought about why."

"*See?*" she said. "Mossy. It's your gift."

"Maybe they just hate me?" I suggested.

"Mossy," she said sternly. The last word on the matter.

She grabbed the screwdriver and proceeded to tighten a loose screw with an unnerving level of intensity. "Anyway, I wonder how our elephant matchmaking service is going. Haven't heard much since Titan got here. What's the word on these mean streets?"

"Well, everyone's pretty hopeful the breeding will be a success."

A bland statement that could have come straight from the head office. But I couldn't locate the right words to describe what it meant to have the elephants together at last under one soaring roof. The thrill of hearing them talking to each other, the comingled smell of them that, for some reason I couldn't explain, smelled far more *elephant-y* than Kira alone.

Sailor grunted as she drove the last turn of the screw. "And what do you think?"

"Me?" I hesitated. "It'd be pretty incredible if it happened."

"Would it?"

I fidgeted with my overalls. "Well, sure. It's a long shot, but I mean, the survival of the species is a big deal, right?"

Sailor leaned over to tickle Maggie's head feathers, and the bird nibbled gently on her ear. "I don't think we're going to Frankenstein our way out of this mess."

"At least it's more natural than what they tried last time."

Sailor looked across, intrigued. "What do you mean?"

"Well, the Pinktons bought African elephant sperm from some frozen zoo in Germany. One of those DNA biogenome projects. Artificially inseminated Kira. It didn't take, though."

"Hmm," Sailor said, and I knew she was holding back her thoughts on that. She adjusted her bun—I noticed she'd used a plastic zip-tie instead of a hair elastic, something I'd resorted to myself many times—and said brightly, "Hey, I have an idea!"

I perked up. No one at Alcatraz ever had ideas. Later I rightfully learned to fear this specific collection of words, but I had no way of knowing then that out of Sailor's mouth they were like pulling the pin from a grenade.

"A little interspecies social program," Sailor said. "We are going to call them . . . Bleat-and-Greets."

I laughed as if dismissing her outlandish proposal. But it's hard to describe to anyone who hasn't lived a life of loneliness how powerfully that casual "we" worked on me.

The flamingo, Pascale, was surprisingly docile and didn't mind being carried around like a baby, so she was an obvious contender for the program. So was the porcupine, Kevin, who was bored out of his brain in his enclosure and needed the stimulation more than just about anyone. The sheep, who loved to move around and were great extroverts, were next on our ambitious agenda, but we'd decided to start with two slightly more manageable and less excitable creatures.

Ten days had passed since Sailor had floated the idea, long enough for her to somehow convince the usually unbending admins to let us trial these Bleat-and-Greets, and I was floating on the rare high of feeling like I was getting away with something. I'd known about the practice of keepers escorting animals through zoos after-hours—you can scroll countless videos of these encounters from the old days—but it had never been done at Alcatraz, as far as I knew. Had no one ever tried? I wasn't sure, but I did know I wouldn't have dared get involved if it had been anyone but Sailor. Her confidence lent me courage.

We collected Kevin first. He was such an affable guy: I took the chance to face-cradle him and coo greetings at his sweet pink snout, which we both enjoyed. I expected Sailor to follow suit, but she just looked on, smiling. Not disapproving but removed in some way. She looped a loose collar around his neck, carefully smoothing the sharp quills down, and wound the leash around her fingers. We buzzed ourselves out of the enclosure, with Kevin trotting beside us like a bristly dog. He took to it so naturally I wondered if he'd once been someone's pet.

"I'd love to get the elephants out as well," said Sailor. I snorted at this idea, picturing Titan and Kira lumbering through the avenues, terrifying everything in their path. "No, I mean it. They're going crazy in their cage."

It was true they seemed restless. You could hear their bellowing day and night. The vets were concerned at first that Titan might have been in musth, the aggressive hormonal condition bull elephants periodically enter into, but that was thankfully ruled out. So what, then? We'd all been so worried they'd hate each other, but instead they bonded straight away, like long-lost herd members. They went from quiet and forlorn to feisty bellowers, as if only together did they find their voices.

The pair lived in the former library, the largest cell in the old prison. It's a beautiful space, compared with the other enclosures, soaring ceilings and light that pours in from the high rectangular windows. It retains the hushed, comforting atmosphere of a library, as if the walls are busy remembering all the books that saved people's lives. Kira had lived in the library since she and Shambala had arrived as juveniles; even then, they'd had to expand the human-size door.

I could tell Sailor didn't want to let the subject of elephants drop. "Why can't they live out in the rec yard, like I suggested? At least there's more space than where they are."

"The air isn't good for them for too long."

"Sure, but why couldn't they build one of those retractable roofs, you know? Like they have over stadiums. Plant some trees out there, build a watering hole. I'm not saying it would be great, but it'd be something."

"I suppose," I said unhappily. As if I personally had any say over the conditions under which the animals lived. I did what I could, I treated all the zoo residents with the utmost care and devotion, and I never once used the electric prods we called buzzkills. I would rather have had one used on myself. I never yelled at the animals or got mad if they failed to act in the way I wanted. No matter what happened—if a creature was in a foul mood, or if it tried to attack you or someone else—it wasn't their fault. But it was obvious that Sailor wanted more for them than everyday compassion. She wanted them to truly live.

"Listen, we are going to get those elephants out to the yard," she said. "We just have to persuade those killjoys up at the admin center."

I was flattered my new friend imagined I could persuade anyone of anything, but I went along with it because I knew it would be her doing the persuading. She could have charmed candy from a chimpanzee.

We moved away from the library, but the elephants stayed on my mind.

"Did you know there's another collective noun for elephants besides 'herd'?" I asked. Sailor shook her head. "A memory of elephants. Isn't that neat?"

"It is," she said. "Very apropos."

"But do you think two are enough, just Kira and Titan?" It was something that had always bothered me. Who would be left to remember?

Anyone else might have asked, enough for what? But Sailor just said, "I'm not sure. I hope so."

We chaperoned Kevin to the flamingo enclosure, and I approached Pascale gently and quietly with some snacks in my palm. I was able to pick her up without any fuss and cradle her in my arms. She knew to tuck her legs neatly beneath her and would sometimes rest her beak on my shoulder. She looked around with great interest as we exited her enclosure. I caught sight of myself in a stainless-steel surface and I looked like a dame from one of the old movies wearing a vivid feathered coat. Sailor paused in the middle of Broadway.

"Bonjour, motherfuckers," she announced in a booming ringmaster voice. "Welcome to the inaugural Bleat-and-Greet."

Heads popped out of doors all along the corridor at her announcement. Most were smiling, although a few shook their heads or rolled their eyes and retreated from our foolishness. There was no hostility, though. Not yet.

Sailor had it all mapped out: she knew which other animals we should visit and which enclosures to avoid for fear of agitating either species. We took Pascale to meet Felicia, the oryx, who lived over on Michigan Avenue. They stared through the shimmering bars, transfixed by each other's toothpick legs.

Kevin the porcupine—highly vocal, like all his kind—was tickled by the tiger salamander, Sweet Pea, and raised his stumpy front legs, emitting a stream of noises ranging from whistles to grunts to a weird teeth-chattering. Sweet Pea responded to this greeting with his perpetual quizzical smile.

"You guys know each other," Sailor informed the pair. "You don't know that you do, but you do. If you were out in the wild you'd live in the same forest, recognize the same plants. Maybe cross each other's paths every now and again."

"Sweet Pea might even give you a hand," I told Kevin.

"What now?" said Sailor.

"So this is kind of mortifying," I said. "But in my first week here I was looking after Sweet Pea and he got one of his hands stuck under a log and it . . . dropped off. I was inconsolable. Convinced I was going to be deported."

"Oh no." She was gallantly trying to keep a straight face.

"It was actually Joseph who consoled me, kindly explained that salamanders can grow back body parts. I was so grateful I nearly cried. Again."

Sailor solemnly saluted Sweet Pea, and we strutted on to the next avenue.

"How did you get them to agree to this?" I asked Sailor after she received a high-five from Vivian, who had emerged from the painted dog enclosure bursting with curiosity. Vivian was one of the keepers who shared my room, and even though she was shy and kept to herself—or maybe because of that—we got along pretty well. She vowed to join us on the next Bleat-and-Greet.

"Oh, it was easy. I just told them we used to do it all the time at the Paris Zoo. The admins seem to have a real hard-on for anything to do with Paris."

"And did you? Do it all the time in Paris?"

Sailor snorted. "No, of course not. Those fuckers were even more uptight than here, if you can believe it. But I always wanted to do it."

"It's a great form of enrichment," I said. "I wish I'd thought to ask if we could do it."

None of the other keepers were really that interested in enrichment, just did the bare minimum—maybe hanging the food on a high branch for the big cats or leaving an inflatable soccer ball for the primates to play with. But I loved thinking up new ways to keep my friends engaged and amused. The admins didn't really care about enrichment one way or the other, as long as you didn't make any over-the-top demands. The only thing they were adamant about was that we couldn't have anything "unnatural" in the enclosures while the tours were on. They'd had complaints in the past from guests about seeing the animals interacting with "piles of trash." Which was ridiculous, because some animals and birds love playing with paper and cardboard and plastic and other stuff that looks like junk. One of the lions refuses to sleep on the "natural"-looking platform we built but insists on squeezing himself into a tiny plastic kiddie pool we once put in there for them to splash around in. The admins let it stay but made us cover it with camouflage netting.

"But that's the thing!" said Sailor, linking her spare arm with mine. "I was totally inspired by you, Birdy." She started calling me that after that day in Maggie's cage, because she decided that I was good with birds, or maybe I reminded her of a bird, I've never really worked it out. "I heard about how you came up with the idea of letting the big cats maul the sleeping blankets from the deer and the camel . . . of course they'd go nuts for something that smelled like prey. And how you introduced the chimps to the dish-washing game and the lexigram and how much things like that changed their lives. It all made me start thinking about what else we could do."

"Oh, I mean, thanks." My face went hot, but I leaped at the invitation to talk about my pet subject. "Thing is, I just noticed the chimps would crowd around, fascinated, every time they saw me washing my hands or scrubbing something clean, so I gave them dish soap and water and some plastic dishware, and it was so funny to watch. They'll literally spend hours at it"—I began to mime the action—"one chimp carefully washing each dish, dunking it in the bubbles, handing the dish to another chimp, who rubs the cloth over it and passes it to the next, who turns it over to dry. Then they solemnly swap positions in the production line and start all over again. It's hilarious." I took a deep breath. "Did you hear about the mirrors?"

"No. What mirrors?"

"Well, after the dishes were a hit, I had the idea to collect some of the shatter-proof mirrors from the barracks and give them to the troop. Bruno and Bones picked them up and turned them over a few times then grew bored, but Stella and Alicia were captivated. Stella worked out she could use the mirror to see her caretakers, even if they were behind her, so she 'spies' on us, then breaks into this wild grin and scampers off when we catch her. And Alicia spends hours staring at her reflection and preening."

"Ha, adorable."

"It really is, although I do worry about the messages she's absorbed about traditional gender roles."

Sailor laughed. I barely recognized this entertaining storyteller inhabiting my body.

"The admins don't care about enrichment because they think the whole razzle-dazzle tour thing is enough," she said. "They can see the animals only through the human gaze."

"The human gaze," I repeated with wonder. "I've never thought of it like that."

"And that," she said, stooping to collect a fallen feather and sliding it under my ponytail elastic, "is why it's all up to us."

The closer we got to the enclosure where Achilles, the crocodile, lived, the more Sailor's body language shifted, from entirely relaxed to the taut intensity of a bloodhound catching a scent. It wasn't hard to understand—Achilles was one of the zoo's biggest attractions, literally and figuratively, the greatest performer Alcatraz had ever known—but I broke into a sweat trying to keep up. Only his dedicated keepers were permitted to interact with him, so I had seen Achilles in action only a few times. The way he could lie still for hours and hours, barely blinking, so motionless you might assume he was dead, then without warning move out of the water with a truly terrifying velocity, his serrated tail lashing from side to side like a scythe . . . the vision never leaves you.

The news of our jaunt must have traveled because Joseph was waiting for us outside the enclosure, arms crossed over his broad chest, the tentacle of his octopus tattoo creeping out of his rolled-up sleeve.

"What are you crazy girls up to?"

"It's called a Bleat-and-Greet," I responded enthusiastically from behind a tickly curtain of peach-hued feathers. "We take animals to meet one another. We're starting with Kevin and Pascale."

"Yes, I can see that." Despite his stern tone, he looked amused by our antics. "Achilles isn't taking visitors today, though, sorry."

Sailor laughed, no, actually *giggled*, which came as a surprise, given how indifferent she'd been to Joseph until now. "Probably for the best. Maybe you and I can take him out for a stroll another day." She flashed him a coquettish smile I knew would demolish his remaining defenses. Teasing banter was Joseph's love language.

"Maybe," he said. The grin, the flickering of the eyes up and down Sailor's body, the puffing out of the chest—all the signals demonstrated the game had worked. Yes, I knew a game when I saw one, even if I didn't know its purpose, which is more than I can say for Joseph. Still, I was glad they might become friends.

"Maybe we could even get the elephants out into the rec yard," Sailor continued in a tone of wonder, as if the idea had just occurred to her. "Let them roam around. See the sky. Get to know each other outside of their cage."

Joseph's lip curled. "Oh, for sure. The elephants. *We'll* get right on that." He turned away as if done with us.

"Guess I got too far over my skis with that suggestion," Sailor remarked as we walked on, but she seemed unfazed, entertained even by Joseph's disdain.

"Joseph's a gambler," I explained, confident that at least in this one respect I was qualified to educate her. "If you get a win, even a tiny one, you have to walk away from the table with it."

"Or." She left a long pause and cast a sly glance my way. "You keep playing until you've completely bankrupted him."

"Well, good luck," I said, mustering all the teasing power I possessed. But even then, back when I barely knew Sailor at all, I wouldn't have bet against her.

As we returned Kevin to his home, I gave him one last snout scritch, pulled a twig from my back pocket for him to chew on, and jotted in my Notes app under Prehensile-Tailed Porcupine: *snout feels like a marshmallow*.

Sailor peered over my shoulder. "Whatcha doing?"

"Oh, I just like to make notes when I observe something interesting about the animals. What they smell like or feel like. Not for anything official, just for myself." I was wary about this disclosure because I remembered telling Joseph this once, and he'd laughed. *"What for? Is there going to be a test?"* But I somehow knew Sailor wouldn't laugh at me.

"Yeah, I do that too."

"Really?"

"Of course. It's important to document every little thing. Someone has to keep the record around here."

"Because we might be the last generation that gets to see these species in real life?"

"*Exactement.* Now who has the best smell, in your opinion?"

I didn't hesitate. "The cats. The small ones, I mean. Precious and co. The big ones smell rank, obviously."

"Or like popcorn, in the tiger's case."

"Right? So weird with the popcorn pee! Binturongs have it too." I laughed in a slightly demented way, intoxicated on camaraderie. "But anyway, the domestic cats, the fur scent is amazing, like caramel, and sometimes fresh-baked bread, or perfume . . ." I struggled to remember any more descriptions, but I think I got the message across.

"How hard is it to get access to pet them?"

"Not sure, I've never tried."

Sailor performed a dramatic eye roll. "Well, come on! Let's try it."

"Now?"

"*Now?*" Sailor mimicked me. "No, next Friday. Let's go, I'll get us inside!"

So, against all my better judgment, we went. Sailor was right, she did manage to smoothly sweet-talk us into the building, but I was right too. When we buried our noses in the soft fur of the purring cats, they did smell like perfume and bread and caramel, and all kinds of other lost things, the specifics of which are also lost to me now. Never mind: some things don't need to be written down.

Paris

Three Years Earlier

Sailor hated the plan from the beginning. There was no longer any gossip or casual talk at the meetings of the Maquis—things had gotten too dangerous for that. Instead, as soon as everyone was assembled, they got right down to business.

Daily life as a keeper had become a battle to maintain hope against all reason. The workers were unhappy. The admins were unhappy. The visitors, when they came, were unhappy. The animals were unhappy. Above their heads stretched rust-stained skies. Air clogged with smoke from controlled burns of deadwood forests all over Europe, a doomed attempt to arrest the mold blight, which continued its march through continents like an invading army.

Sailor came to dread work and lamented never having fully appreciated what she had. The zoo had been so different when she started: more humane, more focused on conservation and education and the bestowing of joy, all the usual ways in which zoos can be good places. Now she felt like an usher at a funeral. Half her day was spent apologizing.

It was Anouk who floated the idea, Anouk who had quickly become their de facto leader. She had been on the activist scene for years, knew her way around grassroots organizing and direct action, and had pretty much seen it all. It felt like a natural choice that she should lead them into whatever came next. But that didn't mean they would unquestioningly follow her into smuggling animals out of the zoo, which was what her plan turned out to be. There was a sanctuary, she informed the group. A vast and amazing place where the animals could roam free, complete *liberté*. Wasn't that exciting? The dubious faces around the table suggested excitement wasn't quite the word.

They pestered Anouk for more details. Who ran the sanctuary? Where was it? How did she know about it? She had a contact there, a reliable person, she assured them. A comrade. "Here. See for yourselves." They passed around her phone, scrolling wide-eyed through a gallery of photos depicting a variety of creatures in a lush wilderness. The shots were zoomed in, the animals slightly fuzzy, as if seen from a great distance. The metadata showed that the photos were all taken within the previous few months.

"You can fake this stuff," said Emanuel, but the tremor of excitement in his voice belied the skepticism. "I mean, a *giraffe*? Could it really be?"

"Yes, really," said Anouk. "Is it so hard to believe a good place still exists?" That appeal to faith might not have worked had it come from anyone else, but they all trusted Anouk for reasons they couldn't even name. She told them she couldn't share many other details, though, for security reasons. The original sanctuary site had been raided, so the group had gone underground, had established a new sanctuary somewhere else, somewhere top secret. Who was this person on the inside? someone asked.

"An old girlfriend, I bet," said Timotei.

Anouk smirked. "None of your business. The important thing is we have a connection, a reliable person, who can liberate the animals if we can get them out. *Ça te dit?*"

While the others grumbled their assent, Sailor gathered the courage to speak. "Isn't straight-up smuggling a bit much?" Her protests were weak, she knew. "We could start with something less drastic."

Anouk just crinkled her eyes, like she was peering through smoke. "No, no. This is the way."

"But what if we get caught?"

Anouk gently pressed a fingertip to Sailor's nose, as Sailor had seen the cats do when they wanted to subdue or placate another cat. For some reason the gently placed paw seemed to hypnotize them.

"Sailor, Sailor, you are so anxious about breaking the rules. The first thing you have to do when fighting for a better life is refuse the elite's rules. The rules mean nothing."

Sailor just as gently pushed the finger away. "They'll mean something when we're all in la prison."

"It will work," said Anouk, amused and unbothered. "You will see."

She was right. They started with an armadillo named Anton, whose enclosure was less-visited than the remaining exotics. Over two days, Daniel and Timotei dug a discreet hole under the wire fencing. The kind of hole an animal itself might dig, were it dreaming of freedom. The enclosure was close to the western edge of the zoo, with a meter-wide gap between the cage and the high perimeter wall. At dusk, when the zoo was closing and everyone was busy with end-of-day tasks, Anouk entered the enclosure, scooped up Anton (who obligingly curled into a ball), and rolled him under the fence and into the waiting hands of Sailor, who was crouched in the dirt between the cage and the wall. She ushered Anton into the calm twilight of a brown paper bag, placed the bag in the butterfly net she'd brought with her, and standing on tiptoe—she'd been chosen for her height—carefully slid the pole up until the net rested on top of the wall, on the other side of which their fellow keeper Yorgos was waiting. She felt tugging on the net and loosened her grip. The net and pole disappeared over the wall, and she turned and walked away, the roar of the motorbike taking off down the street mingling in her ears with the rushing of her blood.

Sailor waited every day for the tap on the shoulder, the summons to the zoo office where the bureaucrats made their decisions. But it didn't come. That was a particularly chaotic week in France—there were riots in Paris, two wildfire fronts joining in the south, crop failures, calls for another national strike—and no one noticed a missing armadillo. By the time one of the keepers alerted the authorities, enough time had elapsed for the Maquis to have plausible deniability in any involvement. The disappearance was put down to natural causes—the animal must have burrowed its way out—the fence reinforced, and life, difficult as it had become, continued.

The mood at the next apéro hour was jubilant. Anouk passed around a photo her sanctuary contact had sent her of the successful relocation: Anton the armadillo, healthy and calm-looking, standing on a cushion of moss, verdant background vignetted so you couldn't identify the setting. Proof, someone said with wonder. Daniel was the one who expressed doubt, scoffing that it was easy to photoshop an image, it could be AI, it could be manipulated. But his objections were waved away, accompanied by much raucous clinking of glasses. Sailor didn't join in. She was too distracted, transfixed by the change she saw in the armadillo. It was as if he had only just begun to comprehend what it meant to live. Staring at the photo, something sputtered awake in her, a bright and terrible flame whose oxygen was hope.

Alcatraz

We began taking walks. Nighttime walks around the island. The walks were Sailor's idea, of course, because before she came along, I stayed indoors after dark, like a normal person. Not out of fear or anything like that. It's just that I only ever felt fully real when I was working, and after the workday was done I retreated into a state of minimal existence, like a robot powered down between tasks. After my shift ended, I would decontaminate at the cleaning station outside the barracks, take a tepid shower, change into the standard loungewear, eat dinner, read a book or watch a movie, then retire to bed. The only interruption to these routines was if Joseph sought me out, and then sex or an argument might be added to the roster. (As a high-ranking keeper, one of Joseph's privileges was a private room to himself.)

Now, Sailor and I gravitated together whenever we had time off—meals, breaks, stolen moments during shifts—but she had a habit of slipping away at night and leaving me to resume my old life.

One evening after dinner in the mess hall, almost two months into Sailor's time on the island, I noticed she had stuck around instead of vanishing. I was with my roommate Vivian, scraping dishes and dishing gossip about the elephants and their much-speculated-upon mating date, when Sailor sidled over.

"So what happens now?" she asked, resting her elbow on my shoulder.

"Oh," I said, confused but pleased, waving to Vivian as she wandered off. "The rec room, I guess?"

Sailor gestured for me to lead the way, and I tried to project confidence as we joined the exodus. We were among the last to arrive at the rec room, and we stood together in the doorway, observing the bodies of our fellow keepers slouched across various pieces of ugly furniture. Most people were playing games or watching sports on their devices, ears closed off, eyes glazed and mouths working in frustration or with concentration. The room was hushed, apart from one corner where a group of men was playing cards and emitting a quiet buzz of malice. Among them was Joseph.

As long as I've known him, Joseph has played cards every night with a group of keepers. The game is called Blind Tiger. The currency is matches: unlit matches are worth ten points; burned matches, five. The intensity with which they play is out of all proportion to the prize. The players hoard matches beneath their mattresses and stash them in lockers, even though no one else would want to steal them, as they have no value outside of the game. There is a swift undercurrent of hostility to these games. On most nights, players' girlfriends sit on the sidelines and watch, their silent presence a crucial aspect of the game's functioning. I had often been one of those girlfriends. There are explicit and implicit rules for being an observer in Blind Tiger. The explicit ones are obvious things like no touching the cards, no commenting on the players' hands, and the implicit ones are more like no breathing in the wrong way if your partner happens to be losing.

"Ohhh . . . kay," said Sailor.

I couldn't look at her. "Do you want to go do something else?" In my panic I hadn't thought through what this activity might be.

"Marvelous idea," she said. "Let's get some air."

"You mean . . . outside?"

She laughed at the expression on my face. "Where else? It won't kill you. Take a walk with me."

I could have argued, given the air was widely acknowledged as being an extremely effective, if slow-working, killer. But I had a sudden distaste for staying in the barracks, so I agreed. I hoped Joseph wouldn't look up and see me, insist that I join him for luck, but he remained transfixed by whatever was happening at the table and I was able to slip out unnoticed.

"Doesn't it drive you nuts staying in one place?" Sailor asked as we retrieved our respirators from the lockers. She was one of those animals that needs to expel energy—I had seen her a few times through the smeared glass rectangle of the door leading to the gym, doing endless mad sprints from one end of the room to the other, her face set in a determination pained enough to rival Feliz's. "It's a known fact you can't think while sitting down," she added as we exited through the air lock.

There wasn't any specific rule at that point against keepers walking around the island after-hours, it was just that no one did it. We left the barracks and walked east past the guard tower, guided by the soft glow of the lights out on the dock, then along the shoreline past the admin center, until we got close to a ruined building that was an Officers' Club in the old days. I had always walked right past without paying it any attention. Sailor stopped in front of the ruin, hands on hips.

"Let's get up on the roof."

I turned at a rustling sound. Two guards stepped out of the shadows onto the path.

"What are you doing?" The eyes of the man who spoke were hooded beneath his cap, and his mouth was concealed by a black bandanna, but with the moon and the dock lights it was bright enough to see his weapon glinting. "You shouldn't be here."

"Hi," said Sailor, pulling her respirator down. "We're just taking a walk. Is that a problem?" She flashed a smile designed to disarm, perhaps not realizing the admins tended to recruit guards not overburdened with human emotion. I could feel the stoicism of this one wavering, though, as he glanced at his companion, who was staring as though bewitched at Sailor. I noticed for the first time that at some point since we'd left the barracks she had lowered the zipper on her leisure suit to reveal a small swell of cleavage. She was also wearing bright lipstick, as she always did. None of us wore makeup, apart from maybe some sunscreen or a slick of lip balm, so Sailor's painted face tended to draw attention.

"Hey, you're Carlos, right?" Sailor said to the first guard. She gave him a playful punch on the shoulder. "I heard you're from Miami. Florida Man! We should get together and trade stories sometime." She laughed, as if enjoying a private reminiscence. The man said something I didn't catch, his voice muffled. He turned his head to the other guy, and they entered into some kind of telepathic exchange while Sailor and I waited. After the guards had grudgingly waved us along, I found my voice.

"Hey, *Florida Man, we should get together and trade stories!*" I choked on a laugh, clapping my hand over my mouth in case the guards heard and thought we were making fun of them.

Sailor smiled, smug as a cat. "What?"

"No one talks to the guards like that. I mean, no one really talks to the guards at all. Not since a few years ago when one of the keepers got in a drunken fight with one and got himself shot."

"No shit?" Sailor seemed intrigued. "Guess those guns aren't just for show. Yeah look, it was cheesy, but it worked, right? Now we can walk without worrying about being harassed. Always be ultrafriendly. Always flatter them. Flirt if you have to. Use this if you have to." She grinned wickedly and rapidly zipped and unzipped her top an inch or so. "Always leave them flat-footed."

The moon slipped behind a cloud and we were farther from the illumination of the dock now, so we both got our flashlights out. I turned around.

"I think they're gone, I see their shadows down near the dock."

"Cool," said Sailor. "To the roof, then." We doubled back to the Officers' Club. It looked so spooky at nighttime, the sightless eyes of its empty window frames and the roofless cavity of its main section sagging like a crushed rib cage. Ivy furred the building's crumbling stone walls. It would have housed bats, if there were any of those still around.

"I'm not sure that's structurally sound. . . ." I called out as Sailor strode to the edge of the building, hoisted herself up onto a window frame, and then climbed onto the narrow stretch of roof that was still intact. I looked around in a small panic, waiting for someone to agree this was a stupid and dangerous idea.

"Come on, Birdy!" Her voice chimed out of the darkness. "It's beautiful up here."

I sighed before following her lead, scrambling with less grace than she had up onto the window ledge. Sailor leaned down from the roof to haul me the rest of the way. It was undignified, but I got there. And she was right, it was beautiful. We weren't very high up, but it felt like another world.

"Isn't this something?" Sailor stretched her arms above her head with a satisfied sigh. "Can't stand being cooped up in the barracks. And it gives us a chance to talk without being overheard."

"Right," I said, although I didn't really understand what we had to talk about that couldn't be overheard.

She wedged her flashlight between her boots and aimed the beam so it lit her face eerily from below. "So that's the scene every night in the rec room?"

"Pretty much."

"Have they always been like that? So . . . apathetic?"

"Not really." I flickered my own light out to play over the humped gray shapes of buildings and the silver gleam of water beyond. It never got truly dark because of the city. "Everyone starts off enthusiastic but then, I don't know. They just sort of give up."

Sailor nodded. "I saw it in Paris too. That doomer mentality. It's a virus that takes hold when a generation feels like there's no future. They retreat into their games and psychedelics and whatever else takes their mind off it. A kind of mass dissociation. Either that or they get really into radical activism and blaze out."

"Blaze out?"

"Yeah, like get arrested. Or worse."

"Doesn't sound ideal."

I said it lightly but I didn't like the way Sailor looked at me then, something hard in that look, like she was trying to figure out whether I was worth investing any more time in. Although perhaps I was just imagining it, because a moment later she was bright and enthusiastic again.

"Listen, though, Birdy, there are good opportunities here."

I was puzzled. "For promotions, you mean?"

She jettisoned a small pebble off the roof. It plinked on something hard below. "No, *mon chou*, I mean for . . . improving things. But it's not going to be easy."

"Okay," I said, approaching the conversation with the same caution I used with the larger predators.

"These blights might be over someday. An old friend in Europe tells me there are signs of recovery in some forest remnants in the north. The moment we're in right now, it's like the days after a terrible earthquake."

She had one of those rare storytelling voices, a campfire voice, and when she talked in that way you felt wrapped inside the circle of light. "You're still shell-shocked, but you can imagine the ground solid beneath your feet again, and you can start to think about rebuilding."

"Getting back to normal."

"Right. Except that's the most dangerous time of all."

"Wait, why?"

"Because we won't be the only ones trying to rebuild. We only have the smallest window, see? There are lots of powerful people with big ideas for the kind of world we're going to make next. And there's us. Whose ideas do you think are going to win out in the end?"

Did she expect an answer? I couldn't tell. I didn't trust my voice to not come out tiny and squeaky, the kid at camp who wants to go home now, so I didn't answer, just hugged my knees and rocked gently. I felt Sailor's arm settle around my shoulder, a comforting squeeze.

"You know what's weirdest about this place? Living with the people you work with. Enforced fraternizing. Any tips for coping?"

"You'll get used to it," I said, then laughed, because I wasn't even convincing myself. "Memorize your roommates' schedules and habits, that helps a bit. Avoid each other. In a nice way."

I knew there was no advice I could give her that would help, though. She was a creature of vast territory, like Feliz.

We stayed there for a while, watching the boats and freighters, alternating between talking and companionable silence. At one point Sailor pulled a silver flask from her pocket and took a deep slug. She didn't offer it to me, and I was glad not to have to refuse. Out at sea, lights from vessels winked on and off like they were talking to each other.

"Have you ever seen fireflies?" asked Sailor in a dreamy voice. "They used to be everywhere. When I was a kid, in spring the whole place would be lit up with them."

"No, we never had them on the West Coast."

"Ah, *quel dommage*, you would have loved them."

"I know," I said wistfully.

Sailor took another sip from her flask, screwed the lid back on, and tucked it away. "When I was a kid, if you were driving you could barely see out the windshield because of all the bugs squished on it. Like, you'd drive into whole clouds of them. But then they just went away." She made a gesture like wiping something aside. "All the windshields were clean."

"Well, the mosquitos and flies are back," I said, the only optimistic offering I could think of.

Sailor and I had a lot in common, but it took me a long time to see the biggest difference between us, and to understand that it could never really be bridged. My generation, we're like animals born in captivity: we accept the state of things because it's pretty much all we've ever known. Sailor was old enough to have experienced a better world. And that knowledge was a sadness she could never shake.

When we left the roof and resumed our walk, Sailor linked her arm through mine, and I had to quicken my step to keep up with her. "We're the flaneurs of Alcatraz," she said, and I smiled and nodded, although I had no idea what "flaneur" meant. I looked it up later and was amazed and enchanted and slightly scandalized at the idea of someone just strolling the streets of a city for fun.

We scrambled down the steep slimy banks near the desalination plant, and Sailor showed me how to prize a mussel shell off the rocks with our multitools. The shells were thin, transparent in places from the acidic waters, but Sailor insisted they would still be good. "We can feed them to Rocco," she said enthusiastically. Rocco was our grizzled old Canadian brown bear, and in spite of having few teeth left, he loved treats of all kinds. We stuffed our pockets with them until our waistbands sagged. The island had always felt sinister at night, but I could see its beauty now as well, how it was both fragile and tough. You could hear the wind and the waves much better at night too, when the day's tasks weren't clamoring in your head.

Just off the path, Sailor pointed out a tiny shrub clinging to a rock. It looked so small and solitary, separated by all those watery miles from its tree kin. There was something so noble about its determination to survive. Or maybe "futile" is a better word.

"I feel sorry for it," I said, bending down to stroke its spiny leaves.

"Don't worry, it's fine," said Sailor. "It will outlive us." Her tone was casual but the words made me shiver.

I had always thought there wasn't time for beauty anymore. That there was something frivolous about it—the pursuit of it, the mindless worship of it as laid out in the old movies we liked to watch. I had thoroughly internalized the notion that usefulness was the only metric of whether something had value. A carabiner was useful. A multitool was useful. Schedules were useful, as were cages and bars. Tranquilizer darts were regrettable but useful. A flower could be useful but only because it might provide food or diversion for a bird or animal, not because it was beautiful. Its beauty was incidental and easily dismissed. But then Sailor arrived, and I realized that even the smallest sliver of beauty matters and can be useful. Not because it makes a difference on some cosmic level, but because it quiets our restless hearts for a moment. It whispers to us that joy is still possible.

Paris

One Year Earlier

After the successful armadillo breakout, they were all keen to try again. Sailor more so than anyone now. Anouk said the sanctuary people were standing by to receive. But almost two years elapsed between Anton's liberation and their next chance. Conditions both macro (political unrest, widespread desertification) and micro (zoo staffing cuts, illnesses, infighting in their little group) conspired to keep the plan on ice. But finally Anouk announced that it was go time.

The operation was more audacious and dangerous in scope, this time involving four sugar gliders. The sanctuary people had expressed a specific interest in the species, which led some of the Maquis to speculate the sanctuary might be located in the Asia Pacific region, where the acrobatic creatures had until recently thrived. Anouk discouraged this speculation, warning that the less they all knew about the sanctuary location, the better.

The breakout was scheduled for evening, as smuggling a group of large dexterous possums during daylight hours was out of the question. Also, free-roaming camera drones had been brought in since Anton's liberation, and the murkier nighttime footage would make it harder to identify any of them, they hoped. Still, Sailor had a bad feeling. "Wouldn't daytime be better, though?" she argued the week before the appointed time. "The gliders will be sleepy then." But Anouk insisted her way was best.

Later, after it had all gone horribly wrong, Sailor would have been justified in feeling vindicated. Instead, she felt only dread as she sat awaiting judgment from the authorities. The room was large and sparsely furnished, and at its center was a sturdy oak galleon of a desk shipwrecked in a sea of beige carpet. The two people on the other side of the desk—starched, smoothly coiffed bureaucrats of indeterminate age—sat in expensive-looking chairs, a comical contrast to her own fragile metal seat, which looked made for a child. She was calm even though she knew what was about to happen.

The kinder-looking of the two spoke first. "Do you know why you're here?"

Sailor pretended to ponder this. "Hmmm. Missing stapler?"

This garnered no response. They simply continued looking steadily at her until the slightly crueler one explained that she was no longer an employee of the zoo, her tenure terminated as of this very moment. They had the evidence in front of them, in case she doubted how much they knew. Here, would she like to view the security footage? (She would not.) It didn't matter. One of them spun the screen on the desk around anyway, so she could watch the infrared video, which featured three ghostly figures stealthily approaching the sugar-glider enclosure. Two of the people were carrying crates. The third figure reached the gate of the enclosure, glancing around a few times, then pressed numbers into the keypad. Nothing happened. The figures spoke urgently to one another, then the third figure tried again. Still nothing. The three of them looked around twitchily but never made eye contact with the camera. That wasn't surprising. The cameras were mobile, moving all the time around the zoo to make it impossible to disable or evade them. After a brief, even more urgent consultation, the three figures hurried away. The camera followed them for a while until they exited the zoo and evaporated into the night.

One of the bureaucrats tapped a button, and the screen went black. Sailor watched the whole thing impassively, her hands folded in her lap.

"Recognize anyone there?" the bureaucrat asked. They didn't wait for an answer, just informed her that what she and her cohorts had tried to do was a serious offense. Jailable. Maybe something worse. However, they had decided not to involve the authorities. As always, they preferred to manage things in-house.

"Do you have anything to say?"

Sailor hesitated for only a beat. "Yes. I'd like a really good reference."

"You would like a what?"

"A reference. A glowing one, preferably. So I can get another job."

The bureaucrats looked at each other. They allowed themselves small, sour smiles. "That will not be possible, Ms. Anderson, as we're sure you're aware. Terminated employees do not receive references."

Sailor ignored this. "There's only one place I want to work." Her voice was cool and controlled. "One zoo. And you're going to help me."

"You're not in a position to bargain."

"I suppose not." Sailor sighed. The bureaucrats must have thought they had her. "I mean, you can word it in your own way, but here's a suggestion for what could be in the reference. 'Sailor Anderson has been an exemplary employee over her decade at the Paris Zoo. She has shown particular skill in working with the primates, the reptiles, and the big cats. Oh, and the pangolins.'"

"This is ludicrous," said the meaner bureaucrat, fingers curled around the edge of the desk. "There will be no reference. And we don't even have pangolins at the zoo."

Sailor looked up. "Oh right, sorry. I forgot you keep them in the other facility. The secret one in La Défense." The bureaucrats blinked in unison. Neither of them moved a muscle, but Sailor could feel them straining to decide how to react. "I guess, like me, those sweet creatures don't have many choices. They don't get to choose, for instance, whether they live a free life or get ground into powder for medicine to fund your little zoo."

The recklessness of what she was doing didn't escape her. Everything from now on was calculated risk. It was like with the animals, there were limits and boundaries to what they'd put up with, but there was no way to discover those limits without testing them. You might wind up with a superficial scratch or a lifelong bond. Or you might wind up dead.

Alcatraz

There came a time, perhaps four months after Sailor and Titan dropped into our lives, when Sailor started joining the trips back to the mainland. I emerged one Sunday morning—it must have been midsummer, because all the zoo's cats were molting and drifts of fur greeted us every morning along the avenues—to see her at the dock, waiting with the other workers to board the scheduled ferry. I raised my hand in greeting, but she didn't see. She had on a small backpack and was facing out to sea. I experienced a jolt of unease that felt wrapped up in various layers: the brooding, overcast weather, the fact she hadn't mentioned it, even though we'd been out late together the previous night, the sense she might never be coming back.

Sunday mornings were sacred on the Alcatraz calendar. It was the only day keepers were permitted to leave the island, save for an emergency, and everyone who stayed behind was granted leisure time to do whatever they wanted. A temp crew from off-island took care of the morning feeds and health tests, and even the kitchen staff got some rest, leaving us to fend for ourselves at breakfast—on those mornings we made our own hot beverages and picked listlessly through baskets of stale pastries.

I'd always disliked Sundays, the way they felt pointless, a filling-in of time before the new week began. But with Sailor abroad they threatened to become interminable. I observed from the top of the hill as the last of the day-trippers boarded the ferry, everyone jostling and joking around, as if summer vacation waited at the other end. The hazy air rippled and my conviction wavered. Would it kill me to join sometime? But as I watched the ferry move out into the bay I thought about how barren it must feel over there now, and the wistful impulse vanished.

One positive thing about Sailor being gone for a few hours was the chance to patch up my cooled relations with Joseph. I had become aware in a peripheral way of his growing displeasure with me, but I'd been pretending it was something that would blow over.

"Oh, look who's decided to grace us with her presence," he declared loudly when I slipped into the rec room and headed over to the corner where he was sprawled. A few of the people around him laughed. But I could tell he was pleased to see me, and when I rested my head on his shoulder, he stroked my hair affectionately, even if it did feel a bit like he was petting his favorite dog.

I half listened as he and the others resumed trading workplace tales from the previous week. The topic of the elephants came up, as it always did, and I began to listen in earnest, hoping for some Kira and Titan updates I could gift Sailor with on her return. But it turned out they were talking more generally about the species. Brandon was explaining about a thing he'd read concerning the concept of *phajaan*, a Thai word meaning "crushing." Used, he said, to describe the breaking of baby elephants. "Barbaric, obviously," he assured his audience, whose faces expressed varying degrees of distaste. "But the book makes the point that a more toned-down version can be useful, like how cowboys used to break wild horses."

A few people started talking then, offering up their own thoughts on breaking versus gentling, like it was just a harmless intellectual exercise, but it sickened me to hear animals being talked about in that way. I steered my thoughts elsewhere, letting my mind drift back to the night before, when I had woken in the darkness to Sailor gently shaking me.

"You have to come outside and see this," she had whispered, her face luminous and spooky in the pale seep of light from the half-open door. My roommates stirred in their bunks but didn't wake. I grabbed my clothes and got dressed in the hallway and we crept, shivering, out into the darkness. Except once we were in sight of the shore it wasn't dark at all. The entire bay was glowing, illuminated by thousands of gently pulsing lights just below the surface of the mirror-smooth water. I opened my mouth, but no sound came out.

"Isn't it a dream?" said Sailor. "Who knew our jellyfish friends were bioluminescent?"

Instinctively I moved closer to the water, mesmerized by the creatures' metamorphosis. A memory stirred, of having read about it once, an extremely rare event in which some jellyfish can produce luminescence en masse in response to some mysterious signal. A once-in-a-lifetime thing to witness. Some part of me wanted to dive in and drown in all that beauty.

"Let's go to the top of the island," said Sailor, grabbing my arm and yipping, shaking me out of my dream state. We scrambled up the hill, tripping over unseen obstacles, laughing and cursing, until we arrived in the shadow of the lighthouse. Sailor and I grasped hands and turned in a slow circle together, hooting with laughter. We were close enough to the zoo building that we could hear answering calls floating through the high windows as some of the nocturnal pack animals stirred and responded. I like to think they were remembering their ancestral songs. The hairs on my arms stood up. Something of a wild animal was coursing through our veins.

I became aware someone was speaking to me. The rec room reassembled itself and I blinked Joseph's face into focus. He clicked his fingers in front of my eyes. "Experiencing a software glitch, babe?"

I feigned a yawn. "Sorry, I haven't been getting much sleep."

"No shit. Wonder if stumbling around in the dark all night with Sailor has something to do with it?"

I made a face of wounded dignity. "We don't stumble around. We have flashlights."

"Whatever." He linked his hands behind his head and leaned back. "I'm not jealous or anything. It's me she wants to spend time with, anyway."

"Yeah, right." I flicked his leg playfully.

"It's true. She loiters around me all the time at work. Can't get enough."

"Seriously?" I felt a pang of hurt. But it was soon salved on realizing what she was up to. "Are you sure it's you and not Achilles she can't get enough of?"

"We're a dream package," he said, and I had to laugh at his indefatigable confidence. "But for real, she knows a ton about crocodiles. Like, more than anyone I've ever met, besides myself of course. Kind of impressive, actually."

I endeavored to conceal my surprise by saying offhandedly, "Yeah, I think she used to work in the crocodilian section of Paris Zoo."

In truth I didn't even know if there had been a crocodilian section at the Paris Zoo. All I knew was I didn't like the creeping possessiveness I felt in vying for the largest slice of my new friend's attention. It made me feel petty. After all, hadn't I wanted she and Joseph to be friends?

I resolved to ask Sailor on her return about both the mainland and her particular interest in crocodiles, but when I saw her the next morning she was sunk in a pensive, untalkative state, so I let her be. We were soon reunited, anyway: on Tuesday morning, the screen showed we'd been assigned to the aviaries together. That sent both our moods soaring. Sailor liked the aviaries as much as I did—she claimed they were her favorite cage in the zoo. Our preferences were very aligned in terms of which animals and birds we favored. We always hoped to be assigned to the same enclosures, but it rarely worked out that way, thanks to the number of keepers and the semirandom system.

The aviaries were a whole section of their own, housed in a new wing adjoining the original building, with a tall atrium and glass front overlooking the lighthouse and the parade grounds. I loved the aviaries not just for the exotics—the toucan with his psychedelic jewel-toned head; the glamorous peacocks; the lone, cheeky kookaburra—but for the smaller, less showy birds as well.

Sailor kept me entertained by describing her reasons for liking various birds. The Australian magpie reminded her, she said, of a scrappy dude hanging around outside the pub spoiling for a fight, but when he opens his mouth to insult you, out pours the voice of an angel. The tufted titmouse was a badass because despite her diminutive size, she didn't let anyone push her around. The blue jays were such ditzy hoarders they kept forgetting all the treasures they'd stolen from other birds and frantically buried, but their coats were so beautiful they got away with it. Her favorite of all the birds, she said, was the humble house wren, because it's small and quiet, so people underestimate it. A homebody, yet during migration it could cover miraculous distances. In Celtic lore, she said, the wren symbolizes kindness and brings good luck.

We worked with the birds until a senior keeper, Prentiss, came to tell us the tour was about to start. He solemnly fist-bumped with Sailor before moving on.

"What's that about?" I asked her as we finished making the aviaries sparkling and presentable. "He's kind of aloof normally."

"Prentiss? Oh, he's a comrade. We have . . . alignment on some issues."

I poured grain into a feeder and felt an eager flurry of wings at my back. "Such as?"

"Let's say, hmm, animal welfare."

"Ah, of course." I hadn't realized there were different positions to be staked out on that issue.

After washing up, we wandered out to the rec yard. The pollution wasn't too bad, so we sat on the patchy lawn with our masks dangling around our necks and tilted our faces toward the shrouded sun. There were a few other keepers around, scattered to the far corners of the yard.

Sailor chewed a leftover biscuit from breakfast with a contemplative air. "You know I've been lobbying the admins again about letting Kira and Titan live outside," she said. "At least here they can see the sky."

"And how's the campaign going?" I teased, as if I didn't already know.

She screwed up her nose. "A big zilch." She put on a high-pitched whiny voice. "'*The air is too impure out there, Sailor. It would damage their health, Sailor. Think of the children, Sailor.*' Bullshit, as usual. The real reason is they want to keep the tours inside. Let the gawkers get close to our superstar elephants. Corral the tourists, give 'em the old showbiz schtick, then whisk them off to the gift shop. Nothing to do with the elephants and their happiness at all."

I attempted to communicate caution about expressing such loud criticisms, mostly through frowny eyebrow gestures, but Sailor just laughed. "Something wrong, Birdy?"

I shook my head and glanced around the yard to make sure no one could overhear. "Honestly, I think they're mostly scared of the animals being stolen if they keep them outside. Gangs have done helicopter raids on zoos before."

She swiveled her neck to look at me. "Really?"

I shrugged. "Not this one. But I've heard stories."

"*Merde*," she muttered, then flopped to the ground, legs stretched straight and arms wrapped behind her head. "Anyway, next we need to convince the admins we shouldn't wake the nocturnal animals up for the tours. It's very disruptive to their circadian rhythms. Or at least equip the exhibits with red reverse light cycle setups like they did in Paris. I mean, honestly, what kind of circus are they running here? Are we the only ones who can see these things?" I had to laugh then. She was like a racoon trying to crack a food puzzle toy: when faced with an obstacle, she'd never give up, but keep turning it round and round until she'd devised a way in. "What?" Sailor said, squinting up at me.

"Nothing. These are, like, admirable missions. But I've been here longer than you, and I hate to say it, but you'll never win the big wars. You have to start smaller. Minor, doable things."

She pushed herself upright, eyes alert with that fanatical light I was starting to both recognize and fear. "What do you suggest?"

I floundered. It had been gratifying feeling as though I was imparting wisdom, but I hadn't thought ahead to concrete suggestions.

"Well . . ." I looked skyward, as if salvation might present itself there.

Sailor followed my line of sight. "Oh my god, you're right," she said. "We need to set one of the birds free."

"Excuse me, what?"

"Well you're right, nothing big obviously, nothing they'd notice. But one of the smaller brown birds, the common ones that everyone ignores."

I felt an upwelling of panic. "But why?"

Sailor looked at me with innocent confusion. "Why not?"

"Because," I began sternly, then proceeded to stutter into incoherence. "I . . . because . . . what . . . just . . . we *can't*." She shrugged amiably, never having bothered to acquaint herself with the concept of *can't*. "Do you know what they do to people who steal animals?"

"No. What do they do?"

"Well, I don't know exactly. But it's bad, okay, just assume it's very bad. Like, the worst it could possibly be. It's a crime, Sailor." I could feel my voice growing hysterical, and I breathed deeply through my nose a few times to calm down. "It's a crime," I said, dropping my voice back to a conspiratorial whisper, although there was no one within earshot. "So, a few years ago, one of the vets, this woman called Hannah, she got caught trying to smuggle something out of the zoo. It was a toucan egg. Everyone was pretty hyped about this egg at the time, because toucans are so endangered. They were worried the male might try to destroy the egg, because apparently they've been known to do that. So as soon as it was laid there were plans to remove the egg from the enclosure and put it in an incubator. But that afternoon, a keeper found the egg missing."

I paused. Sailor seemed to be enjoying the suspense, her wide-eyed gaze focused on my mouth to see what would come out of it next. "Anyway, everyone assumed, of course, that it must have been the male bird. Smashed it, eaten it, buried it, something. But then one of the guards brought some security footage to the admins. It showed this Hannah chick hanging around the enclosure. There weren't good angles to see what she was doing in there, but it was enough. They found her down at the dock, about to board the boat back to the mainland. She claimed she was going to see family."

Sailor leaned even closer. "Oh my god. Did she have the egg?"

I nodded slowly, kind of enjoying myself now. "She was trying to smuggle it out in her . . ." I suddenly realized I hadn't anticipated having to say this part out loud. I had never told it to anyone before: it was one of those stories that everyone seemed to already know, even if they hadn't been here for it.

"Her what? Handbag?"

I could feel my face getting hot. I couldn't look directly at her. "Um, no."

"Oh my god. You mean her *pussy*?" She said the word so loudly I literally flinched, put my hands to my lips to shush her like a librarian. She hooted with laughter, and several distant faces turned toward us. "You mean she just shoved it right up there? Wow."

"Right." I'd intended the story to be a cautionary tale, not a funny anecdote, but I could feel its purpose slipping away from me. "Listen, listen. She got taken away by the guards, whisked off in some police boat, and we never saw her again. The rumors are she got life in prison. Maybe tortured first." I was just making that up, but I justified it as necessary, in the same way a parent might scare their child with a story about monsters to ensure they didn't talk to strangers. "That's what you get for stealing something from the zoo."

"Well, we wouldn't technically be stealing it," she said. "Just liberating it."

"Are you crazy? It's the same thing!"

Sailor must have finally realized my distress was real because she placed a placating hand on my arm and said, "Okay, I get it, shhh, it's okay, Birdy. I wouldn't involve you in anything like that. It's just fun to think about, no?"

Paris

Six Months Earlier

Her years in this city had not always been easy, but one thing she'd never tired of was looking down at Paris through the blueish haze—the metropolis a wavering mosaic of mansard roofs, slender church spires, the serpentine bending of the now-sludgy Seine. Sailor rubbed the side of her thumb on her front teeth as she looked out the tiny window. A maid's apartment, two hundred square feet, tucked in the top floor of a classic Haussmann building. The building had seven floors and ninety-eight steps, each of which had to be climbed to reach her cramped room in the sky. She joked sometimes that she had the best ass in Paris. For some meteorological reason she didn't understand, the attic was often positioned in a layer of clearer air between the haze above and below. She would be sad to leave it.

She'd begun to worry her threat hadn't been enough to move the bureaucrats to action, but finally her reference had arrived. There was nothing keeping her here now.

She sent Anouk a message, the first time they'd been in contact since the disaster at the zoo. Anouk responded right away, as if she'd been waiting breathlessly by the phone.

ughhh I'm so sorry sailor girl, this is a nightmare

                                                                         What the hell happened?

They found out what we were up to. They knew everything, from how we were disabling the alarms to where the drop-off point was. I think someone gave us up

                                Did the sanctuary guys get busted too?

No thank gods. But listen, the gliders are gone

                                                                                                          Where??

Don't know. Don't like it though

    Sailor pulled her duffel bag out from under her bed, unzipped it, and began packing her clothes. She swiped a message back to Anouk:

                                    What did they say in your meeting?

Sacked and banned for life!! big threat. you know those mfs don't have the funds to keep the zoo going. The animals are all going to be sold off anyway. We were doing them a favor

                                                                                         I know

    Sailor slid the phone into her back pocket, folded a sweater under her chin, then another. When she finished, another message waited:

Where are you now?

                          It doesn't matter. On my way back to the states

Fuck, they canned you too? Will you try for Alcatraz?

                                                                    I think so

Ahhh . . . I heard there are no bars on
the cages there. everything is much freer.
maybe a new way forward. incredible

                                    Why don't you apply too? They'd kill
                                            for a star keeper like you

I tried, can't get a work permit ☹ you
know the US is cracking down

                        Ugh, that sucks. What's happening with the sanctuary

gone dark. they can't risk having our petit
"adventure" linked to them you know. they'll reach
out again soon, we just have to be patient

                                    Have you spoken to the rest of the
                                    maquis? what are they going to do?

Everyone wants to work with animals still, but TRUE
conservation this time, grassroots kind. Except Daniel,
he'll probably join a cartel or something! now that they're
starting to get into the exotic animal biz. You know
how he is, he loves animals but he has no morals ☺

                        He wouldn't, would he? Those fuckers are evil.

This is true. May they burn in hell. Listen, I'll send
you the number of my contact at the sanctuary.
Maybe there's something you can do from America?
His name's Mr. Li. I'll let him know to expect you

Sailor looked up. She thought she heard someone coming up the stairs, the telltale creak of the floorboards yielding beneath the weight of a body.

She went to the door and laid her ear against it, listening, but there were no further human noises, just the usual sighing and shifting of the old house and its bones. She went back to packing with one hand, trying to move quietly, as if it made any difference, and with the other she responded:

> Ok but even if I get the job I'm going
> to need to lay low for a while

oh sure, they understand, only if it's safe for you
and the animals. I will help too, as much as I can
from here. Ahh, so jalouse, we will live vicariously
through you! I'll send Mr. Li's details now. Okay,
gotta go. Take care of yourself baby girl, ciao ciao

> take care too. Ciao xx

Sailor resumed gnawing the side of her thumb as she stared out the window. A piece of snow-white trash danced past on an updraft. In another life, she might have thought it was a bird.

Alcatraz

The next time I entered the aviaries, I wasn't on duty there. I'd been assigned to the serval cat in the Africa section and had been having a fun morning playing fetch with him. I'd left the habitat to fetch a broom and was walking along Michigan Avenue when I heard my name.

"Hey, Camille," came the low, urgent call. I followed the sound of the voice and saw Sailor gesturing at me from inside the aviary. She looked ethereal standing there in her cage, light riming her body and a blur of wings fluttering around her head. I trotted over.

"Oh hey, what's up?"

She glanced around quickly and then buzzed the door open, taking me by the arm and pulling me inside. "Just need your help for a second, *mon amie*." She said the French part in a high-pitched trill. There were other people milling around in the avenues and inside other nearby enclosures, workers going about their day, the low rumble of voices and the occasional boom of laughter echoing along the stone corridors, but no one paid us any attention, and the accelerated heart rate that attended most of my meetings with Sailor these days settled into a more regular rhythm. I followed her through the aviary as birdsong filled the air. Two dark-eyed juncos hopped along the path in front of us, pecking away busily. A flash of vermilion flew by, a cardinal on its way to somewhere. My spirits always lifted in that place, and I thought Sailor lucky to have scored two shifts with the birds in such quick succession.

I followed her to the back wall of the aviary, where the new section met the old. Sailor stood in front of one of the elaborate water features, a baroque piece of molded concrete taller than she was, cascading down three levels, like one of those champagne fountains in the old musicals. A few birds were splashing in the shallow pools, ducking beneath the surface then driving the water along their tiny, feathered spines before flicking droplets everywhere. A fine mist settled on my exposed skin.

"Okay, so I just need to do some adjustment to this fountain," Sailor said to me in an oddly formal tone. "It's not working properly. And it would be great if you could stand just . . . there"—she positioned my body carefully a few inches to the right, like a theater teacher moving an acting student onto their mark. "I'll let you know which tools to hand me."

None of this really made any sense to me, but I stood there obediently, waiting for further instructions. There were technicians available to do these kinds of repairs, and while keepers were welcome to fix minor things they noticed in the enclosures, not many people bothered. Why take on someone else's task when you already had a pile of your own? But I knew better than to question Sailor when she was in one of these slightly manic moods.

At the ground near my feet was a red metal toolbox, the kind with drawers that concertina out when you lift the lid. Sailor was crouched down to the side of the fountain, working away at something behind there. As she moved I caught glimpses of what looked like a tiny gap between the fountain and the wall, and I realized there was some kind of damage there, perhaps a patch of rising damp that had rotted the wall. I tilted my head and saw a layer of mesh, perhaps a fine wire, beneath the crumbling plaster. Sailor took a trowel and dipped into a jar of a putty-like substance, then smeared it where the fountain structure met the wall. She half turned and grunted at me, "Hand me those pliers, would you?"

I squatted down and rummaged around in the toolbox until I found a pair of bull-nosed pliers, handed them to her, and stayed down on my haunches, gazing at the patch of daylight filtering through the gap. Sailor looked intently at me, turned her palm upward, and made a lifting gesture.

I was confused for a moment before understanding she was instructing me to stand up again. I obeyed, folding my arms and watching with a creeping sense of unreality as Sailor worked at the wire with her pliers, coaxing the braided pieces of metal apart until she had created a hole around two inches wide. She started humming softly, a soothing tune.

She put the pliers down and slowly twisted her spine a few degrees so that I could see her nose in profile, the tip of her chin. Then she reached into her pocket and pulled something out, keeping her fist closed around it. I could tell she was trying to show me something without looking at me. Perhaps I wasn't entirely surprised when she slowly unfurled her fingers to reveal a tiny cedar waxwing. Perhaps I was so shocked my heart stopped for a moment. The waxwing shook itself into a puffed ball and emitted one sharp, indignant cheep. Then, as swiftly and elegantly as a magician, Sailor extended her arm and delivered the bird through the hole in the wall—that tiny birth canal to the outside world—then withdrew the arm and resumed her plastering-up work and her humming. Within seconds the hole was sealed. Sailor straightened, shot me a friendly, task-well-done grin, rubbed her hands together, and said loudly: "We'll just leave that to dry and then I'll paint it. Good as new. Thanks for your help."

I nodded without speaking and left the aviary, and as I walked down the corridor back to my post, everything was simultaneously the same and altered forever.

The first chance we got to talk about it was a few nights later, on the roof of the Officers' Club. This had become our preferred hangout on the nights when the air was clean enough to breathe. There were forest fires burning in Canada and the pollution counts had been getting steadily worse: some evenings we couldn't risk venturing out at all. Anytime the screen displayed acceptable levels, though, we leaped at the chance to escape the barracks. Nights could be chilly out on the bay, so we brought along scratchy synthetic quilts from the beds to wrap ourselves in.

The guards left us alone, mostly. Sometimes Sailor would pass them a bag of weed or a bottle, presumably purchased during her trips to the mainland. Alcohol and drugs weren't forbidden on Alcatraz, or even discouraged really. I think the admins thought—to the extent they thought of us at all—

that allowing keepers to let off steam in their own time made for happier and more compliant workers, providing it didn't interfere with productivity.

We liked to ramble along the Agave Trail on the southern shore, a great vantage point for viewing the city lights, but we always seemed to end up on the rooftop of the Officers' Club. That precarious, shadowy place felt safe, ironically.

"You don't talk much about your life over there, do you?" Sailor observed on this occasion as we sat, knees drawn, looking out at the shimmering skyline.

"It's not very interesting," I hedged.

"I doubt that. But no probs, I totally get it."

Why did I get the impression she wasn't respecting my privacy so much as plotting another way to get the information out of me, like that raccoon calmly trying new strategies until it cracks the toy open and treats spill out? I considered assuring her no big secret lay behind my reticence. I just preferred living day to day: the only strategy I'd found to successfully immunize myself against both the past and the future. But I decided against it.

"I'm more interested in why you . . ." I dropped my voice to a whisper even though there was no one in sight. "You know, the waxwing."

"I wanted to see what would happen, Birdy," she said at normal volume, taking a swig from her silver flask. At first I had worried the drinking might turn her mean or reckless, like it did some of the other keepers. It seemed to mellow her, though, to shave some of the jagged edges off.

"And? What happened?"

She turned and grinned. "That's just it. Nothing happened. No one noticed a petite brown bird missing. See?"

"Hmmm." I didn't feel like encouraging this line of thinking. "Could just be because there are so many of the waxwings. We pretend they're all rare, but some of the aviary species are thriving in there."

I would be ashamed later at this sulky, irrational reasoning, but at the time it felt righteous. Sailor wasn't bothered by my attitude. She picked up the flashlight and played it back and forth along the edge of the rooftop. I had a brief vision of someone in a boat seeing the light and wondering if it was a signal, some kind of cry for help.

"When you told me about that vet trying to smuggle the egg out in her cooch?" A smile tickled the corner of my mouth against my will. "It gave me an idea. You see, it made me realize that the authorities aren't looking at shit-shovelers like us to do something like that. Sure, they distrust the vets now, and maybe even the guards. They're the elite, people with connections to smugglers and poachers. They know all the channels to the big money. Everyone knows the keepers don't have shit in the way of connections. If any of us smuggled something off the island, where do you think we'd sell it? We'd be picked up the moment we offered the egg to Shady Steve or whoever down at the markets."

Her theory made sense, but I didn't want to give her too much credit. I was still smarting over her having made me complicit in her little experiment. It had taken me a couple of days to realize why she had wanted me there in the aviary—my body had been positioned to block the security camera's restless eye from being able to see what Sailor was doing.

"Well, what about pollution?" I countered. "It can't be healthy out there for birds on the bad air days."

Sailor had of course already approached and cleared this ethical hurdle. "I thought of that, but she'd just fly away from the danger zone, like birds have always done during wildfires. It's a risk, but so is everything else. Freedom doesn't mean freedom from all danger, no?" I declined to answer this unanswerable question. "Anyway, Birdy, my point is, they're not looking at us. We're nothing to them. Beneath their interest. And that can be a very useful place to be."

I suppose I should have known at that moment she had bigger plans in mind than showing me she could set a small bird free and get away with it. But I wasn't ready then.

San Francisco

The city had changed since Sailor had last (briefly) seen it, the year before she left for Paris. She had a couple of weeks to kill until her contract at Alcatraz began. A chance to explore this last, strange port before sailing to her new life. It was dirtier and poorer, like everywhere else, but the air of antic energy in the streets kindled a cautious hope in her. There was a resilience to the people here. The grim reality was threaded through with tiny, bright sense-memories of being brought here as a child: joggling on her mother's lap as a cable car groaned its way up the hill; being fed some kind of rich fish soup from a spoon under a striped umbrella at a café; the pungent but pure smell of sweat rising off the steaming hide of a speckled deer at the zoo. So many things were gone, but others had taken their place. Hawker stalls sprang up like weeds on almost every street corner, a deep, fragrant, dirty fog emanating from their braziers, of spices and dark oil used many times over. Despite its deterioration, she thought it was the most beautiful place she'd ever seen.

A good feeling persisted from the call she'd had earlier with Anouk. The conversation had been one-sided and hurried, Anouk breathlessly letting Sailor know that a few animals had been successfully liberated from what remained of Paris Zoo to the sanctuary. That was all Anouk knew for now, it wasn't safe to talk on these open channels anyway, take care, take care, and she abruptly hung up. But it was enough. It kept Sailor warm.

She walked down to the Presidio. Because of the mold blight there were few live trees left now, and in their place stood rows of carbon-capturing "tree" towers, a forest of glinting steel that lent the waterfront a sinister industrial air. People rifled through the small middens of plastic containers dotted around the shore, sliding choice pieces of plastic into carts and bags and bickering with their neighboring salvagers. Clouds of flies swarmed and settled, swarmed and settled. Occasionally a skirmish would break out. This had been a new development in Paris too, this renewed public passion for salvaging, ever since the oil companies, for years sidelined by the renewables, bullied Kenya into accepting their plastic waste. The sluggish industry was revived, the factories resumed pumping out plastic crap, and the price you could get for bringing discarded packaging to the depots soared. Behind the hills of Marin, Sailor could see red smudges on the horizon where the perma-fires burned. As soon as one was extinguished another would ignite. She assumed it would be that way until all the dead-tree fuel was gone.

A chain-link fence had been erected surrounding what used to be a dog park, and Sailor stopped to look. Attached to the fence were hundreds of laminated posters and sheets of heavy card displaying faded photos of dogs, some with just a name below—Lucy, Artemis, Good Girl, Tiny Timmy—others with poems or long homages to the beloved pet. An array of candles lined the bottom of the fence. A memory wall. It reminded her of the weeks following a disaster when people would search for lost loved ones using any means available. Sailor had always been moved by those spontaneous monuments that sprang up around cities, the chilling way they changed from bulletin boards to shrines over time. When she heard a group approaching, she moved away, feeling ghoulish.

The haunting scent threading its way through the dense warren of the city developed into a full-blown stench by the time she got to the shore. She pulled her scarf up to cover her nose. A man sitting on a bench called out to her. "Hey, tourist!" She didn't like being called a tourist but she looked in his direction, curious. "Give me twenty bucks to swim to that skiff out there." His fingers rubbed together in the sign for money. "I've done it before." He cackled, and she thought she could hear the rattle in his chest, even from so far away.

She laughed and waved him away, moved closer to the water. At first it looked as though the iridescent film floating there was a layer of gasoline on the surface. But close-up, the mass resolved into individual gelatinous jellyfish bodies ruptured and rotting under the noon sun. Sailor stepped back, repulsed. Farther out in the bay, she saw small fiberglass boats bobbing, fishermen dangling over the sides and hauling netfuls of jellyfish aboard.

Alcatraz

September settled in sticky and sullen. You could taste the air gritty and dull on your tongue. Another lonely Sunday morning came around. Sailor had joined the mainland day-trippers, and I was tired of hanging out with Joseph in the basement, so I decided to head up to the zoo and see if I could make myself useful. Maybe I could even steal a glimpse of the elephants without being hustled away by their usual caretakers, who treated us low-status keepers like annoying paparazzi.

As I drew level with the skeleton tree, I heard footsteps on the path behind me and my heart skittered. I can't say why I thought it was Sailor, but when I turned, smiling in anticipation, it wasn't her but another keeper, Lupita.

"Oh, hi," I said, trying not to sound disappointed.

"Hi, Camille. Can I join?"

Lupita was like me in that she didn't appear to seek any fulfillment outside of work. She was often the first to arrive at the zoo and the last to leave. Before Sailor, we sometimes used to walk home to the barracks together. Unlike me, though, Lupita was a highly valued citizen of Alcatraz. She was a primate specialist, had worked in Congo back when there were

The Island of Last Things

still wild troops of gorillas in the mountains there. Now, she was one of the keepers in charge of our chimps. She was older than me, maybe older than Sailor, and the rumor was she'd even met Jane Goodall once, which was incredible if true, because Jane was considered a saint among the keepers. But Lupita wasn't the kind to brag about something like that, and I had never asked her about it because I figured it would embarrass her. I aspired to be like her someday, and in spite of feeling Sailor's absence, I was glad of her company on the walk.

"Hey, did you hear?" She pushed a strand of silver-streaked black hair behind her ear and smiled shyly. My eyes widened. It was unlike Lupita to share rumors.

"No? Tell me."

"Um. It's just . . . there's a new specimen arriving today."

"Really? But there hasn't been an announcement."

She shrugged. "I think it might be one of those public-sourced specimens. You know they like to verify them before celebrating the news."

"Right." I jiggled in my shoes. "What do you think it might be? An Australian marsupial? A fox? Ooh, what about a saola, those horned bovines from Vietnam? Read about them the other day. So rare, even in the old times their nickname was unicorn! But there's a rumor one was found in Laos recently. Can you imagine?"

I was aware of babbling but I couldn't help it, there was nothing more exciting to me than speculating about who our next resident might be. I played scenarios in my head all the time, so it didn't take much prompting for them to spill out of my mouth. Lupita grinned and shook her head. "No idea."

We resumed walking and I let myself enjoy the idea of an addition to the zoo, the sense of continuum a new animal provided. There hadn't been any new residents since Titan. We kept hoping for an influx of arrivals from the shuttered Paris Zoo, but the days and weeks came and went with no sign. No animals were ferried across the water or dropped from the sky. The consensus had been growing among the keepers that they were in quarantine, that it was just a matter of waiting, but something about the silence from the top levels had always felt wrong to me. I was dizzy with the prospect it might finally be happening.

A low humming sound that might have been part of the general ambient buzz of the world separated itself into an unmistakable whirring. The wind picked up, invisible fingers lifting the hair from our skulls. We shaded our foreheads as a gray helicopter dropped through the fog and hovered above the parade grounds, whipping up dust devils.

The unspoken protocol if a new arrival or some other important delivery was incoming was to make yourself scarce. Treat everything as you might an ambulance with sirens blaring, just get out of the way. That's what Lupita and I did as the helicopter's doors swung open and four people wearing hazmat suits and masks emerged, two of them carrying a metal crate, their bodies bent almost in half to avoid the blades. As they came trotting toward us, we scooched to the dirt edge of the path to let them pass, trying to make ourselves small and inconspicuous. They didn't even glance our way, just continued their run-walk past the water tower and down toward the hospital.

Once they had passed, Lupita smoothed her hair back and raised her eyebrows at me. "Guess the rumors were true. Hallelujah!" She smiled and moved closer, as if to hug me, but then seemed to decide against it, turning to continue walking on to the zoo. I took hold of her sleeve.

"Hey. Want to go check it out?" She regarded me with utter incomprehension, as if I had suddenly started speaking a dead language. "Don't you want to see what it is?"

"Um, no. Have you lost your mind?"

I laughed, perhaps a touch wildly, and she looked even more concerned. "Who's it going to hurt?" To be honest, I couldn't quite believe the words coming out of my mouth either. I was the very last person to flout rules, and Lupita knew it.

"Well, us, for starters, if we get caught," she said. "You know how they feel about employees in unauthorized areas. I don't know about you, but I'm going to start work."

What possessed me? I still can't quite explain it, except to say that an emboldening had taken place over the last few weeks. This newfound bravado was just that—not bravery but its foolish cousin. It pulled me along in the wake of the vets who had disappeared into the hospital building. It stayed with me as I crept around the back of the building, the cold and blowy side closest to the water, and searched out the spot Sailor and I had noticed on one of our night ramblings, a small vent in the concrete. It was amazing what the darkness and the training of a flashlight revealed: things you would never have noticed during the day became magically visible to you. Sailor called those little discoveries Witches' Portals.

I crouched down and wriggled until my nose was pressed up against the vent and I was able to get an ant's view of the room. Several pairs of rubber-soled shoes gathered around the stainless steel legs of a table on a gleaming, white-tiled floor. The murmuring of voices drifted across. A reddish light blinking on and off. A strong ammonia-ish smell I associated with bad things.

"I told you," came a voice, the disgusted tone audible even muffled under a mask.

"Yeah, this is a non-breather. Better lock it down in case there's an infestation."

"No signs at all," came a third voice. The feet shuffled around like they were all slow dancing. "Think the poor thing's heart couldn't handle the journey. You can see how thin it is. But better to be sure."

"Get it off the island," said the first voice, which clearly belonged to a person of authority. The feet all moved again and there was the squeak of rubber on tile and the whoosh of closing doors as someone left the room. I got to my feet and walked as noiselessly as I could to the side of the building, where I peeked out to see two of the people who had emerged from the helicopter burst out the front door, holding the same black crate and moving with great speed down the path. I had just enough time to see the label on the side of the box, which read HOLLAND LOP: BRISTOL. So, it had been a rabbit. My eyes stung. I loved rabbits, and I knew Holland Lops were critically endangered. Rabbits were one of the hardest-hit species during the first wave of the fungus, and their collapsed population had a ripple effect on the other species that relied on them—wolves, foxes, birds of prey. It's possible I had just witnessed the end of its kind.

It used to be that people, regular civilians, would occasionally donate animals to Alcatraz. Of course, every zoo had signed a pact never to pay civilians for specimens, to disincentivize poaching, kidnapping, or stealing from the kinds of people who still had pets, so the only incentive left was the thrill of having a tiny plaque engraved with their name mounted outside the enclosure. But even that opportunity had vanished, as there were no animals left that any impoverished civilian could hope to access. And the zoos that used to arrange swaps for breeding purposes—or prisoner exchanges, as Sailor called them—were all gone now. So the only people I could think of who might be in possession of a rabbit were the people who lived in modern fortresses with more security than Alcatraz.

Obviously accepting animals under these circumstances was super risky, which explained why everyone was so cloak-and-dagger about the whole thing. Acquiring new stock from other zoos had been one thing: they all had strict health laws and quarantine procedures. A private citizen could acquire a rabbit or a deer and not realize or care that it had come into contact with the fungus and was a walking bioweapon.

The fungus was the thing we still feared the most. It had already wiped out so many species they hadn't finished recording them all. Researchers grimly announced new extinctions every day, it felt like. (How depressing to be in charge of discovering and recording something that no longer exists, like being an explorer but in reverse.)

Like any catastrophe, though, we had gotten used to it. It was already hard to remember how things were before. But if the blights really were starting to recede, as some people were saying, then a new story would have to be made. Was already being made, if Sailor were to be believed. As I watched that small black box being loaded into the helicopter, I understood her warning in a way I hadn't before. There would be more extinctions, more misery, if the wrong people got to write the story.

Anyway, it wasn't Lupita who snitched on me, I'm sure of it. She would rather have been deported than turn snitch. But someone went to all the trouble of going in the nasty private room in the admin center provided for that purpose and filing a report saying they'd seen me lurking around the hospital. I was called to the admin center after lunch. I hadn't been inside since the day Sailor arrived. My gut clenched walking through those doors, any bravado long fled. I rubbed my clammy palms compulsively down my overall-covered thighs, silently cursing Sailor. Spying on officials delivering an animal was something I would never have considered in my wildest dreams before I met her. So why did I wish more than anything she was there beside me?

I was called into the room at last. The two admins seated behind one large desk glanced up as I entered. A curious thing: while the keepers and vets and other workers were as familiar as, well, family, the admins were rarely recognizable to me. They lived off-island and didn't socialize with the other employees, so maybe I just didn't memorize their faces and mannerisms in the same way. It didn't help that they shared similar bland features and dressed in all black.

Sailor joked they were advanced AI models, but even if robotics had gotten that good, it would have been a pointless expense when human employees were so cheap.

The two admins on this occasion looked irritated rather than angry, but my hands still shook so much I had to press them beneath my thighs as I sat down. The woman cut to the chase. "What were you doing near the hospital this morning?"

I swallowed. I'd already promised myself not to lie. "I'd heard there was a new arrival and I was curious."

The man blinked slowly behind big frameless glasses with tinted lenses. He resembled a horsefly. "It's not your job to be curious, Ms."—he glanced down at the screen in front of him—"Parker."

"I know." I hung my head like a chastised child. "Please don't deport me."

"Hand over your phone."

I jerked my head up. "What?"

"Your phone." The woman tapped the desk impatiently. "Now."

I reached into my pocket and brought out the device, then slid it across the desk.

"We'll be going through your contact lists and messages."

I didn't understand for a moment and then it dawned on me. They must have thought I'd been spying for someone on the mainland, for a smuggler or the people who did smash-and-grabs at vet clinics. I knew what the punishment for those kinds of crimes were. "I would never—" I began, my indignance overcoming my terror.

The admins both raised their hands, as if they could stop words mid-flight. "It's just a precaution," said the man. "You'll get it back tonight after our techs have inspected it."

"In the meantime," said the woman, "your next pay will be docked by half."

A tiny sound of distress escaped my mouth. I transferred most of every paycheck to my mother each month, and though she never said, I knew those meager funds were her lifeline in the campo. I couldn't imagine having to tell her she'd be suffering this month because of me.

Back in the barracks that night, after my phone had been returned to me, I sat on my bunk, staring in trepidation at my screen. I dreaded calling her more than usual. The phone rang for a characteristically long time before her raspy, suspicious voice barked out, "What's happened?"

"Hi, Mom. Why do you always say that?" I laughed nervously. "How are you?"

A deep sigh that ended in a cough. "Can't complain. It's the anniversary tomorrow, you know."

"Yes, I know. I'm thinking about him too. Any new leads?" A polite formality on my part.

"A few rumors here and there. We check everything out."

"Of course. Listen," I said. "There was a bit of trouble at the zoo. I, um . . . the admins docked my wages, but I'm going to make it up to you, don't worry."

She gave a hoarse laugh. I wondered if she was smoking again. "Just my luck."

I had steeled myself for disappointment, or even anger, but she'd changed these last couple of years since Dad had been gone, fatalistic now in a way he would have hated.

"I'm really sorry. I shouldn't have . . . well, it doesn't matter."

"Don't worry about it, hon. I'm fine down here, you know that. We wives stick together. And whatever happened, I'm sure it wasn't your idea."

This stung more than it should have. I had the defensive urge to tell her that, actually, it *had* been my idea this time. I'm capable of coming up with stupid ideas too, you know. But of course I didn't, just reiterated that I'd make it up to her soon, and then we said goodbye, or at least I did. As usual, her farewell greeting was cut off, as if she'd dropped the phone or pressed the button too soon. *Never change, Mom*, I said to myself, but laughing at her inability to master simple devices wasn't the comfort it usually was.

Sailor returned on the late boat that evening, but I never did tell her about what happened. I think I was ashamed. Not just of having been so foolish as to hide out in a restricted area trying to catch a glimpse of a dead bunny, but of not standing up for myself when I was caught. Sailor would never have sat there mutely, accepting the admins' punishment. Sailor would have known what to do.

It felt like cosmic realignment when the chance came, a few days later, to be the first to spill a far more significant piece of news. Although I was so out of breath from running by the time I reached her, I couldn't speak. Sailor was emerging from the commissary, loaded down with bags of pellets, and I grabbed hold of her, doubling over to catch my breath.

"Whoa, Birdy," she said, gently placing the bags down and regarding me with some combination of amusement and bemusement. "Something on fire?"

I straightened up, and between panting breaths blurted out the news: "Did you . . . hear? Kira . . . is . . . pregnant!"

To my gratification, Sailor's eyes widened. I was obviously the first to tell her. I knew so early only because Joseph had told me, having received it firsthand from the specialist keepers who looked after the elephants. It paid sometimes to have friends who had friends in high places.

"Well, I'll be," she said. "It's a late-stage capitalism miracle."

"I know!" I was as hyped-up as a kid at the fair. "I couldn't believe it either! None of us can. But it's true!"

Sailor nodded a few times and then bent down to hoist the bags. "Well, I'm sure the Pinktons are over the moon. Just think of the revenue." I remember feeling a wave of disappointment. It was as if she needed to recollect her skepticism after letting optimism win for a moment. She must have clocked it in my expression, because she added quickly, "Look, it's great news, Birdy. Don't let me spoil your fun."

I skipped off then to see if there was anyone else I could break the news to. I won't lie: despite Sailor's muted reaction, it was one of the best days I'd ever had at the zoo. There were few times to rival its buoyant sense of hope and community. Kira and Titan had done the important work, of course, but we all took ownership of the pregnancy, as if the life growing slowly in Kira represented our own future too.

San Francisco

Back in her rented room, Sailor took out the birding field guide she had carried with her since she'd left Florida. She pushed aside the ratty mosquito net and sat on the edge of the bed. The blazing neon sign above the bar across the street that kept her awake all night was helpful when she needed extra light to read by. The book had a faded mint-green cover featuring an illustration of an aggrieved red cardinal, and it was called *Cawthorn's Complete Birds*. She couldn't remember where it had come from. Her best guess was that someone had given it to her, a relative perhaps on some long-forgotten birthday, but there was no message inscribed on the title page, no clue as to its origin. Still, it was her most treasured possession. More precious for how many of the birds inside were extinct. Its thick pages were so thumbed-through and swollen from humidity they looked deckled. Almost every page contained underlined sentences and handwritten notes scrawled in the margins. At some point around the first big avian die-off, she had switched from keeping notes about the birds she'd spotted and had begun using the book as a kind of journal, a place to jot down notes about anything she saw in the natural or unnatural world she might need to remember.

She flicked to the page where she had written the letter *S*, for sanctuary, and the name, MR. LI. It listed the specs of the California condor alongside a detailed illustration depicting the vulture's distinctive shriveled head atop a preposterously huge body. She loved how the bird resembled a wizened old man drawing a feathered cloak around himself. Maybe she had chosen this particular page because the bird had once represented hope, a Lazarus story that took a dizzying series of narrative leaps from the brink of extinction to miraculous return back to extinction again. Maybe it had just been the page that had fallen open by chance.

She sent a message to Mr. Li saying she'd like to arrange a meeting with someone from the sanctuary, that Anouk had mentioned they had people here in the city. It was probably a bad idea, but she longed for some kind of do-over for Paris. She stared at the screen and rubbed her thumb on her tooth. It occurred to her that they might not respond to text messages, because that was too risky. Better to call instead. While the small green phone shuddered on the screen, she took her book up again and scribbled an asterisk next to sanctuary and a footnote: *The presence of dystopia doesn't negate the possibility of utopia. Anouk believed and so do I. It has to be real.*

After the call terminated, she tapped a message to Anouk and waited, but no answer came there either. She went and sat on the sill of the suicide-proof window, trying to swallow down her disappointment. She had never minded her own company, like some people, but she was beginning to understand that aloneness could be a dangerous state. For many reasons. Even the wash of neon light across her thighs couldn't completely chase away the darkness that had fallen over the room.

Alcatraz

Because I was one of the first keepers Joseph had privileged with the news about Kira, he naturally expected something in return. That was the usual transactional way of things—insider intel about the animals was the hard currency in circulation on our little island. Spending so much time with Sailor must have dulled my usual sensitivity to these transactions, though, because it hadn't occurred to me at the time to do anything but thank him for the news and continue on my way. I wasn't avoiding him or anything, it was just that he spent all his spare time in the rec room and I now spent mine wandering the island with Sailor. But I should have known my lack of gratitude wouldn't go unnoticed. I was headed to my morning shift the following week when he cornered me in the hallway, his breath hot on my ear.

"Camille?" He smiled in an unfriendly way. He reminded me of a jackal. "Don't see much of you these days. Almost forgot who you were."

"Hey, Joseph. What's up?"

"What's up? Oh, not much. Never seen you wear lipstick before. Going somewhere nice?"

My hand involuntarily went to touch my mouth. I had started wearing a pinkish-brown lip color called Vixen I'd bought from Maisie, a keeper who ran a kind of informal commissary on the island, collecting orders and bringing supplies back from the mainland. She could get you anything from Valium to knockoff Chanel No. 5. Even brands of tampons the barracks vending machines didn't stock. I remembered something Sailor had said when someone had commented cattily on her makeup. "This is how I choose to celebrate my face." Joseph's eyes narrowed. I could see him struggling to choose between ridicule and coolness, something to show he was in on the joke. I didn't wait for him to decide but started walking to the exit, and he soon fell into step with me, his arm wrapped around my waist.

"Want to catch up this week? There's a BBC marathon starting Tuesday. We could party after."

He nuzzled my neck, friendly now and maybe even a little contrite. I couldn't help but notice he always responded to any perception of coolness on my part with renewed passion. It wasn't exciting to me, though. On the contrary, I found it tedious. I didn't know much about love, but I knew it wasn't something that needed to be tested periodically like a smoke alarm. Still, I did feel a bit bad about the fact that Sailor had filled up all the time I used to spend with him. "Sure, that sounds fun."

"I mean, as long as your *girlfriend* doesn't mind."

"Who?" I said, feigning ignorance.

"Sailor, man, who else. She's really starting to get on my nerves. Always sniffing around Achilles. She doesn't even try to talk to me anymore. Omar's getting the treatment now."

Omar was the other keeper who looked after Achilles. It was clear Joseph minded less about Sailor hanging around and more that she was paying attention to someone who wasn't him.

When movie night came around, the rec room was full. The old BBC nature documentaries were always a big hit, and not just on Alcatraz: I'd heard they were enjoying newfound popularity out in the world too. If even us keepers longed for worlds populated by creatures and landscapes that felt like they belonged to myth, how strong must the craving have been for mainlanders?

I arrived alone and scanned the room for Joseph. He was standing in a loose cluster of men, and when I caught his eye he gave me a lazy wave and continued talking and laughing. I studied the men for a moment with an anthropologist's eye, fascinated by the way they mimicked one another's stances, hands wedged deep into pockets, the points of their shoulder blades resting against walls so their torsos and hips protruded suggestively.

Joseph had always enjoyed celebrity status among the keepers, a combination of charisma and his elite role. It was the same with the elephant caretakers, but they had been elevated to even more rarefied heights since the news had broken about Kira and Titan's expectancy. To be an elephant guardian at such a time was to work with deities. I could tell Joseph envied them, but being resourceful, he had neatly converted his envy into self-gain. Having special access to his friends meant he got to hear all the elephant news firsthand, which meant he got to carry the information to his favored circle. He talked about the elephants with as much authority as if he tended to them himself.

I found two empty chairs together and sat down, placing my sweater on the other seat. The room was heaving. I remember it was one of the good nights, when a warm camaraderie bound the group together, and it felt like we were one big happy family rather than a loose-knit collection of threads pulled together by circumstance.

Joseph sauntered over after a while. "No Sailor, huh?" He looked over my shoulder, as if she might materialize there. He seemed jumpy, excitable, and it occurred to me for the first time that Sailor made him uneasy but that he was drawn to her anyway. A relatable conundrum.

"Oh, she has a migraine and said she was going to stay in her bunk," I lied.

Joseph pretended not to care, though it was obvious he did. I buzzed with an entirely novel sense of my own latent power. When, earlier, I'd invited Sailor to join us, she had said scathingly, "I think I'll pass, thanks," then shot me a wounded look. "I suppose that means you won't be walking with me tonight?"

I had never had two people vying for my company: never been anyone's favorite before.

"How's Kira?" I blurted out as soon as Joseph sat down.

"*How's Kira?*" he repeated in falsetto, screwing up his nose. "That's all anyone wants to know anymore. No one ever asks *How's Joseph?*"

"Poor Joseph."

He mock-pouted, but I knew he loved it, all the attention and fame-by-proximity. I swooped a quick kiss on his cheek. He turned to me, eyes shining. "Hey, so you wanna know how they knew?"

"How?"

"Well, you know they take blood tests and monitor their hormone levels regularly?" I nodded. "So female elephants when they're ready to ovulate have two surges of LH, luteinizing hormone. Kira had a first surge, then a second, and we . . . I mean they . . . knew after the second surge she'd be ovulating sometime within two or three days, so they only had a really small window for breeding. I swear, we all had some sleepless nights just staring at the cams waiting to see if Titan was going to hear the call, if you know what I mean." I was on the edge of my seat listening to him, I didn't care that he'd practiced this spiel dozens of times. "Look, we all know the mechanics of it, right? But none of us have ever seen it happen in real life before." He laughed and scratched the scruff on his jaw. "Anyway, Titan our man did his duty, and voilà!"

He slid his hand over my thigh, so content he was practically purring. Someone dimmed the lights and we all stared saucer-eyed at the screen as the camera swooped below the waves in pursuit of a pod of orcas. We collectively gasped when the screen exploded with a scene of humpbacks spouting and bubble-netting off some rocky coast, and again when dolphins herded a giant bait ball into shape. We were near the back of the room so I noticed when Sailor arrived after all. She sat just across the aisle, but I couldn't tell if she'd seen me or not in the half darkness. I watched her slide into the chair, her long legs stretched beneath the seat in front. After the movie had ended, a few people brought out bottles, and there were some edibles, and everyone hung around and sprawled on the floor and kind of waited to see what would happen.

Sailor got up at one point and I thought she was coming to finally say hello but she walked straight past us, heading for the whitewashed wall the film had been projected on. On either side of the wall were narrow windows. They had been boarded up for as long as I had been at Alcatraz. Ostensibly, it helped maintain the neither-day-nor-night casino ambience, but it also handily prevented arriving guests from seeing into our squalid lodgings, preserving the notion that we didn't really exist outside our obligation to keep the animals nice for them.

Sailor squatted down in front of one of the windows, and with a calmness that still gives me chills, drew the multitool from her belt and prized off the board covering it. A shaft of light from the dock flooded in and clouds of dust motes puffed out into the room, triggering coughing fits from people sitting close by. Then she calmly stood up amid the growing clamor of protest and moved to the next window and did the same thing, stacking the prized-off boards neatly behind her as she worked.

"Hey!" Voices rose up from all around. "What the fuck!" "Cut it out!" "What are you doing?" I could feel Joseph's body freshly rigid beside me. He was breathing through his nose like a horse. When Sailor was finished she put the tool back in its holster and dusted off her hands.

"That's better," she said, and grinned to the room at large. "You're welcome, vampire bats." She walked cool and unhurried through the crowd as a line of angry faces glowered at her. Some of the faces turned my way as well, and I felt implicated, although I'd had nothing to do with Sailor's small and heroic act of vandalism.

The next time I went into the rec room the boards were back over the windows, but this time they'd been fastened with some kind of tamper-proof metal casing. That was the thing with the little rebellions Sailor waged: they never achieved anything. But maybe that wasn't the point.

After that episode we resumed our night walks, exploring different parts of the island and gathering the occasional wildflower or interesting stone to take back to our rooms. We always avoided the zoo itself; it was one thing to hang out in the nonsecure areas, but I think even Sailor recognized she'd be pushing her luck trying to get inside the zoo after-hours.

Even when bad conditions drove us back indoors, we kept to ourselves. On Halloween, when the health warnings were flashing red on screens all over the island, Sailor invited me to her room so we could cut each other's hair. I usually let mine grow until it was so raggedy I couldn't stand it anymore and then I'd just saw off the end of my ponytail with a pair of nail scissors. So the idea of having someone else do the job with even a shred of care was appealing.

"Wonder where the rest of the ghouls are?" asked Sailor as she ushered me inside.

"In the rec room playing games and stuff," I said. "Just killing time."

"Nothing scarier than that," said Sailor, inviting me to sit in a metal chair and draping a towel over my shoulders. She began snipping my damp hair. I was always interested in seeing other people's rooms, although there was never much to see. Some people tacked photos or inspirational sayings on their walls, but generally the rooms were kept in the state of austerity the admins preferred. Like me, Sailor had a bottom bunk, and like me, she kept a stack of books on her bedside shelf. I studied their spines, hoping to gain some new insight into Sailor's private world. They were mostly serious-looking tomes about animal behavior.

"Hey, that reminds me," said Sailor, following my gaze to her stash. "Do you know what *umwelt* is?"

"No, actually."

"Okay, so think of it this way. We humans assume we're the only ones who center our own lives, who have subjectivity, but of course every other living being does as well. Think about it. Take the dragonfly, she spends so much of her life on the wing, hunting and stalking and eating, and her perspective is minutely focused on her prey, these tiny insects we don't even notice. Her experience is a small subset of the larger world, but to her that's the whole world. I think it's beautiful, her motivation is so simple, so unclouded by any extraneous bullshit. She perfectly understands her world and her place in it." Snip, snip, snip went her scissors. "Every animal experiences life like this. That's why there's no one size fits all when it comes to understanding a species. They each perceive themselves as the center of a very specific world."

"Right," I said. I'd never known anyone who wasn't extremely stoned to talk like this. But I wanted her to keep going.

"We have to get away from anthropomorphism." She stopped cutting, her busy hands still for once. "This obsession with mapping our own human experience onto beings whose perception of the world is often so radically different from our own. I want to understand the *umwelten* of every single creature on this island. Don't you?"

I laughed. "I guess I do now."

Then she told me stories about growing up in Florida, about the infernal humidity of the summers, and how in the winter the iguanas would fall out of trees when the temperature dropped below thirty-nine degrees, and the Burmese pythons would get frozen and have their eyes pecked out by birds. "That was when I was a kid, though," she said. I watched in the mirror as she stepped back to scrutinize her work, then resumed snipping. "It stopped happening because the temperature didn't drop low enough in winter. Which I suppose was a relief for the iguanas and pythons."

"Is your family still there?"

She didn't look at me, just kept busy with her scissors as she said, "No, my parents died soon after I moved away."

"I'm sorry."

"It's fine. They were both sick, they had a rare cancer. Well, rare for other people. Pretty common for the town we lived in. Nothing to do with the superfund site down the road, I'm sure." Snip, snip, snip. "They got to die on their own terms, at least." I didn't know what she meant by this and she didn't offer any further insight, instead pivoting back to me. "Did you have any animals or pets growing up?"

"Sadly, no. Well, unless you count a stray rat as a pet."

"Ooh, tell me."

I hadn't thought about my childhood in a long time. I closed my eyes and placed myself back there, at dusk in the communal yard of our building, an expanse of cracked concrete that acted as a graveyard for broken chairs and sports equipment. A listing basketball hoop was propped against the fence. Eight-year-old me perched on the uneven stairs, counting down the seconds.

"Well, so when I was small, there was this rat that used to visit our backyard. He'd show up at exactly five thirty every day. It was uncanny. He had this routine. He'd duck under this wooden gate leading out to the alley, jump onto the lowest beam of the fence, and *race* the whole way around the fence before disappearing into some dusty half-dead bush. It was the same routine every day at the same time, like a commuter catching the same train, you know? And I was just fascinated by it, by his or her sense of purpose. I think it was my first understanding of how animals mark time, the moment it became obvious to me that we're not the only creatures to keep their own rhythms and routines." Sailor's hands had stopped their work behind my head. I could tell she was listening, really listening, and I was suddenly embarrassed at having gushed on, as if noticing a rat meant I possessed some magical powers of observation. "Anyway, I don't remember when I stopped seeing my ratty friend." Keen to turn the spotlight back around, I asked, "What about the other wildlife in the Everglades? What else did you get there?"

"Well, crocs and gators were the ones all the tourists wanted to see. My parents raised crocs. That's how they made their money, running a small croc farm, letting tourists come and gawk during feeding time."

I forgot she was cutting my hair for a moment, swiveled my neck around to gape at her. "No way!"

Sailor placed her hands on either side of my skull and gently returned my head to a forward-facing position. "The whole operation was hokey, sure, but it wasn't cruel. They really looked after them. They loved them, in their own way."

"Your parents loved the crocs, or the crocs loved your parents?"

"I meant the crocs loved my parents. But maybe that's just wishful thinking. I'm not sure a croc is capable of love in the way we mean it."

"Not part of their *umwelt*?"

Sailor smiled. "Quick study, aren't you, Birdy? Well, I know one thing, my folks were superfond of their kids, as they called them. You'd be surprised how sweet they can be. I mean, they don't show affection like mammals do, but they have their own ways of appreciating you."

"So, they were tame?"

Sailor snorted. "Tame? Uh, no. You can't tame a croc. Only a moron would even try."

"Oh, right. Sorry."

"Did I mention there were a lot of morons in our part of Florida?"

I laughed.

"Anyway, when my dad tucked me into bed at night, we had a routine. He'd stand at the door, switch out the light, and say, 'See you later, alligator,' and I'd answer, 'In a while, crocodile.'"

"That sounds like a nice childhood," I said, and I meant it sincerely.

"Anyway, they're all gone now, and you're done, Birdy."

She brushed the cut hair off my shoulders and it fell like grass clippings to the floor.

San Francisco

There was a corner store Sailor frequented while she was waiting for her passage to Alcatraz. It was the kind of place that sold everything from beer to oximeters to pillar candles depicting Jesus to sacks of beans as heavy as a child. The kind of place that would once have had a fluffy indolent cat snoozing in the gaps between unpacked boxes. After several visits she got to know the owner, a thin, bent-shouldered man named Israel who had lost his wife the year before to lung cancer, an all-too-common end at a time when simply being a breathing human amounted to a pack-a-day habit.

His story emerged in small increments between transactions. The two of them had lived above the shop, but now that his wife was gone, Israel was planning to move in with his sister and her children, who lived in Berkeley. It was too lonely in the apartment, he claimed, and the space reminded him too much of her. Sailor asked him what he planned to do with the apartment, not really with any intention, just casual banter, but when he said he was looking for a tenant an idea came to her.

"Could I take a look?" she asked.

Israel hesitated, then nodded and locked the front door, flipping the sign to CLOSED and beckoning her to follow him. At the back of the shop, he slid a wheeled rack of snack foods aside to reveal a heavy steel door, the kind you might find on a bank vault or a drug dealer's house. "The previous owners were kind of paranoid," he explained as he slid the key into the padlock. The door opened into a dim, airless corridor lined with boxes and crates. Israel flicked a switch, and a naked bulb cast a puddle of light on a steep wooden staircase rising into shadow at the end of the corridor. He glanced at her, wiping his hands nervously down the sides of his pants. "It wouldn't be, you know, official."

"Oh, sure." She shot him a complicit smile. Upstairs were three rooms: a bedroom with a sagging double bed and an elaborate colored-glass chandelier; a tiny bathroom consisting of a plastic shower stall, a cracked toilet and a sink; and a galley kitchen with a two-burner camp stove and a gas bottle shoved haphazardly beneath the counter. The whole setup was so obviously treacherous and illegal—the rickety staircase, the plumbing, the lack of egress in a fire—but it was precisely the thing she was looking for. Anouk had always said you needed a safe house.

They agreed on a price, and Sailor insisted on paying for a full year. Israel looked both relieved and guilty. She celebrated by herself with a tiny glass of pastis in the corner of a grimy bar where multiple screens blaring some sports game allowed her invisibility. She liked how the liquid clouded when she poured the water in, and how the licorice burn of the alcohol jolted her into alertness.

She tapped the number into her phone again then sat with it for a while, taking the occasional birdlike sip of her pastis. Finally she hit call and pressed the phone to her ear. It rang and rang, the impersonal little clicks echoing in her ear, but no one picked up, and after a while the call was ended. She could have been discouraged but she had decided against that. Better to rationalize the sanctuary's silence as a temporary precaution because their operations had been exposed in Paris. They were just lying low for a while. One day they would answer.

Alcatraz

It had been a nice day, a satisfying day. Early November, when the fog-free mornings started to hint at some kind of winter. Inside the zoo, Rocco the bear had started to listlessly pick at meals, a sign of impending torpor, while the reptiles and amphibians were slowing down, preparing for brumation, a state of sluggishness similar to hibernation. Even we humans subtly shifted our behavior, sleeping more and moving with less haste through the shorter days. Strange, how seasons could become so warped and yet the primal impulses persist.

In the morning, I visited the commissary, where the nutrition managers prepared food for the animals. I'd been assigned to Clarabelle the cheetah and I noticed she was stiff and slow. She was seventeen years old, a ripe old age for her species, and while generally in good health, she needed extra assistance to keep her joints working properly.

The commissary was located in one of the nondescript newer buildings, connected to the zoo by a spooky, gray-walled corridor with giant ceiling fans roaring overhead. I loved the sense of purpose the apron-clad employees radiated as they bustled around the kitchens, weighing and chopping and preparing the hundreds of different foods in precise measurements for each of our residents. Stainless-steel prep benches and deep sinks lined the walls. There were ceiling-high shelves stacked with sacks of grains and bags of greens and dried grasses, and in the formidable walk-in fridge—bigger than several of our rooms put together—the various forms of protein, eggs, pink rodent babies for the reptiles (stored in the freezer like nightmarish ice cubes), and Fake Steak for the carnivores and omnivores. I loved the sense of abundance, however illusory.

I approached Leanna, the head nutrition manager. She had her back to me, working at a bench. I watched in fascinated horror over her shoulder as she slit the soft pale belly of a dead mouse and inserted a vitamin pill in the cavity. I wasn't sure which of the creatures this delicacy was intended for—a raptor, perhaps, or a snake, some picky resident who needed to be tricked into taking their medicine—but it made me grateful for our own meat-free diet. Mice were rare and precious commodities now, one of the most expensive of the commissary's line items.

Leanna must have sensed my presence, because after laying the mouse to one side she turned around, her friendly expression in startling contrast to the gory knife she still held.

"Hiya, Camille. What's up?"

"Hey, Leanna. I'm working with Clarabelle today and I was hoping you might have something for her joints."

"You betcha," she said, laying the knife down and tucking a piece of errant hair back under her hairnet. "Come with me, I'll get you some Flexadin."

Like most of the big cats, Clarabelle wasn't fed every day. We tried to mimic their diets in the once-wild, where cats would often go days between eating. That day was Clarabelle's day to be fed, though, so I was glad of the chance to slip her supplements in with the meal. Before I fed her, I treated her to a grooming session. This isn't possible with the other felines, who even in play are capable of neatly separating your hand from your arm, but cheetahs are famously tolerant of humans, especially when reared from a cub, as Clarabelle was.

I sat with her on the floor of her enclosure and groomed her with a special bristled brush. She leaned against my legs, lifting her head slightly when I'd pass the comb over a certain section of her back, head-butting me gently when I brushed under her chin. My mind was blissfully blank as I worked, enjoying the feel of Clarabelle's fur, the beauty of her face with the markings like black tear tracks running down from her eyes; the bulky warmth of her relaxed body resting against my legs. I remember how companionable it felt, to sit there with this creature who, at the very least, trusted me and perhaps even enjoyed my company in return, and how jarring it felt to be wrenched out of this moment by a commotion that exploded farther down the avenue.

Clarabelle and I both jerked our heads up at the noise, a shouting and screeching and banging that kept rising in tempo. At first it was just a cacophony of sound, but before long a voice separated itself from the rest and I realized with a sinking heart that the voice belonged to Sailor. The sound of footsteps walking and running toward the ruckus added to the chaos. With any kind of loud or violent disruption, the zoo instantly transforms into a highly dangerous environment. Animals are hardwired to panic or become aggressive when they sense an altercation, and it can be scary to be in the same space as a creature whose fight-or-flight instincts have clicked into place. Doors clanged closed all around as keepers instantly put space between themselves and their charges. Luckily, Clarabelle was too mellow and too elderly to get agitated. She flicked her ears a little and her eyes widened, but I was able to placate her quickly so I could move out of the enclosure into the avenue to find out what was going on.

I followed the sounds and the general direction of the human traffic, but I already knew where we were going because I knew Sailor had been assigned to the chimps that day, filling in for Lupita, who was tied up in a meeting. Dread followed close at my heels. The shouting and chaos intensified as we got closer to the chimps. There was already a sizeable crowd outside the enclosure, all wearing the bug-eyed expression of rubberneckers gawking at a car crash. Inside, the scene was frenetic, and it was hard at first to see what was happening. I got the attention of someone standing near the door and had them buzz me in. In two of the enclosure's corners were tight clusters of bodies, four or five people each struggling to secure another person who was partially concealed beneath the scrum. One of them was Brandon. I saw his face, blotchy and red with anger, emerge out of the flailing arms trying to keep him in place. In the opposite corner, the other person being held back was Sailor.

I should probably have gone straight to Sailor, offered her help or at least solidarity. But my attention flew instead to the chimps huddled in the corner, their bodies pressed against the wall, screeching in distress with teeth and gums bared. I ran over to them without thinking, dropped down to a crouch and made soothing sounds, stroked their shoulders, trying to calm them down. Behind me, I heard another bout of shouting and the sound of scuffling feet. Sailor must have broken away from her captors, because she appeared, disheveled, at my side, and lifted the smallest chimp, Bruno, who wrapped his arms around her neck and clung on like a limpet. Sailor shot me a grateful look and hoisted Bruno into a cradled position.

I looked out at a sea of faces scrubbed of kindness. The other keepers began to move toward us, spreading into a loose circle, slowly and with purpose, like hunters. Instinctively trying to surround us. I inched closer to Sailor and the chimps moved closer to the two of us. Their shrieking had subsided, but I could hear their frenzied panting and could smell the distress seeping from them.

"It's okay, it's okay," Sailor and I whispered over and over to them, like a lullaby.

As other keepers joined the scene and demanded to know what was happening, the story began to emerge in breathless pieces. One of the chimps, Stella, had been acting up, being defiant and naughty, as chimps can sometimes be. She had yanked a tool from Brandon's belt and scampered to the top of the jungle gym with it. Instead of distracting her or bargaining with her, as I and any other sane person would have done, he grabbed one of the buzzkills and zapped Stella with it. The tool dropped and she followed, thudding to the floor, where she rolled and shrieked in pain and distress. Sailor, witnessing this, got so incensed she grabbed the prod and zapped Brandon in turn.

As the story was being told and then recounted for each new person, two of the admins arrived, summoning Sailor, Brandon, and me to the admin center. The enclosure went quiet then, and people began to melt away back to their duties. None of us spoke as we followed the admins down the hill. In the office, they said they were giving us a chance to tell our sides of the story. Not that I had one. Brandon went first and angrily denounced Sailor, saying the buzzkills were provided for a reason, he hadn't been doing anything wrong, Sailor had just snapped.

"She's a psycho. Look!" He hoisted his shirt up to reveal a nasty red welt on his torso. But when it was Sailor's turn, she stayed silent. She refused to defend herself, so I tried to speak up, planning to explain how egregious it was to use the prods when there were so many other humane methods. I didn't even get two words out before one of the admins spoke over me, as smoothly as if I didn't even exist.

"You, Anderson," he said, gesturing at Sailor. "No mainland privileges for a month."

Sailor leaned forward, locking eyes with him. "No," she said. "Give me something else, please. I don't care what. But I need to get to the mainland."

"Should have thought of that before you assaulted me," said Brandon.

"And you." The admin turned to Brandon. "Two weeks in Waste."

Brandon's neck veins bulged. Waste was the department that dealt with the small mountains of manure the zoo's residents produced each day; the herbivore manure was bagged up and sold in the gift shop and on the mainland for eye-watering prices, while the carnivore and monkey feces was fed into an anaerobic biodigester machine located on the far end of the island that produced biogas to power the zoo. Of course, Brandon would hate being associated with such a low-status department. I wouldn't have minded, and I don't think Sailor would have either.

"Hey, that's just not—" Brandon began, but the admin held up his palm in warning.

"Causing harm to a resident is a strike."

"But I didn't even touch that crazy bitch," Brandon protested, being someone who didn't know when to shut up. "She harmed *me*!" He lifted the hem of his shirt, preparing to demonstrate the welt again.

The admin looked at him, unblinking and unimpressed. "The chimp."

"Oh. Well, the thing is . . ." Brandon looked down at his knees, his face turning an even more livid shade of pink.

"Second strike is deportation."

That shut him up. That shut us all up.

Outside, after watching Brandon angrily stride off in the direction of the barracks, I offered to go to the mainland for Sailor and get her what she needed. She slung her arm around my shoulder.

"Thanks, Birdy, but I'll work it out."

The adrenaline was ebbing away but I was as angry as ever. "Fuck Brandon," I said. "Fuck ever using the buzzkills. Fuck the admins." I didn't care who heard me.

Sailor laughed. "Indeed, a hearty fuck-you to all of them. We're going to burn every last buzzkill before we leave here. Make a big motherfucking bonfire of them. Mark my words."

This thought seemed to cheer her up, because she was completely relaxed after that. But I couldn't get the looks on our coworkers' faces out of my mind. It had been jungle law inside that cage. Certain members of our pack had identified us as trouble, and they were just waiting for a reason to expel us into the wilderness.

We were deep into a Tuesday morning and no one knew why the guest boat was late. Sometimes there were holdups if the weather wasn't cooperating or a VIP was late to board. But this was *late* late. Sailor and I messaged each other to meet up, and we convened halfway along Broadway, standing there with filthy buckets at our feet and hands pressed into our hips, like housewives gossiping over the fence.

"Something's wrong," Sailor said, rubbing her thumbnail along her front teeth, that nervous tic of hers that had become so endearing to me. "There's fuckery afoot, I can just feel it. Thank god I get my mainland privileges back next week. I'm going to do some sleuthing for us."

A familiar wild light shone in Sailor's eyes. To her, fuckery wasn't always a bad thing.

We didn't have to wait long for the answer. A few minutes later, footsteps pounded down the next avenue, and Sailor and I hurried around the corner to where a tightly huddled group had already formed around someone. Between the shifting bodies I could make out enough details—a puff of pale-pink hair; a humpback whale tattoo—to recognize Louise, a founding member of the popular keeper group.

"What's going on?" Sailor nudged the MC, Kyle, who hovered on the outer edges of the scrum.

He glanced at her, annoyed at being pulled away from the drama. "There was some kind of attack onshore. Guests getting mugged, some gang thing, I don't know."

"Come on," said Sailor quietly to me, and I hurried after her as she strode away from the clamor and toward the exit. "Grab a tool from over there"— she pointed at one of the concealed service closets—"and let's go check things out."

Wordlessly, I opened the door and grabbed a shovel from the rack. Sailor ducked inside and hauled a bulging sack onto her shoulder, then cocked her head toward the exit. Heart clamoring, I walked beside her into the daylight. "Stay off the path," said Sailor. "We'll be less noticeable that way."

No one stopped us as we descended toward the bay. The few people we saw outside were hurrying with panicked expressions to various buildings, as if driven by some air raid siren only they could hear. The glossy black guest boat idled down at the dock, and a huddle of people were standing down there, gesticulating. We veered in the direction of the barracks, flattened ourselves against the corner of the building closest to the entrance, and peeked out at the dock. Closer up, it was clear the guests weren't acting like they normally did. There's a scent you become sensitive to when you spend a lot of time around animals: the sour, sometimes sulfurous miasma of fear. The mammalian stress response is particularly intense—almost feral. A few people were crying, and off to the side one guest was berating one of the admins, who stood with his hands clasped behind his back and his chin bowed.

As we watched, a pair of medics emerged from the boat and onto the gangway. They flanked a young businessman type, and each held one of his elbows carefully, as though he were made of some rare ceramic. The man raised his face. He was in just his shirtsleeves, and I could see a spattering of dark stains tainting the snowy-white collar. His left sleeve was rolled to the elbow and a bandage had been wrapped around his wrist.

Sailor and I both turned at the sound of wheels close on the path behind us. Sailor quickly pulled me back into the shadows, but the medic pushing the empty wheelchair was laser-focused on the injured guest and didn't notice us. As she approached the man, he raised his hand and we could hear him protesting, assuring everyone he could walk on his own and was fine to continue the tour.

The admin gave three sharp claps that echoed across the dock. "The decision has been made to continue today's tour," he called out, his authority reasserting itself. Even the berating guest stepped back, as if recognizing his status as alpha had been revoked. The admin continued, "Please rest assured there will be a full investigation of the heinous incident that occurred at our mainland dock today. The perpetrators will be punished to the full extent of the law, and extra security measures will be put in place to ensure no such incident ever occurs again. Now, please, follow our guides to the funicular and enjoy the wonders of Alcatraz Zoo."

The wattage of the admin's smile could have kept the island powered for the week. The guests conferred for a moment. Shortly after, the whole lot of them gathered their things and obediently followed the guide to the funicular, like baby ducks imprinting on the first person they see. When they were out of sight, I let out the breath I'd been holding. "Well, I'm glad he's all right," I said.

"Hmm, sure," said Sailor, shouldering her decoy sack. "We should get back to work before they notice we're gone."

That evening after dinner, we returned to the rooftop of the Officers' Club. The day had been relatively clear and we risked baring our faces to the air. Without respirators the full aromas of the world came into focus: the sweet reek of decaying jellyfish washed against the rocks; the chemical tang of fresh paint; the ashy smell from distant fires. We took turns picking up tiny pebbles from the sticky tar surface and hurling them into the void of the bay, listening for the soft plink as they struck the surface and sank. Sometimes there was no plink and we told ourselves the pebbles had struck a jellyfish. No traces of their magical luminescence lingered—what we had seen that night may as well have been a dream.

"The gangs are getting bold," said Sailor thoughtfully. "Or desperate. The tourists will be spooked for a while."

I weighed a palmful of pebbles, then let them slide through my fingers. They tinkled at our feet, glinting like jewels when the flashlight caught their edges. The mention of gangs brought the cartels to mind, and I turned eagerly to her. "Hey, have you heard that rumor about the cartels and the private zoos they run out of high-rise buildings?" Sailor blinked heavily a couple of times but didn't answer, so I forged on. "Peacocks in the boardroom, floors full of tigers, a rhino in the penthouse, you hear all kinds of things. Can you even imagine?"

I suppose I had been expecting her to share my commingled disgust and fascination. It was well-known that when the blights got bad and the extinction writing was on the wall, various criminal organizations around the world had mobilized to snatch some of the last animals out of the wild. A thing to make you sick. Those animals could have had a much better home here, at Alcatraz, with the other lasts of their kind.

"Can I imagine, Camille?" I was used to her teasing tone, but there was a new note of coldness in it. "Can I imagine a more vertical version of this prison?"

"Well, it's just a rumor." Her reaction stung, like I was being accused of something. "Probably not even true."

She drew her arm back and threw a stone with particular vehemence across the void. I followed its trajectory and my gaze wandered beyond, between the illuminated towers of the bridge, where the dark humps of freighters and tankers were lined up like a malign pod of whales. "Oh, unfortunately it's true enough. Friends of mine back in Europe have tried to destroy those miserable operations."

I think I might have gasped. "So those places are *real?*"

She laughed at my foolish tone of wonder then grew somber again, rubbing the side of her thumb on her front teeth repeatedly, as if calming herself. Sometimes she reminded me of the animals, with the rituals they invented to keep themselves from going mad.

"Of course they're real. They attract evil morons who bring briefcases full of cash for the chance to pet baby tigers. But I don't want you thinking about those sick places. What if I told you there was another place where the animals roam free, like, completely free and wild?"

"There's no place like that." I crossed my arms like a teenager resisting unwelcome information.

"Oh yeah, Miss Never-Left-the-Island? What would you know about it?"

I ignored her needling. "Like a wildlife reserve or something?"

"Right, a sanctuary. A huge territory far from so-called civilization."

"Where?"

"The location has changed. No one knows exactly where it is unless they get invited there. That's deliberate, to keep the animals safe. There are people hired to spread disinformation."

"So the animals roam completely free? I guess I don't buy it. Where on earth is there enough wilderness left for that to be possible?" I didn't mean to sound skeptical. I wanted it to be true more than just about anyone, but there's a lot of country between what you want to be true and how the world is.

"Well, as I've heard it, a billionaire couple . . . she's Indian I think, and he's from New Zealand? Bought up these huge tracts of wilderness decades ago, when there was still enough undeveloped land left. Over the years they accumulated all these rare plants and created these specific habitats, with the plan to bring endangered animals there and give them freedom. The air is clean, there's plenty of unpolluted water. They protect it all with a private army." Her voice was dreamy and it seemed to come from far away, as if disconnected from her body.

"Where do *you* think it is?"

"The most credible rumor I've heard, it's located in China's Hunan province, maybe near Zhangjiajie National Park. Or even inside it. You've seen the photos . . . those wild sandstone pillars rising out of the jungle like natural skyscrapers?"

"Of course. Holy shit. Really?"

"Yep. Apparently the owners did a secret deal with the Chinese government, set up the sanctuary deep in the heart of the park. It has cliffs so steep-sided the bulldozers won't ever get in. The animals just live there, without anyone bothering them."

"Wow. Imagine if that were real."

She turned to me again, her eyes hooded in shadow, her mouth set in a serious line. She placed her thumb under my chin and gently tilted it upward. "Do me a favor, huh, Birdy?" I nodded, ready to agree to anything. "Promise me you'll start imagining a better world than this one."

San Francisco Bay

Sailor carried all her possessions in the battered but sturdy black duffel bag that had traveled with her across several oceans and time zones. It was a beautiful morning. The smog had burned off early and the bay was smooth as glass during the crossing. She sat up on the bow deck so she could get a good view of the island as they approached. The ferry went at a decent clip and the breeze gusted her hair around her face, so she had to keep pushing it back behind her ears. No one took photos or pointed out landmarks or acted like tourists at all, as they would have in the old days. Everyone on the boat either worked at Alcatraz or for the ferry company, or had some business with the island, making repairs or unloading deliveries. Sailor was the only person on that ferry with excitement in her heart.

She stood up as the boat drew closer to the island. From the shore it had looked small, a bit disappointing even. An inconsequential hump of land rising out of the vast bay. But now that they were closer, she understood how immense and imposing and permanent it was. How, in approaching it, one might feel a terror that was lodged in its very stones—the terror of men knowing they would never again leave.

She put one hand on the rail and used the other to shade her face. She could have taken a photo, but she decided not to. It wasn't the sight of the island that thrilled her anyway, stirring as the first impression was. It was the smell of it. Lifting her chin, she closed her eyes and inhaled deeply through her nose. And there, beneath the other scents on the breeze—the vegetal funk of biofuel, the stomach-churning rot of dead jellyfish, the deep briny cleanness of the sea—she found what she was searching for. This far away, she couldn't identify the species exactly. A mammal, almost certainly. Perhaps it was an elephant, or a monkey, or a deer. Perhaps just a rat scurrying through the undergrowth. It was possible, wasn't it, that life still teemed both inside and outside the enclosures? That this cursed place might offer a tiny fragment of what the world used to be? Another chance.

It didn't really matter what creature she could smell. All that mattered was that she was about to be among animals again. She thought about what Anouk had said, the rumor that there were no bars on the cages in this place. It intrigued her, the rapturous way people spoke about this last great experiment; the mystery of what happened on the tours; the impressively leak-proof culture surrounding the island's business. Was it possible the Pinkton family had, against all odds, pioneered a new model for what a zoo could be?

Leaving Paris, she had been racked with doubt, but now she clearly saw the path she would take. She would work hard while she waited to hear from Anouk. She would lie low, if she could manage that, but all the while she would keep her eyes open. She would fill herself up with learning so she would be the best asset possible when she finally made it to the sanctuary.

For the first time in months, she opened up a tiny chink in the armor painstakingly built around her wounded self and allowed happiness to slip inside.

Alcatraz

Sailor loved the Arboretum at first sight, just as I had. Because it wasn't a section keepers would ever be assigned, she had no legitimate reason to visit, which naturally made her itch even more to get inside. After the raid on the guest boat, Sailor set her sights on growing a tomato there. Why, I'll never know. Maybe it was her novel way of convincing me a place like the sanctuary could exist. If she could prove that one tiny, beautiful thing from the old world persisted, wouldn't that prove an entire other world was possible as well? Maybe I'm overthinking it and she was just hungry for something that wasn't Fake Steak. Anyway, I had to break the news it wasn't going to be possible.

"There's no rule against planting a tomato there," Sailor countered. I tried to explain the reason there was no rule was that it had never occurred to the authorities that anyone would attempt to plant something not already sanctioned as belonging there.

"Well, that's their problem, isn't it?" she said with a wicked smile. "They need to have better imaginations."

What she craved, she told me, was a real tomato. Not one of those tasteless pale imitators that passed for tomatoes, but a real, honest-to-god ripe red tomato nodding heavy on the stem: bursting with juice, fragrant as summer. She'd carried a tiny packet of modified heirloom seeds with her all the way from Paris, she told me, somehow evading the sensors and the quarantine scans, and had been looking for the right place to plant them. They were the super-fast-growing GM variety France developed after the famine in the south.

Her descriptions of this magical hypothetical tomato were irresistible enough that I agreed to help her get access. Gill had a soft spot for me, and Sailor knew it. A while ago, he and I had convinced the admins to let us use some of the nutrient-rich herbivore manure as fertilizer for the garden. After it was approved, I was given the task of transporting the shit from the enclosures to the Arboretum, which added to my daily workload, but it had cemented an alliance with Gill. Once the demand for manure spiked—for fueling the power plant that ran the island and selling to the elites—the admins frowned on using it for such frivolities, but Gill must have convinced them somehow to let him keep a tiny allotment.

Unable to come up with any other reasons why we shouldn't try, I arranged for Sailor and me to drop by one evening after our duties were completed. As an offering, we brought a small cartload of manure. Gill greeted us at the entrance.

"Ah, a hostess gift!" he said, steepling his hands at his heart. I could tell he was pleased at the prospect of showing us around his leafy kingdom. He loves talking to anyone who'll listen about his pet subject, biophilic design, the idea that architecture and design can reconnect people with nature. He dreams of repopulating Earth with trees and flowers and animals, his vision a world where humans exist in service to nature instead of the other way around, but I've observed him cut himself off when he gets too enthused talking about it because, like me, he knows it's dangerous to dream. He's an evangelist without a church. No wonder he and Sailor got along right away.

We walked single file as Gill pointed out various plants, providing both their scientific and colloquial names. He talked about the plants like he was introducing dear friends. *This is the spider orchid*, he would say, inviting us to admire a delicate starfish-splayed bloom. *And this is the desert rose*, as he gazed lovingly at a sturdy little tree sprouting flamboyant pink flowers. He would stop every few seconds to caress a leaf or press his nose gently to a flower, and Sailor and I would mirror his actions, as if under a spell.

It was humid in there, like a sauna. Like a rainforest, I guess. I inhaled as deeply as I could, savoring the good, wholesome smells of earth and leaf and flower. My nostrils prickled. After the barren soil of the island, where even the hardiest of plants struggled against the elements, visiting the Arboretum could overwhelm your senses.

At one point, Gill excused himself to answer a call, and Sailor whispered in my ear: "Quick, let's do it now." She glanced around, homed in on a section just ahead of us where a strip of bare soil ran behind a row of nodding palms, and made a series of frantic gestures in my direction. We moved stealthily toward the area, Sailor keeping up an inane stream of prattle in case anyone was listening. We were parallel to the palms when we heard Gill's voice growing nearer again. We exchanged a harried glance, then, staying as close to the path as we could, pulled from our pockets the seeds we'd emptied out of the packet and sort of flung them in the direction of the soil. We careened back to the center of the path, me quickly crossing my arms and Sailor plunging her hands into her pockets.

Gill approached with an apologetic smile. "Sorry about that. Where were we? Oh yes, the rhododendrons. Follow me!"

I made a point of not looking at Sailor as we continued the tour. As always when she convinced me to aid her in some quasicriminal enterprise, I worried the thundering of my heart would give the game away.

I had largely forgotten about the tomato seeds when Sailor came to me a few weeks later and announced we needed to go see whether it was time to harvest. She'd been counting the days and had decided the plants would have had time to fruit. Having gotten away with planting them in the first place, it seemed reckless to me to invite new scrutiny by revisiting the scene, but Sailor insisted and, as per usual, after a weak attempt at resistance, I relented. I secured a visit with Gill the following week, and we appeared at the appointed time.

"Can't get enough of my tours, huh, ladies?"

We smiled with what I hoped looked like sincerity. Gill contemplated us for a moment before waving us inside. He held a pair of pruning shears, and the sight of them for some reason sent a flutter of fear up my spine. I considered making some excuse for needing to leave, but Sailor placed her hands on my shoulder blades and gently propelled me along in Gill's wake. We got to the palm section and Gill turned around slowly. He raised his eyebrows ever so slightly as he looked into our faces—both of us with innocent expressions frozen in place—then he stepped neatly off the path and bent down behind the palm trees. The soft click of the pruning shears, then he reemerged holding a perfect tomato on a fuzzy green stem. He dangled it in front of our contrite noses. It smelled, as Sailor had promised, like sunshine, but that didn't mean I wanted it to be the last thing we ever smelled. I had a vision of Gill lifting his radio to call the guards, of Sailor and I being unceremoniously hauled out of the garden and dragged through the avenues, then bundled onto a ferry and deported. All over a tomato.

There was a heavy silence as we three stood and contemplated that blameless fruit. Gill spun the stem between his thumb and forefinger. The glossy red globe rotated. Sailor and I stared, hypnotized. He abruptly pinched the stem and the globe came to a stop, then he reached out, took my right hand, gently prized it open and placed the tomato in my palm, covering my life line. He folded my fingers over.

"You could have just asked me," he said. His tone was mild, containing only the tiniest hint of scolding, and when I looked at his face I saw the beginnings of a smile there, an acknowledgment that we three shared something that perhaps not all the residents of this rock could fully appreciate. "Now get the hell out of my Arboretum."

That night, we broke into a disused storeroom on the top floor of the barracks, wrenched the filthy, complaining window open a few inches, and wedged a shoe under the sash. We performed a solemn ceremony with the tomato, sprinkling it with salt and pepper and passing it back and forth, puncturing it gently with our teeth and taking tiny nibbles, chewing with our eyes closed as the waves boomed against the rocks below.

"To forbidden fruit," Sailor announced, holding a shred of tomato up to the window, a red crescent moon floating against the smeared sky. We both let out the hoots of laughter we'd been holding in since we left Gill. I don't think it's hyperbole to say it was the most memorable meal of my life.

The closer Sailor and I became, the more distant everyone else seemed to get. After the episode with Brandon and the chimps, tribal lines were drawn. People would stop talking when Sailor and I walked by, and we no longer got invited to any extracurricular activities. Schoolyard stuff, but still. Hostility from Brandon and his pack was to be expected, I suppose (he still bore the scar from Sailor's attack), but I was quietly wounded when Joseph too started aiming unfriendly looks our way. The admins had put an end to our Bleat-and-Greets, and I wondered aloud if one of the other keepers had complained.

Sailor shook it all off, but it clung to me. I would lapse into long silences during our night strolls, unable to focus on fairy tales like the sanctuary when the ground beneath our own feet felt so unstable.

"Look, we need to distract you, and everyone else, from all the depressing shit," Sailor declared one evening, as her first Christmas on the island approached. I had been especially morose on this occasion, and I could tell she was itching to turn my mood around. "And I have an idea."

Her idea wasn't to do with enrichment for the animals this time, or sowing secret seeds. She wanted to throw a party. As far as I knew, there had never been a party on Alcatraz, at least not one to which the workers had been invited. I objected at first, worried that word of an unsanctioned party reaching the admins would be another mark against Sailor, and maybe me, should I be implicated as her accomplice. But she just waved me off.

"A party will be good for morale," she said, as if it were all decided. "Everyone will pretend to hate it, but they'll love it, trust me."

We abandoned our evening walks for a while in favor of meeting in a large barracks storage closet we'd commandeered. Inside this war room we drew up lists and discussed tactics. "Hors d'oeuvres, definitely," Sailor said during the first of these meetings. "Trays of hors d'oeuvres." I looked skeptical, but she plowed on. "Some of the cooks will help us if we make it worth their while."

I shrugged. "If you trust them. I mean, you've tried their food."

"Aha, but party food doesn't have to be good, Birdy, it just has to be small. The regular shit they serve, just cut into bite-size pieces. What about music? We could make a playlist, project videos on the white walls. Oh, and we need to order some of those sky lanterns, the ones you put candles in and release. They sell them in Chinatown."

I laughed. "Why don't we just have a champagne fountain as well?"

Sailor clicked her fingers. "Yes, brilliant idea! You can't have a party without champagne."

I'd thought I had laced the words with enough sarcasm that even she couldn't miss it, but apparently not. Still, it didn't take me long to get caught up in the fever of planning. Only occasionally did I have to step in and quash Sailor's ambitions.

"Costumes!" she declared at one point. "I know a place on the mainland that could bring them over, they used to supply the San Francisco Opera. Incredible stuff. Like a dream." I didn't have to say anything, just lowered my chin and gave her a stern look. Even trying to imagine some of the keepers in elaborate opera costumes made my mouth twitch.

"No? Too much? Okay, strike that. Back to the music. I've decided we need a live musician, just to open the event, and then we'll switch to dance music. And I know just the person. She's a cellist, a knockout."

"Sneaking an unauthorized person onto the island? That's crazy. You know the admins are cracking down on that kind of thing. Why don't you just ask permission? I think there are forms."

Sailor laughed. "Come on. You know what they'd say. Fuck their forms. It's easier this way."

"What about the guards?"

"The party will be inside, so it's outside their jurisdiction. Besides, I'll pay 'em off if I have to. Any more objections?"

"I'll let you know," I said, but we both knew I didn't need any further convincing. The idea of the party surged through my blood like an intoxicant.

The night arrived too quickly and not quickly enough. We'd invited every keeper and gardener and some of the vets as well, and though I saw these people every day, I was beset by nerves. Sailor had managed to bring previously unheard-of luxuries from the mainland: string lights; *papel picado*, the cutout tissue paper decorations they used for fiestas in Mexico; and flowers, impossible fat bunches of them, white and purple and nodding on long delicate stems, that arrived in a big insulated box on the morning boat. Somehow the flowers are what stand out the most when I think back. We piled the blooms into whatever we could find—buckets, jars, coffee cups. We strung the lights up along the corridors and wound them around the tables in the common rooms. We draped Mexican *papel picado* from hooks close to the ceiling, and they fluttered gently in the breath from the forced-air vents.

One of my tasks was to prepare the rec room for the concert. Sailor left me to get it ready, claiming she had other work to do. With fumbling hands,

I arranged the seating in concentric circles around a stagelike area containing one lonely chair. Sailor still hadn't returned by the time the party was due to start. I tried not to feel deserted: I had my instructions, after all, and fulfilling instructions had always had a calming influence on my nerves. I stood sentry outside the rec room door, wearing a slinky black dress Sailor had lent me, makeup on and hair loose and brushed to a shine. I held a sheaf of papers in my clammy right hand, and as the people began to arrive I handed them out. Sailor had designed them using heavy paper she'd found somewhere. Programs, she called them, as if the word might transform our dingy rec room into a Beaux Arts opera house. The font was curly and old-fashioned, elegant spider's legs trailing across the creamy pages.

"A concert, huh?" said Louise, taking a program and scrutinizing it, then rolling it into a funnel and staring through it at me. "Is Sailor going to sing for us?"

"You'll see," I said in my best mysterious hostess voice.

"Whatever," she said as she wandered off, opening her hand to let the crumpled program flutter to the floor. I didn't let her disdain bother me—at least she'd come along. She wasn't the only one, either.

"Hey, nice dress," said Joseph, sidling up to me. He had his arm flung around Ali, and she clasped his waist, her hand wedged into his front jeans pocket. She served me a brazen look she'd probably rehearsed in the mirror. I understood what was happening. It was important for alphas not to break eye contact. I didn't know her very well—she was lucky enough to work with the elephants, so our paths didn't cross all that often—but she was a member of Brandon and Louise's pack and had presumably hooked up with Joseph too. I gave her a weak smile. No doubt I was supposed to feel jealousy at this display of intimacy between them, but I had no room tonight for extra feeling, and I wordlessly ushered them into the rapidly filling room. Sailor had suggested people dress up for the occasion, but no one had, besides me. They wore their leisure suits or sweatshirts and jeans, but all of them had turned up and they seemed curious in their carefully detached way, so I knew that would be enough for her.

Where was Sailor, anyway? I kept glancing over my shoulder into the corridor, a sick feeling rising. Hovering near the doorway, I swiveled back and forth, like a broody bird on a nest, between the buzz and rustle of the room and the silent gloom of the corridor. I checked the nearest screen and saw that it was already ten minutes past the official starting time of the event.

But right at that moment Sailor appeared like a vision. She wore billowing white trousers and a plunging black silk blouse split almost to her navel. Her skin was luminous, her lips glossed to a high shine. She looked like a movie star. Beside her was an equally tall, beautiful woman wearing a flowing white Grecian-style dress. It had a braided ribbon edge that ran along the neckline, swooped under her rib cage, and passed around her waist several times. The hem swirled around her ankles like smoke. She carried a curvy black case that came up to her chest.

Sailor flashed me a conspiratorial wink before guiding the woman and her instrument through the doorway. My view was blocked, but I felt the tenor of the room change. The clamor of casual conversation shifted abruptly into a higher register before subsiding into a low hum. Two latecomers elbowed their way past me, and my heart caught for a moment at the sight of the familiar guard uniforms. But when I saw their faces I recognized them as friendlies—guys who were cordial when Sailor and I took our night walks—and they soon found seats toward the back and settled in, their faces impassive.

The cellist took some time, affectionately liberating her instrument from its carapace and arranging herself on the chair, the cello cradled against her wide-open thighs like a lover. The room was silent, eyes following her every movement, enthralled. I'd bet none of the people in that room except maybe Sailor had ever seen a musical instrument besides a guitar or a set of drums in their lives. Certainly not one like this. Its burnished red-gold wood gleamed in the dull, harshly lit room with an almost supernatural luster. That long-dead tree must have been honored to sacrifice itself for such an object.

She lifted her bow and began to play. I find it hard even now to describe the music itself. It amazed me that so many sounds could come from the one instrument, like she was coaxing a whole choir's worth of voices out of those strings. She played for an hour without stopping, her face moving through an elastic series of moods: at one moment her features would bunch up as though in pain; at the next they would be lit with a kind of religious ecstasy like those marble saints you see in churches. The room was emptied of everything but the music.

When she finally finished—completely spent, her body flopping over the cello, hair damp with exertion—there was a long moment of silence before the room erupted in thunderous applause, whistling and stamping of feet and whooping. I thought the windows might shatter. The cellist lifted her weary neck, pushed the hair off her face, and smiled, dipping her chin in appreciation.

I hoped she might mingle after the performance, but Sailor swooped in to rescue her as the crowd pressed around, bustled her and the cello out the door, down the corridor, onto the dark shore, and off the island. There was the newest of new moons that night, so she would have been delivered from the brightness of the barracks into darkness. There was a boat waiting to whisk her back to her life, whatever that consisted of. No guards intervened. Her exit from Alcatraz was quiet, efficient, unremarkable. As though she had never been here.

Back in the barracks, the party changed tempo. The music was turned up so loud you could feel it reverberating in your molars. Someone sloshed a drink in my cup. I had never tasted champagne before. (Of course, we couldn't get champagne in the end, it was actually sparkling wine from Taiwan, and we could only get hold of a dozen bottles, but it still felt impossibly decadent.) After a while the room began to move in a different way. It began like a rumor, a small thing that grew in intensity as it passed from person to person. Shoulders began to sway and waists began to swivel. Arms rose above heads, elbows bent, and faces blurred with a kind of hypnotic pleasure. If it seems ridiculous to describe the basic act of dancing, well, that's only because it all felt novel to me. I had never been to a club before, never lived in a place where moving one's body to music was considered a worthwhile pastime. Of course I had seen people do it before, in movies and shows and occasionally on the streets of certain neighborhoods, small spontaneous outbursts of joy, but never up close, in bodies with which I was familiar. The transformation was captivating. There was a wildness to the dancing, a loosening of the collective consciousness of one's own body in relation to the world. These were people who in normal life disdained demonstrations of physicality beyond the purely functional. We were servants to our jobs, and those jobs required every ounce of our physical energy along with a sort of psychological hygiene that ensured we never let ourselves get carried away. We weren't huggers. We didn't give each other massages or back rubs. And we certainly didn't dance.

I looked around for Sailor. Eventually I found her, talking animatedly with Prentiss at the far end of the room. Even he seemed loosened from his usual seriousness, his eyes crinkling with laughter as he leaned in to listen to her. Sailor caught my eye at that exact moment, said something to Prentiss, and barreled toward me, enfolding me in a sweaty embrace. For such a slender person she carried a lot of strength in her upper body, and I felt my ribs creaking. I wrapped my arms around her back and sort of patted at her damp silk shirt. She flung her head back. Strands of hair caught in her lipstick.

"Isn't this great?"

I nodded vigorously. Before I could object, she grabbed both my wrists and began to jig backward, pulling us toward the dancing. Torn pieces of *papel picado* floated from the ceiling like confetti.

After a while, with trembling legs and hair plastered to our necks and much inebriated laughter, the entire creature of us gravitated to the exit of the barracks and out into the night. I was surprised to find it had been raining. The downpour had rinsed the island clean. The whole dock area was a mirror, slick and beautifully treacherous. The guard tower sparkled as though studded with diamonds. There was a faint pinkish glow out in the bay, like a memory of bioluminescence. Or maybe the wine was making me see things that weren't there.

Everyone spread out around the dock, drinking and smoking and talking with the meaningless intensity that accompanies the waning hours of a bender. A few of the guards wandered over, accepted gifts of wine and pills and whatever else was being passed around, resting the butts of their weapons on the ground in a break from the seriousness of their jobs.

I can't remember who I talked to or what we talked about. The whole scene has the tint of unreality about it, up to and including the part when Sailor—who had been goofing around with a clutch of people out on the dock—pitched butt-first into the bay. I had coincidentally been gazing in an unfocused way at the dock at the exact moment it happened, and under the flooding illumination of the dock lights, I witnessed in perfect detail the almost comical moment her foot caught the edge of the dock, her body folded in an elongated V, and she tumbled backward into the jellyfish-infested water. A sharp animal sound of distress flew from me and I leaped to my feet.

The splash elicited shouts and yelps and screams, and one hoot of laughter that was immediately cut off. People went running from everywhere toward the dock, a stampede of people slipping and cursing, clutching each other for support. By the time I arrived under the floodlights, Sailor had already been dragged back onto dry land and was lying flat on her back, water streaming from her hair and clothes, tendrils of seaweed tangled around her feet. She had lost a shoe. She sat up and several people clapped her drunkenly on the back, either in congratulations for being alive or in an attempt to clear her lungs of contaminated water, and she began laughing in a slightly unhinged way. "I kept my mouth shut!" she yelled. Someone helped her get to her feet, and she leaned down and slowly hitched up her pants. Her calves were striped with jellyfish welts. She must have been very drunk or high, because instead of seeming alarmed, she raised her right fist into the air and whooped. The people around her cheered.

Once it had been confirmed that Sailor was going to be fine—she adamantly refused to return to the barracks, so someone fetched some antihistamine lotion and painkillers and we patched her up under the stars—it was decided we could still, in all conscience, set the lanterns loose, given we had gone to the trouble of getting them and everyone had so far survived the night. I was sitting next to her, applying the last of the lotion to her stings, when someone yelled out: "Hey, Sailor, is it your birthday or what?"

She peered out into the night, thrust her silver flask into the air. "It's all our birthdays!"

There was more cheering. "Here's to Sailor," another person called out, and everyone raised whatever they were drinking.

"Thanks for paying for all this shit!" someone else yelled, to ripples of laughter.

"Well, you can't take it with you!" Sailor shouted, her neck bent back to look up at the stars. Then she took a deep drink from her flask. I nudged her, holding out my empty cup. Sailor snatched her flask to her chest and wagged a finger in front of my nose. "None of the hard stuff for you, Birdy. You couldn't handle it."

I pouted but I didn't really mind, because I already felt woozy enough. I had just wanted to draw out the night.

A solemnity fell over the group as, with blankets draped around our shoulders, we lit the candles and placed them inside the delicate rice-paper sky lanterns. Someone counted down from three and we all released the lanterns at about the same time, a flotilla of hot-air balloons lifting into the sky.

Some were picked up on a breeze right away and pulled out to sea, growing smaller and smaller until their points of light became indistinguishable from stars. Some lingered, as if reluctant to leave the party so soon. One dropped in the water, fizzled out, and sank. The breeze off the water was bone-chilling that night, and people began to drift back inside once it was clear the ceremony was over. But I stayed out on the dock, hugging my knees and watching until the very last lantern blinked out of sight. It was so beautiful.

What can I tell you?

It was so beautiful.

For a whole precious hour the next morning Sailor and I were the toasts of the town, the belles of the ball. Instead of avoiding our table as they usually did, the other keepers crowded around, eager to recap the night in the presence of the sorceress who had made it possible. Louise even insisted on getting coffee for us, and Sailor pinched my leg under the table as our formerly disdainful colleague carefully carried the brimming cups over. I won't pretend it wasn't all gratifying, seeing Sailor surrounded by so much admiration.

Then the admins arrived. Three of them, casting a shadow over the sunny scene with their black suits and their hard expressions and their synchronized strides. The noise in the hall dimmed and sputtered to silence. It was unusual for the admins to enter the mess hall, so much so I hadn't ever noticed the dusty lectern and microphone set against one wall for the purpose of addressing us. Which one of the admins proceeded to do.

"It has come to our attention that an unauthorized event took place last night." A wincing screech of feedback from the mic. "A member of the public was brought onto the island without clearance. The island's security was compromised, with guards failing in their patrolling duties while the event took place. Every employee who attended this event will forfeit their next month's salary."

A tidal wave of protesting voices flooded the hall, but one crested to the top.

"Come on now," called out Sailor, getting to her feet. "That's not fair. I was the one who organized it. There's no need to punish everyone."

The admins studied her with cold indifference, then looked away, as if satisfied there was nothing to be gained from paying her any further attention. A different admin addressed the hall this time. "Every employee. A month's salary. No exceptions."

Sailor's cheeks blanched. She opened her mouth to protest further, but the admin who'd just spoken shook their head in warning, then the three of them turned heel and strode out of the hall. There was a moment of silence as everyone stared daggers at the departing admins, but then people began to redirect their ire at Sailor and me, and we sat there, cowed, as the pendulum swung back against us.

That night, after Sailor and I exited the barracks, intending to discuss the situation outdoors as usual, a guard stepped onto the path in front of us. He had a balaclava pulled down over his face, exposing just his eyes.

"You need to get back to the barracks," came his muffled voice. "A curfew is now in place."

My mind froze. "A curfew?"

He didn't answer, just minutely adjusted his hold on his assault rifle. That tiny gesture was enough to make my scalp tingle. I glanced at Sailor. She had her hands on her hips; she practically bristled with indignation. "Oh yeah? On whose authorit—"

The last syllable choked off as the guard—it was Carlos, I realized with a shock like being drenched with cold water, the same guard who had let us continue on that long-ago first night walk—lifted his gun and used the muzzle to gently push down the zipper of Sailor's hoodie, then let the muzzle rest there in the channel of her cleavage. She opened her mouth to say something, then snapped it shut. Carlos slowly lifted the rifle again. Sailor shot him a tight smile and steered me by the elbow back in the direction of the barracks.

San Francisco

The whole way on the ferry she thought with growing hunger of the meal she was going to buy from one of the city's hawker stalls. Several months had passed since she had arrived on Alcatraz, and she was finally returning to the mainland. She felt a changed person from the one who had first sailed there on a tide of cautious optimism. Some of the hopeful edges had been sanded off, but there were compensations. She had found allies. One, for sure. Her mind was already ticking over with possibilities.

But for the moment all that mattered was food that didn't look and taste institutional. She couldn't wait to savor the specific gritty pleasure of balancing a fragrant bowl of spicy food on her knees while inhaling vehicle fumes. When she disembarked, though, and began walking the streets around the Embarcadero, she couldn't find so much as one. She almost wept with disappointment. Eventually she spotted one of the vendors she recognized from last time, when she had been waiting for her passage to Alcatraz. He was sitting on the same corner, on a plastic crate, rubbing his forehead, a cigarette smoldering between his fingers, his portable stove cold.

She approached him with the controlled wariness she used to approach animals. "Hi. Not selling today?"

He looked in her direction but as if he couldn't quite focus. There were reddened patches around his eyes. "Not today. Not tomorrow."

"Why?"

Then he looked at her again, actually got a bead on her face this time. His voice was incredulous. "*Why?* There's nothing to sell. Lady, where are you from?"

Sailor, embarrassed now, waved in the vague direction of Alcatraz. This didn't seem to mean anything to him, and she was glad. It suddenly felt like a bad idea to be admitting she lived on an island of relative plenty. She pushed some money into the vendor's hand and walked quickly away before he could refuse it. The gesture felt wholly inadequate but she didn't know what else to do.

She wandered in the direction of the tourist wharf until she reached a long line of mostly men waiting to reach a small booth shielded with metal bars. The booth was so far away she couldn't quite read what was written on the sign above it, so she approached one of the more benign-looking men, a grizzled fisherman who reminded her of an uncle she had liked. "Hey, what's going on here?"

The man looked at her with tepid interest. "Waiting for a license."

"A license to do what?"

He laughed darkly, like he'd been waiting for this question. "To fish, kiddo. They just brought in quotas."

"For the jellyfish?" The man shrugged: What else? As she turned away, she heard shouting and some kind of scuffle underway in the line. The sickening sound of flesh and bone hitting flesh and bone. She deliberately didn't look back, didn't want to know any more about what was going on. Her plan had been to find somewhere else to eat, but as she plonked down in the dirt of a nearby park she found she'd lost her appetite.

First she tried Mr. Li, with little hope of an answer. Then she called Anouk and left a message. "Hey it's me, Sailor. I would love to know what's happening." She tried to keep it light, shave the frantic edge from her voice. "It seems like, I don't know, everything's gone dark. The sanctuary, Mr. Li, you, everyone. Look, I'm at Alcatraz now and I'm willing to help in any way I can, but I need to hear from you. It's too risky to try anything if I don't have someone I trust taking possession on the other side. Anyway, call me. Let me know you're okay."

As she was burying the phone back in her bag, a voice sounded close behind her.

"Hey, sorry to bother you."

She turned, hackles up. The man was youngish, maybe thirty, with a striking face and straw-colored hair pulled back into a neat bun. Around his neck was a tiny cowrie shell strung on a leather cord, and the fleshy part of his earlobes were stretched around two black gauges that you could have shot a bullet through if you were an exceptionally good shot. He raised his palms to her. "I didn't mean to scare you. It's just, I think you might be Sailor? I'm from the sanctuary."

The relief at hearing those words was so sudden and unexpected she almost lost her balance. She took a few stabilizing deep breaths, buying time to retrieve her native suspiciousness. In a friendly but wary tone, she said: "How do I know you're for real?"

He displayed a set of tidy white teeth. "Like, a code word or something?"

"I mean, no . . ." She bristled at this gentle attempt to ridicule her. "But, you know what? Sure."

He made a placating gesture. "Of course, of course, I'd do the same, man. Can't trust anyone these days. Anouk and Emanuel said you'd ask something like that."

"You know Anouk?"

"Sure. Paris Zoo. She's a legend, man."

"Where is she?"

He shot her a quizzical look. "I thought you'd know that."

"And you know Mr. Li as well?"

"Of course." He had a serene face, almost childlike. "Anyway, I'm Johannes. Can we go somewhere and talk?"

"Ugh, I'm sorry, I can't. I have an appointment. I'm already late, actually." It was true, and she found herself regretting it. He looked disappointed too, and she tried not to feel gratified by it. "But, I mean, I can come back next Sunday? That's the day the staff ferry goes."

"The staff ferry," he repeated. "From Alcatraz."

She felt a new surge of pride in her role, with its proximity to the animals. The thing someone like him must surely crave above all else. Even if the promise of the zoo had proven illusory.

"That's the one," she said. "So what's your role at the sanctuary?" She said the word in the way he had said Alcatraz. Tinged with awe.

He blinked slowly. Impossible to ignore the fact of his eyelashes, which were long and dark and lush, like the fawn at the Paris Zoo they'd all joked looked like a fashion model. "I'm in charge of recruitment." He stumbled over the word, as if it were new to him. "But I'm going to be working with the animals soon."

"Oh, cool."

They smiled goofily at each other, communicating across some silent plane of understanding. Don't fall for it, she warned herself. You know what happens. Just because he might be the kind of person who'd ruin his life to protect one tiny rodent, that doesn't mean he's a person worth ruining *your* life for.

"I've really got to go," she said, salvaging some dignity. "Same time next week?"

"Yes. Give me your number."

She gave him her number, and they went their separate ways. She was surprised—maybe a touch flattered—when a message arrived from Johannes not ten minutes later, fixing a time and place to meet, as if he hadn't been able to wait to contact her again. A flicker of warmth flared in her belly. It had been a long time since she had been pursued.

Alcatraz

Most people would have kept a low profile after the fallout from the party, but it wasn't long before Sailor was floating another scheme. Winter had dug in its heels, and although fires still smoldered in the distant hills, the cold cut deep on our small nation out in the bay. This was the season too, when dangerous storms gathered without warning and lashed the island, shutting down all the boats and ferries and sending the animals spiraling into states of panic.

One of these storms racked the island for three days without letting up. There was no time to seek Sailor out for our usual debriefings: I was constantly required at the zoo to placate and calm the residents as gale-force winds made the windows shudder in their casings and the sea surged through the Golden Gate, spraying bitter-cold spindrift across the island.

On the fourth day the wind eased, and the chaos inside the zoo faded as the cortisol and adrenaline emitting from the scared animals finally began to ebb away. Excused from my duties for the afternoon, I sleepwalked my exhausted body to the laundry room to wash my reeking clothes. Sailor found me there, robotically pulling clothes out of a machine, and engulfed me in a bear hug as if she hadn't seen me for months. The laundry room was quiet that day, only two other keepers in there. They glanced at Sailor and me, then slid their gaze away, leaving before the drying cycles were complete, clutching their warm, clammy clothes to their chests and hurrying out as if we might be contagious.

I leaned into her embrace gratefully, resting my forehead on her shoulder and closing my eyes.

"So, Birdy, do you think everyone enjoyed the party?"

I disentangled myself with a laugh. "Apart from the fact they all blame us for the punishment? Yes, definitely."

"Yeah, I thought so too. It was pretty great, huh?"

"It was the greatest," I said, and we beamed at each other in the shared knowledge that it had all been worth it.

"Rough few days up there," Sailor said, tilting her nose in the general direction of the zoo. "I heard you were amazing."

I shook my head. "I don't know. I feel so helpless when it's like that, running from enclosure to enclosure, trying to work out who needs you most."

"Yeah, me too." Sailor helped me feed clothes into the dryer. We sat on adjoining fiberglass chairs, their brittle surfaces webbed with cracks, arms folded over our chests and staring with a kind of hypnotized boredom at the overalls and underwear spinning around.

"Listen, speaking of animals in cages," said Sailor after a while, "I've been thinking. How about we go see the famous Achilles one of these days?"

I dragged my eyes away from the whirling laundry, trying to process what she was saying. "Wait, you haven't seen Achilles yet?"

"No, not properly! Just glimpses. He wasn't out the first day we did the tour because he'd eaten something that disagreed with him, remember? Ever since then I've been trying to get that fucker Joseph to let me inside, like he promised. Now he's saying it's against protocol or some bullshit. But I bet he'd let you in." She shot me a coy glance.

I wasn't in love with this proposal, especially given Joseph appeared to have turned on me as well, but I wanted to be useful to her, and I felt bad about everyone shunning her after the party. "Sure, I could try," I said tentatively. "He's done it before, snuck me in to watch a feeding. If you stand quietly in the tunnel and then get straight back to work it's usually okay. I can ask him about it if you want."

I prayed she'd say not to worry about it, but I knew the futility of such a prayer. This was her dream, and I knew why now. Crocodiles were a link to her past, they were family to her, and this might be her last chance to ever meet one. All of our last chance.

She grabbed my hand and squeezed it. "Birdy, you are my absolute favorite person in all the world."

"Stop," I said, even though I loved to hear her say it.

Despite his turning up to the party with Ali, I chose to believe Joseph still felt something for me. I knew too, he could be easily lured into bed if the conditions were right. I could feel my currency depreciating with alarming speed, though, and I knew I didn't have much time to deliver on the promise I'd made Sailor.

There was one narrow conduit to his attention: Blind Tiger. I hadn't been to a game in so long, my appearance at the table a few nights after Sailor and my talk in the laundry room garnered some raised eyebrows and smirks, but otherwise people ignored me. Joseph didn't react when I took a seat near him, apart from glancing briefly my way. He happened to be having a good night, hand after hand going his way, and by the end of the card game a pile of matches teetered in front of him. A pragmatist in every other way, Joseph's only deviation from strict rationality was his superstitions about Blind Tiger. If an evening's session went particularly well or particularly catastrophically, he would attribute the wins or losses to a specific thing—it could be a lucky item of clothing, or a weather condition, or the fact that someone had sighed during an especially tense play. All the players harbored these little superstitions, but Joseph was particularly susceptible. I knew when he triumphantly swept up his haul that night and looked over my way, he'd decided which lucky object had tipped the game his way. His gaze flew right past Ali, who had been at his shoulder all night, and fixed on me, his returned angel. It made sense in a ridiculous sort of way, I suppose. I was the unusual factor in the evening's entertainment, therefore my presence must have ushered in his good fortune. I knew we'd end up sleeping together that night—it felt preordained. But did Joseph trust me? I wouldn't have bet even a handful of matches on it.

I waited until a postcoital moment to broach my agenda: the possibility of sneaking Sailor and me in to see the crocodile. Joseph was always at his most emotionally vulnerable, pliant, and suggestible after sex. He was like a big cat in that respect. Lionesses, for instance, often use the moments right after the act of mating to make their escape, when the male is completely docile, happy to sleepily watch his conquest saunter away now that he's had his fun.

Joseph propped himself up on his elbow to look at me through half-closed eyes. His intricate tattoos gleamed dark against the sheets.

"Ah, so now you haughty bitches want something from me." There was no venom in his voice. I guessed he was thinking about second chances. He grinned and ran his finger down my sternum, making me all shivery. "Yeah, I could make it happen. When do you want to come by?"

I suggested the next time bad weather cut the island off. The work was always lighter on those days and the admins thinner on the ground. Joseph frowned, lay back down, and rubbed at the stubble on his cheek. I was pressing my luck, but he must have been in a magnanimous mood because he yawned, rolled over onto his belly, and said lazily, "Sure, whatever. Just don't bring a cast of thousands or anything. Just you and Sailor. If you get me in trouble and I get demoted to, I don't know, fucking . . . *salamanders*, I'll mess your shit up."

I kissed him on the back of the neck, lightheaded with victory.

The following week, we got the chance to take Joseph up on his promise. We arranged to meet him at the enclosure, once we'd finished our morning tasks. Achilles had one of the special enclosures, four cells knocked through and combined with a cut-through—the wide corridors prison guards once used for moving quickly between cell blocks—to form one of Alcatraz's largest exhibits. The room had been fitted with a deep pool and a pipe that carries the water in and out of the bay. Achilles doesn't need pure water, in fact he prefers it brackish, so the system just removes the harmful chemicals and pollutants, and a mesh filter stops the jellyfish from getting in. I knew all this because Joseph loved to explain the mechanics of the enclosure. He knew nepotism had gotten him the job, but he took great pride in it, and I'd always liked that about him, even if his bragging did get a bit tedious sometimes. Like when someone whose admiration he craved—say, someone like Sailor—was on the scene. I was worried about how she'd be around him, but she was on her politest behavior. She listened to everything he said without interrupting or correcting him, even though she was an expert, thanks to her parents' farm, and had no doubt forgotten more than he'd ever know about all things crocodilian. She acted fascinated by every detail, and I could see Joseph opening up, his chest swelling at finally winning her attention.

The keepers gain access to Achilles's habitat via a corridor enclosed by electrified fencing: we call it the tunnel, because it's narrow and kind of spooky. The tunnel leads to a high wooden tower. At the top of the tower is a three-sided platform, and the keepers stand on the edge to dangle the crocodile's food on a long pole, great hunks of bloody lab-grown meat that he leaps out of the water to snatch, massive body twisting and jaws snapping. The whole contraption is carefully designed to offer the impression that the humans are in some danger, although of course they're not. The guests go nuts for it, though. The spectacle of the human, alone and vulnerable atop the tower, and this prehistoric monster lurking in the water below, just the ridge of his snout and a pair of beady eyes visible, is mesmerizing. Heart-stopping, sometimes quite literally. (One of the many reasons guests are required to sign a release and waiver before entering the zoo.) On the few occasions I've been lucky enough to witness a feeding, I've spent the following days vibrating with the primal joy-horror of it all.

As was the protocol when dealing with dangerous or unpredictable animals, Joseph and his partner, Omar, had lured Achilles into his holding pen with some treats, then locked the double-steel and guillotine doors between the holding pen and the main habitat as they showed us around. We got only a glimpse of Achilles from the back as he sashayed down the path, but Sailor's face transformed at the sight. "Oh, what a beautiful boy," she cooed, dropping down to the floor and extending a hand in the direction of his retreating tail. "Who's a magnificent beautiful boy?" It was almost funny except I could see she wasn't putting on an act but was genuinely enchanted by him and desperate to interact. She wasn't intimidated by him at all.

I hadn't visited in a while and had forgotten the unnerving atmosphere of the enclosure. A fecund earthiness and humidity rose from the tropical plants arranged in a dense, junglelike formation around the central pool, and a smell radiated from the pool itself, a dark base note of decay. No doubt Achilles preferred it that way, but I kept my distance from the water. It was black and rank, sheened with a layer of grease and dotted with scraps of some gray-green vegetation. Sailor had no such qualms, crouching down on her haunches to gaze into the stagnant water with a kind of avid hunger. I guessed it made her homesick.

After Joseph's tour ended, he must have been momentarily floating on a dopamine high because he asked if we'd like to stay for the feeding. Sailor said yes so quickly the word had the staccato shock of a gun firing. Joseph grinned and swaggered off to release Achilles back into his cage. We moved back into the tunnel to watch the show.

Omar emerged first, carrying a bucket brimming with a viscous mess of Fake Steak that was somehow no less disgusting for not being real. He swung the bucket in his only hand. His right arm ended just above the wrist in a pale puckered lump. During the tours he made sure the stump was highly visible during every movement, and all the employees let the guests assume he had lost the hand to a crocodile. It was a better, or at least more dramatic, story than the truth, which was that the hand was mangled during a momentary lapse of concentration at the steel factory he worked in before he made it to Alcatraz.

"Do you know a croc can go for months without eating?" Sailor asked me. "Years, in a pinch. The metabolism slows down until they're almost comatose. Somewhere between cryptobiosis and hibernation. A perfect and miraculous animal, almost goddamn indestructible. Almost. Remember the spate of mysterious croc killings that happened a few years into the blights? Body parts scattered around the mangroves?"

I shivered. "Ugh . . . I must have blocked it out."

"Yeah, well, it wasn't a mystery to me. When their prey suddenly vanished en masse, the crocs had no choice but to find new sources of protein. A few disappeared Floridians later and the locals took matters into their own hands."

"Oh no, that can't be true."

Sailor grunted.

The familiar metallic buzzing of the outer door opening made me snap back to attention. There's nothing quite like witnessing a fully grown saltwater crocodile sway past to make you acutely aware that there's nothing but a fence—suddenly as insubstantial as a paper screen—between you and a solid ton of carnivorous apex predator. I turned to Sailor, expecting her face to mirror my own misty-eyed reaction, but instead her expression was neutral, even cold.

"That crocodile is not well," she said. She narrowed her eyes and leaned closer to the shimmering wire fence, which buzzed quietly, ominously.

"How do you mean?" I had always considered myself especially observant, but Sailor seemed to possess a sixth sense when it came to seeing animals' invisible distress. I never could match it.

"Look at that little hump in his back. Osteomalacia, maybe. And his teeth, they're almost transparent at the ends instead of opaque. Vitamin E deficiency, probably. And see his tail . . . it's too rigid."

As he slowly made his way to his pond I scrutinized his posture, trying to see what she was seeing, but I couldn't find anything that looked particularly wrong. I wasn't an expert like she was. We stood and watched as Achilles slid into his pool, submerging completely before resurfacing, his enormous snout resting just below the water, his eyes both sleepy and watchful.

"Interesting that this is the only enclosure they keep natural during the tours," Sailor said as we watched Joseph climb the tower. "No simulation needed."

"It seems to work."

"Are you kidding me? The tourists go wild for it." She refused to call them guests. "A croc doesn't need all the smoke and mirrors to hold your attention. Not that the other animals do, either. But you know."

My heart fluttered as Joseph paused on the platform tower. He hesitated for a moment, head slightly bowed, as if praying. I knew it was all part of the act, but it still thrilled me. Then he raised his head, rummaged in the bucket for a hunk of Fake Steak, loosely tied the glob of "flesh" onto the end of the pole, and lowered it over the edge. Achilles exploded out of the water with such speed and violence that both Sailor and I jumped, even though we'd been expecting it. A wave of fetid water sloshed onto our feet. Achilles snatched the food off the string, spun ninety degrees, and splashed back into the pool, thrashing around for a few seconds as though his dinner were still alive and needed to be subdued. Then he sank from sight. The pool was deep enough that he could disappear completely into it, and that was somehow more terrifying than when he was visible.

High above us, I saw Joseph turn his body in our direction, anticipating something—applause?—but I couldn't bring myself to praise him in front of Sailor as I normally would have. I just waved up at the tower, my arm flopping around like a fabric doll. We stayed and watched Achilles's fearsome acrobatics until the bucket was empty. Then, as Joseph was climbing back down the steps, Sailor said, "I'm going to go talk to him about Achilles's condition."

"No, don't," I blurted out.

"Why not?" She stood with hands loosely on her hips, amiable but perplexed. In that way she was like Joseph: she couldn't comprehend why anyone would want to thwart her perfectly reasonable desires. What could I say that wouldn't sound pathetic? Because his fragile ego won't like it? Because he might not say anything now but is sure to punish you for it afterward? I stayed silent as she strolled into Joseph's waiting jaws. They were too far away for me to hear the interaction, but I watched anxiously as Sailor confronted him, her posture friendly and relaxed, his increasingly rigid and furious. She leaned down and took a piece of Fake Steak from the bucket, shook it around as if for emphasis, flicking droplets of some engineered bloodlike substance onto the walls. When Joseph wagged a finger in her face and abruptly turned and walked away, I felt it evaporate in an instant, like bad magic, any last chance at friendship or even civility.

I knew from that moment on they would be sworn enemies. And so it was, and so it will ever be.

San Francisco

Sailor arrived early. That was a thing she'd always liked to do in the before-times. The luxury of those stolen moments alone, nursing a glass of wine and surreptitiously watching patrons come and go in the fly-specked mirror behind the bar. Not that there was any of that Parisian glamor in the place Johannes had chosen, a tiny, heaving noodle bar near Jackson Square. There was a profusely sweating bouncer at the door, and she could see the outline of his gun holster. Her eyes widened when she saw the prices on the menu. *Crammed in here with the last of the big spenders*, she thought. Weird choice.

The only seats she'd been able to get were at a narrow aluminum bench at the window overlooking the street. It was a steamy night and the windows had all been cranked open. She had done her makeup and changed into a nice dress in the apartment above Israel's store, feeling jangly with anxious anticipation and kind of foolish, wondering what Johannes would be like to talk to. Radical conservationist types—"radcons," she and Anouk sometimes called them—could be intimidating. And anyone involved with a sanctuary like the one he worked for was bound to be high-status, the kind who didn't suffer fools. She would need to be on her best behavior.

At the appointed time she felt rather than saw his presence materialize beside her. He was wearing a long-sleeved shirt and had his hair pulled back into that neat bun. They went to the counter and ordered noodles from a cashier whose weary face was partially obscured behind a veil of steam. "All plant, for me," said Sailor. Johannes ordered the special of the day. While they waited for their food, a server brought over a small ceramic jar and two thimble-like cups, and they took turns pouring each other shots of the eye-watering liquor, some unholy blend the restaurant was selling for a similarly eye-watering amount.

"Here's to millionaires' moonshine," said Sailor, aware she was trying to charm him. As Johannes brought the cup to his lips, his shirtsleeve slipped down his arm and Sailor saw he had a small Y-shaped scar darkening the flesh below his wrist. She had a similar one on her inner thigh, from a cattle leech back in the Everglades she hadn't noticed until it was too late. Absurdly, it made her feel closer to him. "Listen, sorry about the fuckup in Paris," Sailor said, anxious to address the issue so they could move on. "We had everything set up perfectly, I swear. It should have been easy to smuggle the sugar gliders out of there, we had a van waiting and everything. We think someone snitched."

Johannes wiped his mouth with a napkin, nodded slowly. "I like them," he said after a while. "Big eyes. Stripe down the head. Very cool."

"Yeah, man, they are very cool." She found herself tickled again by his odd manner. "What else do you like?"

He frowned down into his empty cup as if the answer might be there. "Big cats mostly. Big things."

"Big things."

"An elephant would be excellent."

"Oh yeah, the ultimate get. Kind of impractical, though, no?" She was enjoying the banter now. It was fun imagining the escalating, wildly impossible zoo breaks that might have happened if the whole thing hadn't fallen apart.

"We're still interested," he said, "if you have any connections on this side."

"What are you looking for, specifically? Like, is there a particular species the sanctuary wants to acquire?" She was so hungry to know more, she worried her tone made her sound like an amateur.

Johannes looked straight at her for the first time since they'd begun talking, and she felt the first stirrings of unease. His eyes were blue-green and had a strange, almost inhuman sheen to them. He didn't answer right away, just stabbed with his chopsticks at a tangle of noodles and brought them to his mouth, chewing slowly. Sailor, glancing into his bowl, saw something gelatinous and iridescent just below the surface. She pushed her own bowl away and dabbed at her mouth with a brown napkin made from some kind of scratchy fiber.

The waiter hustled them out of there as soon as the dishes were cleared. On the sidewalk, Sailor extended her hand again. "That was really nice," she said. "I've missed talking to animal people."

Johannes didn't look at her but shifted his gaze around, as if searching for something or someone. "Let's go have another drink. Somewhere quiet. I want to talk to you about something else."

"I can't," she said quickly, instinct kicking in. She'd always loathed the forced bonhomie of stretching a night out beyond its natural boundaries. "Sorry, I have to meet friends."

"You don't have any friends here."

The icy certainty of the words made the hair on the back of her neck rise. Then he flashed a just-kidding smile, and she relaxed again. It was just the odd manner, she told herself. She'd known a lot of people like this, it came from working around animals all the time. You could lose your ability to communicate effectively with humans.

A couple entering the noodle bar jostled them as they pushed past, and Sailor was surprised to find Johannes leaning close into her side, in that familiar way in which lovers reduce the space between them. It seemed so unlike something someone like him would do that it took her several seconds before she realized the slight pressure in her lower back was the point of the knife Johannes had pressed there. She couldn't help herself: she laughed. At the absurdity of it, at her own stupidity, at the idea that she had come this far just to die in some back alleyway over a failed animal smuggling.

"Just walk," he whispered.

Alcatraz

As a brand-new year slouched in, I continued, on occasion, to attend Blind Tiger sessions. Not always enthusiastically. The curfew had turned Sailor and me into house cats, and she especially found it intolerable. At first, she sulkily retired to her room or a quiet corner of the barracks after dinner to read or listen to shows, but soon she started disappearing altogether. Sometimes she'd be gone for hours on end. I worried she might have found another flaneur and was out there defying the curfew with someone else. But I never saw her with anyone else, and if I peered outside on those evenings made darker by her absence, I saw no one but the guards. I would slink back to the rec room, and she'd reappear later that evening or at the breakfast table and it was as if she'd never been gone. I could have questioned her, but she gave off an aura of polite discouragement that shut down inquiry.

The Blind Tiger games bored me beyond belief. They always had. In the old days I'd managed to hide my boredom and frustration, but when I returned to the table this time it was as someone who had tasted a superior form of escapism. I made my feelings known by fidgeting behind Joseph (the correct, subservient position for girlfriends and hangers-on during Blind Tiger), sighing loudly during tense moments, and tapping obnoxiously on my screen. All of these were known transgressions, and it wasn't only Joseph who shot me foul looks or outright told me to quit it. I didn't care. No one had told me what a heady stimulant not caring was.

After one particularly nasty session during which Joseph lost to his main rival, Brandon, the situation came to a head. Joseph lumbered up from the table like an angry bear, dragging me away by the elbow. He pulled me into a dank hollowed-out nook in the corridor some people call "the waterfall" because it leaks when there's rain. It's the place everyone goes to for either sexual trysts or arguments you don't want other people to hear.

"What the fuck is your issue, Camille?"

I drew my neck back like an animal who's trying to avoid being stroked. His bulging forehead vein repulsed me. "I'm not sure. The question is sort of vague."

This was the kind of answer that typically enraged him.

"You've really grown a mouth on you since you've been hanging out with Sailor, haven't you?" I sensed a shifting of his mood from generalized anger at losing the game to a highly specific desire to hurt me, and in spite of my newfound bravery I had enough sense to want to avoid getting hurt, so I didn't say anything. But as the seconds ticked by with my back up against the waterfall, I realized all of this was his problem. It was no longer anything to do with me.

As if sensing this change in me, Joseph's face suddenly switched to a conciliatory mode. He leaned closer, head tilted, as if he were going to kiss me. "Look, let's just get back on track here. Nothing hotter than makeup sex, hmmm?" His voice was low and smoky. Seductive. "You thought so a few weeks ago." I glanced down and saw he was cupping the bulge in his pants.

It's true I used to be very into sex with him. He would admiringly call me his demon, his little nympho, because especially if I was bored or had had a stressful day I'd crawl into his bunk after lights out, or message him to meet me in the shower room, and it would feel good at the time, but I'd always get sad after. I loved the intimacy of conjoined bodies, but it took a while for me to realize it wasn't Joseph I wanted, not even that part of him, it was the few seconds of comfort it brought to have our bodies pressed together in the dark, the frisson of cells rubbing against cells. Those seawalls against the tide of despair. That was the addictive thing.

I laughed—I swear I wasn't making fun of his manhood or anything,

I was just struck by how absurd the situation was and how much I longed to get away from it. But his face distorted again, and I saw that I had really triggered something, some primal force that was now propelling him like a branch hurled along a swollen river. He pulled a fistful of matches from his pocket and brandished them in my face. This was also patently absurd, the petulance of it, but I had no urge to laugh this time. Then he snatched a folded piece of cardboard from his back pocket and scraped one of the matches across it, letting the others fall to the ground. I only realized it was a flint when the flame was warming my face. I recoiled as any creature confronted with fire would, stepped back and collided painfully with the wall, my heels scraping the stone and sending a dart of pain up my calves. It amazed me that such a tiny incendiary device could generate such heat.

I didn't want the whimpering sound to escape my lips but it did. Joseph seemed pleased. When the flame burned all the way down to his thumb he swore and dropped the remains of the match, shook out his fingers, then placed his thumb briefly in his mouth. It was pure instinct—the burned flesh seeks a cooling place—but he must have quickly realized the optics of this, and he removed the thumb and placed both hands flat on the wall behind me, pushing his face so close to my own that it no longer read as a face but instead as a series of colors and textures. Tiny rivulets of blood veined the white of his eye. "See what your selfishness causes, Camille?"

A small fire of my own sputtered into being. "I'm sorry, Joseph," I said, dredging up the most rueful, pathetic, beta voice in my arsenal. I let a beat of silence float between us. I let the idea of reconciliation suggest itself. I lifted my cramped arm and stroked his cheek, savoring the manly coarseness and the warmth of his blood pressing beneath his skin for the last time. "But I'm going to need you to fuck off and leave me alone."

The rumor crawled in with February. It traveled like a shameful secret, spoken only in low tones in quiet corners. I think we all feared that speaking it openly might cause the worst-case scenario to manifest, bringing calamity down on all our heads.

Achilles the crocodile was sick, the rumor went, ailing with something no one had yet been able to diagnose. The Squeaky Shoes appeared in the zoo every day, the sight of their white coats sending not only the chimps and monkeys into a frenzy of alarm but the humans too. It became a superstition to avoid the crocodile's cage, unless you happened to be one of the chosen ones, like Joseph and Omar, who tended his needs. For the first time, we pitied them. Their jobs had always seemed so secure, but now, with their famous charge ailing, who knew what their futures would be? Their own fates were intertwined so tightly with that of Achilles, we knew if he disappeared, they would too.

Sailor was the most distressed of all. I knew Achilles's plight felt personal to her. For most of us who had never encountered the species before, certainly never in the wild, Achilles was almost a creature of mythology. But for Sailor, he was a fully realized being with whom she felt an almost painful kinship.

One late afternoon I found her standing a few feet away from the entrance to the crocodile enclosure, leaning back against the wall, staring intently through the bars and gnawing on the side of her thumb. I remember her lipstick had smudged at one side of her mouth, a smear of pink marring her cheek. I approached her as I might have a skittish animal, not entirely sure she was aware of my presence. She moved her head slightly at the movement, then switched her gaze back to the enclosure. Frightening sounds were emitting from the cage. I leaned in and gently rubbed the lipstick mark away. She smiled weakly at me, then gestured toward the chaos.

"I told you there was something wrong with him," she said, and I was shocked at the inconsolable note in her voice. Her eyes were glassy. "He's malnourished, I keep trying to tell them. Sure, crocs can go a long time without eating, but when they eat they need real protein, not that Fake Steak crap. He hasn't had a proper meal in years. And now he's getting weaker."

I finally forced myself to look inside. A small group of vets was crowded into the enclosure. Joseph and Omar were nowhere in sight, no doubt banished while the examination was being carried out. Some held instruments and pads, while others were engaged in quite literally wrestling with the enraged Achilles. One bearded vet was dancing around trying to find a soft place on the croc's underbelly to target with a dart gun. Achilles's snout was bound closed, jagged teeth poking out and the edges of his mouth tilting up in a macabre grin. His tail was lashed around with cable that had been bolted to the wall. But still his rage filled the room. A weakened crocodile is still a dangerous crocodile, especially if he feels he has nothing to lose.

I couldn't watch for long. I know I'm cowardly, that truly good zookeepers should be stoic, but I can't stand seeing any animal in distress. It has always sickened and angered me to see the animals restrained. Sailor, though, she never looked away. I knew she felt it keenly, the bitter irony that this miraculous predator—this last link in an unbroken genetic chain joining our time with that of the dinosaurs—managed to survive every calamity from the Cretaceous era on, but it couldn't survive us. If crocodiles were going to pass from this Earth, Sailor wanted to bear witness to that passing. I wished I could be more like her.

There was something about the way Sailor felt about Achilles that I'd not seen in any other keeper: respect and love mixed up. A feeling beyond wanting to tame or befriend him. I know some people, people like Joseph, consider it wrong to feel so much for the animals under our care. He sees it as a sign of weakness. Other people, like the protestors, see it as a moral failing, to be more concerned with the welfare of animals than that of humans. Intellectually speaking, I sympathize with the wretched plight of my own species, but the reality is that the most wretched humans aren't in front of me and the animals are. The animals have no one to speak up for themselves. (*Neither do the people*, counterargue the protestors in my head.) The animals are doomed without our help. (Protestors in my head: *ditto the people*.)

It's just that the animals matter in a way that's hard to define. They matter not only because a particular species will die out if we don't lock its last members away in here, but because they belong to us, to the whole story of this Earth, and without them the story would not be as beautiful or as profound. Anyone who has ever stopped to watch a hummingbird beat its tiny wings to a stillness as it draws the nectar out of a flower with its long, curled tongue will know what I mean. The natural world is beautiful even when it is terrible, even when it is engaged in ritual slaughter. Any antelope who has ever felt the hot breath of a lion on its neck will know what I mean. In that last moment of its life, the antelope surely regrets that it will never again experience the thrum of the savannah under hoof, the generous shade of the acacia tree, the smell of water running over smooth white rocks. It wishes not to have to leave this beautiful world.

The natural world and the nonhuman beings in it are part of what makes this life worth living. If we kill all the beauty around us, we kill a part of ourselves. These thoughts whirl around pointlessly in my head, never resolving, just coming back to their starting point like a snake devouring its tail.

Hush now.

While Achilles declined, Kira thrived. Nature giving and taking away, if you believed in that sort of thing. We all stole any chance we could to peek into the elephant area. Her keepers would examine her by placing her favorite treats into a special custom-built steel chute, like a corral for cattle, with scales to weigh her and open sides, and I longed to see this sight I'd only heard breathlessly recounted.

One afternoon I happened to be passing by (that was going to be my cover story, anyway) when I saw Kira entering the chute. It was a Tuesday and the tour was wrapping up, the guests milling around out of sight in the gift shop. Most of the zoo had returned to its nonmagical state, people bustling around and getting things back to normal. I knew I should keep moving, but I couldn't resist stopping to watch. Kira's keepers and several vets stood by as she scooped the fruit into her mouth and began slowly chewing, her dark-lashed, intelligent eyes taking everything in. Two of the vets passed ultrasound wands along her sides and belly while a machine hummed nearby, then peered intently at a screen. I don't think I took a breath the whole time. If only I could have spent all day observing her.

A small crowd had formed by then, and when there was nothing left to see, we all made moves to disperse. Brisk footsteps approached and then I heard Brandon behind me, talking in a low, gleeful tone to someone.

"Did you hear? She fucking locked one of them in!"

"*What?*" A woman's voice. "Oh my god."

"Yeah." He laughed, quick and vicious. "She's lost it."

At that moment two guards strode past, hands at their weapons and a get-the-fuck-out-of-our-way air swirling around them. Everyone in the vicinity obliged. A pit opened in my stomach and I grasped at the sleeve of the first person I saw. It was my roommate Vivian.

"What happened?" I asked her.

She regarded me with kindness, like she felt sorry for me. "Apparently a guest got locked inside a cell."

"Jesus, are they okay?"

Louise butted in then, wielding the same gleeful tone Brandon had used. "Well, apart from having a meltdown and threatening to sue, the guest seems fine. Luckily the enclosure was empty, or else—" She mimed shooting herself in the temple.

I dreaded asking, but I had to know. "Do they . . . know how the guest ended up in there?"

"Someone accidentally locked them in," said Vivian quickly.

"Yeah, such a terrible accident," said Louise smugly. "Bet you'll never guess who." Before I could open my mouth, she said, "Here's a hint. It rhymes with 'jailer.'"

Vivian took Louise by the elbow and gently steered her into the stream of traffic along the avenue. "Sorry," she mouthed over her shoulder as they moved away.

Someone else spoke then, but the inside of my head was a crackling radio broadcasting the same message over and over—Oh no, oh no, oh no—and I shoved past them, my only mission to find Sailor. Apart from harming an animal, the next worst crime on Alcatraz was harming a guest. I didn't know what the authorities would do to her, I just knew I had to try to stop it. I struggled to remember what enclosure she'd been assigned that day. Then it came back to me: the Asia Pacific section.

By the time I arrived, there was already an audience of gawkers. I maneuvered to the front and saw the two guards talking in low, ominous voices to Sailor, whose back was pressed against the wall of the enclosure. She didn't look scared, though, just defiant and a bit annoyed. I waved, trying to get her attention, but there was too much going on. The guards held her upper arms, firm but not rough, like they were helping an old lady across the street. As they hustled her out of the cell and out into the corridor, she caught my eye and winked. I opened my mouth to protest but no sound emerged, and by the time I gathered my voice to call out *Hey, where are you taking her?* they were already out of earshot.

The two days that followed were hijacked by a familiar misery. To have someone you love disappear is to have a hole gouged out of your life. No one knew where they had taken Sailor. Coates, our resident spy and knowerof-all-things, reported that he had seen her being taken to the admin center, and he swore she had never come out again. For once, no one believed him. It was far more likely she'd been deported, the consensus went. Under cover of night, probably, for discretion's sake. It made my jaw ache with hatred, how casually they all talked about it.

Then, on the third day, biblically enough, she reappeared. In her usual spot at the breakfast table, as if nothing had happened, tapping on her screen and ignoring the rising hum of curious voices that filled the mess hall. She looked up at my rapid approach, her hair a little wild but her eyes clear and brimming with mischief as always.

"Hey, I've got something for you," she said. "Come sit."

I was so choked up with relief I had to gulp down some water before I could speak. Sailor rummaged in her pocket and pulled out a dented candy bar, a brand I remembered from my teenage years. She slid it across the table to me.

"Voilà. A little gift from the dungeons of Alcatraz. Can't vouch for its quality, sorry."

"What . . . dungeons?"

"That solitary confinement cell in the basement of the admin center? Not an urban myth, as it turns out."

"Oh my god. Sailor, are you okay?"

She snorted. "Sure I am. They didn't get time to set it up properly. It's basically a storeroom, loads of boxes and junk piled everywhere. Dusty as fuck and my allergies were a nightmare, but it wasn't too bad. Found some old user manuals for forklifts and read them cover to cover. Ask me anything at all about hydraulic lift cylinders."

I laughed, incredulous and impressed by her refusal to let anything crush her spirit. "I thought you got deported," I said, my voice breaking mortifyingly on the last syllable.

"Hey, it's okay, Birdy," she said soothingly. "I'm flattered you cared. But slightly offended you thought they could get rid of me that easily."

"Fair enough," I mumbled, swiping my nose and attempting a smile. "What the hell did you do, anyway?"

Sailor laid her hand dramatically on her chest in faux indignation. "What did *I* do? More like what did the psycho guest do."

"Okay, what did the psycho guest do?"

She'd obviously been dying to tell someone, because she had the whole spiel ready. She folded her arms on the table and leaned forward, locking me in her gaze. "So, the tour has long ago passed by and I'm working in the Australian marsupial area, right? I've just taken the quokka out of the enclosure and put him in the nesting area, out of sight so he can get some sleep, poor nocturnal baby. I need a tool, so I leave the enclosure for a second. I swear it was just a second. And on my way back I see this tourist, he must have slipped away from the tour without anyone seeing, and he's got his camera out and he walks into the cell, like just brazenly walks in there and starts looking around."

"Seriously?"

"Right? Like, the motherfucking nerve on this guy. I figured he wanted to get a photo of himself with the quokka up close. The adorable goofy face on them, people were always harassing them in the wild for selfies in the old days. Anyway, I decided if he wanted to spend some time in there, he could be my guest."

"Sailor! No."

"Yes." She grinned wickedly and took a sip of coffee.

"How are you—" I floundered around for words. "How are you still here?"

She ignored my question. "My big mistake was letting him see me. He went nuts. He's threatening to sue, you know, but he won't get far with that. Thank you, ironclad liability wavers. Also, he was in there for, what, fifteen minutes, tops? What a giant baby." She wrapped her hands around her mug and smiled, cheered by the memory.

"But so that's it?" I asked. "They're not going to punish you any further, right?"

"Apparently not. Guess I'm valuable to them, at least for the moment."

"Of course you are," I said loyally, and then we switched to discussing all the things that had happened in the forty-eight hours she'd been away, which, if you work at a zoo, can be a surprising number of things. I knew she wanted to know about Achilles, but he was no better, so I deflected by talking about how exciting it had been to watch Kira's ultrasound, and my enthusiasm must have been contagious because she expressed great envy over having missed it.

Sailor seemed to quickly forget about her brief incarceration, but a question lingered in my mind. I knew I appreciated Sailor's rare value, but I doubted the admins did. So something else had saved her.

San Francisco

Johannes continued to press his body close to hers as he steered Sailor past all the places she'd noticed on the way to the noodle bar. Those places looked different now, in the way everything tends to look different when you have a knife at your back. When they arrived at a nondescript office building on Washington, he pushed the door open with his shoulder and shoved Sailor into the lobby. She could have tried bolting, but something told her that her languid companion was capable of moving with deadly speed when he needed to. Johannes put his free arm around her shoulders, a tight grip that to a casual observer might have looked like the proprietorial affection of a husband for his wife. He nodded at the security guard, who barely looked up from his screen, and ushered her into the elevator.

"Where are we going?" she asked as they ascended, and he didn't answer but she hadn't expected him to, she had just wanted to hear a human voice.

On the twelfth floor the doors opened and he motioned her to move ahead. They were facing an empty open-plan office space. It looked to be long abandoned, the computers all ancient gray boxes, a blanket of dust settled on all the surfaces, a stifling air of neglect. Cords coiled from sockets like exhausted snakes.

Johannes leaned against a desk. He tucked the knife away in the inner pocket of his blazer and his hand reemerged holding a gun, like a parlor trick. He balanced the Glock lovingly in his palm before placing it down next to him, its muzzle pointed at her like an open mouth.

"I don't like crowded places," he said, almost apologetically. "Easier to talk here. Get to know each other better. I'm an admirer. You were so close at the French zoo." He said this in a sympathetic, encouraging way, like his admiration might make up for kidnapping her, or whatever this was. "What's Paris like, anyway?"

"Fine."

"I have a friend there. He's in the exotic animal business as well."

"That's nice."

"A lot of his merch came from Paris Zoo, actually. You might know him?"

"I doubt that. I don't think we're on the same side of the business, if you know what I mean."

Johannes shrugged. "Seems to me like you are. Maybe you just haven't been as successful yet?"

The barb shouldn't have hit home, but it did. "You don't know anything about me."

"I know enough. I know you know about smuggling. I know you're in a position to start up again, now you're at Alcatraz."

"And how did you come to know all that?"

Johannes looked at her steadily, that same deadened light in his eyes. She understood it now, and why it disturbed her. It was the look of a person whose conscience had never fully developed. Someone else might have characterized the look as reptilian, but Sailor loved reptiles.

"My French connection told me you were on your way here," he said. "We help each other out sometimes."

She felt the first chill of comprehension. One of their former colleagues in Paris must have given them all up to one of the cartels there. Maybe that explained why Anouk had stopped answering.

"So I guess you're not from the sanctuary, then."

The man's neutral, emotionless gaze transitioned then into something closer to contempt. "There's no fucking sanctuary."

"How did you know you had the right person?"

"You think you don't stand out in this cesspool? The way you look. The way you smell."

"Excuse me?"

"Like someone who works with wild animals." His smile was friendlier now. "I'd know that smell anywhere. Also, I overheard you leaving that message. Took my chance."

"I suppose there's no Mr. Li either." She didn't even bother making it a question, and he didn't bother answering.

Johannes pushed away from the desk and glanced at his phone. "Listen, I need you to do something for me, Sailor."

Her name in his mouth made her shiver with repulsion now. It pained her to remember she'd found him attractive at their first meeting. Beauty could be a good disguise, god knows she'd used it herself from time to time, but she was ashamed to have let his appearance lull her into thinking him safe. Johannes had commenced cleaning his fingernails with the tip of his knife like some wannabe gangster from a movie. It made her want to laugh, although she was smart enough to stifle the impulse. If her years at the zoo had taught her anything, it was that no creature was as dangerous as a man being laughed at.

He looked her up and down, from her scalp to her toes. But this too felt performative. Her radar told her he wasn't really interested in that, for whatever reason.

"Let's go," he said, his voice patient, like he was trying to corral a child. "We're going up to the roof."

"The what?"

"I want to show you something. Come."

Johannes headed out of the room and Sailor reluctantly followed, her eyes drawn to the strip of tanned flesh and glint of metal that flashed from his waistband. He entered the elevator and she stepped in after him, stared resolutely ahead as they ascended ten floors. They emerged into a world of sleek mirrored walls, black marble floors, and gilded columns. An executive floor. The kind of place where common people are never intended to be seen unless they're there to clean. As with the offices below, a thin film of dust had settled over the surfaces, and the silence was so deep it felt like the space had forgotten sound.

Johannes led her to a door marked STAIRS and Sailor's heart hammered faster. He pushed it open and took the stairs two at a time like a kid, flinging the door at the top open and waiting for her with a strange look on his face. Pride? Something like that. She emerged into the glare of the rooftop, squinting and shading her eyes with her arm.

He gently swiveled her shoulders so she faced the center of the roof. She'd heard about fancy offices and hotels with swimming pools on the roof but had never expected to see one with her own eyes. Johannes released his grip and nodded. She walked slowly through the skeleton doorframe of a half-built structure resembling a greenhouse, approached the edge of the pool, and peered over the side. This one was past its prime, the painted blue tiles flaking in places and patches of rust blooming on the metal ladders. But it was still impressive, an Olympic-size fuck-you to all the pool-less surrounding buildings. The cavity was about halfway full, the water no longer chlorinated but green and greasy-looking. For a terrible moment Sailor was convinced Johannes had brought her here to drown her. She imagined him pushing her head beneath the surface and the water flooding her lungs. She glanced at him and he was staring into the pool as if transfixed, still with that proud look on his face. She understood then that he was seeing the future. A time when the swimming pool would contain something more interesting than algae and slime.

Alcatraz

The week after Sailor's release, I happened to find myself after a shift had finished standing next to Joseph at one of the cleaning stations.

"Oh hey," I said, lathering up.

"Hey," he grunted. He was monosyllabic with me by then, so I was used to that, but I noticed his expression was one of permanent worry now, his mouth drawn into a tight line. He squeezed his fingers into fists as the water poured over them, skin stretched white over the knuckles. I had been feeling slightly bad about telling him to leave me alone (actually, *fuck off* and leave me alone, my brain helpfully reminded me), so on an impulse I said: "Listen, I'm really sorry about what's happening with Achilles. I'm sure it's just something minor, but it must be stressful for you guys."

He swiveled his neck like an owl and fixed me with a stare so hostile it made my whole body turn cold.

"Funny you should say that, *Camille*." He spoke my name like it was a lie he'd found me out in. "Ever since you and Sailor visited the enclosure that time, he's been going downhill. Did that bitch poison him or something?"

I raised a chicken-wing arm and turned the faucet off with my elbow. "You must be kidding. Poison?" It galled me he would try to blame Sailor for a problem whose cause was so clear. "Shouldn't you be more worried about malnutrition? I mean, that's obviously what's wrong with him."

"For the last fucking time, it's not malnutrition! We feed him all the time!"

I opened my mouth to say something about it being less to do with the quantity he was being fed than the nature of the protein, but I had a feeling Joseph wasn't in the mood to be schooled on his own area of expertise, so I just shrugged. This appeared to enrage him because he slapped his hand down on the side of the sink, and water and suds flew everywhere. I jumped back a step, slipped, almost overbalanced. Instinctively I raised my hands, as if protecting my face from a blow. He looked shocked then, took a step back of his own.

"Anyway, just stay out of my way, both of you. And tell Sailor to stop creeping around Achilles, or I'll report her to the admins."

And he stalked off, arms tight by his sides, flicking the water angrily off his fingertips. Another mess someone else would have to clean up.

When I told Sailor about the encounter later her eyes widened. "Poison, huh? That's an interesting theory."

"Wait, you think Achilles has really been poisoned?"

"Well not literally. But his body is turning on him because he's not getting the right nutrients. Eating away at him from the inside."

I didn't like this theory any more than Joseph's. Sailor seemed distracted. She said she had to go see the admins about something, and though I would normally have asked her about it, I sensed she didn't want me to. There was a lot of activity in the admin center around this time, people entering and exiting the building with somber expressions. The continued presence of the Squeaky Shoes only heightened the sense of dread.

In huddles in the rec room after-hours, keepers talked in low voices about Achilles, stopping only if Joseph or Omar were in earshot. Joseph particularly radiated a dangerous energy that cleared a space around him wherever he went. Even his usual acolytes avoided him, which spoke volumes, I thought scornfully, about the loyalty of his pack.

The collective mood wasn't helped by an unannounced visit from Mr. Pinkton halfway through February. The admins often took these opportunities to have the boss address us, but on this occasion his presence was indirect: his helicopter glowing noxious green on the landing pad; his goons posted like smartly dressed gargoyles outside the admin office. I wanted to talk to Sailor about what it might mean, but I couldn't find her all day. Usually I had a radar for picking out her distinctive stride even from the other side of the zoo, my ears attuned to the frequency of her cackling laugh, but the zoo felt empty of her. They made me increasingly nervous, these vanishings, especially after the incident with the imprisoned guest. She didn't turn up that night either, and after lights-out I worried myself into a state of low-pitched terror.

The next morning I was shuffling, sleep-deprived and twitchy, at the back of the line of keepers on the way to get assignments, when I became aware of an excited hum of chatter pulsing from the direction of the rec room. A premonition rippled across my neck. I quickened my step, squeezing through the entrance with a few other stragglers, but I didn't even have to look up to know. Joseph's and Omar's names had been replaced on the assignment screen. But that was as far as my premonition had taken me. I gaped up at the names that blazed in their place: DEV KOLLURI and SAILOR ANDERSON.

My shock wasn't only about the promotion—although it was unheard of for such a new keeper to land a stellar assignment like this one—but because Sailor had kept it from me. I turned away from the screen and bumped hard into someone, mumbling apologies before trying to maneuver my way out of the suddenly stifling room, desperate for air. I emerged into the corridor to find Joseph at the center of an adoring group. People were slapping him on the back and holding up their palms for high fives. What was happening? For a moment I entertained the possibility Joseph was leaving Alcatraz, and somehow the group was trying to console him by acting like it was a big victory, a final display of sycophancy before the memory of his time here ebbed away. But the longer I hovered outside the doorway, the more the details of the scene suggested a different reality. Joseph's expression was far too genuinely euphoric for someone whose coveted role had been given to his nemesis. Something else was going on.

As I was trying to puzzle it out, Joseph happened to glance over and catch my eye. He winked. I smiled and gave him a limp thumbs-up, then slunk back into the rec room to avoid the humiliation of walking past him and his admirers. I looked again at the screen, wondering if I'd hallucinated the news: no, it was still there, plain as day, the names Sailor and Achilles linked together like lovers. But for the first time my gaze widened to encompass the other postings. Joseph's name was still there, but under a different assignment this time. The elephants. Kira and Titan.

I walked alone to work in a daze, thinking about Joseph and Sailor, about how thin the line could be between fortune and misfortune, and trying not to feel left out.

It was clear right from the start that Joseph's popularity would soar even higher thanks to his new posting, but Sailor didn't seem to generate the same adoration. The next morning I found her alone at breakfast as usual. Her face lit up at my approach, and she slid across so I could sit beside her.

"Congratulations on Achilles," I said shyly, and she screwed up her face and playfully punched my arm.

"Listen, I wanted to tell you but they swore me to secrecy until it was official. They basically kept me locked in the admin center until this morning. Not the dungeon this time, so I suppose that's an upgrade. It's not exactly a reward, anyway. Everyone's treating me like even more of a pariah than usual, in case you haven't noticed. It's like the kiss of death being assigned Achilles. Dev is distraught about it."

She laughed, that wonderful corvid's cackle, and I joined in, selfishly relieved to know her newly exalted status wasn't going to change our friendship. She could play it down all she wanted but I knew she was over the moon about getting to spend time with Achilles, and I was suddenly and unequivocally happy for her. How often do the people we care about get exactly what they want?

"So how did it all come about?" Now that the unbreakable nature of our alliance had been established, I was bursting to hear all the details.

"Ha, well. I had a word with our pal Mr. Pinkton. What? Don't look so shocked. He's not some god, you know."

"But . . . how? What did you say to him?"

Sailor smiled. "Everyone's open to persuasion, Birdy. You just have to work out the angles. They were desperate for an answer to the Achilles problem. Their investment was looking somewhat rocky, and you know how these people are about their investments."

"You're the perfect keeper for Achilles, even they must have been able to see that," I said. "Thank God Joseph got switched to elephants, though. You might have had to borrow one of Mr. Pinkton's bodyguards otherwise." I stuck out my tongue and mimed a blade across my throat.

Sailor side-eyed me. She blew on her steaming ersatz coffee. "I wouldn't say *God* had anything to do with it."

It took me a moment. "Wait. Are you saying you persuaded them to put Jos—"

Sailor put her finger to her lips. "Now we don't want your boyfriend getting the wrong idea about me. Loose lips sink ships."

"Huh?"

"It was an expression about a million years ago. Anyway, it's not even a big deal, it's not like he would have been booted out, being untouchable and everything. Pinkton royalty. I just made a teensy suggestion, that's all. Planted an idea. But still, don't say anything. Joseph's cockiness is insufferable, but imagine if he was *grateful*?"

She gave a dramatic shudder, and I laughed along, but I was touched by her stealth generosity. She was right that the admins wouldn't have dared deport Joseph, but she didn't know him as well as I did. For Joseph, being demoted to regular keeper status would have been worse than deportation. It would have been like a little death. Sailor had saved him.

"So listen, Birdy, enough about Broseph. There's going to be an announcement later today."

"Oh no, what now?"

"Nothing dire, don't worry. Just . . . interesting. The Pinktons are buying the other zoos."

"They're *what*?"

"Yep. Paris. Singapore. Berlin. Sydney. What's left of them, anyway."

"Why? I mean, they're just shells now, right?"

"Sure, but it's good real estate and the infrastructure is still sound, mostly. I guess the idea is to prepare for the future. Expand the franchise. Get in before anyone else does."

"He told you this?"

"Wouldn't say told me directly. I just happened to be in the room."

"Convenient."

She shot me a grin and angled her mug toward mine for a toast. "A good talent to cultivate, Birdy. Being in rooms at the right time."

The announcement about the zoo acquisitions came later that day, just as Sailor had said it would. But there was an extra announcement that surprised even her. The tours were going to be increased, we were informed, from once a week to once daily. Effective the following Monday. The admin who delivered this piece of explosive news left the kind of pause that anticipates a swelling of applause. Instead, the vibe of the room changed from the dutiful boredom that usually accompanied assemblies to confusion and outrage, a slow-building burr of voices like a giant machine starting up.

The admin tapped testily on the mic. "The Pinktons thank you for your continued service to Alcatraz." Never had such anodyne words sounded so distinctly like a warning.

We dispersed after that, off to our own political corners to discuss this development, with all its exciting and worrying ramifications. As I left the barracks I overheard Prentiss talking to another keeper. "This is outrageous," he said with the quiet, righteous passion that was his hallmark. "We have to do something."

I didn't hear what the other keeper mumbled but I certainly wouldn't have faulted them for responding, *Like what, exactly?*

I waited just outside for Sailor, who finally dawdled out with the stragglers.

"Can you believe it?" I asked her, all keyed up from a storm of feelings. She cocked an eyebrow in a manner that meant yes, she could, as ever, believe whatever ridiculous thing was happening. "On the one hand, I guess this means there'll be more funds for the zoo. That's good, right? On the other hand . . ." I didn't need to elaborate on why this new regime wasn't optimal. "Why do you think the Pinktons are doing this now?"

Sailor sighed. She seemed tired. "They're trying to raise money to fund the other zoos. It's an animals arms race out there, Birdy, and they're not the only interested bidders."

I was sorry I had asked, but also anxious for answers, so I forged on.

"Do you think they'll be able to fill the tours *every day*? I mean, they're crazy expensive."

"Oh, you would be surprised at how many masters-of-the-universe types are still around. Elites from all over who made out like bandits when things went to shit. There's always been a waiting list for the tours."

"There has?"

"Yep. And now every one of those ghouls will get to visit the end-of-the-world zoo, yippee." She said this in an inflectionless way that scared me. But before I could sink too far into glumness, Sailor nudged me. "But hey, guess what? We are officially no longer under curfew. Got the message this morning."

She held up her palm and we high-fived, but there was a somber feeling even to that usually exuberant exchange. I was thinking about the animals, about what a daily tour routine might do to them, and I knew Sailor was too.

You'd think it would be hard to avoid someone within the limited habitat of a small island, but I had surprisingly few occasions to run into Joseph after he was reassigned. He had his routines and I had mine, plus the now-daily tours kept everyone in a state of distraction. The afternoon boat always carried a full load of eager guests, and their needs and demands became inescapable, as did the stress of keeping the animals from suffering under the increased scrutiny. Perhaps wary of the optics of catering solely to the ultra-high-net-worth set, the Pinktons had even debuted a special charity day on which orphaned children could experience the tour. With the new schedule, there was barely enough time to eat, sleep, or even pee. Joseph was the last thing on my mind.

It came as a shock, then, the morning Sailor and I arrived in the rec room to find I'd been assigned to work the elephant enclosure, because it could only have been Joseph who requested me, given he controlled the rosters for Kira and Titan's section. Sailor and I shot each other a look. Like every other keeper on Alcatraz, we were always trying to sneak glimpses of Kira and her magnificently swollen belly, but most of the time we had to be content with the daily dispatches about her health, dispassionate rundowns of bloodwork and stats. To get to see her up close was a dream. She was seven months along then, around a third of the way through her gestation period.

"Damn, I'm so jealous," said Sailor, looking longingly at my name on the screen. "You have to tell me everything!"

I assured her I would, and she headed off to her own duties with Achilles.

Ali, who must have been lurking close by the whole time, appeared at my shoulder. I'd heard on the grapevine she and Joseph were officially a thing now. "We're doing a major floor-to-ceiling cleaning of Kira and Titan's enclosure and need help," she said, in a tone designed to quash any ideas I might have about spending time with her precious charges. She sniffed and pushed her hat down on her forehead, shot me a lupine grin. "Help with shoveling, if you know what I mean."

The thing neither she nor Joseph ever understood was that I didn't mind cleaning up after the animals. Shoveling elephant shit wasn't a punishment for me in the way it was for them. I knew they often bribed newer keepers to do this part of the job, and I just felt sorry for them that they could spend so much time with those incredible creatures and not want to serve their needs in every way. Still, it was strange they'd specifically chosen me to help with such a routine task, especially given how tense my relationship with Joseph had become. But I was so euphoric I didn't expend much energy pondering it.

As I was lacing up my boots, Sailor returned. I heard her distinctive footfall as she strode down the corridor toward me.

"What happened?" I said, squinting up at her. Her eyes had that wicked gleam they got when she was busy cooking up a scheme. "What did you do?"

"So listen, the vets are doing a full checkup on Achilles and they made me leave the enclosure."

I laughed. "Let me guess. You were trying to tell them how to do their jobs?"

"*Moi?*" Sailor drew her shoulders back, pretending to be offended. "How rude. But yes, pretty much." She grinned, stretching each arm over her head in turn. I could feel the energy sparking off her. "Anyway, I'm supposed to help someone else out, so I told them I was coming to observe the elephants. Broseph won't let me in the cell, obviously, but I thought I could loiter around anyway. At the very least it will annoy him."

I shook my head at her but my heart was glad. By the time we got there, the elephant enclosure was a hive of activity. One of the assistant crew, Jorge, was at the top of a ladder, enthusiastically scrubbing a wall, while Joseph, Ali, and another senior keeper were tending to Titan and Kira. Titan seemed agitated, swinging his gargantuan trunk around, while Kira was swaying gently on the spot, almost like she was meditating. Her sides were swollen with the growing calf I pictured curled there behind her ribs.

"You go ahead," said Sailor, pushing me gently in the direction of the action. "I'll stay out of the way. Don't want to mess up your big day."

"Oh, you're here," Joseph said as I stumbled into his presence. He was all brisk business, his manner distracted and tone impersonal. Sailor hung back in the shadow of a doorway, but I made the mistake of glancing back at her and Joseph followed my gaze. His face clouded. Sailor gave him a loose-wristed salute and loped away.

"Hi," I said brightly, smiling at everyone. "Just let me know what I can do."

"We're taking them out into the yard." Joseph delivered this seismic piece of news with impressive offhandedness. It was possible he'd been practicing. His mouth twitched into a smile at my incredulous, mouth-agape response, and he handed me a shovel. "All right, all right, don't get your panties in a bunch. You're the only keeper I can trust to not rile them up, that's all. We need a calm vibe out there."

"Oh my god, Joseph, thank you," I gushed, not caring how I sounded. "I'll do whatever you need."

He grunted. "Yeah, you'd better. Hope I don't live to regret this little experiment." His gruff words didn't match his countenance, though. He looked like a kid being told he could open all his birthday presents at once.

While the team prepared Kira and Titan for their short but historic journey, I was instructed to stand near the door and ensure no one tried to enter the enclosure. Occasionally I'd peek out to check on Sailor. She was paying visits to enclosures up and down the avenue, and I could hear her laugh ringing out from time to time. The keepers had almost finished getting the elephants ready when her head appeared around the side of the door. She beckoned me over with an air of clandestine urgency. I couldn't tell if she was genuinely afraid of Joseph seeing her in his territory or playing it up for my amusement, but the second option was definitely more in character.

"Hey," she said. "So I've been summoned to Maggie's enclosure. Apparently, she's attacking anyone who tries to enter her cage. One keeper's already in the hospital getting a gash stitched up, and now everyone else is too scared to approach her. Useless." She shook her head. "Anyway, peace out for now. Don't do anything too exciting without me."

"Good luck with Maggie," I said, although I knew she didn't need luck. Sailor was the only person beside me whom the bird was always calm around. "But hey, you won't believe this," I said, my voice going all the way up at the end. "We're taking Kira and Titan out to the yard, just like you always said we should."

"No. Way." She gently pushed me backward, and I nodded ecstatically.

"Well, well, well. I wonder how Joseph got that idea? Maybe he's not a lost cause after all."

"I should go," I said, aware of heightened activity in the room behind me. "But come back after, I'll tell you all about it."

"Thanks, Birdy," she said, blowing me a kiss. "What a day."

Then it was time. I remember reading once about a circus in New York City that each spring would march their elephants through the Queens Midtown Tunnel to Madison Square Garden, where they were to perform. The tunnel was closed off, and people would line the route to cheer the elephants along. I'd always been enchanted by the vision of these majestic creatures taking over the city for a day, the sound of their trumpeting blaring like wild music through the urban canyons.

I recalled it now as we solemnly walked our elephants along the avenue to the corridor that joined the zoo with the old rec yard. People cheered and clapped, and we keepers accompanying Kira and Titan felt like the minders of movie stars. Joseph had warned me not to touch them but to stay close so they'd be calmed by my presence. As I walked alongside I could see the individual folds in their skin, the ingenious network of crevices that absorb and retain water, and it took every ounce of willpower I had not to reach across the few inches separating me from them. He couldn't ban me from smelling, though. My nostrils tingled with the earthy, honeyed scent rising from their hides.

Outside, the air was clear enough to see the blood-orange towers of the bridge rendered sharp against the blue sky. I took a few puffs of my EZ-Breathe anyway, because it was better to be safe. There had been understandable concern about how Kira and Titan might react to this unfamiliar environment, but all our anxieties evaporated the moment they took their first outside breath. At the end of the ramp, Joseph and the other keepers stepped aside and the elephants moved as one into the open space, calling out and lumbering with unhindered glee toward various objects strewn around the yard—a section of large plastic tubing from some construction project; an inflatable beach ball; two truck tires. I watched with teary happiness as Titan approached the tubing and lifted his front legs onto it, then ponderously and slowly rolled across it and spilled onto the other side. The elephants took turns trotting after each other, ears fanning and tails swinging. They found a spigot in the wall and below it a shallow basin in which water had accumulated, and Kira siphoned up water with her trunk, then jetted it over her back. When they had tired of those pursuits, they both gravitated to the tires and plonked down in them like overgrown toddlers.

I sidled up as close as I dared to Joseph, who was looking on like a tough but doting father. "How do they get along with her being pregnant?" I asked. "Looks like they're happy together."

He scratched his ear and hesitated a good long moment, as if considering not answering me. But he loved talking about the elephants, just as he had loved talking about Achilles; these charismatic residents conferred a status on him that was unequal to any other pride in his life. "They weren't too keen on each other when she first tested positive, she got kind of hostile and protective, we had to separate them." I suppressed a smile: classic Joseph to boastfully present this detail as insider intel when he hadn't even been their keeper back then. "But they're better now. Hell, they're both elephants, aren't they? They might be the last two on Earth. They don't really have a choice." He fixed his gaze on me. "Like if you and I were the only two people left on Earth, I guess we'd have to find a way to get along." He turned his head and spat in the dirt. We stood for a moment together, watching the elephants reveling in their good selves, in the closest they might ever get to their proper *umwelten*. I jumped when Ali's voice sounded next to my ear.

"Hey look, a pollinator drone."

Joseph and I turned. She had her hand out like you do when you want a butterfly or a hummingbird to land on it. A few feet away hovered a gleaming striped object, slightly larger than a honeybee but doing a fairly decent impression of one, complete with a convincing layer of fuzz. But there was something off about it, like all the ersatz pollinators, a kind of uncanny valley wrongness. Between the beating of its wings, I thought I spotted a corp logo on its back. Joseph took a step toward it. "Hey, cool, I've never seen one of these close up before."

"What's it doing here, so far from home?"

"Don't know," said Joseph. "But the corps give you a reward if you turn in rogue ones."

I stared at my fellow keepers. An alarm deep in my lizard brain went off. Something to do with a piece of arcana I had filed away long ago. I stood slack-jawed for a moment while I fully retrieved it. Then the words came shooting out of me. "Quick! The elephants! The bee!"

Two faces looked at me uncomprehendingly, and then the words reached them as if I'd shouted them down a long hallway. They remembered too: elephants are terrified of bees.

"Fuck," said Joseph, and he lunged for the drone. It swooped out of his reach and headed for the other end of the yard, where Kira and Titan had risen from the tires and were busy siphoning water from the basin and squirting it into the air.

"Fuck!" said Ali.

"Fuck!" I yelled. It was all we could seem to say. Then we were all sprinting down the yard, uprooting clods of dirt.

"You!" yelled Joseph, spinning around and pointing at me, his face twisted with fury. "Get the fuck out of the way! Somewhere safe. *Now!*"

I hesitated for only a moment—even my calming presence wasn't going to help things now—before running back to the building, missing every second step of the stone staircase. By the time I got to the top, my breath ragged, the elephants had spotted the drone and were freaking out as predicted. Joseph and Ali darted nimbly around the bellowing creatures, calling out and trying to calm them, but of course anyone who's ever witnessed a melting-down toddler or a terrified animal knows there are few workable solutions beyond riding out the storm as best you can and making sure no one hurts themselves. I stood there helplessly, squeezing my hands together.

Joseph yelled something to Ali and she nodded and they both jogged to the side of the yard closest to me, where the ramp was. They were halfway up the ramp when the drone pivoted from the elephants and headed for them. I still have no idea why: perhaps it was programmed to follow certain kinds of movement.

"Let's lead it inside!" I heard Joseph call, and they raced toward the door with the drone gaining on them. "Buzz us in, Camille!"

I ran to obey, so absorbed in my task I didn't even notice her until I was right on top of her. Sailor, returned from her mission with Maggie. She held the door open with one hand, and with the other she calmly reached out and snatched the drone from the air just as Joseph and Ali reached us. Sailor's hand jerked around as the drone whined furiously inside, but she had a strong grip.

"Get it inside," snapped Joseph, annoyed that she'd beaten him to it. "Put it somewhere safe, away from the animals."

Sailor looked steadily at him as she slowly clenched her fist. The crunching sound was horrible to hear. She opened her fingers, and we all watched, hypnotized, as she plucked the mesh wings off the crushed bee, one on each side, blew them off her palm, then let the remains of the drone fall to the ground. Ali's gaze swung between Sailor and the elephants, who were still rocking and lowing in distress. I could see she was torn between confronting Sailor—now clutching the wrist of her injured hand as blood dripped onto the concrete—and placating Kira and Titan. Joseph barked something impatient at Ali and she sped off toward the elephants. Then he turned his attention to Sailor. I instinctively stepped closer to her, a protective move like we had once performed with the distressed chimps. Joseph's eyes were blazing.

"What the fuck did you do that for? We could have got a lot of money for it."

"Oh, for real?" She glanced down at the ruins. "Damn."

He shook his head in disgust, but then his face softened and he began to laugh. "You are one crazy-ass bitch, has anyone ever told you that?"

Sailor cocked her head at him and tucked her bleeding hand beneath her armpit. "A few people have mentioned it over the years."

Joseph laughed again, and Sailor even smiled a little in response, or maybe it was a grimace of pain. "Well, you can explain it to the corps when they come sniffing around for their property." He didn't sound mad anymore. The weirdest part, when I look back on it, was the whole thing felt like a private moment between them. Not a stalemate, nothing like that, but like they had reached an understanding of some kind. "I'm going to make sure my elephants are okay." He jogged away and then called over his shoulder, "You should get that hand looked at."

I had never really been in love with him, but I felt some generous feeling rise in me then, a kind of love by proxy, at how much he cared for the elephants. When I looked over at the seawall again, he and Ali had somehow managed to calm Kira and Titan, and they resumed their bathing and exulting as though nothing had ever happened to breach the perfection of the day.

I knew Joseph considered himself to be made of tougher stuff than someone like me. He prided himself on his thick skin, to the point where he'd half convinced himself that was why he'd been assigned the crocodile and then the elephants. But that afternoon shook him, I could tell. Seeing how scared the elephants were forced him to consider how fragile they were. Of course, I had always known this. Having a thick hide doesn't shield you from the terrible things this world has in store.

I took Sailor to the hospital and sat with her while the nurse treated the gashes on her hand.

"Another victim of Maggie the eagle, huh?" he said.

Sailor hesitated, then said, "Yeah."

She didn't flinch when he applied the stinging lotion. He bound the hand and ordered her to take the rest of the day off. I walked with her back to the barracks, although she scoffed when I offered her the crook of my elbow as we walked down the hill. "I'm not an invalid, Birdy. It barely even broke the surface."

She refused to enter the barracks itself, convincing me instead to sit with her for a moment down by the dock. It was eerily quiet down there. After the raid on the guest boat, the protestors had been banned on Mr. Pinkton's orders and the free-speech zone dismantled. The only relic remaining was a scrap from a hand-painted sign caught in a piece of chain-link fencing, flapping furiously anytime it caught a breeze. I didn't miss the protestors, but their rocking boats and droning chants had become such a fixture of the landscape their absence felt weird.

"Why did you do that?" I asked.

"Do what?"

"Destroy the drone."

"Because it was most likely a spy."

"Really? Who'd want to spy on us?"

Sailor picked at the hem of her overalls. "Promise you won't laugh?" I raised my hand courtroom-style and she said, "My enemies."

I found myself with no urge to laugh. "But what do they want?"

She sighed. "The usual shit. Power. Prestige. Money. To hoard all the remaining good things. To see other people suffer and to be insulated from that suffering."

"But what do they want from you specifically?"

"Something they're never going to get."

I wanted to probe further, but Sailor told me I should get back to work before anyone noticed I was missing.

"I'll let Joseph know you're okay," I said, only half joking.

"Oh, I'm sure he's superanxious. What did you ever see in that jerk, anyway?" She winced and cradled the hand.

I looked down at my shoes, caked in elephant shit. "I thought he was hot, I guess."

She sniffed dismissively. "Well, those chemical imbalances can happen to anyone."

I considered this for a moment. As often happened when I was around Sailor, the urge to be honest asserted itself. "Actually, I think I just liked being chosen by him, like I was someone important, you know?"

Her pained frown turned into a laugh, as if my truth telling were a panacea. "Oh, sister, I've been there. You know what really helps, though? Realizing none of us are important in the slightest. Not me, not you."

"Thanks, that's really reassuring."

"Ha, and you can probably guess how important I think would-be alphas like Joseph and Brandon are."

"Hmm." I put a finger to my temple, pretending to consider. "So what is important, then?"

If ever a question was rhetorical, it was that one. Sailor shot me a conspiratorial smile, and we both raised our eyes to the long white building on the hill, that place of last refuge for the best things left in the world. Glowing like a beacon, like a warning.

San Francisco

Johannes led her to a door at the end of a hallway on the fifteenth floor. He pressed a key card to the sensor and it opened with a soft whoosh. Inside was a huge ballroom designed to contain hundreds of people. Stretching as far as she could see into the distance were cages. There were huge custom-built cages like the kinds they used to use to transport tigers in a circus. There were cages running the entire length of the ceiling, presumably for birds. There were cages with elaborate locking mechanisms, and cages within cages. It was like a nightmarish art installation. Johannes turned to look at her.

"We'll start moving the specimens in soon. It's going to be like nothing you've ever seen." Sailor didn't answer. She tried not to look at the cages, but they filled all her visual space. "So." Johannes smoothed his hair back, leaned against the wall, and studied her. "Here's where you come in. First off, we want a big cat. A jaguar, preferably."

She laughed this time. She couldn't help herself, it was so ludicrous. "Wouldn't it be smarter to start with something smaller? A sparrow, maybe?"

Something flickered across those dead green eyes. Not rage or anything as volcanic as that. More like annoyance at a bug who keeps evading being swatted.

"Used to be, people would pay a lot for animal skins," he said, curling his right hand into a half fist to examine the state of his fingernails. She had to admire how calm he could make his voice, almost singsong. "A crocodile bag, a snakeskin pair of shoes. But you can get way more for the live animal now, so no one bothers with that. And yet, there's still a trade for exotic skins. Huge demand for paper-thin suede on the black market now." He looked up, an expression of innocent inquiry lighting up his features. "I wonder where they're getting those skins from?"

Sailor's mouth went dry.

Johannes tugged at the skin on his wrist. "This . . . this makes the softest suede. You wouldn't believe it. The customers can't tell the difference. Or maybe they can, maybe they just don't care."

"Why are you asking me to do this?" she croaked out. "Why not one of the other workers?"

He raised his palms to demonstrate the question couldn't be answered. Or wouldn't be answered. It occurred to her that perhaps she wasn't the first person the cartel had approached.

"Listen, I'm really looking forward to working with you," he said, as if she were a new colleague at the bank and he was talking up the virtues of working at that particular branch. "Our organization is pretty new, but we've got big plans. Like, *big*."

In any other situation she might have been touched by his childlike enthusiasm, but the thought of supplying animals for the cartel made her want to throw up.

"Listen, I'll try, okay, but I can't promise any—"

She didn't get the whole sentence out before the force hit her. For one deranged moment as she was sailing through the air she thought some external neutral action had occurred—an earthquake flinging an object at her; a projectile crashing through the window—but it was simply his hands casually shoving her and forcing her body backward in space. Her coccyx bone hitting the edge of a cage hurt more than the shove had. It knocked the air out of her and she crumpled to the floor. He strolled closer to her, contained and focused as a cat.

She scuttled backward along the strip of carpet running down the middle of the room between the cages, shoulders drawn, waiting for the next blow. Even without his weapons, he was stronger than she was. Keeping eye contact was the only defiance she had left. But he didn't touch her again. Instead, he reached across and swung open the door of a large cage. Sailor glanced across and back, sizing up the cage and the intent in his eyes. He cocked his head and made a sweeping gesture with his hand to indicate she should step inside. It was so big she could walk through the entrance without stooping. Like it was made for her, or somebody like her.

Johannes shut the door to the cage and locked it with an old-fashioned metal key. Sailor thought about telling him that the setup was all wrong, they didn't have the proper safety mechanisms in place. The cage was intended for something big, and zoo protocol dictated there should be at least three heavy-duty doors between the captive animal and any humans that interacted with it, one of them preferably a steel guillotine door. She guessed it would just anger him, though, so she stayed silent. She realized she was wheezing and focused on trying to slow her breathing.

Johannes crouched down and looked through the wire at his catch. His hair had slipped from its bun during their tussle, and he smoothed it back.

He said, "I feel like we got off on the wrong foot."

"Oh, you think?"

He smiled then. He seemed to enjoy her sense of humor. "What I mean is, you think I hate the animals and I don't."

"I don't think that. I don't think of you at all."

She knew it was a risk, but he just shrugged. "Are you sure about that?"

"Are you flirting with me?"

He laughed, ever more delighted with his catch. "Maybe."

"Wow. I hate to think what your next stage of seduction might be."

He waggled his finger at her like she was a naughty pet. Which didn't seem too far from the truth. "You know, I wanted to be a vet when I was a kid."

"Oh yeah? What happened?" Her breath was coming slower now. A tiny relief. "Let me guess. Cartel life pays better."

"Sure. But still. I envy you."

"I get that a lot." Sailor made a sweeping gesture to indicate her surroundings.

"For real, though. Getting to be with animals all day. What's that like?"

All her cocky bravado fled her then. There was such yearning in his voice, and it broke down her defenses. "It's the best thing in the world," she said.

Johannes didn't respond, just nodded and looked off into the distance, at whichever other world contains the choices we don't make.

When he finally turned to leave she couldn't help it: a whimper escaped her. At the doorway he stopped, reached into his back pocket, and took out the key. He turned it around a few times in his fingers, then he walked back, stooped down, and placed it gently, almost tenderly, on the ground just outside the cage door. She could smell the clean, citric scent of whatever product he used on his hair.

She heard him leave, heard the clunk and whine of the elevator, but she elected to wait until long after his departure before she opened the lock and released herself from the cage. As the light at the windows turned slowly from silver to lavender to black, she thought about a time not so long ago when she had been inside another cage. She'd known fear and adrenaline that time too, but there had been something else. It spread warmth all through her, remembering how it had felt to cradle the chimp, crouched next to Camille—sweet Camille, who hated trouble but had chosen to run toward it—while all those unfriendly faces looked down on them. A feeling so rare and pure she felt sure she'd never know it again. The feeling of knowing she'd found her pack.

Later, she couldn't remember how she got out of the building, only that as she limped through the streets her adrenaline was pumping so hard it kept the pain at bay. Back on the island, she locked herself in a bathroom stall and took dozens of photos. She examined shoulders and clavicle, where a series of vivid bruises were already blooming. She tried to imagine being separated from this tender skin in which her physical self resided. She was the last of her kind. Wasn't there some responsibility in that?

Various scenarios presented themselves. She could do her time at Alcatraz then simply disappear, make a new life someplace they couldn't find her. But cartels had networks everywhere and would ferret her out no matter how far she ran. She could resign from Alcatraz. But no, she couldn't bear the thought of giving up her time with the animals. They were all the last of their kind too, and she owed them something. She made a decision then, the only one left to her. The kind that isn't really a decision at all.

Alcatraz

As the days grew longer and the one-year anniversary of Sailor's arrival approached, I buried myself in my work, trying to ignore the pall of unease that had settled over the island. Kira's belly was getting heavier—and the prize pool to guess the details of her baby's arrival was growing richer—but the situation with Achilles had only gotten worse. He'd failed to improve under Sailor's stewardship as we'd both hoped, despite her insistence on providing round-the-clock care. Early on in her new role she convinced the admins to procure a supply of black-market meat by claiming the Fake Steak was slowly killing him. The meat arrived at night, stealthily, aboard one of the helicopters, and Sailor swore Achilles perked up after the first few feedings. But after the supply ran out the admins informed her they wouldn't be able to continue because the Pinktons' connection had vanished. Instead, the crocodile's medications would be increased, because other zoos had seen success in the past with a different cocktail of meds.

Sailor raged about it to me in private. "He doesn't need more goddamn medication! He needs to live like a crocodile." But even she knew the Pinktons always got the last word.

It didn't help that the daily tours were grinding everyone's nerves to dust. It felt like no sooner had we recovered from one disruptive performance than another was upon us. The animals were becoming more stressed and less predictable, and there was a dramatic uptick in keepers visiting the hospital to patch up various injuries. While most of us kept our grievances to ourselves, Sailor wasn't so circumspect. She didn't care if the guards or admins overheard her complaining about the conditions she called intolerable for both humans and animals, and for reasons I couldn't yet fathom she never seemed to be disciplined for it.

But she wasn't the only unafraid one. Prentiss, one of the only keepers I'd ever heard Sailor praise, began to make his previously concealed feelings known. He started sitting with Sailor and me at dinner, and while I liked him well enough, the extra scrutiny he invited was unpleasant.

"It's an outrageous betrayal of the original charter," he loudly declared one night, in between taking furious stabs at the food on his plate. Heads swiveled our way. "Alcatraz is supposed to be a safe environment. We need to demand the zoo be converted into a purely conservation environment, pronto. No public access!"

Sailor nodded along while I stared in mortification at the table. It turned out Prentiss had always hated the tours, a common ground on which he and Sailor could enthusiastically meet up. I had no desire to join them there. Not that I didn't also resent the new frequency of the tours, but I would never rail against them as a concept. I knew enough to understand the symbiotic nature of these shows: without the guests there was no Alcatraz, and without Alcatraz there was no us.

But if Sailor and Prentiss knew that, they didn't show it. When I dipped back into the conversation they were animatedly discussing unionizing the workers. Unionizing! The image of Mr. Pinkton coming to the bargaining table was hilarious, if you chose not to imagine what would happen to the person who proposed it. The only right we'd ever had was the right to work here, and for most of us that was more than enough.

I stood up, indicating I was going to clear my plate and would see them later, and Sailor gave me a distracted smile and went back to listening to Prentiss. I made a point of looking straight ahead as I walked stiff-necked to the cleaning station, but I could feel the eyes on me anyway. It didn't matter that I didn't take part in these incendiary discussions: I had the mark on me just the same.

Then, one drizzly Saturday morning, our last timber wolf died. His name was Franklin, and he had once been part of a family pack of three wolves on the island. For two years he had been alone. He was a magnificent seventy-pounder with a silver-gray mane, bright white muzzle, and yellow eyes that regarded his world—what was left of it—with weary suspicion.

I was working in the snake enclosure when I heard a commotion coming from one avenue over. This old building has a way of both absorbing and distorting sound, so you can feel like you'd heard one thing and find out later it had been something completely different. I rushed out into the avenue—momentarily forgetting I still had a royal python draped around my neck—to find several other keepers emerging from their enclosures too, heads cocked and alert. There was no mistaking the note of distress in the call we'd all heard. Clanging rang out as people dropped their tools and doors swung shut behind them. There were a few minutes of confusion as everyone tried to work out where the sounds were coming from, until finally I heard someone shout, "Hey, over here! The wolf!"

A dozen or so of us arrived to find Prentiss cradling Franklin in his arms. The keeper was rocking back on his heels and crooning softly, Franklin's lolling head and huge front paws in his lap. There was something nightmarish about the way the wolf's body was positioned, something unnatural.

"He was fine a moment ago," Prentiss moaned. "I don't understand what's wrong with him!"

Four vets came running up, their soles slapping the concrete floor. The primates went absolutely bonkers as they passed, hooting high-pitched warnings, leaping and ricocheting off the walls of their enclosures. Most of the animals had learned to hate the sight of the Squeaky Shoes, but the great apes especially took exception to them. The chimps could be sweet and affectionate, but they held grudges.

Ignoring the outraged screeches, the vets hustled everyone out of the way and entered the enclosure, moving gingerly to surround the human-wolf tableau on the ground, their eyes fixed on Prentiss as though he were the dangerous one. A vet bent down and gently peeled Prentiss's hands from Franklin's fur, then pulled the keeper backward so the wolf slumped to the ground with a soft whumph. The same vet hooked his elbows under Prentiss's armpits and raised him to a standing position, then shoved him out of the way and rejoined his colleagues, who were all crouched on the floor examining Franklin.

One of them began performing CPR, while another got the paddles ready. They worked on the wolf right there, on the floor, as we all watched with breath held, but there was no response from Franklin's limp body. Then they all rose as one, an imposing, white-coated human wall of clinical expertise, and a stretcher materialized, and they hoisted the wolf onto it and carried him away to the hospital.

Later that day, two helicopters touched down on the helipad. One was a generic gray zoo chopper; the other was jade green and glossy and contained Mr. Pinkton. We assembled to hear him give a eulogy for the lost wolf. This was a tradition of sorts at Alcatraz. He had done the same when the jaguar before Feliz died.

Sailor sought me out in the barracks afterward. I was lying, red-eyed, in my bunk, staring at the slats above and trying to remember the last moment I'd had with Franklin. The banal tragedy of never knowing when something is happening for the last time. She seemed sunk in thought, not exactly distressed like I was, but disturbed in some way. "Care to take a stroll, Birdy?"

I nodded and scrambled to my feet, and we exited the barracks into a lavender twilight. Both choppers had departed and the island felt morbidly still. As soon as we were out of earshot of the guards, Sailor said, "Don't you think it's kind of convenient that it was Prentiss who found him? Prentiss who got assigned that enclosure today? The same Prentiss who's been agitating about docked wages and unions, getting on the admins' dicks about eliminating the tours?"

"What are you saying?" I sniffed morosely. "They deliberately killed Franklin to punish Prentiss?"

"Well, no," she said, in a way that convinced me she had been thinking just this. "But I think they knew Franklin was in his last days."

"They're going to deport him, aren't they?" Prentiss had scared me with his radical outspokenness, but he was a good person and my anger simmered at the injustice of such a punishment.

"Of course," Sailor said. "Troublemakers always get thrown into exile. If they're lucky."

Wanting to lighten the mood, I punched her lightly in the arm and said, "Surprising you haven't been deported then," but she didn't respond. "Hey, I'm only joking, sorry."

She blinked and then grinned at me, and I saw that she had returned from some faraway place. "Oh, don't think they wouldn't try something similar with me, Birdy."

"They'd better not," I said darkly, then we both laughed because who did I think I was?

That's when she told me about why she'd so far evaded any serious punishment for her various infractions. It turned out every time she'd "disappeared" she had been inside the admin center, where she'd been summoned to help try to secure more animals for Alcatraz and the Pinktons' future zoos. Specifically, the animals that became available after Paris and all the others had closed. This had been the condition under which her tenure at the zoo continued.

I started to ask *Why you*, but realized I already knew why: they assumed she still had connections in Paris. "I always wondered what happened to the animals after the zoos closed," I said. "We all did."

Sailor shook her head. "You don't even want to know. It's a shitshow out there. That's why the Pinktons are so desperate to get their hands on the merchandise, as it were. Before the cartels and the private collectors and fuck-knows-who-else gets them. Pinkton's got scouts all over the world tracking down leads."

"Wow. And were you able to help them?"

"Not really. I mean, all my Paris contacts have scattered to the winds. But I did find out something interesting. Something top secret."

"What?" I asked in a reverent whisper.

Sailor put her finger to her lips and led the way down to the agave garden, a lonely, unused path we sometimes traveled on our walks. The wind had picked up and it howled around us, setting our shirts and pant legs flapping, but she spoke close to my ear anyway.

"Remember the sanctuary I told you about?"

I nodded, my heart skittering.

"Some of the animals made it there."

"That's amazing," I said, and Sailor gave a satisfied smile. I couldn't help adding: "Do you think any animals will come here?"

"Probably. Depressingly. I mean, money talks. Anyway, it sucks about Prentiss," she said ruefully.

"It does," I said, and we stared out at the city, thinking about our fallen comrade.

As Sailor predicted, Prentiss never returned to Alcatraz. Put on a boat during the night without even the chance to say goodbye to his friends. Word drifted back that he ended up working in a windowless shipping warehouse somewhere, the kind with suicide nets installed. He was blameless, we all knew that, but this was how it always was when an animal disappeared. Someone had to pay.

San Francisco

Johannes was waiting for her at the Embarcadero. She saw him as soon as she stepped onto the gangway to exit the ferry. Bracing himself with one foot pressed against a wall, watching the boat come in. More boyish than she always pictured him when she was back on the island. Almost harmless. He looked genuinely pleased to see her, as he always did. He framed it as a treat, their getting together, like old friends with a standing date to play chess. As if she had a choice. Well, there were always choices, but if she didn't help him, he'd find someone else who would. She'd seen the way he looked across at the island. Ravenous, half-demented with desire. Dreaming about opening up the white building on the hill to get at what was locked inside. And Sailor—Sailor was the skeleton key to his dream. No matter how bad things got, she had sworn to herself, she wouldn't pass that burden on to anyone else. So she kept coming back.

Tight-lipped, she strode so briskly he had to practically jog to keep up. When he drew even, she said under her breath, "We can't be seen together." Already she'd clocked that Lupita, one of the other keepers on day release, had shot them a curious look.

"That hurts me, Sailor," he said. He put his hand to his heart and grinned, as if this was all a great lark, and she burned with hatred for him. "I don't have to use this, do I?"

She blinked, uncomprehending, and he opened the flap of his blazer ever so slightly so she could see the bulge of his weapon. She swallowed, a tide of fear rushing in to displace the hatred. A quick shake of the head.

"Good," he said, sounding relieved. "I feel like we're beyond that, don't you?"

"Sure."

"There's a place near here where we can talk."

They traveled through a maze of alleyways and arrived at an abandoned open-air shopping mall. Papered-up windows, shuttered play areas, small heaps of detritus blown into doorways. The forlornness of a former ice-cream booth, its soft-serve machine coated in a thick layer of dust. Johannes made a beeline for a particular bench that looked slightly cleaner than the others, and she realized this must be a regular place for him. It was both strange and slightly pathetic, like all his choices. He wiped the seat down and gestured for her to sit, then sat beside her, rolling one shoulder, then the other.

"This is nice," she said, looking around. The eyes of perfume models on billboards staring down at them, artificially joyous smiles frozen in perpetuity. "Real fallen-civilization vibes."

He laughed, amused as ever by his prize. "It's quiet."

The panic that attended being near him was rising like bile. She felt a clawing desire to delay the conversation that lay in wait, and glanced down at his smooth brown hands, fingers outspread on his knees. His nails were buffed to a pearlescent sheen. She didn't think she'd ever met a man so fastidious about his appearance.

"How on earth do you keep a tan like that in this foggy city?"

"I use a tanning bed."

"Those things will kill you."

He shrugged. "Got to die of something."

"I guess."

"You guess, huh?" Needling her. Then, as if a switch had flipped, he became instantly serious. "So here's the deal. My bosses want a timeline for the jaguar transfer."

Try to regulate your breathing, she told herself. Don't let your fear show.

"I'm working on it. But it's not simple, you know. There's a ton of security. Complicated logistics."

"They also want to know how you plan to pull this off on your own."

Sailor grasped around inside her panic and made a split-second decision. "I have a helper."

"Someone we can trust?"

"I trust them. They don't know anything about this and they won't ever know. They think they're helping me with something else. But they're the best there is."

Sailor watched Johannes consider this. "I believe you," he said at last. "You know why I believe you?"

"No." She hated his weird gangster gallantry. She hated how raspy her voice was.

He reached across and covered her hand with his own. A loving gesture, under some radically different set of circumstances. One of his rings pressed into her flesh, leaving an indent like the bite of a small creature. Her blood quickened.

"Because, my love, we know where to find you."

Alcatraz

There might have been more fallout from Prentiss's unceremonious deportation if the zoo hadn't soon after received a shipment of meerkats. They'd supposedly been in quarantine since Singapore Zoo closed and had finally been released into our care, although when the admins called an assembly to announce the news, Sailor dug her fingers into the back of my leg, and we exchanged a subtle look. More likely the Pinktons had won whatever bidding war or confrontation had gone down.

It was nominally spring by then, and many of the animals were responding by nesting, preening, and looking for mates they would never find. Spring is supposed to be hopeful, but in a place like this its arrival ushers in a sense of sadness. So the presence of new life, especially of such a busy, energetic variety, was mood-boosting enough to lift some of the gloom, even for Sailor, who was still smarting over how they had dealt with Prentiss. I was bothered by it too, but part of me hoped something good might come of it, that Sailor might at least see his expulsion as a cautionary tale. It certainly seemed that way for a while. She didn't become subdued, exactly, but she kept her head below the parapet, and I was relieved when each day ended without any new crisis.

On my most optimistic days, I warmed myself over the sputtering flame of an idea—that Alcatraz might be entering a kind of golden age. There was Kira and Titan's future baby, the first to be born in captivity since the blights began. A miracle, by any measure. And now there were the meerkats, and the promise they represented. If they had survived against the odds and made it all the way to our island, why shouldn't other animals follow?

The guests, not surprisingly, couldn't get enough of our pregnant elephant and our new arrivals. The MCs had trouble dragging the guests away from the meerkat enclosure to continue the tours. "It's like herding cats," Sailor told me after witnessing a particularly recalcitrant group one day. "The MCs are beside themselves." We made fun of the guests, but in truth, we keepers weren't much better. We would all make excuses during the day to pass by the enclosure, casting looks of envy through the shimmering bars at whichever keeper had scored the assignment. Unlike some of the established animals, the meerkats appeared to have developed no sense of their own mortality, or even of their confinement. The parameters of their world—consisting entirely of the simple and easily met needs of food, water, shelter, and the company of their own kind—were perfectly pleasing to them. They were in utter harmony with their *umwelt*.

There's a common perception about animals in captivity that's been around way longer than the quarter century I've been alive and will no doubt exist until this island crumbles into the sea, that small enclosures are horrifically cruel. But here's a zookeeper secret: some animals like small spaces. There are certain creatures that will wither away in captivity—great white sharks, migratory birds—because they don't think like we do, they think in terms of continents and oceans, and they cannot be separated from their instinct to roam. But plenty of others seem content to lead sedentary lives and never display signs of restlessness or cabin fever. They can even become lazy, which is why enrichment is so important. Given half a chance, an animal whose material needs are being met will take the opportunity to sleep more. They're like humans in that way. Sailor and I came up with precise calculations: if in the wild a creature would normally spend, say, ten hours a day sleeping, but in the zoo environment they're able to sleep for fifteen hours, then we need to keep them awake and occupied for those five hours to give them a chance to act out their natural behaviors. Insofar as that's possible. Of course, there are exceptions, and they tend to be tragic—the jaguar, the lone wolf, the elephants forever searching for their lost matriarch.

Perhaps I've given the impression that Sailor and I were in complete accord when it came to the animals. But our philosophies often diverged. Sailor wouldn't agree that some animals thrive in small enclosures. She also wouldn't accept that the animals loved us and sought out our company, no matter how we wanted to believe it so. She felt it was okay for us to love them—crucial, even—but where we slipped up was expecting that love to be requited.

We argued good-naturedly about all this. I took the position that in an ideal world every animal and bird and reptile would live its life free in the wild, but given the state of our world, the moral imperative for humans was to help protect the remaining species before they all went extinct. Sometimes—in fact almost always now—that meant zoos. Or this zoo. The last one. Sailor never bought it, though. She would just give me a skeptical look when I tried to justify how essential the zoo was. She was a radical and I was bound so tightly to the status quo I couldn't see beyond it.

While we were on a break together one evening outside the meerkat enclosure, watching the mob wreak delightful havoc, I mentioned the common perception that animals haven't developed our sophisticated cognition because they're too busy chasing the lower parts of Maslow's hierarchy of needs—food, shelter, etc.—and therefore don't feel as deeply as we do. What if that isn't true, my theory went, and instead animals have just as rich and complex inner lives as we do? Especially in captivity or in a domesticated situation. Maybe captivity actually *encourages* it, because the animals have more time in which to develop personalities and pursue the kind of recreation that leads to discovery. I'd seen it with my own eyes, creatures using their ample spare time to solve puzzles or become fascinated by their own reflection in a mirrored surface or subtly change their language to communicate with creatures they wouldn't normally encounter, like us. Think of Koko the gorilla. Think of Alex the parrot.

I presented these thoughts to Sailor like a gift. She pondered for a moment, nodding, and I grew certain she was going to agree with me this time.

"Interesting," she said. "I accept it's possible that captivity fosters a deeper inner life. But what about if that makes life even more torturous for them? I mean sure, a tiger could be lying around thinking about cat calculus, but they could also be thinking about wanting to kill themselves. If they develop a heightened ability to feel things, to reason and worry, wouldn't that be exacerbated by being locked up?"

I didn't have any answer to that. I still don't.

I've said Sailor and I shared everything, and that was mostly true if you don't count her mysterious visits to the mainland. But there was one other incident she kept from me. I knew only because I happened to witness it. It took place just after a tour had wound up, as I was making my way from the commissary to the enclosures with buckets of feed. The last of the guests had exited through the gift shop and the zoo had lurched back into life, like a giant stretching after a sleep. I was walking along the second-story catwalk on Michigan Avenue when I heard Sailor talking, low and unintelligibly, to someone whose voice was unfamiliar to me. I didn't want to be nosy but I was curious, so I leaned my head over the railing, intending to catch her eye and wave or exchange a few words of banter, I don't really know what I had in mind.

I saw Sailor huddled outside Feliz's cage, her head bent while a strange man berated her. I stared at my friend's neck as an awful feeling traveled up my own, a prickling like the anticipation of thunder. I didn't like how close the man was standing to her, and I liked even less that she had twisted her body away from his, as though she feared him. The man had black ear gauges and golden-brown hair pulled back in a bun, and as he turned I saw the lanyard around his neck indicating he was a guest on tour.

I watched as he gestured mockingly toward Feliz's enclosure. "What is this shit?" His voice rang out loud and clear, like he didn't care who heard him. That was typical of guests. "I came here to see a magnificent wildcat, not some mangy . . . whatever that is."

Anger spiraled through me. I was sure Sailor would leap to Feliz's defense. She raised her face, and while she forced a polite smile I could see the rage in her eyes. "I can't do anything about the state of the animals," she said. Her body was still and calm but those eyes were as livid as I've ever seen them. "Sir."

The man drew his shoulders back and for a hot blinding moment I thought he might try to hit her. I placed the buckets on the floor. But the man seemed to think better of it and took a step back. I let my held breath out. Another keeper hurried past, glancing with mild interest at the scene. It was unusual enough to see a guest outside the tour group, let alone talking to a keeper. Although Sailor was more than that, she was a high-ranking employee now, so I suppose they assumed she had some business with the man. The two of them watched the other keeper out of sight, then the man spoke again.

"You're going to have to do better than that, Sailor," he said, so quietly this time I had to strain to hear. It shocked me not so much that he used her name—we all wore name tags while tours were on and were trained to encourage conversation if a guest approached us—but the way in which he said it. There was menace but something else too. I'd heard that tone before in married couples on tour. It was something to do with ownership. Like she belonged to him.

San Francisco

During the crossing, the sea rolled under the ferry's hull like a living thing. Sailor's gut churned and she wished she could flee back to the refuge of the rock. An unexpected turn of events, this aching desire to stay on Alcatraz. To miss it during those brief but harrowing hours she spent ashore.

She continued to try the number for the sanctuary whenever she returned to the mainland, although more as a comforting reflex than with any expectation of a response. It didn't occur to her to give up: there would be a way to find them when the time came, she was convinced of that. But she no longer tried to contact Anouk. Not because she didn't miss her or had ceased to worry about her welfare, but because she knew—in the same intuitive way she knew about the sanctuary—she'd never hear from Anouk or any of the others from Paris again. That world was lost to her, and there was nothing to be gained by trying to find it.

Two new preoccupations loomed in the forefront of her life now: Alcatraz, and her reunions with Johannes. She could have refused to see him, but what good would that have done? Better to meet him here, on neutral soil away from inquisitive eyes, than have him visit her place of work again. The memory sent streams of shame and rage rushing through her.

She had barely got out the first few words of the justification—"Listen, about the jaguar"—when he interrupted her. A pebble of importance in the mountainous scheme of things, but it was infuriating knowing he could cut her off anytime, and she didn't dare reciprocate, not unless she wanted a taste of the back of his hand again.

"The plan has changed," he said. "No jaguar."

She swallowed her angry retort. Maybe if she stayed obedient and quiet, he'd relent and set her free. *Maybe*, she heard Anouk's voice chime in her head, *they'll build mansions on the moon and you could go live in one of them!* That was the kind of thing Anouk would say to the new keepers when they expressed naive ideas about zoo life. The Anouk in her head—possibly the only place she existed anymore—was right, though: displaying meekness would only make someone like Johannes crueler. Better to let him believe she loved engaging in their usual witty repartee than let him sense her fear.

"Can't *wait* to hear what else you have in mind," she replied with as much sass as she could muster.

"Oh you're going to die when you hear."

He told her what they wanted, then waited with bright-eyed anticipation for her next parry. But she felt deathly tired suddenly. Her shoulders and neck slumped forward, as if her bones had rubberized.

Perhaps she'd been wrong about his disdain for weakness because he switched into a more genuine, sympathetic mode then.

"You know, my bosses wanted to know what the holdup is, but I told them these things take time. I told them a helicopter would help. They said okay, we can maybe do a chopper, airlift the animal out." He must have misinterpreted the reason for her horrified expression because he added, "Don't worry, we've done it before. It just takes a lot of cojones to dodge the gunfire."

"Listen," she said, urging her body into an upright posture again. "We don't need any of that. I'll make it work."

Johannes's mouth twisted with skepticism, or maybe he was sulking about his daring prison break being taken off the table. Sailor had to stop herself from grabbing his arm and shouting in his serene face. Instead she counted to three in her head and found her calmest voice.

"Don't worry, okay? I have another plan. It was going to work for the jaguar and it will work for this. I just can't talk about it yet because the details are still being hammered out."

How crazy it felt to be talking to this man—this person who wouldn't blink an eye at murder, who talked about skinning human beings as if he were discussing the weather—like she was a mother trying to placate her child. When she was the one who felt like a child, wailing into the darkness, desperate to be consoled. But there was no one to say it to her, the words she was saying to him, and she knew there never would be now.

Hush, everything is going to be fine. Don't worry, don't worry.

Alcatraz

When did the small transgressions start to give way to the larger ones? It must have been a process, but it was one that played out beyond my notice, because I was woefully unprepared the day Sailor shared her big plan—the culmination of all her little rebellions—with me.

We were sitting on a rocky cliff edge set at the northwestern end of the island, a precipitous and windblown locale Sailor had begun to favor for its isolation and the booming soundscape of waves that covered our voices. With a little imagination, you could easily pretend you were the only ones alive out there. I was in that half-dreaming state I sometimes fell into beneath the dome of the night sky, trying to make out individual landmarks within the smudged pastel glow of the city skyline. I heard her say the words, I understood each of them as discrete words, but at first I couldn't make sense of how they related to one another. I turned slowly toward her, scared already of the words, of the power they had, now that they were released and could never be unsaid.

"You want to smuggle the crocodile off the island?" I thought by repeating the words they might lose some of their power, but instead they seemed to swell monstrously the moment they left my mouth.

"Exactly," Sailor said in a matter-of-fact tone, as if she already knew I'd agree. "Are you in?"

"No," I said, shaking my head so hard I could feel things rattling around in there. "I am emphatically not in."

She laughed in a dark, almost cruel way. "Oh, come on. You've seen him. It's all for Achilles. He deserves to live a good life."

"Yeah, well, so do we," I said, but this straightforward truth didn't have any effect on her. She seemed haloed by an otherworldly light, some wicked intent streaming through her. "I don't understand," I said desperately. "Why would we risk everything?"

Sailor appeared to ponder this. "Can't you feel it?"

"Feel what?"

"If we don't do something they're going to win." Her voice was low and ominous, like when a freighter's horn sounds through the mist.

My lips quivered with cold. "*Who's* going to win, Sailor?"

She took a deep breath in through her nose, a loving but exasperated gesture. "The Pinktons of the world, that's who." Her voice was so soft it was almost a whisper. I had to lean close to hear. "The donors. The cartels. The animals will keep disappearing and the climate refugees will keep coming, and one day all of us will be crowded into a tiny area to fight for our lives, our own little Alcatraz."

I flailed about for something to lighten the mood, but my mind was a panicked blank. "What about the sanctuary?" I said at last, turning to look at her.

Sailor blinked slowly and it was the most amazing thing, it was as though that word—"sanctuary"—was a homing beacon, leading her back to safety.

"Yes," she said, "exactly, the sanctuary. That's what we have to keep our sights on." Focus restored, she grasped my hands, almost crushing my fingers. "Listen, Birdy, it's going to be a bit complicated but it's going to work. We're going to get him off the island and we're going to take him to that sanctuary we talked about." With her fingers pressed against mine, a jolt of recognition went through me, recalling the very first day we met, when we had spontaneously clasped hands watching Titan's arrival. Except her hands had been warm then, and this time they were cold. It felt like several decades had passed since that day instead of only a year.

"I don't know," I said in my smallest and most wretched voice. In that moment I swear I had no intention of even considering what she was asking. But she was smart, my friend. Instead of trying further to persuade me, she just sat there in companionable silence, eyes closed, holding my hands inside her own, as if she were protecting them, until my mind had uncoupled from the present and wandered back into some of the events leading up to this night, back to when Sailor had tried to improve Achilles's diet and been shut down, and when they had casually thrown her in a dungeon just for trying to share a few moments of lightness with us, and when the Pinktons had increased the tours because money mattered more to them than the happiness of the animals, and when they had deported Prentiss to send a message to anyone who might stand in the way of their plans, and my heart cracked and then hardened, and a faint rage began to beat there. I'm not sure it has ever stopped.

Sailor, as if expecting and sensing this inner shift, spoke then, as sincere as I'd ever heard her. "Here's the thing, Birdy. I can't do it without you."

She must have known how those words would work on me. Even as I resisted, I could feel myself being drawn in by my hopeless desire to be indispensable to her. Talk about an Achilles's heel.

In the days that followed I pinned my hopes on desperate things. I hoped she'd been sneaking too much from her flask the night she suggested breaking Achilles out. I hoped she'd tell me it was all a joke to test my loyalty. I hoped she'd see the lethal, treasonous folly of even thinking about such things. But the rational part of me knew she had meant it and there would be no changing her mind.

Sailor would only talk about "our" plan when we were on the move or on the cliff edge, backs against a rock and feet dangling over the void. Never indoors or even close to a building. I didn't need to be told why, but it scared me even more that she was finally exercising caution, as if all the other forbidden things she'd done had only been a practice run. The other keepers and the guards thought us insane, swaddled in our coats with beanies pulled down over our eyebrows, striding through the darkness, our breath curling like smoke. Sometimes Sailor insisted we wear respirators, even when the air pollution was low, and those were the times I knew we were going to be discussing the kinds of things that could get us thrown in prison for real. It made me feel sick to even consider breaking the rules at the best of times, but this, this was egregious, unthinkable. Except that Sailor *had* thought of it. Sometimes it seemed like it was all she thought of.

"What about if something happens to him while we're trying to get him out?" I remember asking one night as we rounded the corner of the Agave Trail. "You get prison time for killing some types of scarab beetles, for fuck's sake!"

Sailor stopped and faced me, her hands on my shoulders. "Listen to me. I'd never let anything bad happen to Achilles. And if I'm not around, you have to take over looking after him, okay?"

"Don't talk like that."

"We all have to talk like that. Everyone should make plans for when they're not here anymore."

"Like a will?"

"No, not a will. Who gives a shit about that old-school bureaucracy, like it matters who gets some old fucker's money after he croaks. No, I mean protecting the things you love if you're not there to protect them anymore."

"What are you talking about?"

I was close to frustrated tears. The moon slipped out from behind a bank of clouds, revealing the silhouettes of freighters out at sea. They seemed suddenly to gain sentience, to be observing us. I shivered, feeling some ancient curse stirring.

"Hey." Sailor cupped my face in her cold hands. "Hey, Birdy. Come on now. All I'm saying is that I don't intend to stay on this island my whole life. But I'd never ask you to leave if you're not ready. So I want to make sure there's someone left who cares about the animals like I do. Like we do."

Fine. She placated me then, as she always managed to do. But even she couldn't turn illogic into logic. Strip away all the emotional appeals, and the logistics of it were still impossible. A crocodile isn't a toucan egg or a cedar waxwing. He is an apex predator with a jaw strength of 3,700 pounds per square inch and the dentition to crunch through bone. Not to mention, the specific crocodile in question lived in a militarized zoo on an island pummeled by storms and patrolled by a private coast guard who were trained to shoot to kill. So, the question remains: What changed my mind?

Listen, I could try to weave a story about how I valiantly overcame my risk-averse nature and found courage. Or that my fears were quelled once the details were fully explained and laid out. Or that I remained scared but decided the moral justice of freeing Achilles outweighed the personal dangers to his captors. The truth is, I was terrified Sailor was going to leave me behind, and out of that terror emerged a kind of reckless conviction.

San Francisco

There were more people clogging the city's arteries than she'd ever seen before. She mentally sorted them into two categories: eye contact—vendors, couriers, hawkers of various things—and eyes downcast—refugees, immigrants, the untethered, people fleeing one calamity only to find themselves snared in another. It all made her feel lonely. And gave her a strong sense that whatever was on the verge of happening, she was no longer part of it and could only observe as it streamed by.

She stopped at a run-down souvenir stall and impulsively bought a plastic Eiffel Tower key ring for Camille, who'd always seemed entranced by Sailor's stories about Paris. What harm was there in propping up the fantasy of the city as it existed in her friend's imagination? She slipped the tacky bauble into her pocket and worried it between her finger and thumb as she made her way through the crowded streets. The problem remained how to protect Camille. Not just during the terrible and daunting task that lay ahead, but also after that. Sometimes she reminded Sailor of her younger self, and in a funny way this was a consolation, because Sailor herself had been naive and scared at the beginning, when Anouk had taken her under her wing. And after all, she had leveled up, hadn't she? But on the other hand, Camille was a different person than even the softest version of Sailor had been. More sensitive, less quick to anger. Sailor ran her thumb along the side of the Eiffel Tower, no closer to peace of mind.

After her appointments were done there was still some time until the ferry, so she took a graffiti-covered cable car to Chinatown and wandered the streets, wrapped in the comfort of her anonymity. Because she could never be sure she wasn't being followed, she had become adept at maintaining spatial awareness at all times, but she saw nothing that struck her as suspicious. Maybe Johannes really did trust her.

She slipped inside a narrow bookstore and in the neglected history room in the back corner, after quickly casing to ensure she was alone, she performed the rote gesture of trying the sanctuary. But this time the call tone sounded slightly different—quicker and shriller than usual—and she had to put a hand out to a bookshelf to steady herself. She cleared her throat, panicking about what to say if someone answered. It had been so long she'd given up on rehearsing a spiel. There was a soft click and a pause in which she would later convince herself she heard breathing, then the call ended. Her eyes unexpectedly brimming, she buried her phone away in her bag and hurried out. Just an allergic reaction, of course, to the dust accumulated on all those unturned pages.

On the street, her attention was caught by a glossy limo pulled up to a stoplight. It took a moment for her eyes to adjust to the lightly tinted window. Inside the car, a woman in a bright pink coat had her nose pressed to the window, and she was holding up a sleek white rat to the glass, as if it had requested to watch the world go by. As the lights changed and the driver slowly moved into the next block of snarled traffic, Sailor raised her hand in a wave. The woman was oblivious, possibly only seeing her own reflection, but Sailor could have sworn the rat met her gaze, its pink nose twitching and eyes gleaming with the secret knowledge of its own kind.

Alcatraz

The next time we visited the rooftop of the Officers' Club, I noticed Sailor running her hands over the stained stone columns and peering up into the shadowy recesses before we clambered up.

I wrapped my arms around my chest. "What are you doing?"

In the weeks since Sailor had announced her plan, I had become a vibrating bundle of neuroses: a woman of backward glances, worn-down tooth enamel, compulsive foot-tapping. Nerves jangling at the commonplace sound of a foghorn. Sailor didn't answer, but she didn't need to: I knew she was checking for surveillance devices. That should have been consolation, proof I wasn't the only one on edge, but instead it made me feel worse.

I swung between wanting more details regarding how the Liberation of Achilles—the LOA, as Sailor insisted we call it—was going to work, and wanting to speak about anything else. For the most part, Sailor kept a veil of secrecy draped over what would happen when we left the island. *If* we left the island, I always silently added.

"The less you know the better, Birdy," she assured me the first time I pestered her about specifics.

"Like the low-ranking henchman in a heist?"

She laughed. "Sure, if that's how you want to think about it."

"So I can't give anyone up when they torture me?"

"*Mon dieu*, girl! No one is going to get tortured. It's just easier if I handle that side of things, that's all. My sanctuary contacts prefer it this way as well."

She knew mentioning the sanctuary soothed me, and I couldn't even resent the trick, because it clearly soothed her too.

That night on the roof, she finally stopped being evasive. She had set a date for our leaving, she informed me. Four weeks from now. It would be a new moon on the night she had chosen, dark enough to provide cover. Her friends had confirmed their part in the escape. All I had to do was be ready, and help her devise a plan to get Achilles to the waiting boat.

Oh, was that all? I shivered as though I were naked to the biting wind instead of wrapped inside my warmest coat.

Sometimes, on the rare occasions when the zoo experiences a moment of silence, I like to stop and listen to the water making its way through the buildings as though through the veins of a sleeping giant. It is carried around the island in pipes ranging from tiny tubes to echoing chambers taller than a baby giraffe. It pleases me to imagine the water running along these channels in the darkness, secret rivers flowing beneath our feet and above our heads. The tributaries are never still. Gurgling, trickling, gushing, dripping, rushing.

The challenge of breaking Achilles out of Alcatraz came down to one factor, as far as Sailor was concerned: we had to get him down to the water. Sailor's friends from the mainland would be waiting near the island, she told me, and would use their high-tech boat to sneak us and the crocodile away to the sanctuary.

"These friends," I pestered her. "How do we know we can trust them?"

"They're legit, don't worry," she said. "But, Birdy, listen, it's dangerous, all right? Better if I'm the only one who deals with them. In fact, better if you don't even know their names for now. All we have to worry about is getting that big boy down to the water."

We batted the problem back and forth, always referring to the future act itself as liberation, never smuggling or kidnapping or insanity. Never speculating, not even once, about what exactly it would look like if we failed.

"We need to sneak him out through the building somehow," said Sailor. "Maybe through the pool in his cage. Where does that lead to? Is there a pipe we can slip him through?"

The pipe was too small, I explained. The pool emptied via a drain not large enough for a full-grown crocodile.

"Well you've been here longer than I have, Birdy." I could hear the exasperation in her voice. "Think!"

It was as though her impatience dislodged something in my brain, because at these words a memory broke loose. "So, okay, listen, I've just remembered there's an old sewer pipe running through the basement. I saw it once. Kind of spooky. Not sure if it's in use anymore. I think it empties out into the bay . . . or used to."

"Wait, what? Tell me more."

I didn't have much more to tell, but it didn't matter. I could see the gears working in Sailor's head.

The new problem was getting access to the basement. It was off-limits apart from the maintenance crew and the guard who worked that section. There was nothing top secret or sinister there, as far as any of us knew, just some machinery and generators. It wasn't as though anyone was agitating to get down there, so it wasn't a high-security zone, but you still needed clearance and a good reason, neither of which were at our disposal.

"Who's on duty there?" Sailor asked.

"It's usually Benjie."

"Hmm, okay. Let's work out how to get past him."

Pulled recklessly along by the success of my first idea, I found myself saying brightly, "I think I know how." Sailor looked intently interested, so I forged on. "Benjie has a routine," I explained. "Every day at four thirty p.m. he meets Wesley for a cigarette at the entrance. And I've noticed he always leaves his jacket and his ID hanging in that staff closet near the basement stairs. The basement doesn't need a fingerprint like the enclosures, just the ID chip."

"So you're saying we could 'borrow' his ID while he's having a smoke?" Sailor said. "That's not a bad idea."

I stammered into a tangent about the routines of creatures both wild and captive. How when you work with animals you notice that they tend to do the same thing at the same time each day, even if that's just selecting a particular seed first or licking a particular paw. How my childhood friend the rat demonstrated this principle through his habitual, meticulously plotted movements around our yard. "Humans are the same," I said in the final windup. "That's how I know Benjie will briefly leave his post every day at four thirty for his cigarette. That's when we could sneak into the closet and take the pass."

A beat of what I hoped was awed silence passed.

"Or," Sailor said. "Hear me out. What about if we just asked Benjie if he could let us down there?"

I laughed because of course she was right. "Yeah," I said. "That could also work."

Sailor and I stood on the dimly lit landing, staring into the void that led to the basement. Benjie stood with us, and I noticed with a kind of appreciation that his black pants were unusually tight, snug around his muscular thighs. I'd never paid him much attention before: the guards were a monolith to me. He wasn't looking at me, though, but at Sailor.

"What do you guys want down there anyway? Some privacy?"

He said this with a hopeful leer. Sailor tossed him one of her easy smiles, and I marveled at her ability to remain relaxed in tense situations.

"I told you, Benjie, we're amateur ghost hunters. Camille here read on a paranormal site that the basement is haunted, so we wanted to go down there and check for supernatural vibrations." She opened her jacket and pulled her flask halfway out of the inner pocket, shook it while giving him a lascivious wink. Benjie laughed, and I blushed to the roots of my hair, not fully interpreting the implications flying around but guessing enough of the gist to feel teenager-awkward. The explanation and Sailor's demonstration seemed to satisfy him, and he flashed his pass to let us in, one hand resting lightly on his pistol, legs planted wide like he was straddling an invisible horse. I think he knew how good he looked in those pants.

Down we went. I can't recall which of us started the giggling, but it quickly infected the other until we were both wheezing with laughter, clutching each other as we descended the twenty steps. I wondered if Benjie was still standing at the top, watching us, but I didn't dare look back. When we arrived at the bottom, Sailor snapped into seriousness and keyed in the code Benjie had given us. The door swung open and we were hit with a blast of stagnant air. A panel of overhead lights clicked on as we passed the threshold, and the door whooshed shut behind us. The farthest corners of the basement were obscured in shadow. Large pipes ran overhead and along the edges of the walls, and the sound of rushing water, a muffled backdrop up above, was thunderous down here. It felt like being inside one of those machines in hospitals that keep people alive.

After a few minutes the dankness gave way to a subtler but more pungent smell, an off-putting mix of earthiness and rusty metal, like old blood. I hadn't been in the basement for a long time, not since my orientation as a trembling neophyte, but I remembered the smell, and I remembered the sewer pipe. It didn't look like anything from where we were because it was covered by a large manhole. When you opened the manhole there was a short drop into a carved-out tunnel with a pipe that ran off in two directions, one back toward the zoo, and the other sloping down to the cliffs. I remember someone joking it would make a good waterslide.

The manhole was at the farthest end of the basement, concealed from sight by the generators and other equipment. We wended our way through and stood, looking down on it. The cover was heavy and old and looked as if it hadn't been moved in years. The two of us pulled on the oxidized iron handle, straining and groaning, until it reluctantly peeled away from its seal and we were able to hoist it open. I opened my hands and my palms were streaked red with rust. A blast of stale air rushed up. Sailor knelt and stuck her upper body down the hole, playing her flashlight around.

"This will do nicely, Birdy," she said, emerging. She put her palm flat for me to slap it. Her skin was striped red as well, and I felt like we were performing a blood oath. I took my turn looking inside. There was a shallow, sludgy trickle of water at the bottom of the pipe but it didn't smell bad like I expected, just pleasantly mossy, like the way Sailor had once described me. It might have still been in use as an overflow from the showers or something, but clearly they had replaced most of the old pipes with new ones when the prison had been converted into a zoo.

I pulled myself back into the open air and wiped my hands. Sailor's cheekbones jutted stark and ghoulish under the unforgiving light.

"Did you hear it?" she asked.

"What?" I pretended not to know what she meant, because I didn't want to admit it scared me.

"The ocean!" She cupped her hands around her mouth and made a kind of moaning that sounded uncannily like the sound I'd heard traveling up the pipe. "The sirens, they're calling us."

"Oh, cool. Is not answering an option?"

"Absolutely not! Listen, we could easily fit Achilles through here, then basically slide all the way to freedom. We have to find out if it's still open at the other end, and where it empties to."

"Oh, no. No way."

"Birdy," she said, giving me a wheedling look. "There's no other way."

"I'm not going down there. You're not going down there."

"*Au contraire*," she said breezily.

"But we don't have any of the . . . stuff we need."

"What stuff? We just need our two bodies."

"Yeah, that's what I'm afraid of, our two bodies being found wedged and rotting in a sewer pipe."

"It's just a reconnaissance mission, Birdy. In and out. We'll come back once we know what tools we need."

It had been one thing to stand outside the pipe and look in, my feet firmly on the ground. It was another thing entirely to descend into that terrifying void. Sailor went first. I felt a flutter of anxiety as first her legs and feet, then her torso, then her head and shoulders disappeared. Swallowed whole. But then I heard her voice, faint and low like she was trying to whisper, telling me that it was fine and to come on in. Claustrophobia pressed down on me, but I lowered myself in anyway. I was determined to be brave, because if I had to do this for real, I couldn't afford to lose my nerve. There wasn't much water in the pipe, thankfully, just a rusted, greenish sludge. The tunnel wasn't big enough to stand upright, so we proceeded on hands and knees, me following Sailor. The worst part, in a way, was the voices. They echoed in my ears, their murmured utterings never resolving into words I could understand.

"Who is that?" I gasped, peering into the gloom at the soles of Sailor's boots.

She tilted her head up. "It's just sounds from the shower room. Nothing to worry about." Perhaps in a bid to distract me, Sailor began to tell a story about being a child in Florida. "I think it's my first memory," she said, her voice floating back to meet me. "I was a toddler, and I remember rolling around on a rug like toddlers do. But it wasn't just me. There was a small caiman right next to me, rolling around as well. Like a brother from another mother."

"A small what?" My own voice sounded trembly and weird.

"A caiman. Family: Alligatoridae. Order: crocodilian. Picture a miniature croc with a short, blunt snout. Real cute."

"Oh. I've never seen one."

"I think there's even a photo of it somewhere. If you want to know why I turned out the way I did, it's because my parents let me play with large reptiles." She laughed, and her mirth pinged off the walls.

"That sounds fun," I said, and meant it sincerely.

"Yeah, it was."

I don't know if it was the unfamiliar surroundings or a simple desire to offer a story in return, but I finally felt safe enough, deep in that treacherous tunnel, to talk about my own family. "Did I ever tell you what happened to my dad?"

Sailor stopped descending and I could sense her entire attention trained up toward my voice. No way out but through, now.

"So . . . I told you my dad used to drive for Mr. Pinkton, right? Well, one day when he came home he was really jittery and angry about something, but he wouldn't tell us what it was. Mom got so mad at him, but he just clammed up, told us not to worry. He started acting really erratically after that, like not leaving the house whenever he wasn't working, and drinking a lot. Snapping at Mom and me. And listening to those, you know, conspiracy theory guys, late into the night."

"Ugh, I'm sorry, Birdy."

I crouched there, wishing I hadn't started.

"Anyway, one day he just didn't come home from work. Mom called the Pinktons' office and they said they hadn't seen him. Mr. Pinkton had to get a backup driver. I remember they seemed really pissed about it." I laughed, even though the memory was the opposite of funny. "Mom was totally distraught. She called the Pinktons' office every day, getting increasingly hysterical, but they swore they didn't know where he was. The police just brushed us off, of course. People disappear all the time, you know?"

"Yeah, I know," came Sailor's voice. "I'm so sorry."

"Mom got obsessed, she started listening to all the same conspiracy stuff. Government plots, corporations who had inconvenient people disappeared, that kind of paranoia. She'd chase any lead she heard about on these forums. One big theory was that there are these hard labor camps dotted around South America for the purpose of building, I think, doomsday bunkers for rich people? And the idea is random people are trafficked to work in them. She went to Argentina to investigate one of these rumors and she just sort of stayed there."

"She left you behind?"

"I wanted to go with her but she insisted I stay. I'd already been offered this job, Dad set it up before he disappeared, and I think she wanted to know at least one person in her family was safe."

"Did you ever find out what happened to him?"

"No." I took a shuddery breath. "For a while I had this whole fantasy about how he'd hit his head and blacked out or something, was living a second life somewhere without knowing he'd ever had a family. But that was just kid stuff. I think now it was something more mundane. Got hit by a car or something. His body taken to one of those homeless morgues. I certainly don't think he's alive and working on a doomsday bunker chain gang in Argentina." It felt necessary to state this so Sailor didn't think I bought into the conspiracy theories too. "But you know, it brings my mom comfort. She lives in the campo with a bunch of other women, widows I guess, all looking for their lost loved ones. That's why I don't go back to the mainland. There's no one there for me anymore. Anyway." My head ached. I felt wrung out by this unplanned confession. "I miss him. He was a good dad. A good person."

"Of course he was," Sailor said. "May his memory be a blessing. But I wonder." I fancied I heard the soft rubbing of thumb against tooth.

"Wonder what?"

"Oh nothing. It's just, driving for Mr. Pinkton. Wonder if someone saw him as a potential courier."

"Courier? For what . . . drugs?"

"Maybe. Or maybe something way more valuable. Hey, we should get going, I think I see light at the end of the tunnel, so to speak."

She was right. A watery light had begun to illuminate the sides of the tunnel. Within a few seconds I could no longer hear the voices over the muffled booming of the sea. The light grew steadily brighter until it dazzled us. When we reached the end, there was a perfectly round hole covered by a set of heavily rusted crosshatched bars. Ivy had grown across the bars. We squatted down together on the slimy floor. Dark blue diamonds of sky peeked through the patches between the ivy. We shuffled closer, peered out through the grating as a thin but steady trickle of liquid dribbled between our feet into the sea below. We were positioned above a rocky cove on what I guessed was the leeward side of the island.

"Perfect," Sailor whispered. She reached through and pushed aside tendrils of creepers to reveal a wedge of ocean, the white sail of a distant boat. The bars were so rusted the surface crumbled beneath the touch. We opened our fingers and let the breeze whip the reddish flakes away. Maybe it was my imagination, but the air smelled so clean.

"Come on, we should get back," Sailor said. She turned to face the gloom of the tunnel. The way back was easier. I knew what to expect and the darkness didn't seem so oppressive this time. The voices were still swirling around, but they had lost their creepiness. As we picked our way back up the clammy slope, I hoped Sailor would tell me more stories from her childhood but she didn't, she just kept up a quiet almost melancholy humming, like it was a private conversation she was having with herself.

We climbed out of the tunnel and back into the mindless roar of the basement, pushing the manhole cover back into place and wiping our hands on the rags we kept in our back pockets. I had no idea how much time had passed. It might have been an hour or a week. "Wait." At the door that led back to the world, Sailor tousled her hair and smudged her lipstick with the back of her hand. When we got back upstairs, Benjie was waiting, still wearing that lecherous grin. He reeked of smoke.

"Find any ghosts, girls?"

Sailor winked at him. "Baby, the place is lousy with them."

He seemed to find this extremely funny, clutching the gun at his side as he laughed. Then he waved us away while making a shooing noise, like we were chickens.

At Sailor's insistence, we returned to the scene a week later. I tried unsuccessfully to make her reconsider the whole idea.

"I've got a bad feeling about this," I said. An impressive understatement. "I think people are getting suspicious."

She shot me a sharp look. "Who?"

"My roommate Vivian, for one. After we got back from the basement last time she made a big deal about how weird the barracks smelled, like musty water or something. She said it smelled, and I quote, 'haunted.'"

"Well, you should put your clothes through the machine before going back to the barracks, dummy."

I mumbled some sullen retort. Her unbothered attitude about life-threatening situations could really be irritating. But of course I went back with her. Scared of being caught out and scared of being left behind.

Now that we knew the dimensions and had determined the tunnel would suit our needs, we just had to measure the opening and unfasten the bars at the other end to make the drop-off into the waiting boat on the night of the escape. It was around a twenty-foot drop from the pipe opening to the water. I fretted this last detail: How on earth would we get Achilles into the boat? Sailor assured me her friends would be arriving with all the stuff—a winch, a harness, pulleys, years of experience handling animals—and while it all sounded outlandish, she had a way of describing various futures that made them materialize in your mind's eye like magic.

Still, I listened with a stone in my gut. We agreed it would be too risky to convince Benjie to let us down into the basement again, so we decided to try my original plan of swiping his pass while he was out for a cigarette.

"It's so weird the way people started smoking again," said Sailor. "You might not know this, but everyone stopped smoking for years and years. And then, boom."

"What's your theory?" Again, I knew she'd have one. We loved our theories.

"My theory is people decided everything else was fucked, so it didn't even matter anymore. They might as well kill themselves in the manner of their own choosing."

"Plausible," I said.

The operation proved simple. At 4:28 p.m. we slipped down to the shower room, pretending to have business there. We loitered while watching from a discreet distance as Benjie checked the time, slicked his hair back, and headed up to his rendezvous with accelerated lung cancer. I kept watch while Sailor ducked inside the storeroom. She came out seconds later and we hurried to the basement stairs. I was scared as Sailor held the pass up to the door sensor, but it opened with no trouble. I went inside while she returned the pass, closing the door but for a tiny crack, which I used to peek out. After what seemed an eternity, she returned.

"Benjie won't know a thing," she said, closing the door softly. "But let's be as quick as we can. Headlamp on."

I swung my backpack off my shoulders and pulled the headlamps out. I didn't feel as claustrophobic as I had before. We had illumination now, and there was a calming sureness in knowing where the tunnel led. Weirdly, it was Sailor who seemed nervous this time. When we reached the end of the pipe, Sailor reached into my backpack and pulled out a small hacksaw and began to saw through the edges of the bars. She worked her way around the circle. The bars were welded together in the middle and it didn't take long before the whole thing folded down into our hands. Sailor pushed aside the vines. There was a boat out there again, but this one was sleek and black and much closer in to the cove. I could make out a figure on deck, looking up at the island. I shaded my eyes to try to see better, but the boat was too far away to make out any details. I turned to ask Sailor something, but I never got the words out. If you've ever seen a rabbit or a deer stand stock-still, assessing their environment while their body remains so minutely poised for flight it's as if time has stopped, you might understand the pose my friend stayed in for a few suspended seconds. Then she shook herself out of it and lifted her right hand in a fluttery wave. I looked down at the boat and thought I saw the person there make some kind of answering gesture, but I couldn't be sure.

"Let's wait here for a moment," Sailor said. "Out of sight."

We crouched in the shadows and watched the boat bobbing on the slight swell. After a while we heard a telltale low buzz, and another vessel came into view—a guard boat on its patrol around the island. The boat in the cove pivoted and sped off, so fast and quiet it could have been flying.

"Three minutes," Sailor said under her breath. She gave a curt little laugh, reached out and pulled the vines down to better cover the entrance, and then we propped the bars back into place. It would be easy to move it aside once the time came. Then we made our way back up the pipe to the basement.

Sailor never did show me the photo of her as a baby in Florida, but I keep a copy of it in my brain nevertheless. A rosy-cheeked infant wearing a diaper and a sleeveless cotton top, sleeveless because it's Florida and it would have been swampy and hot. She is smiling toothlessly at the snub-snouted reptile who is indistinguishable to her, at this tender age, from any other kind of friend. There is a potted plant in the corner, a long brown sofa, and striped curtains framing open French doors, beyond which can be glimpsed a line of palm trees. I don't know why I bothered to furnish the imaginary house of Sailor's memory, but the scene is stubbornly immovable now. It's her history, but it belongs to me as well.

San Francisco

It was the last time they would see each other before the big event, if all went well, Johannes told her. He had business out of the country and wouldn't be back until the night before the breakout. The operation, as he called it.

"We're getting so close," he said, pacing in front of the bench where she sat. As restless now as Feliz. "I wanted to take you to see our headquarters, you know, the office tower we visited on our first date? But there's a lot of work going on there right now, finishing touches for the big opening. The Palace of Exotics. Man, it's going to be like nothing else on Earth."

"I'm very happy for you."

"A high-rise full of animals." With his hands he traced a tall column in the air. "Can you fucking believe it?"

Sailor licked her chapped lips. "Sure I can. A multistory petting zoo." *For rich freaks*, she silently added.

"The best anyone's ever seen," said Johannes dreamily.

"No doubt."

"It hasn't been easy, you know." He ceased pacing and fixed her with a stern look. "We've had to fight to get the good specimens before your bosses snap them all up." For a moment Sailor was confused, then it dawned on her that he meant the Pinktons. Talking about the family she worked for like it was just another cartel. Although she'd reached a point where it was getting harder and harder to tell the difference. She rode a wave of nausea. "Anyway," Johannes added, "there's more good news."

"Oh?" Willing the nausea away sometimes meant being frugal with her words.

"There's going to be a good job for you at the Palace, after. I've made sure of it. You and your accomplice."

She turned her head, pretending to cough. It bought her a few seconds to compose her face. Important to not let the scorn show. How desperate must he think her, that she would jump at a job working in his creepy petting zoo. As desperate as most people were, she supposed. He didn't know her parents had left her a big enough inheritance to fund an escape to somewhere far from here when all this was done. Despite her best efforts, the words came out tinged with anger.

"That's if I survive the breakout. What do you think will happen to me if the Alcatraz guards catch us in the act? They won't be as lenient as the Paris Zoo. Have you seen how militarized the island is?"

"They're amateurs," he scoffed. "I've been there, don't forget. You think we can't outgun them?" He paused, a boy soldier waiting to be praised.

"I'm sure you can."

"I just have to know we can depend on you, Sailor."

"Yes, sir. I'll get you this crocodile or die trying." The jokey words curdled in her mouth.

Johannes bent and squatted on his heels facing her. He placed his hands on her thighs. She could feel the warmth of him through her jeans. She wondered how far she'd get if she started running.

"We've tried these raids ourselves, you know," he said gently. This inexplicable desire of his to win her over. "They're very expensive. Too many casualties. Too much attention. My bosses prefer this way now. More discreet. Better odds of success."

He lifted his shoulders to indicate it was all just business in the end. How many animals you could fit in a skyscraper. How many casualties were acceptable. Whose life was worthless and whose was worth something. Numbers in a ledger.

Alcatraz

How do I begin to describe what happened next?
My heart.

At two in the morning on the first day of summer, Kira went into labor. We were all sound asleep in our beds, everyone but the night watchmen and the vets, who were called when Joseph was woken by an alarm linked to the cam in the elephant enclosure. Just as first light was burnishing the spires and towers of the city, Kira gave birth to a stillborn calf.

She lost gallons of blood, our Kira, but she survived. That was a blessing, I suppose. The previous morning at breakfast we had all checked the daily update and animatedly discussed its findings, as had become the tradition, because she was almost halfway along and we'd begun a countdown to the due date. We were like fans following the fortunes of a beloved sports team. Kira's stats had been fine, the pregnancy proceeding normally (whatever normal meant in a species that had dwindled to the edge of extinction). To wake into a day in which hope has been neatly removed is a flavor of despair none of us had quite tasted before.

Everyone cried. Even Joseph. Even the stoic admins and the toughest of the guards, whose stern mouths quivered when the news was broadcast. Even Mr. Pinkton, who arrived with his family in his green helicopter to mourn with us and then departed with a look I'd never seen on his face before. I almost felt sorry for him.

I say everyone cried. But Sailor didn't. Not because she had a hard heart, but because she had always known. She hadn't poured all her hope into the new baby because she had seen how these things turn out. I think, if anything, the loss of the calf hardened her resolve.

Animals had died before, but nothing had ever affected morale like the death of Kira's and Titan's calf did. Things changed after that. Time both crawled and sped up. Everyone grew superstitious. I saw keepers who I knew to be atheists blessing themselves before they entered enclosures. Arguments broke out like spot fires throughout the day—one would be stamped out only for another to ignite along the next avenue.

I kept to myself. No matter what other task I might be doing, my mind stayed fixated on the idea that the calf's death represented something larger. After all, Kira and Titan could mate again. There could be another pregnancy, maybe a live birth next time. But I couldn't shake the conviction that the tragedy was a mirror in which our own predicament had suddenly become visible. All of us were trapped on this island, our futures stillborn. If Sailor and I didn't get out soon, we were as doomed as the elephants.

I didn't learn to love the plan for the Liberation of Achilles, exactly, but its necessity became clear to me in those final weeks. Like how a conscript might feel on the edge of some just but bloody war, the mission had become bigger than my feelings. As the days dripped away, I walked around with dark shadows under my eyes and itchy, blotched skin. My hands shook when I held the hoses and carried the feed buckets. It seemed impossible to me that on a day not so far in the future, this island would no longer be my workplace, my home, the entire circumference of my world. I had learned how to be a zookeeper on this rock. I had entered and exited my first romantic relationship. I had made the kind of friend you only make once in a lifetime, if you're that lucky, and even though this friend and I were planning to leave the island together I still found myself swamped by nostalgia for the days we'd passed here in each other's company.

If I expressed doubts and questions about my involvement, Sailor was always ready with a detailed answer.

"How will we get Achilles down to the basement?"

"Didn't you notice the freight elevator?" I hadn't noticed it. "Behind a stack of boxes, near the manhole cover. Rarely used, I'm guessing. We enter upstairs, near the showers. I've scoped it out, no cameras in sight. We can get him in easy."

"What about if we get separated on the night?"

"We won't. But if we do, there's a safe house near the wharf. A room above a corner store called the Blue Mermaid. I've told the owner, Israel, to expect you. You'll find me there."

Whenever my resolve begin to falter, I had Sailor tell me stories about the sanctuary. She was only too happy to oblige. I don't think it was just to humor me, I think she derived some emotional nourishment from it too, this task of weaving a fantasy of the life we were going to live once we got off the island. The night after the stillbirth, I had never needed that vision of our shared future more urgently.

"Remind me what it looks like," I implored.

"The sanctuary is the most beautiful place you've ever seen," Sailor began. It felt like she was talking to me from some distant point, her words floating across the oceans and continents, like she was already there and was waiting for me to arrive. "It has these sandstone pillars that reach into the clouds. It has vast open plains, and savannahs. It has waterfalls and rivers. It has deep forests you could get lost in, and meadows full of wildflowers. There are no factories or power plants, no buildings at all, apart from small cottages and huts that blend in with the scenery. The air is clean and the water is pure and uncontaminated."

As she spoke, my terror evaporated.

"And what about the animals?" I hugged my knees tightly to my chest, a child prompting a parent to read a favorite book, though having memorized every word.

"There are so many birds you sometimes can't even hear yourself think. There are big cats and primates and antelope and giraffes, and elephants, great herds of them that move across the plains on quests to find new succulent plants and watering holes. Sometimes they're not after food or water at all, but just setting out to visit friends. There are monkeys swinging in all the canopies, and in the forests and meadows, if you lie down on the ground and pay attention, you can hear the insect life all around you, this hidden kingdom working above and below the earth. And there are bees, more bees than you can imagine, pollinating the plants and flowers."

"I can't wait to see the bees."

"Me too," said Sailor.

The anxiety crept back again. "Are you sure they'll let us be keepers?"

Sailor hesitated, and I wondered whether she had some doubts too. The sanctuary probably had long waiting lists, impossible CV requirements. "We'd qualify, wouldn't we, having worked at the very last zoo?"

"Yes, of course they'll let us be keepers," she said after a while. "They're waiting for us, remember? We just have to get there. But the thing is, you don't see the animals." I must have looked confused because she added quickly, "At least, not often. Not like here. But that's the beauty of the sanctuary, you see?" All the time she'd been talking, Sailor had been staring out at the water, but she turned now and met my eyes. "Remember how I told you about choice and control, how important it was?" I nodded. "Well, at the sanctuary, the whole focus is choice and control. The animals all have agency. They're completely free to act on their natural impulses, whether that's to wander the plains in full view or hide in a hole in the ground. There's no intervention, no feeding, no manipulating of behaviors. No fences."

"So they're all in there together?" I asked. "What about if they eat each other?"

"Well, they sometimes do, of course. That's how things are in nature. You know that." I nodded. "The rangers, us, we're just there as stewards."

"Stewards," I whispered. I liked the sound of that.

I could see it so clearly when she spoke: the intense lush green of the plains, ribbons of mist winding around the peaks of the mountains, our community of rangers happily lost in the jungle.

Increasingly, Sailor wanted to extend her time outdoors. We would finish talking, our conversation naturally winding down, but when I'd suggest returning to the barracks her face would twist stubbornly. *You go without me*, she'd say, and I'd reluctantly gather my things and head back, teeth chattering and stomach muscles clenched against the cold that always descended late at night. Sailor was much hardier than me, in case that isn't already apparent. She drew strength from some deep inner well. I would invariably stop and look back and would see her lanky silhouette etched against the slightly paler dark, resting on her elbows on the rooftop of the Officers' Club, or with her spine pressed against a rock on a slope tipping down to the shore. She would sip frequently from her flask, ever more frequently as the scheduled day of our escape grew closer, and that was the only sign I ever saw that perhaps the stress got to her too.

San Francisco

She entered Israel's corner store like just another customer, carrying a black duffel bag and greeting him on her way to the vault door that led to her apartment. It had become a kind of haven for her, a place to rest and plan after her tasks on the mainland were done. Israel nodded and smiled in her direction but didn't stop from his work pressing stickers onto cans with a price gun. She was always hypervigilant entering the bodega, but she'd never felt the slightest twinge of being watched. Perhaps the cartel didn't care what she did outside of working for them, especially now that they were so preoccupied with their big opening.

Inside the apartment, she dropped the bag on the bed and stood to the side of the window, looking out. There weren't many people around, and none of the vehicles parked nearby were occupied. She unzipped the bag and drew out the gold bar she had bought that day, the culmination of her saved wages and the last piece of the collection she had been amassing these last months. It didn't even look real at first, something cartoon-like about its heft and shape, like a burnished brick a villain might hoist through a window. But the more she looked at it, the more affecting it became. Even lacking the covetous desire for precious metals, she had to admit there was something of the sacred in the way the gold shone. Something primal that stirred in her at the weight of it.

Shaking the mood off, she crouched and opened the safe beneath the sink and slid the bar inside with the other pieces. There were stacks of gold coins, strings of gleaming necklaces, yellow cuff bracelets embedded with colored gems, a few diamond-studded watches. In a velvet pouch, two wedding bands that were more precious than the rest put together. She allowed herself a minute to admire the sight of such old-fashioned treasure. Not just numbers on a screen, but a small fortune made solid and touchable. Cumbersome but still portable. Accepted the world over, unlike so many currencies now.

After she locked the safe, she stayed rocking on her heels for a few beats, eyes shut. She was so close now. If she had been unwise to involve someone else, especially someone who'd come to mean a great deal to her, it was too late to lament. There were certain safeguards in place, but it was all a risk beyond anything she'd attempted before. She hoped she would be forgiven, although she had no expectation of it.

She rose and slung the empty bag over her shoulder. The sun was setting. A wind from the north was picking up, and the rotting edges of the windowpanes shuddered. Looking out, she caught a sliver of bay flashing molten gold through the buildings. Alcatraz just out of sight, suddenly precious now that she was on the verge of leaving.

She was so tired of leaving, but there was something exhilarating in it too. A new world out there beyond the horizon, waiting for her. Waiting for all of them.

Alcatraz

On the last day, it rained. I woke from a fitful sleep before dawn to the sound of it drumming on the roof of the barracks. My heart lifted a little. That telltale sound promised a reprieve. I ducked outside to check in case I was imagining it. Sheets of rain gusted sideways against the dock, and the island was socked in by a wall of fog. Surely the conditions would make our departure impossible. But I emerged after breakfast to find the rain had cleared and the day was crystalline, the dissolved world beyond our shore made whole again.

I had to remind myself with each step to perform normality for my roommates, especially kind, sharp-eyed Vivian, whose antennae for trouble were finely tuned. We chatted as we laced our boots—about what, I couldn't have said under torture—and I must have been convincing enough because she acted as though nothing was amiss. All the while we interacted, one scene played over and over in my mind, as stark and vivid as if it had already happened. Sailor wrangling Achilles while I dragged a hunk of Fake Steak along the floor, leaving a wide bloody trail for Achilles to follow. Our prize crocodile sashaying along the avenue, the crushing mass of his tail sweeping great half-moons in the dust. On his way, without even knowing it, to liberation.

I was assigned to the farm that day. I have a photographic memory for these things. I could tell you which enclosure I had worked on any significant day over the last nine years. The day after I arrived on Alcatraz, for instance, it was the snakes. I remember, after overcoming my initial fear of them, being surprised and enchanted by how different in personality they are from one another, and how subject they are to mood swings, just like we are. One glossy green tree snake sulked for hours because I moved one of his favorite sticks. The first time I slept with Joseph, I had spent the day with the sweet, goofy capybara, upon whose accommodating back you could place any object—a cup, a book, another animal—and it would still be there when you next checked. (Capybaras want to be friends with everyone and everything. It's a wonder they've survived so long with that innocent attitude.) The most important day, the day when Sailor arrived, I was her orientation guide. That one is easy to remember, but I have a whole catalog of them. A little useless superpower of mine.

I didn't see Sailor in the morning; we had agreed we were both to go about our duties as normal. It made sense to avoid being seen together too much. I was happy with this arrangement, relieved really, because I had a notion the very sight of Sailor would set off a tornado of panic in me. I had a lot to do, anyway. Not just my usual work duties, although I intended to fulfill them as carefully and diligently as always. I needed time to say goodbye to my favorites. To the birds and animals, of course, but also to the plants, to the island itself. This place I had expected never to leave until either I died or the last of the animals did.

As I moved through the paces of my day, my body felt hollow and weightless, and everything appeared extra-sharp, the contours of objects standing out like paper dioramas. I made excuses to visit the cages of the creatures who had taken up special residence in my heart and I said my silent goodbyes, trying my hardest to make sure my inner turmoil wasn't transmitted to my furred and feathered and scaled and quilled friends. I was desperate to remember everything.

So many of the animals are sensitive, exquisitely attuned to the emotional state of those around them. They can pick up the smallest frequencies of distress or anger, and it can make them act in ways that clueless keepers disapprovingly call "erratic." It's not erratic, though, to be influenced by the mood of someone close to you. Humans do it all the time.

I must have been successful in my emotional masking because none of the animals seemed to pick up anything out of the ordinary. They let me stroke and talk to them as usual, or if they were the kind who were indifferent to humans, they ignored me as usual. The dissonance between my internal state and the normality of the zoo lent the day a disturbingly surreal aura.

I think it was the birds that tore at my heart the most. They were the most indifferent of all the zoo's citizens, but I'd always loved them despite my love never being reciprocated. I thought I understood them too. They abhorred touch not because they didn't feel affection, but because being wary of touch was rooted in survival. To be unable to fly was to invite death.

I entered the aviary—with the keeper's permission—and once inside stood still, listening to the clatter of beak on branch, breathing in the sharp stink of the droppings coating the floor, feeling the breeze of wingbeats passing close to my head. Birdsong rang and crackled through the air. Some might have been singing about inconsequential things—the seed they had just spotted; a branch they were planning to head to; the feeling of the sun slanting through the glass—but I was sure others were singing of grief.

Ever since I'd known this day was coming, I'd been secretly honing a new theory that some humans are wired with a migratory instinct, just as some birds are. The wild urge to be free, to set off for distant places, no matter the risk. You see it in the tanagers and warblers and orioles. During the season, while the resident breeds continue their usual behaviors, the travelers begin to sicken, to stop eating, to spend whole days perched at the very top of the aviaries, flapping and squawking at the sky they will never breach. Even when raised in captivity with every material need provided, the urge to press on to the distant breeding or feeding grounds can't be eradicated. They yearn to follow the great flyways along which they have never traveled, because the coordinates are written on their generational memories. They know about a world without ever having seen it, and the memory lives inside them, beating in their tiny, feathered chests and tormenting them like a curse. Was it so strange, then, that Sailor and I also yearned for a world we'd never seen?

Of course, birds aren't even the only creatures to migrate. There was once an incredible animal called a narwhal, a pale, medium-size porpoise with a slender ivory tusk jutting from its lip like a needle, whose migratory instinct was so strong, no marine facility in the world was ever big enough for them to survive in. Many facilities tried, assuming that like some of the dolphin and whale species, the narwhals would learn to accept the parameters of their new world, trading freedom for abundant fish. But the narwhals simply gave up. They died within weeks of being confined. A global ban on keeping them in confinement was introduced. Not that it helped much. Now, like the polar bears and so many others, they're gone, fading pages in the book of our collective memory.

Back in the farm enclosure, I stroked the velvety flanks of Yasmin the cow, laying my cheek on her neck and feeling her jaw move as she ruminated on her cud. I swung between pitying her for being so sedentary and envying her ability to be happy wherever she was. Then I knelt in the straw to let the goats gambol around and butt me with their tufted heads. They eventually got bored and skipped off, and something came over me as I knelt there—an intense, bone-deep weariness unlike anything I'd ever experienced before. I lowered my spine to the floor of the enclosure, where all the animals stood and lay and pissed and tracked shit around, spread my arms wide like I was making snow angels, and closed my eyes. I tried to draw the barnyard funk into my nose and mouth, to make it part of me. Something wet touched my wrist.

I turned my neck. "Oh, hello, Summer."

It was the bunny, my sweet little friend come to check on me. Close up, his eyes were black and convex, the orbs opaque and glistening like motor oil. His nose twitched manically and his foot reached out to repeatedly tap my arm. A rabbit is programmed to assume a fellow rabbit has come to grief if they're prone and still. "It's okay," I told him in my most soothing voice. "I'm not dead." I gently cradled his face, flattening his ears so only his tiny lagomorph facial features protruded between my palms, a solemn medieval nun wearing a habit. After I released him he performed a few leaps in the air and flopped over on his side, which basically translates to *Isn't life fun?* in Rabbit. We talked for a short while longer, then I resumed my duties.

I didn't say goodbye to any of the keepers. I didn't want to risk anyone's safety. After my shift was over, I wandered the avenues, just walking and breathing it all in for the last time. I wanted to bottle the various scents of the zoo and take them with me. I fantasized a coat lined with pockets that would hold tiny glass vials of each individual fragrance, so I could reach in and remember them anytime I wanted.

Instead, I reached into my pocket and pulled out my phone. It was four in the afternoon. Eight hours to go.

Sailor didn't appear at dinner. I sat with a group of keepers who, to my relief, were in a particularly raucous mood, shouting and gesticulating across the table, which meant my own silence went unnoticed. I felt like I had a pill stuck in my throat. I went through the motions of eating in case anyone was watching, raising the fork to my mouth occasionally and pushing the food around on my plate into different patterns. I wondered how long the boat ride would be, where Sailor's friends were planning to take us first. The journey would be long and no doubt dangerous. Maybe this was the last chance I'd get to eat for a long time. That prospect propelled me over to the buffet to find something portable to take with us. People had finished eating and were clearing the tables, the room filled with the clangor of scraping chairs and plates being stacked together. I settled on four hard pucks—some unholy cross between a falafel and a scone—which I bundled inside a napkin.

We had agreed it would be too dangerous to pack our bags as if we were leaving forever. It was important we kept up the impression of continuity and normality. I returned to my room, relieved to find it empty. My roommates were probably getting ready to play cards or watch a show—impossible for me to imagine such a carefree life now. I placed the food pucks inside my backpack, although they were already stale and I couldn't imagine a circumstance under which they'd suddenly become appealing. I was having trouble imagining my future circumstances at all. I packed a water bottle as well, a warm scarf, my phone, my inhalers, some medication. None of these were unusual items to bring on a nighttime walk around the island, an activity my cohorts had long ago accepted as Sailor's and my harmless eccentricity.

The feeling of dissociation grew stronger and more disturbing as the minutes ticked by. The gestures I made barely belonged to me. I wished Sailor would appear, or at least check in with me. For the thousandth time, I convinced myself she was planning to leave without me. Maybe she had left already. I stepped outside the barracks and peered into the shadows. Was that someone moving down by the dock? Was that a boat's engine I heard beneath the soughing of the wind? The movement down at the dock resolved itself into the shape of a guard, strutting along the foreshore, moving his head from side to side, as if keeping time with a beat. Technically, the guards weren't supposed to listen to music or watch videos or take calls while on duty, but many of them flouted those rules. The job was largely boring, once the thrill of brandishing a weapon and feeling like some badass warrior seeped away. I was glad for their inattention. Hopefully it would make the terrifying task ahead of us a fraction easier.

I felt something touch me from behind, a jab in the small of my back, and I jumped and emitted a strangled yelp.

"It's just me," came Sailor's low, reassuring voice. She stepped around me and into the sallow light. Her face was serious, gaunter than I'd ever seen it. The skin around her eyes was puffed and her pupils were enormous and inky black in the gloom.

"I'm scared," I said. It felt good to admit it out loud.

"I know." She reached out and took my hands and squeezed them. "Me too. But you're going to be fine, Birdy. You're going to be amazing."

There was something off about her demeanor. I couldn't put my finger on it. I told myself it was just that she'd been hitting that flask of hers. Even that explanation was worrying, though: I had hoped the dangerous job we had committed ourselves to might be carried out in a state of sobriety and utter clarity. But I didn't dare question her, not at this late hour.

"We should separate now," she said. "I've got some things to do before we meet again. See you up at the zoo just before midnight."

She rummaged around in her pocket, then withdrew her hand and flicked it open to display a palm full of small ivory-white pills. She closed her hand again and gave me a somber smile. "I got them from one of the vets. Animal tranqs, but they'll work on humans too. This should keep our friends occupied for a while."

The short glimpse of those pills caused an abrupt and violent reassociation with reality. Everything became sickeningly clear. Not only were we about to smuggle one of the zoo's priceless specimens off the island, but we were also going to drug the people in charge of making sure such things never happened. The last, nightmarish piece of the puzzle. I tried to say something, some words that might constitute a verbal protest, no matter how feeble, but Sailor put a finger to my lips and shook her head.

"I know what you're thinking," she said. "But of course I'm not going to drug the guards against their will. I'm not a monster. I'm going to *offer* the pills to them, that's all."

"Will that work?" I could barely speak. The invisible pill in my own throat swelled.

Sailor's mouth twitched into a grim smile. "Oh, it'll work. I've done it before."

"*What?* Never mind, never mind." My hands flapped around like startled birds. "I don't want to know."

Sailor pulled me in for a quick hug, then pushed me gently back toward the barracks. "Just act normal, you little weirdo," she said, and it was good to see her laugh again, good to be gently teased, as if everything was the same as it had always been.

Before I even reached the barracks door, I reached a conclusion. There was only one way I was going to survive this night, and that was by fundamentally changing how I thought about it. Rationality was pointless in a situation like this. Delusional confidence was the only approach that made sense. The depraved, radical, unstoppable energy of the only manned mission to Mars or the first person to ever eat an oyster—that was what I needed to bring. A light flared into existence, and the light was a story. This very night, we were going to bring that magnificent, ailing crocodile with us into a new life, somewhere far across the ocean, far from anything that could hurt any of us ever again. I let myself believe for the first time that we were really going to pull this off.

At a few minutes to midnight I set out for the zoo. The island was quiet now, most of its residents asleep and dreaming. The new moon sulked behind a bank of stratus clouds and a few low-enthusiasm stars punctured the darkness. As I walked up the hill, I continued saying my silent goodbyes. Goodbye, rock. Goodbye, skeleton tree. Goodbye, water tower. Goodbye, morgue. My backpack bumped against the buttons of my spine, a soft, rhythmic thump-thump like following footsteps.

Sailor was waiting for me at the entrance to the zoo. She held a large black canvas duffel bag at her side, containing the tools she had gathered for the mission. The Fake Steak was inside, no doubt. I knew she'd been squirreling away her meals for the last week, stashing the globs of protein who knows where. I'd offered to stash mine as well, but she'd said it might draw too much attention. She already looked skinnier to me, her cheeks more hollowed out, and I made a resolution to share every scrap of food I ever found with her once we were off the island.

A guard was at the entrance too, of course, there was always a guard there and I had known and been prepared, but somehow seeing the sturdy, undeniable reality of him spurred my heart into a gallop. I hoped Sailor had wrapped the Fake Steak well so we didn't leak a telltale trail of blood. The guard was Benjie, our friend from the basement. As I got closer, I saw he was grinning. No, that doesn't describe the expression, really. More beaming, his mouth stretched wide, like he was watching some wonderful, wholesome movie in his head. I glanced at Sailor. Her lips were pressed together and she refused to look at me. I looked back at Benjie and he seemed to see me for the first time. I was only a few inches shorter than he was but he looked down at me as though he were a giant inspecting a mouse, his chin tucked into his neck, a look of benevolent wonder flooding his young face. He looked between me and Sailor then said: "Yeaaahhh, lovely ladies."

"Heeeyyy," said Sailor. "Lovely ladies, just passing through."

He pondered this for a long moment, then started nodding slowly and with great satisfaction, like he had finally had some confounding scientific anomaly explained to him.

"Go ahead, please." He took his hand from where it had been resting on the gun slung diagonally across his chest and waved grandiosely toward the zoo beyond. Sailor smiled at him, grabbed my hand, and we walked quickly past the entrance, through the doors and into the zoo. Once we were inside and out of earshot, I turned to face her. "Oh my god, he is tripping balls!"

"I know," said Sailor, and she burst out laughing. "Holy shit."

"I don't think I've ever seen someone so high."

"Right? He was, like . . ." And she did an impression of his big, goofy face that made me emit a strangled squeak. Deep inside the zoo, some nocturnal creature answered. Every time the bouts of laughter subsided, one of us would start it up again, until our scrunched faces were red and stained with tears. I had forgotten how good it could feel to laugh over something ludicrous, how that rush of serotonin was better than any drug.

"I needed that," said Sailor breathlessly, once we'd finally recovered enough to consider moving on. "Phew."

I let Sailor lead the way, and she headed to the avenue where Feliz lived, as I'd assumed she would. I knew she'd want to say goodbye to him. Many of the residents were slumbering but some were at their most alert. An owl hooted as we passed, his entire head swiveling to watch our passage, amber eyes stern with avian judgment. I could hear the chimps stirring in their enclosure and hoped they'd return to their dreams without causing a ruckus.

We arrived at Feliz's enclosure. I had skipped his cage on my private goodbye tour, thinking I couldn't bear to see him. He didn't alter his step when we came into view, just kept pacing with his eyes focused on something far away, his huge silken paws tracing the same path, back and forth and back again. His mouth hung open, revealing a patch of stippled pink tongue. Sailor sank to her knees. "Hey baby, hey baby," she said, pressing her fingers against the bars. I remained standing, biting my lip and glancing around. "We were supposed to be the caretakers," Sailor said, her voice melancholy. "I'm sorry, Feliz. We should have found a way to take you as well."

I strained my ears for any suspicious sounds beneath the familiar animal ones, but the night was quieter than ever. I drew a deep breath in through my nose and exhaled through pursed lips.

Sailor got to her feet. She swayed gently, blinking and staring down at Feliz. "Let's go say goodbye to some of our favorites," she said, and I didn't tell her I'd already done this. Even if the delay hurt our chances, how could I deny her the same gift? We passed beneath one of the massive skylights and Sailor craned her neck and pointed at a smudge of stars gleaming far above us. "Look!" I'd never heard her express innocent wonder in that way before. I clenched her hand.

"It's nights like this I wish I didn't have to leave."

"Why don't we stay, then?" The shameless speed at which I barreled toward a way out. "Only Benjie has seen us. We can just go back to the barracks!"

Sailor stared at me. I swear I saw her pupils dilate as I watched, like ink spreading on a white cloth. "Oh no," she said, and she wore a sweet smile. "It's too late for that. But everything's going to be okay, don't you worry, Birdy."

I was starting to get tired of that trite reassurance. Everything was patently not okay. Even if we decided not to kidnap Achilles now, we were both in deep shit and Sailor surely knew that. As we passed the elephant enclosure, I pressed my nose to the bars of the old library to watch Kira and Titan for a moment. I expected them to be asleep but I could see the reflection of the moonlight glinting in their black eyes. A shadowy pyramid rising from the floor resolved itself into a pile of browse someone must have put out for them. The elephants were occupied with hooking the tender branches in their trunks and bringing them to their mouths, but they lifted their heads at the sight or smell of us. Sailor, beside me, whispered, "Go on in." She buzzed me inside.

Kira and Titan continued looking at me as I entered, their long-lashed eyes taking in my unexpected presence. They didn't move, but I detected an invitation. I approached slowly with outstretched hand. The two were only a human's width apart, and I was able to stand between them. Their slowly flapping ears brushed the top of my head, and I touched each of their necks, savoring the sensation of their hides under my palms—warm, wrinkled, and bristly to the touch but not as rough as I'd always imagined. I closed my eyes and felt the muscles working as they chewed, felt the life—precious, against-all-odds life—pulsing beneath my fingers. I was certain they were still grieving. "I'm sorry," I whispered into Kira's ear, and her head quivered gently, as if she understood.

Then we were on the move again. I thought Sailor had a specific destination in mind, maybe to see Maggie the eagle, but instead it was the start of a meandering journey around the zoo. I trailed in her wake as she skipped and danced and sang softly to herself or the animals. It was endearing at first, but after a while I began to get scared. It was nearly one in the morning and we were no closer to completing our mission. Surely every moment wasted here was more time for the guards' high to wear off and for them to hazily recall and examine the lost hours of the evening.

"Hey, when are your friends arriving again?"

"Friends?" She seemed confused.

"Jesus Christ. You know," I pressed her. "The ones with the boat?"

"Oh, right. Friends." She laughed. "They'll be here soon."

"If we're going to do it, let's do it," I said. "If not, let's just go back."

I had crossed into a state of quietly hysterical exasperation, standing with hands on hips outside the meerkat cage. Sailor blinked slowly, as if I were something fascinating just starting to come into focus. I waited for her to talk, to snap back into her brisk and decisive self.

"Thank you for being my friend, Camille," she said softly. "You don't know what it's meant to me."

When you're angry, the arrival of kindness is so unexpected it can undo you. I stuttered out something, maybe, "I'm glad you're my friend too, Sailor."

"I know you want to go," she said. "And we're going to get there soon. Just a few more goodbyes."

By the time we arrived at Achilles's enclosure, another mood had settled on Sailor. I saw it in the slump of her shoulders, the dulling of her eyes. We stood at the entrance. I waited for her to use her ID to open the door, but she hesitated, swaying gently, lost in thought. Alarm hammered in my chest. Finally, she spoke, and her voice was so different from before, all broken and choppy.

"We only got to be young for such a short time."

That was the first and last time I ever saw Sailor cry. I didn't move to hug her or console her. I don't even think she was talking to me. Moments later, as I stood there, arms dangling uselessly by my sides, she squared her shoulders, wiped her face, and buzzed us into the anteroom of the crocodile's lair. I worried the security cameras would pick up the vibrations of my fear. Oh, but Sailor had disabled them, hadn't she? Somehow the thought didn't console me much.

I've always had this visceral reaction when I'm anywhere in Achilles's vicinity. The bone-deep human fear of a primordial creature against whom one has no natural and few unnatural defenses. Bullets have been known to bounce off the hides of crocodiles. Injured crocs have taken down whole boatloads of fishermen. His kind have been around for millennia; we've been around for a blip of that time. How angry the crocodilians must be that they won't outlive even our puny species. The idea that we would need to enter his lair soon set off a fight-or-flight reaction in my amygdala. My armpits got damp and my breathing grew quicker and shallower. I couldn't see Achilles, but I could smell him. Somewhere close by, waiting.

Sailor, on the other hand, appeared perfectly calm, as if none of the other moods of the evening had belonged to her and she had stepped up to reclaim her true self. It was the only thing that made me feel better. The preternatural confidence that came over her whenever she was close to

Achilles. Sailor the swamp rat, the crocodile girl. She was so beautiful and wild to me in that moment.

"Listen," she said. "So, I gave Achilles a tranquilizer earlier. He's in his holding pen. He'll be mellow as a marsh." She laughed softly at her own nonsense. "We're perfectly safe, there's nothing to worry about. Come on, let's go up to the tower. I want to get a sense of where we're going." She grabbed my arm and pulled me toward the tower.

"What are you talking about?" I said, trying to shake off her grip.

She acted as though she hadn't heard me, practically running to the door that led to the tower room. Seeing no choice but to follow, I climbed the stairs after her, up to the feeding platform above Achilles's pool. The holding pen where Achilles waited and dreamed was in shadow and I couldn't see any movement in there, but still I felt weak at being so close, an intruder in his territory. I had a flash of panic imagining the power going out suddenly, the doors all swinging open, and I almost lost my balance. Of course there were contingency plans for such blackouts, great generators stored beneath the building designed to kick in if there was ever an interruption to the current. Standing on the platform, hugging my arms around my body, that was cold comfort.

The part of me not paralyzed by fear in that moment was fascinated by our new vantage point. I had never been up here before, had never been invited, not even when I was sleeping with Joseph. It was dizzying, much higher than it looked from the ground, the lonely viewpoint of a diver about to launch into an Olympic pool. There was even a different soundscape up here. We were closer to the skylights, to the giant exhaust fans, to the air vents, but somehow that didn't fully explain the unnerving low shrieking of the air at this height.

Sailor hummed under her breath. My friend had clearly ingested something that was clouding her usually sharp judgment, and I was sickeningly certain now that it would fall to me to get the three of us to the basement, down the sewer pipe, and into the waiting boat. Much as I cherished Sailor's company, I wished fervently in that moment for some relief from it just being the two of us. Honestly, I would have welcomed a shout from below from Benjie, demanding to know what the hell we thought we were doing. I would have submitted to being marched out of the building, even deported. But no shout came. There was no one coming to save me.

I took a tentative step forward and peered over the edge of the platform. The pool looked even more sinister at night. I don't know how to explain it, but it didn't possess the normal properties of water. There was no glistening, no light refraction, no sense of what lay beneath. Instead, it seemed to absorb all the light. I stepped back, training my gaze on the ceiling to restore a sense of normality and permanence.

Sailor stopped humming abruptly, as if she was listening intently to someone else speaking. I turned and saw an emotion ripple across her face. Astonishment? Happiness? Some combination of the two, I think. Surprise at how good she felt in that moment. Then she turned to me and grasped my hands. "Listen, I love you."

I waited. She had started, as if there were something more to tell me, but she didn't say anything further, just dropped my hands and stepped off the platform into the darkness.

Achilles must have been waiting patiently in the pool because as Sailor fell, I felt rather than saw a monstrous energy surging and lifting from below, like a geyser exploding through the earth's crust, the snapping of jaw and slapping of tail, an obliterating splash as bodies smacked the water, the sounds of thrashing, and then silence. I screamed. As if a conductor had cued an orchestra, the zoo erupted around me with answering screams and shrieks and bellowing and pounding of cages and walls. The animals made sounds they'd never made. It was as though the bars disappeared and the zoo itself dissolved and we were transported to a jungle, each of us exposed and terrified and finally confronting our existence on the razor's edge between living and dying. Something toppled over and the echoes rang through the empty avenues. I don't know what happened next, maybe I blacked out or wandered out of time, because I didn't remember anything more until I woke up the next morning in my own bed, tiny scratches all over my face and arms, the sheets crumpled and streaked with dirt and blood and tears and god knows what else.

Florida

She arrived craving stone crabs. But the towns close to the Everglades, which usually coalesced around the great seasonal orgy of these creatures, were quiet as she passed through. The festival had been canceled. The crabs were all gone. She'd been working in Paris for only a year, but already the country she'd lived in most of her life felt unrecognizable, in the grip of some wasting fever. As she approached her parents' place, she realized she'd been subconsciously listening for the ubiquitous screaming whir of the airboats as they flew along the mashes and canals, but they had vanished too.

The truly eerie part for Sailor, though, was the way the beauty of the place hadn't diminished one bit. If you didn't know that hurricanes had recently drowned several townships and that the mangroves had been moving steadily inland to escape the encroaching high salty tides, you wouldn't notice anything amiss. She had been given to believe the planet's decline would be abrupt and devastating: one moment gazing upon vast Edenic beauty, the next confronting a smoking wasteland. But here nature still felt ascendant. The secretive dark waters and the high sheen of the palm trees and the rippling river of grass, it all made Sailor's throat ache in the same way it always had. If she could be laid to rest anywhere, she would choose to have her body rowed through a canal shaded by a mangrove canopy, as the rasping bark of pig frogs serenaded her and dragonflies alighted on her eyelashes.

She pushed aside this morbid fantasy as she bounded up the stairs to the family home, a red wood-frame house with a wraparound porch built close to the marsh. A faded wooden sign featuring the silhouette of a crocodile swung in the light breeze. The farm and its vast warren of watery pens stretched out the back. Her parents were at the door to greet her. Frailer and more sunken into themselves, but with ready smiles as always.

Over the course of three days, Sailor tried every form of persuasion she knew to urge them to come away with her. Move to another state, another country, higher ground at least. But they gently refused every entreaty. This was where they belonged, they told her, here with their kids, and they intended to stay until the end. Would she like to see the kids now? They had missed her, apparently, even the shier ones who tended to hide in their dens or stay semisubmerged near the tangled roots of the mangroves.

When the time came for her to leave, they pressed a gift into her hands and returned to their formal parental pose to see her off, arms wound around each other's waists. Their eyes were cloudier than the last time she had seen them. She wondered if she just appeared as a blur to them both now. She took the steps down briskly, as if her lost cause didn't sting and the trip had gone exactly as planned, and when she reached the car she stood with one hand on the open door and the other shading her forehead, looking back up at them.

"See you later, alligator," her father called out.

Sailor raised her hand in a salute. "In a while, crocodile."

She was relieved her voice didn't crack on any of the words. It was important to keep up the pretense. The pretense they would all see one another again.

Alcatraz

How to fill the breaks in my memory, those little absences where the rest of the story lies? I'm not sure I would want to retrieve them even if I could. It wasn't just the night in which Sailor fed herself to Achilles, but the days that followed as well, when I was losing parts of my mind in solitary. It had changed since Sailor had first been sent there. Oh, yes. It was no longer a repurposed storage closet, an accidental space in which a prisoner could read pamphlets and pilfer candy. They had restored it to its original purpose, a temporary hell leached of light and sound and warmth and comfort. A place to be ambushed by memories. A place to come face-to-face with your shattered self.

Hunched in the corner of the cell in total darkness—I had groped my way there because to sit in the middle of the floor without the comfort of a wall was to risk falling out of time again, and a corner provided at least some sense of solidity, a reminder I was still anchored to this earth—I recalled a story I'd heard about one Alcatraz prisoner who spent weeks in the hole. The trick he devised to stay sane was to pull a button off his shirt and throw it into the cell, then spend however long it took groping for it in the darkness. Once he'd retrieved it, he'd throw it again, no doubt becoming expert at interpreting the particular echoes as the button clanged off surfaces. Fine-tuning and perfecting his bat-like sense of where the tiny plastic disc existed in space. I wished I had a button. They stripped me of everything but a plain beige tunic, and there was no other object in the cell but the mattress, a blanket, and a bucket. "That's to relieve yourself," the person who locked me in told me. A dispassionate stranger. I don't know where she came from, I never saw her again. As if there could ever be any relief.

I didn't have a button, so I replayed Sailor's death. A pitiless beam projected on the darkness, the scene flickering in an endless loop. The smooth grace with which she moved away from me and sailed over the edge; the snap of Achilles's jaws; the stench of fetid pond water rushing through my mouth and nose. Slide, snap, rush. The first dozen times I replayed the scene, I lost myself in a storm of choking tears, unbelief and grief pouring out of me, but after a while the storm's remnants drained away, and I was filled instead with a cold fury at Sailor. I wanted to rage at her for leaving me. For lying to me. Most of her deceptions had been lies of omission, and I could forgive those, but she had said she'd never let anything bad happen to me, then she had brought me to Achilles's cage so I could watch her die.

Solitary was unspeakable, but I knew it was only the beginning of my punishment. A week after being imprisoned, I was released and told to report back to the admin center the next afternoon for a briefing. A guard escorted me from the dungeon and up the stairs and out into the world, his huge hand clamped around my upper arm as if he were trying to keep me from becoming airborne. It was simultaneously the longest and shortest journey of my life. He left me at the pathway, pointing helpfully down toward the barracks in case I'd forgotten where it was located. I walked in a shaky daze back there, hands cupped around my eyes to shut out the blinding intensity of the sun.

I stumbled into someone at the bottom of the path close to the dock and rasped out an apology in my unused voice, accepting that for the rest of my time on the island I would be a pariah. I felt hands gripping my shoulders and I pried my eyes open, gingerly, with a great deal of pain. The light like needles piercing my skull.

Joseph came into view. For a moment I thought he was going to kill me, right there on the dock in front of the world, for having endangered Achilles.

I didn't mind the idea at all. I wasn't brave—I hoped it would be quick and as painless as possible—but I was entirely willing, even raising my throat to him, as if I expected him to run across it with a knife. Instead, he pulled me to his chest, holding so tightly I could feel his heart pounding. "I'm so sorry," he murmured into my hair.

I hobbled to the barracks with the intention of scrubbing every inch of my unwashed body, but I didn't make it to the showers. I opened the door to my room and saw something black and rumpled lying on my bed, a hulking shape suggestive of a corpse. It was Sailor's duffel bag. Someone must have found it on the platform of the croc tower and brought it here, to let me know we'd been found out. Whatever was in that bag would implicate me beyond doubt in Sailor's doomed kidnapping scheme. So why then weren't there guards waiting outside the door to arrest me? Why did the barracks ring with the emptiness of an abandoned building? I sat down heavily on the thin mattress of my bunk.

My hands were steady as I unzipped the bag, even if my nerves screamed. I wanted to be anywhere else on this cursed Earth, but I made myself stay and go through with it. This last rite of our friendship. It was the closest I'd been to Sailor since she had stepped away from me on the platform edge, and I could have sworn a tiny puff of the precious already-fading scent of her wafted up as the zipper parted and revealed the contents of the bag.

Inside there was no leash, no Fake Steak, no rope to tie Achilles's snout, no damning smuggling tools. There was only a pile of Sailor's personal things. The first item I pulled out was familiar in a way that made my vision swim—her silver flask. I uncapped it and put my nose to the neck. The smell of whatever had been in it still lingered. Up close, it smelled chemical, medicinal. It occurred to me that maybe it had never been booze at all.

Next, I took out her phone, which she must have unlocked before she died. Nudging aside the twinge of discomfort I felt at breaching her privacy, I began scrolling through it, because I somehow knew that's what she had wanted me to do, and after a few seconds I got up and locked the door to the room. Then I sat cross-legged on the cold floor and slipped down the rabbit hole she had left for me.

It was bewildering at first, so many messages and photos and videos and calendar appointments, along with short journal-like entries on various significant dates. Most of the appointments she'd had were with the same person, a Dr. Hinckley in the Mission District, and below each reminder were brief, terse descriptions of symptoms and treatments. In a separate ziplock bag were neat stacks of receipts, invoices, cards, and notes fastened with rubber bands—the flotsam and jetsam of a busy and perilous life. I barely noticed as the light dimmed, and when there came a hammering at the door some many hours after I'd first locked myself in there, I didn't even raise my head. Let them break the door down if they wanted to get in so badly. I heard low, concerned voices whispering outside and then the clacking of receding footsteps.

I learned more about Sailor's parents after going through her things, more than she had ever told me. You could tell how much she loved them, and how it had stripped her heart raw to leave them at the end. Her mother and father had made a pact together when they were both very sick, it turned out, had stockpiled morphine, and when the time came they had grasped hands and walked into the den and given themselves to the crocodiles, freely and with immense love. It must have always been in Sailor's mind, this unthinkable last option. Some part of her decided that if she had to die, she wanted to die like her parents had. When her time ran out with the cartel—when she could no longer delay or fob them off and they demanded their pound of flesh, their ton of crocodile—she had performed the act that seemed the most natural thing in the world to her. To die in the way one chooses, among the creatures one loves the most.

Sailor herself had been sick for a while, with the worst kind of Lyme disease, the new kind that no one has yet survived. Her trips to the mainland hadn't been fun jaunts to meet a boyfriend or girlfriend or take in the city air. Instead, visits to the doctor for the medication to keep her functioning, and encounters with the man I now knew as Johannes.

I thought about the time I had seen him berating Sailor in front of Feliz's cage. I thought about the boat Sailor had waved to in the cove and how defiantly she had turned her back. It made me shiver to imagine Johannes's incandescent rage when he learned Sailor had robbed the cartel not only of the crocodile, but also of the chance to exact revenge on her for failing them.

Or maybe he wasn't angry at all, but sad. That he'd never get the chance to own a crocodile now. That he'd never see Sailor again.

I regretted the hours I had spent in the darkness, cursing Sailor for betraying me, because after sifting through it all—all the artifacts of her brief and shining life—I finally understood the obvious. *Listen, Birdy*, I could hear Sailor saying. *I was never going to deliver Achilles to the cartel. Are you kidding me? All I needed was for those stupid fuckers to believe I was going to do it.*

She must have done a decent job because they could easily have found a way to get to her. Johannes's little visit to the island proved that. That's why she had to keep up the pretense when she was with me, so the hatching of the plan and the conversations about how it was going to work would seem believable. My reluctance probably added an extra touch of vérité.

I like to think part of her sincerely believed the feat was possible, though—not the part about condemning Achilles to an even worse life in a swimming pool atop a skyscraper, not that of course. The part about the sanctuary being real, and the possibility of getting Achilles and ourselves there. I think it *needed* to be possible for her to have peace, and to lend me the courage to do what I'm going to do.

If you knew from the start how small you were going to have to shrink your dreams in order to fit them into the shape of your life, how could you bring yourself to even begin?

Once I had absorbed everything there was to absorb, I looked to see if there was anything else in the bag. Just one more item, it turned out. A book. An old birding field guide called *Cawthorn's Complete Birds*. Almost every page was scrawled with marginalia: names, numbers, stray thoughts. I found a rough ink drawing Sailor had done, of a Y-shaped symbol. Beneath it, a scathing note to herself: *Not a scar, a tattoo, you idiot. His gang sign.*

Then I found Mr. Li, and myself. On the page devoted to the common wren, her favorite bird, was my name, circled several times.

I felt sick that she had left all of this lying around where it could have been found while she was still alive. Evidence—enough to put her away forever. Enough to get her disappeared, if that were more efficient. It seemed so risky, so unlike her, my falcon-eyed friend who had always arranged everything down to the last detail and who always hated and mistrusted authority. But I think all along I understood. Because isn't that what I'm doing as well, writing all this down despite how much it might cost me? In the vanishing hope that if I don't make it, someone might find it and understand why we did everything we did.

Alcatraz

The only reason I'm here to tell this story is that the crocodile lived. Not only that, he thrived. The other keepers filled me in, crowding around me in the mess hall at breakfast, hovering but never touching me, as if I was a curiosity that fascinated and frightened them in equal measure. Like the primates will do when something new appears in their cage. It was a miracle, they said, no one could quite believe it. Within days of Sailor's death, Achilles began to show signs of recovery, as if he had somehow absorbed not only her nutrients but also her spirit. At least there was that for us all to cling to. A silver lining in these dark days, no?

That was the part they told me. No one dared tell me about how he jealously guarded the remains of her body for a week, lashing out so viciously at anyone who tried to enter his lair that the keepers had to just give up until every scrap of her was gone and Achilles let them approach again. Although someone must have dared to, otherwise how would I know? Well. Some things are just known. They're in the water and the wind, waiting to be told.

It turned out Sailor had lied to me about one more thing: the security cameras. They had been on the whole time, recording the night's adventures. It must have seemed obvious to the admins and ownership and our fellow keepers that Sailor had been the main culprit, and the other participants—like me, and the guards—had innocently been maneuvered into her diabolical but also inexplicable secret plan. No one could understand why a person would do such a thing. I don't think any of them wanted to understand. Sacrificing yourself for another was something they couldn't comprehend.

I was famished but I found I couldn't face eating in the mess hall. Hearing the knives and forks clanking against the plates set my teeth on edge. After everyone departed to start their shifts, I sat in the echoing emptiness of the mess hall until the time came to head up the hill to my appointment with the admins. At the crest of the hill, a flash of movement caught my eye. It was right at the upper periphery of my vision, so I had to crane my neck back to my shoulder blades to see it. I squinted into the bright white sky. Etched there, like a stroke of calligraphy ink, was a bird, quite low—perhaps forty feet above my head—flying in a straight, determined line toward some unknown destination. It had found an updraft and was letting the air carry it along, its wings outstretched and still. It didn't look down.

My fingers opened and my ID pass fluttered to the ground. Only when the bird had vanished out of sight did I realize I was kneeling on the clammy earth, my hands clasped together and pressed to my sternum. I stood slowly, wiping the mud off my knees. There was no way of knowing, of course, no identification one could make from that distance that would prove it definitively. But I knew in my heart it was the cedar waxwing Sailor had set free.

At the entrance to the admin center, I faltered. To be this close to the place of my confinement, the dungeon in which I had almost lost my mind—the effect was immediate and visceral. I was about to run away, screw the consequences, but at that moment someone emerged from the building and swept past me with barely a glance, and their appearance broke the spell somehow, because I was able to slip through the door in their wake and force myself up to the front desk.

The person manning the desk looked up incuriously, their manner only vaguely convincing of a human going about their day. A perfect career bureaucrat.

"Yes?" the person said.

"I'm here for my appointment. Camille Parker."

Formality was the only option in this room, with its studied air of neutrality and the steady hum of a machine emanating from some unseen source. This declaration caused the person to look, if anything, even more bored. They gave an almost imperceptible sigh and gestured to a rigid green sofa beneath the window. "Wait over there."

I sat for what felt like a very long time, without anything to do but listen to the various clinical sounds of the room. My ears began to pick out the low chirping of a smoke alarm; the drone of the air-conditioning; the very faint undulating tones of two people talking in another room. But after a while a familiar roaring whir displaced all the others, growing louder and louder, and I might have thought I was having an aural hallucination if the admin didn't jerk their head up as well. They rose and left the room, a slight twitch about the neck. I wondered whose helicopter it was. A group of VIP guests was the most likely. But it could also be a new animal delivery. That thought no longer excited me like it once had. I don't know why it didn't occur to me who it really was until the admin returned and said curtly to me, "Mr. Pinkton will see you now."

I followed the admin down a corridor and into an empty boardroom. The air hummed at a slightly different tempo in there, I noted.

"Wait here," the admin said, as if I were in a position to do anything else.

I took up what I assumed would be the expected pose, sitting with my hands in my lap and eyes downcast. I had never been alone in a room with Mr. Pinkton before, and when he entered, my only thought was that for such a slim man he took up a surprising amount of space. Was it surprising, though? Power is expansive.

I rose from my seat but I wasn't sure whether I should bow or shake his hand or avoid looking at him or some other protocol altogether, so I resorted to a kind of dipped chin curtsey that almost capsized me. I righted myself and Mr. Pinkton gave the faintest of smiles. As he closed the door, I glimpsed just the hands of his two henchmen posted outside, held in loose fists at their sides.

"I don't usually do this," he said, lifting the back flaps of his suit jacket as he sat down. "Speak directly to workers about their employment. But your father was a good man. Never had a better driver. I was sorry to lose him."

I swallowed painfully and aimed a tepid smile of my own at the wall behind his left ear.

After enduring a silence in which I failed to speak, he said, almost blurting it out, "I felt very bad about what happened to him. I mean, his disappearing like that. I wish I could have stopped it."

"Thank you," I said, like a fool, but I couldn't think what else to say.

He fiddled with the cuff of his shirt, held together with a jeweled cuff link that probably cost more than my annual wage. "These gangs." There was suppressed rage in his voice. "They can't get to me, to people like me, so they go after my circle. My employees."

At his words, something clicked into place in my brain. Sailor had been right, then. One of the cartels must have pressured my father to help them steal animals, thinking proximity to the Pinktons would afford him opportunities. It made me proud and broke my heart that he must have refused them, just like Sailor had. But for Mr. Pinkton, my father's disappearance must have unearthed a different kind of pain, because here he was, seeking absolution. Forgiveness for his involvement in my father's death, however minimal his culpability might have been. I felt a shift in my feelings toward him, another tide turning. Awestruck gratitude and reverence—that was the default position of every employee on this island when it came to Mr. Pinkton. I had never dreamed there was another way to feel about him. But sitting there, breathing the same air as this iconic figure in whose shadow we had always labored, I saw how mundanely, disappointingly human he was, after all. Incredible and faintly comical that someone like Mr. Pinkton, who had everything in the world, could still be brought down to earth by a wretched feeling only commoners should have to experience.

"I'm very sorry about your friend too," he said after a moment. "Uh, this . . . Sailor Anderson."

It was so pathetic, given the circumstances, but the thing I was most worried about was crying in front of him. I looked at the ceiling and blinked furiously.

"A terrible, terrible thing." He cleared his throat and went on. "However. I think you can see our position here. The Alcatraz ownership position. It's really a question of harmony. The, uh, event was very disruptive to the Alcatraz community. *Hugely* disruptive. How would it look to keep on one of the employees involved in this regrettable disruption?"

He left a much more expectant pause this time, and I got the message loud and clear: I was expected to answer.

"Bad?" I offered.

"Exactly," he said, tapping his pointer finger on the table. "Very bad. A very bad precedent. So I'm sure you'll understand that we have to terminate your employment."

I narrowed my eyes and nodded, feeling nothing, looking at nothing.

Mr. Pinkton sniffed impatiently. "However, because I like you and I liked your dad, I've ordered this news be kept confidential. None of your colleagues will know. You'll simply get on the ferry on Sunday and not come back. That sound okay?"

For the first time, I looked Mr. Pinkton directly in the face. Am I flattering myself if I say he faltered for a moment? He scratched his ear and looked away, but I saw it exposed in that split second: he was afraid. Not of me, of course not. But of what he saw in my face. The knowledge we shared that they would never stop trying. A jaguar or a crocodile was worth the lives of a thousand cartel soldiers, everyone knew that. And even if they never succeeded, their attempts couldn't be kept from the guests forever, and one day the guests would stop coming, and that would be the end of this little end-of-the-world experiment.

Mr. Pinkton got up and pushed his chair back, the superior, distracted smile of his class back in place. "I won't shake your hand," he said. "Contamination protocols, you know."

"Of course," I said.

"Good luck."

"You too," I said, but he was surprisingly quick in his movements for an old man, and he was already halfway out the door. I doubt he even heard me.

Back in the barracks, I retrieved Sailor's bag from my locker, opened the bird book, and found the page. The name in block letters: MR. LI. A long string of numbers and a country code I didn't recognize. An asterisk I hadn't noticed the first time, and a footnote so minuscule I had to bring the page to my nose to read it: *I knew it was real!!! Tell them I sent you, Birdy.* No indication of when she had written it, but the ink looked fresh enough. I went to the Officers'

Club, stepped just inside its ruined walls to conceal myself, and called the number. I didn't expect anyone to answer, so when a clipped voice came on, I almost dropped the phone. We spoke for only a few seconds, but it was enough, it was all I needed for the time being. A kind of proof of life.

Alcatraz

I could tell it was early. My roommates were still asleep, the room stuffy with our communal exhalations. It would have been nice to have had more sleep on a day on which I was planning to travel, but it couldn't be helped. There wasn't much preparation to be done, beyond packing Sailor's things, along with my own few meager possessions, into her duffel bag. My first time off the island, and I had no real idea of how people normally prepared for their days out. I could only recall generic details that might have been borrowed from movies or books. Things like packing an extra sweater in case the weather changed. Filling your water bottles in case you can't find clean water along the way. Stashing trail mix in an inside pocket of your backpack. A hat and sunscreen so you don't get burned. Telling someone where you're going in case you get lost.

The ferry wasn't due to leave until nine, so I wandered up to the Arboretum. Gill was generous with his time as always, paused what he was doing to show me the spider orchids that had just started blooming again. He was proud as a new father at this achievement that was both tiny and momentous.

"You should apply to work with me in here, Camille," he said, placing his hand gently underneath a bloom and stooping down to inhale its subtle scent. "You obviously have an affinity for the plants. I could let the admins know I need a new apprentice."

I looked up at him, surprised. "They'd let me do that?"

He shrugged. "Who knows? Things have been going downhill so fast, I couldn't promise the sun will rise tomorrow. But it's worth trying."

"Thanks, I'll look into it." Much as I'd always enjoyed the balm of the plants and flowers, it had never occurred to me to aspire to work in here. I suppose I've been so single-mindedly committed to the animals, with their flesh-and-blood needs and their inescapable demands, that these other gentler living things have been obscured to me. I regret that now. There was always so much more than I have allowed myself to see.

"I worked in the zoo for a minute, you know," said Gill. "Before you got here."

"I didn't know that. What happened?"

"I couldn't handle how brutal it was. At least the plants want to be here. They're happy to have me look after them, I think. For as long as we have left." He checked the time and gave a quiet yelp. "Eek, I have to excuse myself. I'm expecting a shipment of birds of paradise on the morning boat and I need to prepare a space for them."

"An exchange," I said, smiling.

"What do you mean?"

I was embarrassed then and wished I hadn't said anything. "Oh, it's just that I'm leaving on that same boat. Going to the mainland for the day. The flowers in exchange for me."

"Ah." He slipped off his gardening glove and put his hand gently on my shoulder, looking straight into my eyes, his own dark eyes twinkling. "Well, lord knows I covet my birds of paradise, but that's hardly a fair exchange." The scene wavered and I had to turn my head while Gill gallantly pretended not to notice. "Wait here, I have something for you." He returned holding a small box, its top punctured with air holes. He lifted the lid. Inside was a pale, gnarled bulb that resembled garlic. "My night lily," Gill said, gazing down at it with affection. "It never thrived here. Will you plant it somewhere for me?"

"But I'm just going to visit family. I'll be back later today."

"Nevertheless."

I stared down at the bulb, then gave the smallest of nods. Gill replaced the lid and carefully tucked the box into my backpack. I mumbled a farewell and quickly walked away without looking back, although I got the impression Gill stood there watching me until I was out of sight.

On the way back to the barracks, I made one final stop. It was easy in the end, much easier than I'd anticipated. There was a doziness to the morning, a sense that all was permissible provided you were discreet and didn't ask too much of anyone else. That might be just the mood I'm in today, though, coloring the way I see things. Possibly everything is the same as it has always been, and there will be someone waiting for me at the other end to take me into custody and sort me out for good. I have an intuition that won't happen, though. The belief has taken root inside me: I think they are done with me.

At the appointed time I lined up with the rest of the motley crew headed for the mainland. There were twenty or so keepers, a few off-duty guards, a gaggle of admin types, two maintenance workers in their green overalls with fluorescent orange stripes across the shoulders, all the freight guys who load and unload the cargo, plus the boat's crew and the people who work the snack bar. It was cloudy earlier, but by the time I joined the line it had turned into a dazzling day. As I waited I took a few puffs of my inhaler, but it was more out of habit than necessity. My lungs felt full and clear.

When I got to the screening point close to the embarkation ramp, I noted with an upwelling of satisfaction that Benjie was one of two guards on duty at the dock. I had presumed he would be because this was his new posting, a demotion I suppose after his misadventure at the zoo. Still, there had always been a faint chance he might have swapped a shift with someone or been indisposed somehow. Seeing him here made me feel that other things might also flow successfully on this day.

After the person in front of me was cleared and moved onto the ramp to board the idling ferry, I stepped forward into Benjie's eyeline. He gave me a sheepish grin, as though the memory he was referencing was of us having shared a wild night out at a bar. I examined my feelings for traces of resentment toward him but there was nothing. It hadn't been his fault, after all. He was an innocent bystander, if such a character is even possible.

I handed him the black duffel bag and he scanned it then handed it back to me. He lowered his voice. "Sailor asked me to give you that. I left it on the bed for you after she, you know . . ."

I nodded, not trusting myself to say anything. He jerked his chin a couple of times, a gesture I understood to mean he wanted me to stretch my arms and spread my legs apart so he could pat me down. I looked at him. I had been practicing this look. It was a look that invited him to enter into complicity with me. Not even for my own sake, but for Sailor's. I'd worked it out at some point in the hole, although I suppose I'd known it for a while—I think he had always been in love with her. Unlike a lot of the other guards, Benjie was always nice to me and Sailor, and she encouraged him, knowing she would need him one day. How did she know he would fall in love with her, though? I guess she couldn't have been sure. Every plan requires calculated risks. I tried to remember this as I flirted with my own calculated risk: transmitting an unspoken message to Benjie to let me pass through without a search. Never mind that I've never had a fraction of Sailor's talent for this.

He hesitated before saying loudly, so his partner could hear, "You're good to go." As I passed I gave him the tiniest of smiles, and then I boarded the boat on which I hadn't set foot since the first time I was brought to this rock. I chose a seat in the back, away from everyone.

San Francisco Bay

Because it's such a rare, beautiful clear day, everyone is outside on deck. I can hear their chattering like birdsong floating through the open windows. I had thought I wouldn't want to look back at the island, but I find myself doing it anyway. Naturally I'm familiar with the dock side of Alcatraz, where our home the barracks looms, but I never get to see it from the water. I have to admit the sight is stirring. The rock itself, so forbidding and craggy, like the setting for a dark fairy tale. The zoo building, glowing white and stark at the crest of the hill, its inhabitants hidden from sight lest we love them to death. The lighthouse, standing lonely on its ridgeline like a monument to vigilance and longing. The sea foaming around the base of the cliffs.

The island grows smaller as I watch, and I finally turn to look the other way. The Embarcadero looms in the distance, growing larger and more solid as the boat chugs its way to the shore. Ever so gently, I pull the zipper of my jacket down a few inches, lift the edge and glance down, as if I'm checking the lining for the manufacturer's label. I can see the top of the warbler's downy head and one of its eyes, alert and glossy like a button. It emits the tiniest of chirps, which thankfully no one could possibly hear over the sound of the engines and the rushing of the wind against the smeared glass. I can't tell whether the chirp is indignant or simply an acknowledgment of our shared aliveness. The bird seems comfortable in there. She doesn't struggle or attempt to flap. I made a special pouch for this purpose, a silk cocoon that perfectly fits in my inner pocket, a secret repository in which to hold her close to me. I wonder if it pleases her that we are finally heading in the right direction. At this time of year she would be preparing to migrate, her inner compass pointed toward the flyway she has only ever traveled in her dreams. While I can't promise she will live a long or even a happy life, I will see to it that she gets the chance to soar, if only for a little while.

I watch the other passengers collecting personal possessions, smoothing down hair as they make their way toward the exits, impatient no doubt to finally feel their feet on terra firma, casting their thoughts ahead to the people they are going to see, the meals they are going to eat, perhaps other darker thrills toward which they have been yearning.

I stay seated and still, watching the shore come closer. I can feel the bird's tiny heart beating against my own. I pretend Sailor is with me again, and that we are going home.

Acknowledgments

With enormous thanks to my agent, Sharon Pelletier, who championed this story from the start and knew just the right home for it. To Caroline Bleeke, whose editorial vision, insight, and generosity are otherworldly, and to the team at Flatiron, a young but already legendary imprint I'm so proud to have on the spine of my book—Mary Retta, Jen Edwards, Emily Walters, Erin Kibby, Jeremy Pink, Alexus Blanding, Megan Lynch, Marlena Bittner, and Malati Chavali, thank you all.

To Elizabeth Beilharz, whose close reading, insights, and stellar company continue to make me a better writer, reader, and person. To the world's finest zoo architect, Greg Dykstra, whose intel and anecdotes about zoo design helped me think more deeply about animal happiness, and Andrea Dykstra, who always provides nourishment both culinary and emotional. To cheerleaders extraordinaire Jane Barratt and Jennifer Paull. (*Merci* for the French slang, Jen!) To Laura Kirar and Richard Frazier, who create magical environments for creative communities in Mexico and beyond. To Glenn McCulloch, whose encouragement always means a great deal. To Arras Wiedorn, who generously shared fascinating behind-the-scenes experiences of zookeeping, and to animal allies everywhere—all the zoos and conservation groups and wildlife refuges devoted to the welfare and happiness of the beings in their care.

To MacDowell, a sanctuary for artists and one of my favorite places on Earth, where I began writing this novel. To San Francisco, an excellent city full of ghosts and great stories, although with fewer jellyfish than this book depicts. To my beautiful Aussie family, whose affection and enthusiasm spans hemispheres. Lastly, to Adam: your love is the greatest thing in my life.

About the Author

Emma Sloley is a MacDowell fellow and Bread Loaf scholar. She is the author of the novels *The Island of Last Things* and *Disaster's Children*, and her work has been published in *Literary Hub, Catapult, Joyland*, and many other publications. Born in Australia, Emma now divides her time between California and the city of Mérida, Mexico.

Recommend *The Island of Last Things* for your next book club!

Reading Group Guide available at
www.flatironbooks.com/reading-group-guides